BY JAY NEUGEBOREN

BEFORE MY LIFE BEGAN

A NOVEL

Jay Neugeboren

Simon and Schuster
New York

THIS NOVEL IS A WORK OF FICTION. NAMES, CHARACTERS, PLACES AND INCIDENTS ARE
EITHER THE PRODUCT OF THE AUTHOR'S IMAGINATION OR ARE USED FICTITIOUSLY.
ANY RESEMBLANCE TO ACTUAL EVENTS OR LOCALES OR PERSONS, LIVING OR DEAD, IS
ENTIRELY COINCIDENTAL.

COPYRIGHT © 1985 BY JAY NEUGEBOREN
ALL RIGHTS RESERVED
INCLUDING THE RIGHT OF REPRODUCTION
IN WHOLE OR IN PART IN ANY FORM
PUBLISHED BY SIMON AND SCHUSTER
A DIVISION OF SIMON & SCHUSTER, INC.
SIMON & SCHUSTER BUILDING
ROCKEFELLER CENTER
1230 AVENUE OF THE AMERICAS
NEW YORK, NEW YORK 10020
SIMON AND SCHUSTER AND COLOPHON ARE REGISTERED TRADEMARKS OF
SIMON & SCHUSTER, INC.
DESIGNED BY GRANGER, NICHOLS/LEVAVI & LEVAVI
MANUFACTURED IN THE UNITED STATES OF AMERICA

1   3   5   7   9   10   8   6   4   2

LIBRARY OF CONGRESS CATALOGING IN PUBLICATION DATA
NEUGEBOREN, JAY.
BEFORE MY LIFE BEGAN.

I. TITLE.
PS3564.E844B4 1985   813'.54   85-1912
ISBN: 0-671-54372-5

FOR MARY WEINBERGER

AND TO THE MEMORY OF
ARNOLD WEINBERGER (1907–1983)

BOOK ONE

1

ALL THE MEN were trying to kiss my mother, so I kept pulling at her dress for us to get away. Pink and blue streamers caught in the dark curls of her hair, and tiny dots of silver, on her bare shoulders, sparkled under the light from the lampposts. In the middle of the street Louie Newman was standing on the roof of Dr. Kaplan's new Buick, trying to dance with a skinny woman who wore a shimmering black dress, and it seemed to me that the sequins on the woman's dress glittered like the scales on an enormous fish. I didn't feel well. I wanted to go home, to be in my own room. I pulled harder and I thought I heard my mother's dress tear—I stopped pulling at once, scared—but she didn't seem to notice. Her dress was made of a pale lavender silk-chiffon, dark-purple irises swirling around one another toward the ground. I saw a man's lips pressed against her lips, but she was laughing too hard for him to keep them there. I'd never seen so many happy people before in my life. Everybody was dancing and singing and shouting and hugging each other and throwing paper in the air. Above the noise and the lights and the stores and the apartment buildings the sky was black. Where was my father? Could I tell him, later, what my mother was doing with the men? Would he see that her lipstick was smeared at the corners of her mouth?

The war was over. I was ten years old. I was living my first life. We were ankle-deep in paper—confetti and streamers and newspaper—and I began kicking, trying to make tiny sprays of color explode into the air between our feet. I heard the fire engine's bell and siren now, above the music and the shouting and the noisemakers, coming toward us from Linden Boulevard. I looked up. A long wavy piece of orange crepe paper floated down and caught across my mother's forehead and cheek. She brushed it away with her palm. Mr. Lipsky, our butcher, shoved a bottle toward her and she grabbed it by the neck, tilted her head back, and drank. I wanted to smash the bottle on the sidewalk, but I couldn't see the sidewalk through all the paper.

I was ten years old. I was living my first life, and though there would be times in the years to come—more than I'd ever care to count—when I'd yearn to go back, when I would have traded all the happiness of my second life merely to have stood for a few seconds in the place where my mother and I stood on that warm summer night so long ago, what I wanted more than anything in the world in the moment itself was for my life to fade, to disappear, to be blacked out. And yet it seemed to me, then, impossible that the moment itself would ever end.

"Come *on!*" I said. "We gotta get home."

She took another drink from the bottle Mr. Lipsky handed her and I watched him kiss her with his tongue and put his hand on her shoulder, near her breast. I thought of him cutting fat from lamb chops on his chopping block. I pulled harder and she shoved him away, told him to behave himself. I saw Tony Cremona carrying a brown paper bag, and when he saw me looking at him, his face lit up.

"Hey Davey—c'mere," he called. "C'mere and see what I got."

I let go of my mother's dress and pushed through to Tony. He opened his bag and showed me the firecrackers inside. I glanced back, saw the skin of my mother's thigh, like raw flesh, where I'd torn her dress along the seam. Now the fire engine was closer, and all the firemen were waving their hats and cheering. "*The war is over . . . ! The war is over . . . ! The war is over . . . !*" In the back part of the fire engine, up high next to the man who steered, a fireman in a black raincoat and red hat was waving an American flag. Sammy the Dalmatian stood totally still, frozen against the wooden ladders and silver hose couplings. Tony took my hand, to pull me with him. The paper was so high and thick that I felt as if I were trying to march through snow.

"You go on with Tony," my mother said. "Okay? Be a good boy, Davey. Let Momma have some fun, yeah?"

"Will uncle Abe come home now?"

"*Abe!*" my mother cried out, as if someone had stabbed her. I wanted to put my arms around her but I was afraid she might push me away. "Oh my baby Abe!" she cried out again, and I wished there was something I could do to take her pain away. "Oh my precious Abe!" Tears streamed down her face and I wanted to ask her why she was crying if uncle Abe was coming home. Mr. Lipsky put an arm around her shoulder. Furious, she shrugged him off, and I thought of a wild horse, its eyes crazed with fright. She looked up at the sky and mouthed Abe's name but I heard no sound. Her brown eyes seemed larger and more beautiful than ever, as if she and not my father was the one who was half-blind. I touched her skirt. She blinked. She took a quarter from her pocketbook and pressed it into my hand. "Here, sweetheart." She kissed me next to my mouth. I could smell her perfume, like fresh lilacs.

What would you be ready to die for?

"You and Tony go get yourselves some candy at Mr. Fellerman's. For a celebration, yeah? Your uncle Abe is coming home, darling. He's coming home now. Everything will be all right."

The dark brown of her eyes seemed to fade to hazel, the black center to a glistening violet. I wished I were in bed, her tucking me in under cool sheets and kissing my closed eyes.

I followed Tony across the street and into the alleyways between my apartment house and the next one. When we were on the other side of all the empty ash cans Beau Jack had lined up, Tony lit a match and threw a firecracker down but even though I could smell the burnt sulphur, I didn't hear it go off, the noise from the street was still so loud. *What would you be ready to die for?* That was the question Abe had asked in one of his letters, the question he said he asked himself every morning when he woke up and every night before he went to sleep, the question he told me I should begin thinking about.

"Wanna light one?"

I lit a match and touched it to the stem of a firecracker but I held it in my hand so long, staring at it, that Tony had to slap it away. Tony lit some more. I wondered: were I grown up and a soldier, would I be brave enough to throw myself on a Nazi hand grenade in order to save the rest of my buddies? But because I couldn't imagine feeling anything afterwards—not even when I saw them all standing in a circle looking down at me—I couldn't find an answer to the question. I bent my head sideways so I could hear the firecrackers going off. I wet my fingertips on my tongue and wiped them on the ashes after the explosions and sniffed in the fragrance.

We walked to the end of my building and out into the big courtyard behind. I didn't see Beau Jack there in his chair. I imagined he'd been too shy to go out and celebrate with everybody else and that he was sitting in his room in the cellar, listening to the news on the radio. I thought of how happy he would be that the war was over, that Japan had surrendered the way Italy and Germany had already done.

No people sat on the back fire escapes, but most of the windows up and down the street were lit up. Tony and I climbed the wooden fence that separated the buildings on my side of the block from the ones on

Linden Boulevard. We watched out for the barbed wire at the top and jumped down to the other side, where the ground was lower. It was dark, but we knew the alleyways and backyards of our neighborhood by heart.

"Wanna come home with me?" Tony asked. "I got some cherry bombs and bottle rockets and M-8os saved up."

"I gotta get to my own house soon," I said. "I think my father's there waiting for me."

We ran down the ramp into the cellar of building 181, the German police dog barking at us from inside the super's apartment. Tony knocked over a garbage can and I did too, and we kicked grapefruit rinds and orange peels and coffee grounds and other junk around on the cement floor and then we dashed out fast. I was laughing out loud with Tony, but inside I was thinking of my mother on the corner of our block, without me. We went through a small courtyard, down again into the front part of the building, past the furnace and the boiler and the coal bin and the other bins where people stored things, and out again into another alleyway, the one where the older guys played Chinese handball after school. We were running and we couldn't stop quickly enough when we saw the three men standing there, as if they'd been waiting for us.

Tony touched my hand. "Let's beat it," he said.

I started to run back the other way but one of the men grabbed me from behind and squeezed so hard with just his fingers and thumb that I thought he was going to crunch the bones on the back of my neck. Tony was wailing. I took a deep breath, then kicked backwards with all my might and I got the man who was holding me in the shin. *I'm coming, Tony*, I called out, inside my head. *Just hold on a few seconds more and I'll get to you, buddy. . . .*

"Hey, stupid—it's the Voloshin kid," one of the men said. "Lay off."

The man let go of me at once. He flicked on a cigarette lighter in front of my face. It lit up his face too and I saw that it was Spanish Louie, a Sephardic Jew who worked for my uncle. He popped the silver top down, but I drew a picture of him inside my head first—the downward drooping folds of his eyelids, the way his fat lower lip jutted out and covered the crevice in his chin—and I held it there, inside me.

Tony was bent over, his forehead to the ground, his ass up in the air, but I didn't move toward him. I hoped he knew why I didn't—that they wouldn't try anything else now that they knew who I was—but I was afraid he might think I was scared, or that I didn't care. In my head it was as if the three men were huddled around a campfire, warming their hands, only there was no fire on the ground—just a girl propped up against the wall, staring ahead with a dopey look on her face, the skirt up around her waist.

"Hey Davey my boy," one of them said, buckling his belt, moving toward me. "We were just havin' some fun, right? To celebrate the end of the war."

I looked straight into his eyes—it was Little Benny Shapiro, another one of my uncle's men—and he gave me a big grin, as if we were old friends. Little Benny wasn't much taller than me or Tony, even in the high-heeled elevator shoes he wore—maybe five-foot-one or two—so he didn't have to bend over to put his arm around my shoulder. I saw Tony look toward us. I went rigid. I didn't want Tony to think I was a friend of Benny's. I didn't want him to do something stupid that might make Benny hurt him more. I kept my arms pressed to my sides, concentrating my eyes on Tony's, hoping he'd stay quiet.

"Hey—no hard feelings, huh?"

Little Benny reached into the inside of his jacket, where I could see his holster strapped across his chest in its harness, the square black handle of his gun toward his heart. He drew out an enormous money roll, snapped the rubber bands off, counted out five dollars, stuck them in my shirt pocket.

"You and your friend go have a good time, yeah? You get a steak and put it on his cheek and he'll be okay. What he does is say to everybody, 'But you should have seen the other guy—' Right, Davey?"

Little Benny leaned back and laughed, then buttoned his jacket at the waist—it was the kind of jacket that musicians wore, with only one button and wide lapels—but I didn't smile at him or look at the money or try to give it back. He grabbed my chin between his thumb and his index finger and pressed so hard I felt my teeth cutting through my lips.

"But you ain't never gonna tell your uncle what you seen, right?"

I didn't say anything and he squeezed harder.

"This never happened, right?"

"You want me to see that the other kid here don't talk?" Spanish Louie asked. "I could clip his ear off."

"It's Angelo Cremona's kid," the third man said. I squinted. Avie Gornik was standing against the wall, picking at his teeth with a folded-up dollar bill. Avie lived with his mother over Mr. Berg's drugstore. He was an old man, fat and bald, who spent his free time during the day in the stores, shopping for her. She never went outside their apartment. "Should I fix him good so Angelo knows we don't wanna make a second visit?"

"He your friend, Davey?" Little Benny asked.

I nodded.

"Any friend of Davey Voloshin is okay by me," he said.

"They shouldn't go in alleys at night," Spanish Louie said.

"Yeah," Little Benny laughed. "It can be very dangerous to go in alleys at night."

"What about the piece?" Avie asked.

"Turn her over and leave her a glass of water for when she wakes up." Benny laughed in a tense, high-pitched way that made me hate him even more. He sounded like a woman. He bent down and kicked the girl. She flopped onto her side and I heard her head crack against the cement.

They didn't look at Tony or me again. They walked out side by side, taking up the entire width of the alley. I saw the bulge in Spanish Louie's back pocket, where he kept his blackjack, and as soon as I was sure the three of them were gone I went to Tony. I tried to lift him.

"You're a fucking dirty Jew," he screamed, shoving me away. "Goddamn dirty Jew! Dirty Jew! Dirty Jew!"

"Don't say that."

"I hope the Nazis had time to cut off your uncle's cock—!"

"Shut up," I said, and I grabbed his wrist. He was wheezing in and out so hard when he spoke that I had to concentrate to make out his words.

"Who's gonna make me?"

He jerked his arm away, looked up at me. When I saw how swollen the left side of his face was I tried not to show anything. His lip was bleeding badly. I offered him my handkerchief.

"I don't need anything from you, you crummy kike."

"Your face looks real bad," I said. "Does it hurt?"

He sniffed in, wiped his nose with the back of his hand.

"A lot you care."

"You should get home right away and do something for your face."

"My old man got guys can take care of them real good. They ain't such big shots."

"It's all swollen and purple."

He stood up, shrugged me off when I moved toward him to help.

"I ain't a dumb sissy," he said.

"I didn't say you were. Just that your face is swollen and cut and you gotta get some first aid for it."

"We ain't soldiers."

"So?"

"So what?"

I shrugged. "It's your face," I said. I pointed to the girl. "Do you know who she is?"

He walked over and stared down at her.

"It's Mrs. Davidoff's dumb daughter Rosie," he said. Nobody knew Rosie's age. She lived in a special home for people like her during the winter. The rest of the year she sat in front of Mr. Davidoff's grocery store on Rogers Avenue, knitting long scarves. "Who cares anyway? We ain't playing soldiers I said before. Didn't you hear me?"

"Is she alive?"

He bent over. "Yeah. She's breathing."

He moved away then, but he walked crookedly and there was no time for me to get to him before he scraped his cheek against the brick wall.

"Jesus Christ!" he screamed. "Jesus fucking Christ! My old man's gonna be so angry with me I don't know what to do. Jesus Christ! Jesus Christ!"

He kept veering from side to side, his left hand out in front of him to keep from knocking against the walls of the alleyway. I went back, picked up his bag of firecrackers and ran after him. Could I help Tony and Rosie at the same time? If I called her apartment and her mother and father were there I'd have to disguise my voice so they wouldn't think I'd been in on things. Outside, Linden Boulevard was even more crowded and noisy than my street had been. Cars were stuck out in the middle of the road, honking their horns, crowds of people waving flags and dancing in circles with each other.

"Here," I said. I grabbed his arm and turned him around, shoving his bag at him. *"Here!"*

He took it without looking at me and I wanted to do something—anything!—to change things, I was just so scared that he wouldn't ever want to be my friend again.

"I'm sorry," I said.

I wanted to say more, but he disappeared into the crowd.

I walked back toward my own street. A few people said hello to me and one old woman pinched my cheek and tried to hand me a Hershey bar from a shopping bag. At the corner of Martense Street and Rogers Avenue, I couldn't find my mother. I crossed over to where Mr. Weiss's tailor shop was, but she wasn't there either, so I crossed back and walked up our street and climbed the black iron fence in front of our apartment house. I got my sneakers wedged in good between two of the sharp points that stuck up—we would climb up there when we needed to see what time it was on the Holy Cross tower on Church Avenue, a block and a half away—and I looked all around until I spotted my mother on the other side of Rogers Avenue. Her mouth was open wide, her teeth bright, her head tipped to the side, and she was laughing in a way that made her look more beautiful than ever. She gave her head a shake and confetti swirled down from her hair onto the people around her. I'd never seen so much paper. I watched her smile and thought of how she smiled the same way when I drew pictures for her, landscapes of trees and mountains and barns and lakes.

The lobby of our building was quiet. We lived on the third floor, in apartment 3B, and I walked up the stairs, took the key out from under the doormat—my father wasn't home from work yet—and let myself in. What would happen to Tony? If his brothers found out that he'd let himself get caught by my uncle's men, how rough would they be on him? In the kitchen, I looked up the Davidoff number, put a dish towel over the mouthpiece of the telephone. I told Rosie's mother where she was, but hung up when she started screaming questions at me. I went to my room, got my ruler and pencil and scissors from my desk, then took a copy of the *New York Post* from the newspaper rack in the living room and brought it with me to the kitchen table. Starting with the sports pages, I drew lines with a pencil, up and down and back and forth, across the photos of all the Dodger and Giant and Yankee players. There was an article from the day before about the Dodgers who'd be coming back as soon as the war ended, guys I'd never seen but had read about—Pee Wee Reese and Pistol Pete Reiser and Cookie Lavagetto and Billy Herman and Ed Head and Kirby Higbe and Hugh Casey—and I cut their faces into little squares, first sideways and then up and down. I cut through five pages at a time. I brushed the squares of newsprint with the side of my hand to the edge of the oilcloth and into a paper bag I took out from under the sink. I nicked the oilcloth a few times—it was an old green-checkered one we'd been using ever since I could remember—and smoothed the nicks down with saliva.

When I finished with the *New York Post* I went into the hallway where the incinerator was, found the comics section from the previous Saturday and brought it inside. Scorchy Smith was on the front page, frying Japs with his flamethrower. I smiled and ruled lines across Scorchy and the Japs and the palm trees and the B-24 Super-Fortresses and cut the comics into squares. I'd sent my Uncle Abe a few sets of drawings I'd made of Scorchy Smith and the pictures seemed so good to him he thought I'd traced them. So I sent him more, and I also sent him some of the actual comic strips so that he could compare the sizes—mine were a little smaller—and see that I'd done the drawings myself, free-hand.

When I was done pouring the pieces of paper into the bag I twisted the top closed and shook it up and down so that the colored pieces would mix with the black-and-white. Then I looked out the window and I felt even better because—as if my finishing just when I did *made it* happen—there was my father walking along the street from the No-strand Avenue end, coming home from work.

There were still big crowds at both ends of the street—our block was one of the longest in the neighborhood—but in the middle, where my father was, he was all alone, and I watched him walking under the lampposts and felt happier than I had all night because I knew I'd be by myself waiting for him, to give him the good news.

I cleaned up the kitchen table, put my ruler and pencil and scissors back into the desk drawer, then turned out all the lights in the apartment, locked the door and got into the front hall closet. That was where my father always went first when he got home, to hang up his coat or jacket. I set the paper bag down at my feet, but away from me so it wouldn't rustle, next to where the carpet sweeper was, and I waited. It was broiling hot in the closet, but the soft wool of my father's black winter coat against my cheek soothed me. I wondered how hot the subway had been for him. I breathed in through my nose, the odors of wool and camphor and stale cigarettes—my father smoked over three packs of Chesterfields a day—making my eyes tear.

I imagined listening to his footsteps coming up from the second floor landing—he always stopped there, to get his breath back—and then I imagined myself running down the street with him toward the corner where my mother was, and of how we'd throw my confetti into the air, and of how some of the pieces of the comics would stick in his hair. I saw him smiling proudly, one arm around my shoulder, his other arm around my mother's waist. I saw him pulling us to him from either side, to give us kisses.

His key was turning the lock and then, through the slit at the bottom of the closet door, I saw that he'd put the foyer light on. I held my breath and while I did it occurred to me for the first time that because it had been such a hot day he might have gone to work without his jacket, but I was afraid to move my hands and feel around to find out. My eyes pressed closed as tightly as I could get them, I tried to see him when I was looking down on him from the window, and when the picture came into my head I breathed out: his thin summer jacket was folded over his right arm, the newspaper rolled up just above it, chest high.

A second later the closet door opened and in the yellow foyer light I saw the pale skin on the back of his hand—he was reaching for a hanger —and I pushed out toward him and began shouting that the war was over.

"What are you—crazy or something!?"

He dropped the hanger and it bumped me over my right eye. He reached in, snatched me hard on my right arm, above the elbow where my muscle was, and dragged me the rest of the way from the closet.

"What are you trying to do—give me a heart attack? Are you crazy or are you crazy?"

He shook me hard—he had tremendous power in his hands—and then shoved me away from him.

"I just wanted to surprise you," I said.

"I don't need surprises."

"But the war's over, Poppa—and Uncle Abe will be coming home now! Momma said so."

"Wonderful."

He pushed by me but there was no anger on his face now. He looked tired, the way he usually did at night after work. His right eyelid was drooping down behind his thick glasses—he was blind in his left eye, from having lost all sight there when he was six years old—and when he hung up his jacket he slipped his hand into its side pocket and came out with a crumpled pack of Chesterfields. The cellophane crackled like the sound of fire.

He walked away from me, to the kitchen.

"You're all sweaty," he said, over his shoulder. "You should dry off so you don't get a chill."

I followed him into the kitchen.

"Aren't you happy that the war is over?"

He was at the sink, running cold water over his wrists to cool himself off. His glasses off, he looked at me sideways with his good eye, then splashed water on his face.

"I'm happy the war's over," he said, but his voice was flat.

I showed him my bag. "I made confetti."

He was reading his newspaper. He held it in one hand while he opened the door to the icebox with the other.

"What?"

"I made confetti."

"I thought you said spaghetti. Did Momma leave me supper?"

"We never ate," I said. "I think we forgot—I mean, I don't think she ever got to make supper—we were too busy being excited because of the war being over." I heard the sentence in my head that I could use to get him to do what I wanted: "Momma's down at the corner with everybody, but she sent me back to get you so we could all celebrate together, like a family."

"So?"

He was at the kitchen counter again, slicing a piece of American cheese for himself. His cigarette stuck to the corner of his lower lip.

"So I waited for you so we could go to the corner together. Don't you want to come? I got enough confetti for both of us. I made it all myself."

He exhaled, smoke curling toward the ceiling, and when he looked at me and nodded his head up and down a few times it was as if he were really listening to me for the first time.

"Sure, Davey," he said. "Sure."

He washed the stub of his cigarette under the faucet, forced it down the drain.

"Momma's expecting us, you said? She's really waiting for me?"

I nodded. "Sure."

"Sure."

I went into his bedroom with him while he changed. When he lifted his hands up over his head, to pull his undershirt off—he wore the sleeveless kind with straps that hung loosely across his shoulders—I stared at the hair in his armpits and at the way the muscles rippled on his upper arms. Even though he was a small, thin man, I was always amazed at how powerful his arms were from tying packages all day at Gordon's, where he worked on the Lower East Side. Gordon's was a men's clothing store that sold merchandise on the installment plan. Sometimes on school vacation I'd go to work with my father and watch him at the counter next to the cash register and be proud of the way he could snap the twine off with his bare hands, without using a scissor or a knife.

"Should you take your air raid warden's stuff?" I asked.

"What for? The war's over."

"I don't know," I said. "But I saw some of the men wearing their old Army hats and parts of their uniforms, so I thought maybe you should."

We walked downstairs. When we got to the lobby he put his cigarette out in the standing ashtray and lifted my face up toward his, his hand under my chin.

"You like it when I get dressed up in my air raid warden's stuff?"

I nodded. I figured he knew that I sometimes took the stuff out of his closet when my friends and I played war—the helmet and arm band and silver whistle and flashlight and gas mask.

"So listen," he said, smiling. "Maybe if I don't have to turn the stuff back in, I'll let you have it. Okay? Would you like that?"

"Would I!" I exclaimed, and I couldn't keep from lunging toward him, from hugging him around the waist as tightly as I could. "Oh Poppa!"

"Well, I ain't promising," he said. "It depends on if they make you pay or not—that gas mask must of cost a few good bucks. But if I don't gotta pay, maybe I can let you have it."

He patted the top of my head and I let go of him.

"Okay? It's a deal?"

"It's a deal."

We went outside and started toward the corner. "I'll tell you something else. Listen. Sure I'm happy the war's over, but you know the one thing I'm sorry about?"

I thought of saying something about Uncle Abe coming home, but I didn't.

"What?"

He looked at me in a very serious way, shaking his head up and down. His good eye was moist.

"I'm only sorry F.D.R. didn't live to see this day. He was a wonderful man, President Roosevelt. He . . ." He stopped. "Come. Momma's waiting."

At the corner, we found my mother right away. Her lipstick was on straight and she gave my father a big hug and kiss.

"So look who's here finally!"

Before my father could say anything about what I'd said to him to get him there, I tugged on her dress and showed her the bag with the confetti.

"Where'd you get it?"

"I made it," I said. "I cut it all up myself. It took me a long time."

"Ain't he something?" she said to my father. "Ain't this little one something?"

"You want some?" I asked.

"And why not?"

She reached in and took a big handful. Then I pushed the bag toward my father and he took a big handful too. Between them they'd taken more than half.

"Hey Sol—" she yelled at my father. "Guess what?"

"What?"

"The war's over!" she yelled, and she threw her confetti into his face.

My father tried to laugh, but when some of the pieces of paper got stuck in his mouth, he gagged. He coughed and spat and my mother turned him around and pounded him on the back with the flat of her hand.

"Raise up your hands over your head—"

My father looked at me, his hands in the air as if he were being robbed, and I saw that his eye was tearing badly. He stopped gagging.

"So what are you waiting for?" he asked me. "Throw already."

I wanted to get a really good effect, so I tore my bag down from the top on two sides to expose the rest of the confetti, balanced the bag on my hands from underneath and gave as hard a toss as I could, upwards. All the confetti went up in a kind of clump, though, and as the clump fell only a few pieces detached themselves and fluttered. My mother was leaning on my father's shoulder, laughing at him, picking pieces of paper from his face and hair. I looked at the empty paper bag and I felt embarrassed.

People were cheering and pointing towards Rogers Avenue, where I saw a silver-gray DeSoto come along, men on both running boards—five of them—and they had guns in their hands and were shooting them into the air as if they were cowboys riding a stagecoach. Little Benny was in the front seat, wearing a brown felt hat pulled down on one side, shading his eyes. He was grinning from ear to ear, as if he'd just won the war himself. When my father saw who they were, he spit on the ground, three times.

"They should rot in hell," he said.

"Shh," my mother said. "C'mon, Sol. Someone will hear."

I looked at the ground where my father's spit had gone, and it seemed to me that the mounds of paper that had risen almost to my knees by now were ocean waves. I imagined myself standing at Coney Island, knee-deep in the water, holding my father's eyeglasses in my hands while he swam out, arm over arm, to get cooled off, and I saw how frightened I was, that if he went too far he might disappear under the waves and never come back.

A few feet away from me Marvin Ellenbogen, who lived downstairs from us in our building, was going around picking up bunches of confetti and streamers with his hands and stuffing it all into an A & S shopping bag. I stared at him for a while—things seemed quieter somehow—and then I hunted around until I found a bag and I did the same. I pushed over to Marvin and raised my bag up over my shoulder and tossed the whole thing at his face and this time the stuff sprayed out beautifully. For a second I found myself wishing that Tony Cremona could be there to see, and when I thought of him, my heart bumped. Then I threw the bag away and just started scooping up as much paper as I could hold in my hands and arms and heaving the stuff at Marvin while he did the same back to me. I lost sight of my mother and father, but that was just as well, I figured, because I knew my father would probably have had that sour look on his face again by this time. I knew that he was probably beginning to think that when Abe came home from the Army he would have to quit his job at Gordon's and go to work for him again, no matter how much he didn't want to.

2

ON THE MORNING that Lillian called to tell us Abe's troopship had arrived and that she was going to have a big welcome home party for him that night at her house, my mother and father were near the end of one of their fights. I'd heard some of it between dreams—it was about money again, and how my father didn't earn enough but still kept forbidding my mother to get a job—and when I went to the bathroom in the morning my father's small blue canvas satchel was at the door. Whenever I saw it waiting there by itself I knew he wouldn't be coming home after work. He did that sometimes, and stayed in a hotel for a few nights or with one of his two brothers. Usually, he'd explain to me afterwards, he left home not to punish my mother for anything she'd done to him but because he felt her life would be happier without him in it.

He was still home when the call came. My mother and I were eating breakfast and listening to "Rambling with Gambling." Through the window at the end of the kitchen I could see bands of snow about an inch high on the railings and stairs of the fire escape, white on orange, and I narrowed my eyes and stared, to see if the snow was perfectly level or if it had begun to melt in places.

My mother turned the radio down, and as soon as she got the news about Abe—the phone was on the wall between the table and the icebox and she put one hand over the mouthpiece and whispered to me that Abe was home but that we couldn't say hello to him because Lillian said he was asleep—tears started down from her eyes, sliding along the crease lines around her mouth.

She asked a lot of questions about how Abe looked and how he was

feeling—it was January 1946, five months since the war ended—and if
he'd asked about her. She apologized to Lillian for crying like an idiot,
and while she carried on I thought of all the drawings I'd saved up for
Abe and of which ones I would take, even though I knew that taking
them would mean showing them to him in front of other people.

"Is it really true this time?" I asked when she hung up.

"It's really true."

She switched the radio off and stuffed the antenna wires that came
out of the back—the copper showed through in spots, smooth orange
between the thin twisting lines of red and white—into the wooden con-
sole. She turned in a circle like a little girl, looking around the room as
if she didn't know what to do next, then she leaned over the sink,
knocked on the wall, called into the bathroom to my father that Abe was
home, that Lillian was making a party, that he should come home early
from work. He didn't answer. He was coughing again, the way he did
every morning, and I imagined him bent over the toilet bowl, hands on
thighs. My mother went into the foyer, came back with her pocketbook.
She sat next to me, took out the compact that had her initials, E.V.,
engraved on the gold cover—"E.V.—get it?" she liked to say to people.
"My initials and name are just the same!"—and inspected her face,
twisting her mouth this way and that, running her tongue around between her gums and her lips. She rubbed rouge into her cheeks, and
then, while she smiled at me over the mirror in her compact, she put on
fresh lipstick from a brass-colored tube that looked like a machine gun
bullet, and blotted her lips with a tissue.

"There!" she said. "What do you think?"

I shrugged and tried to keep eating. But it was hard to get the hot
cereal to go down smoothly. The grains of Ralston stuck at the back of
my throat and all I could think of was what it was going to be like to
actually see Abe again. I'd only been in the second grade when he left
for training camp four years before. He'd had a furlough once after that
and had met my Aunt Lillian in Atlantic City while their daughter Sheila
came and stayed with us, but I never saw him again before he was
shipped overseas. Abe had been a hero and had killed a lot of Germans.
Once, on a postcard, he said that he'd killed two Nazis just for me, and
what I wondered—what scared me—was if killing somebody up close
would change you in ways that you couldn't ever change back, even if
you didn't know the person and even if you knew the other person would
have killed you first if he could have. I wondered if he would still like
me.

"Listen," my mother said. "We'll go to Poppa."

"But I have school."

"That's what we'll do, okay? Just the two of us. We'll go to Poppa and

give him the news that Abe is coming home and I'll talk him into coming
to the party. Forgive and forget, right?" She reached toward me. "You'll
come with Momma, darling?"

"I have school," I said. "I told you."

"So I give you permission—how often in one lifetime does your uncle
Abe get home from the war?"

"Will you write me a note?"

She smiled. "I'll write you a note."

My father came into the kitchen, lit a cigarette, blew a puff of smoke
toward the ceiling. Three tiny pieces of toilet paper were stuck to his
cheek and chin where he'd nicked himself shaving. My mother put her
arms around his neck, from behind, but he twisted away and pointed a
finger at me.

"You take good care of your mother while I'm gone, do you hear me?"

"Oh Sol!" my mother exclaimed. "Sol darling—not now, all right?
Didn't you hear who was on the phone?"

"I thought you weren't talking to a good-for-nothing like me anymore."

"Life is so short, Sol. Why should we use it up fighting?"

"So your brother is coming home and that makes everything jake,
huh?" My father sniffed in. "Wonderful. Last night you told me I didn't
have a pot to piss in and this morning—"

"Sol! Please—!"

"—and this morning, now that your big shot brother is coming home
you start in with all the hugging and kissing. Sure. Wonderful. Everything is hunky-dory as long as Abe is around."

I thought of how cold the radio said it was outside. I imagined the
snow on the fire escape as being made up of millions of tiny white grains,
like sand, and I felt sad that Abe was coming home now instead of in
the spring or the summer. If he came home in the spring or summer, I
knew, he would take me to a Dodger game at Ebbets Field. I thought of
me and Tony and Marvin and the other guys sneaking into the bleachers
and of how proud Abe would be of me for the way we did it. My mother
was gone. My father was searching around on top of the table as if he'd
lost something—he was too proud ever to ask me to help him look for
anything—and what I saw inside my head was the lush green of the
grass of Ebbets Field before a game began. I saw the men walking
around the base paths, dragging the enormous pieces of weighted-down
cloth they used to smooth the dirt paths. I saw Abe laughing his beautiful big smile and waving to people he knew in the stands and I saw how
happy I was to be next to him. Now that he was back, though, I wondered if I could still stay friends with Tony. Tony's father worked for
Mr. Fasalino the way my father worked for Abe, and Mr. Fasalino and

Abe controlled different territories. According to my father, Mr. Fasalino's organization had been scared to go too far while the war was on and we were fighting against Italy, but now that the Italians weren't our enemies anymore he figured Mr. Fasalino would try to move into our territory as soon as Abe got back.

My mother set my father's satchel down on the chair next to me, took out his set of clean underwear, laid the tops and bottoms on the kitchen counter, and folded them down with her hands.

"For me this once, all right? Just meet us at Lillian's tonight. Is that asking too much of a man I've been married to for fourteen years?"

My father cocked his head to the side, and from where I was sitting below him the white of his blind eye was soft and milky. When the two of them got angry, my mother's cheeks would fill with color and my father's would go pale and gray. It was as if their fighting made him older and her younger. My mother's hand was on the back of my neck, but I wasn't sure she knew she had it there. I tried not to hear the words they said to one another—I hated it when he acted like a beggar—and I thought instead of the questions I could ask Abe, the ones I'd been saving up about what the war had been like, and who were the bravest soldiers, and whether the Australian Commandos were really the best of all, even better than our Rangers, and if he'd ever been scared he would die and what he'd imagined during a moment like that.

"If I hurt your feelings," my mother said, "then I apologize right here with the boy as witness, okay?" She stroked my neck slowly and I didn't move. "Look—I know you mean well, Sol, but what would be so terrible if we had a little extra money? I think it would be a terrific job, being a comparison shopper. Anybody meets me in the store, they would think I'm a regular shopper, like I'm supposed to look like. I'd get to move around a lot, from store to store. I could save us some money too. I—"

"No wife of Sol Voloshin is gonna work so long as he's alive. Do you hear me?"

"I hear you. But I'll say it again, that I'm sorry and that at a time like this what I think is bygones should be bygones and we should be like a family. Like a *family*, Sol, all right? Do you hear me? Did I ever want more than we should be a real family together, the three of us, with no secrets? Only when we fight I get scared that it's gonna be like Momma and Poppa all over again and you can't ever understand that, how all I want is for us to love one another."

"Sure. I'll love you and you'll love Abe and Abe will take care of the whole world. Tell me another one."

My father touched his underpants, on the counter, but he didn't put them back into his satchel. I was afraid to look directly into his face because I knew he might look at me in a way that would make me want

to help him find the words he could use to make her stop being angry
with him. But if he left her for good and never came back, would she be
happy then?

"And listen, Sol—I'll try not to nag you about money no more either,
so you can see that it's okay by me if you go. Sure. Only if you go, Sol,
you don't ever have to come back, because do you know why?"

I thought he might give her his old line about how when the war
ended in Europe it would start in Brooklyn, but he didn't. He just stood
there, his silence making the look I'd seen a thousand times before begin
to spread over her face—her eyes narrowing, the left corner of her
mouth curling upwards, her neck going stiff—and I went rigid too, so
that I could be ready for anything she might say. I wanted to get out of
the room—to grab my schoolbooks and coat and galoshes and to slam
the door behind me and leave them to scratch at each other with their
words—but I knew that if I moved and tried to get away they'd only
switch their attention to me.

"And you say you love me," my mother said. "Don't make me laugh,
mister. If you really loved me you wouldn't talk to me the way you do."

"Not in front of the boy, all right, Evie? Please."

"Not in front of the boy. Sure. But if you want to rant and rave in
front of him and I say not—if I get down on my knees for you to stop,
like I been doing—that's all right, huh?"

"Look. If I'm there tonight, I'm only liable to say the wrong thing and
take away from your good time. The truth is I don't trust myself around
Abe."

"Listen, mister, if you think a pip-squeak like you can take away *my*
good time, then you got another think coming. I'll tell you a secret," she
added, moving toward him. "You don't make me happy and you don't
make me unhappy. You don't got the power in you."

"Evie, stop already. The boy."

"He ain't hearing nothing he ain't heard before and if he don't like it
he can pack up and get out too. You think I need you two? What can
you do for me that I can't do for myself? Tell me that. Come on. Tell
me."

My father slumped into a chair. The ashes on his cigarette were getting long and I was frightened they'd fall on his hand and burn him. I
tried to make their faces go away by remembering war movies I'd been
to—*Guadalcanal Diary* and *Back to Bataan* and *Destination Tokyo*—
and I imagined going to them with Abe so he could tell me which parts
were true and which parts were made up.

"Whatever you want, Evie," he said. "Whatever you want."

My mother laughed at him then and when she did I felt that she was
laughing at me too.

"Sure. *Now* you'll do what I ask, when it suits you, right? When you don't want to be embarrassed in front of your precious son. You ain't nothing, Sol. Did you know that? You're less than nothing, if you want the truth. You ain't—"

"*Stop it!*" I cried out. "*Stop it already!*"

My mother turned to me.

"Well, well," she said, mocking me with her eyes. "So look who's butting in now? What's the matter, *bubula*—you're afraid your father can't fight his own battles?"

I stood and screamed at her with all my might to stop—to just stop it already, that I had said to stop it—and while I went on shouting the words I looked for something to grab on to, but the only thing I could see besides the radio was my bowl of cereal. There was still some Ralston in it, in a grainy brown crescent along the outer rim—so I lifted the bowl into the air with both hands and smashed it down on the table.

"*Now* do you believe me?" I shouted. "*Now* will you stop it?"

"See?" my mother said, her voice suddenly gentle again. She came to me and got down on her knees next to my chair. She started to stroke my hair and my cheek. I couldn't move. "See what we're doing to the boy? Oh Davey—what are we doing to you, darling? Tell me what we're doing to you, my baby—"

"I'm not your baby," I said, and I backed up against the icebox. "All I want is for you to just shut up. The both of you. *Just shut up shut up shut up*—" Once I started screaming I couldn't ever stop myself, and even though we'd been through scenes like this before, while it was taking place and I was screaming my lungs out at them the strangest thing was I felt at the same time that I was outside the scene too, watching it all happen as if somebody else were throwing the tantrum— as if I couldn't figure out how a boy like me could ever get so crazy.

"My poor baby," my mother said. "My poor little Davey."

My mother took my father's hands away from his face. She lifted his cigarette from his lower lip and set it down in the ashtray.

"For him, Sol," she pleaded. "For him—it's for him we gotta stop all this crap."

"Crap is right," he said. "Sure, Evie. Whatever you say. Sure. So listen. I stopped already, in case you didn't notice. Didn't I stop? Did I stop or did I stop?"

My mother kissed my father on his forehead, came toward me. When she smiled at me this time all I saw was her mouth, like the heart on a Valentine's card, bright red wax and enormous, as if it were triple its regular size, with a dark opening in the middle for her tongue, and what I wanted to do more than anything in the world was to have a baseball bat in my hands—a beautiful Louisville Slugger—and to be able to swing it around and smash through her lips and teeth to the back of her skull.

"My sweet little Davey. My little baby. Your Poppa and I stopped our fighting, see? Didn't we stop, Sol?"

She was still smiling, and when she tried to put her hand on mine I leaned back into the windowsill, frightened that she might tell Abe about my tantrums.

"Stay away from me," I said. "I'm warning you. Do you hear me? Stay away from me."

My father stood in the entranceway to the kitchen in his good winter coat, the soft black one that was part cashmere.

"I'll go straight to Lillian's from work."

I stayed where I was, my fists opening and closing at my sides. My father pointed a finger at me again.

"You calm down and listen to your mother, do you hear? You're only making things worse."

I fought to control the rasping sound that came from my chest, but I couldn't, and I wanted to smash his head open too for switching and taking her side, for doing her dirty work for her. Didn't he know that this only made her despise him more?

"We'll all be away from each other the whole day, we'll feel better," he said. "You'll see."

"But do you see what we do to him? He won't even let his own mother touch him. Remember when he was a baby and he used to hold his breath? Didn't I tell you then?" She clucked inside her mouth. "Someday. Someday, Sol—didn't I warn you enough times?—someday Davey's gonna kill somebody with that temper of his and I won't be responsible. That's all I got to say."

The front door closed. I imagined the way my father would look, slouching down the stairs from landing to landing. My mother moved around the kitchen as if nothing had happened. She cleared the table and put away my father's satchel and picked up the little white chips from the broken plate with a damp cloth, and what seemed craziest of all to me was that she actually seemed happy again all of a sudden, as if the scene had somehow given her what she wanted. When she talked to me her voice was sweet and relaxed. It was almost as if she were talking to herself. She went on and on the way she did sometimes, while I stood there, frozen.

"Listen. If you want to turn into a statue, Davey, you can keep standing there—it's all the same to me—or else you can show how really smart you are and go wash your face and comb your hair and put on a nicer shirt, for visiting your grandpa. So you won't go to school and I'll write you a note. What's the big deal, a smart boy like you? In the meantime I need to get dressed and do my eyebrows, so you got time to think over what happened. It wouldn't hurt to apologize either. You don't want to come with me to visit Poppa, I won't force you. The same goes for Abe's party. You want to come, come. You don't, don't. Only I know you want to see your uncle Abe a lot, don't you? I mean, even though I know that deep down your father loves me, if he talks to me the way you seen him do it makes me feel he don't and the feeling spreads everywhere inside me so there's no room for anything else, and I get scared, and he gets more scared, and then you see the way things get out of hand, yeah? I mean, I told him right on our honeymoon that I knew he *loved* me—let's face it, he worshiped me, who didn't know that?—but I told him I was just a funny kind of girl that way, that I needed to be told it every day of my life and in the right tone of voice or else I get—well—sad was the way I put it back then. I do get awful sad sometimes, Davey. Like when you were born and your father came to me in the hospital with his hands full of the most beautiful yellow roses and you were lying on my breast under the sheet, and I asked him if he still remembered what I said to him on our honeymoon and he promised me he would never forget. But he forgets. I mean, he forgets, don't he? You're the witness. He forgets all the time. . . ."

Beau Jack was shoveling snow from the sidewalk when I got downstairs. His dog Kate was tied to the fence with a chain, and I took off my mittens and brushed her fur behind her ears. She got up on me, her front paws against my chest, and I put my arms around her neck and let her lick my face the way she liked to. She was part Labrador and part basset hound, with black fur like warm silk. Some people made fun of her because of the way she looked, her top half sleek and long and her bottom half slung low to the ground, with big front paws that went out sideways, slue-footed—but I loved Kate and I visited Beau Jack in the cellar sometimes just so I could feel her fur and let her lick me.

"My Uncle Abe's coming home from the Army," I said. "We're gonna have a party for him tonight at my Aunt Lillian's."

"That's real good," Beau Jack said, but he didn't smile at me. He leaned his shovel against the fence. His Dodger baseball hat was set at a slight angle on his head, tilted down at the right side where the ear was missing, from a war injury. What he had instead of an ear looked like a little brown mushroom cap. "I like to see the boys come home."

"I mean, he's not coming home today. He came home yesterday, but the party is for tonight."

Beau Jack's skin always seemed dusty in the winter, as if coated with a thin layer of dried-up salt spray from the ocean. I'd been thinking of trying to draw him for a while, but I was afraid because I couldn't figure out how I could get the color of his skin—the exact shade of brown showing through the pale white—onto paper with just my pencils.

"Listen, Davey," he said, leaning down toward me. "You want to see the most beautiful thing in the world?"

"Sure."

"You come on with me then."

I followed Beau Jack into the building. I liked being close to him because even in the winter he gave off a wonderful fragrance, like peanut oil that had been frying for a while. On the fourth floor he stopped.

"You go on in first. But be quiet."

He unlocked the door. The foyer smelled like fresh paint. The walls were bright yellow and the room was empty.

"You go on," he said. "Go on now."

He closed the door behind us. I went into the living room. It was empty too, without furniture or carpeting, and the venetian blinds on the two windows were drawn up to the top so that the room was full of bright white light. In the middle of the ceiling two wires hung down from the fixture, tied together with little plastic caps on them. The parquet floor gleamed as if it had a thin sheet of glass on top of it. I smelled the wax. The walls were bare, painted in a soft powdery gray, and where the electric wall fixtures had been there were round cones sticking out that looked like women's breasts.

"Isn't it beautiful?" he asked.

He drew me with him, out of the living room and into a bedroom. The bedroom was bare also, painted in the same gray, the color the sky was sometimes on a cold day before snow came.

"Spent lots of hours getting it ready, but it was worth it, don't you think? Oh yeah. If you ask me I think there's nothing more beautiful than a home that's all clean and empty and fresh-painted and ready for some new family to come live in it."

I went into the kitchen with him and admired everything: how white and shiny he'd gotten the refrigerator and stove and sink, how he'd put shelf paper in the cabinets, how crystal clear the windows were. I told him that I had to go, that my mother would be waiting for me.

"What I do is I use newspapers on the windows. It has chemicals in it that makes them shine." He smiled. "That's what I like to best of all, you see—to get a place ready before somebody starts to live in it. But you know who's moving in, Davey?"

I shook my head.

"Gone to be a boy your age in the family, somebody you'll have to play with."

"What's his name?"

"Don't know." He led me back along the corridor and out the door. Under the surface of his skin—along the flat planes of his cheeks and under the brown pores that were pitted like the perforations between postage stamps—it seemed to me that there were shades of purple. Without the purple, I thought, the brown would not have seemed so deep and beautiful.

"Stanley maybe. Or Steven. That be the boy's name. Steven. His father's a dentist."

When we got back downstairs my mother was next to the fence with Kate, waiting, and Beau Jack told her about the apartment and the family that was moving in, so that she wouldn't get angry with me.

"We're going to see my father," she said. "I'm hoping that maybe this time we'll be able to talk him into coming home to live with us."

"You're a good woman, Mrs. Voloshin," Beau Jack said. "You're a good daughter to that man."

"Wouldn't that be nice, Davey—if your grandpa came and lived with us?"

I looked down. Kate licked at my right hand and I slipped it into her mouth so she could nibble on it. My mother laughed. She leaned on Beau Jack's arm.

"I think he's afraid we'll make him sleep out on the fire escape, this one is, but we wouldn't do a thing like that, would we?"

"Oh no," he said. "We don't put the boy out there. What we do if you got no more room is you send him down to live with me."

"My brother's home, you know—Abe—so maybe he'll figure out something for us." She paused. "You remember my brother?"

"Everybody knows Abe," Beau Jack said.

"Things'll be different again now that he's home. Sure. Maybe we'll move down to Mrs. Farber's apartment when she moves out and that way we'll get an extra bedroom." She pressed Beau Jack's arm with her gloved hand. "We got first call on that, don't we?"

"I told Mr. Fogel you first in line."

"Or else Poppa can share Davey's room with him for a while. We'll get one of those nice hi-risers, so the room will still be just as big in the daytime. Sol don't like the whole idea, and my father ain't coming home with us right away, only you gotta start planning these things ahead."

"Oh yeah," Beau Jack said. He took his shovel from against the fence and the metal scraped along the sidewalk, giving me chills. "You got to plan things."

My grandfather's old age home was on the Lower East Side, a few blocks from where my father worked, and we had to change trains twice to get there. We walked up the six flights of stairs to his floor—the elevator was broken—and when we came into his room he was sitting up on the side of his bed with his feet on the floor, his head to his chest.

"Shh," my mother said. We took off our coats—my mother was wearing a Persian lamb coat with a mink collar that her father had given to her before he sold his fur store—and she tiptoed toward him, going around his bed to the far side, laying our coats across his blanket first. The room was about half the size of our gym at school and there was nothing in it except beds, wooden chairs, and, along the wall opposite the windows, a row of old metal lockers, one for each of the twenty men who lived in the room. The lockers were different colors—gray, brown and green mostly—but none of them had been painted for a long time and the rust showed through where the paint had chipped away.

Five other men were in the room, two of them taking naps under their blankets, three sitting on chairs next to their beds. The man in the chair next to my grandfather's bed was reading a book with Hebrew words in it. He had a lump on his neck that ran from just under his ear into his collar in an oval shape that made me imagine for a second that there was a hand grenade under the skin.

My mother sat on the bed alongside my grandfather, reached into his lap and stroked one of his hands.

"*What?*" My grandfather's head jerked upwards. "What do you want from me? What?"

"I'm sorry, Poppa. I didn't mean to wake you. You must have been sleeping lightly—like a feather, yeah?"

"Is Davey here?"

I came around in front so he could see me.

"Hello, Grandpa," I said, and I leaned forward and kissed him on the cheek. He took my shoulders in his hands and pressed me to his chest.

"You're a good boy, Davey." He turned to my mother. "Why didn't you call me first?"

"I wanted to surprise you."

My grandfather slipped his feet into orange carpet-slippers, walked to where the lockers were. He took a key from his sweater pocket, opened the lock, fumbled around inside until he found what he wanted. On the inside of the locker door there was a mirror and a calendar. He looked into the mirror and opened his mouth wide, as if inspecting the fillings in his teeth.

He handed me a Clark bar. Half the wrapper, at a diagonal, was faded to pale orange, as if it had been lying in the sun for a long time.

"This is for you. I was saving it."

"Oh Poppa!" my mother exclaimed. She hugged him, but he just sat there stiffly. "Didn't I tell you how much your grandpa loves you?"

"Thank you, Grandpa."

"You're a good boy, Davey." He looked at my mother. "I always said he was a good boy, didn't I?"

My mother chewed on the corner of her lower lip, and I hoped she would give him the news about Abe right away so we could get it over with. My grandfather and Abe hadn't seen each other since before I was born. My grandfather had not even come to my parents' wedding, he hated Abe so much.

Two old men limped into the room, leaning on one another. My mother waved to them, but they didn't come to say hello. My grandfather wasn't friendly with the men in his home. Most of them were observant Jews who spent a lot of time downstairs in the sanctuary and library, praying or studying. My grandfather didn't believe in religion and he sometimes made fun of the other men for their beliefs.

"Why don't you eat your candy bar?" he asked me.

I looked toward my mother, for permission.

"Sure. Why not? That's what he gave it to you for—to eat."

"He's a good boy," my grandfather said. "He's a nice quiet boy. I like that. He doesn't say much."

"Oh yeah," my mother said, ruffling my hair. "He's a real quiet one, this one is. You never know what he's got spinning inside that gorgeous head of his."

"All right," my grandfather said. "You came for a reason, Evie. So talk to me."

The Clark bar was hard as a stone, and while I tried to bite a chunk out of it I wondered again—as I did each time we visited—why it was my mother kept looking with so much love into the face of a man who treated her so badly. I agreed with my father—that there was nothing she could ever do that would please her father, so why did she keep trying? Did she think that if she could figure out what to do to make him love her, he would get back together with Abe—that they would all be a family again the way they'd been once upon a time? After our visits to him she usually explained to me that her father hadn't always been this way, that when she was in high school her girlfriends had envied her, to have a man like him for a father—that he'd been very handsome, a sharp dresser, a man who liked to tell jokes, a man who always had a good word for people. But no matter what she said I could never imagine a picture of what his face had been like when he was younger.

Sometimes I tried to make the faces of the old men in his home younger by taking away their wrinkles and their beards and by moving the position of their eyes downwards in their faces, but most of the time it seemed impossible for me that these old men had ever had other lives. I knew that some of them had once been wealthy, that some had fought in wars—a man on the floor below my grandfather's wore a medal on his bathrobe given to him by the Emperor Franz Joseph—and often when my grandfather made me walk to his locker with him so he could give me candy, I would glance in the mirror and try to imagine how I would look when I was an old man, at the end of my own life.

"Abe is coming home." My mother let out a long breath of air. "I mean, he came home yesterday—last night, Lillian said."

"I don't know any Abe."

"Oh Poppa," my mother said, and as she took both his hands in her own I saw tears glisten in her eyes. "He's *alive*—Abe is *alive*, Poppa! He could have been killed every day, but he's alive, and he's home, don't you see? Your own flesh and blood. Forgive and forget, Poppa. Please?" She closed her eyes and tried to get control of herself, to stop herself from trembling. "Listen. Lillian's having a party tonight and I asked permission for you to come and even she thought it would be wonderful. So don't you see?"

My grandfather pulled his hands away and spoke to me: "What are you staring at? Go. Go look out the window. You don't have to listen to this kind of talk."

I went to the window and looked at the city, at rooftops with pigeon coops and clotheslines and chimneys and smokestacks and water towers, at iron ladders and brick ledges all edged with narrow layers of snow. My mother was begging her father not to make her choose, and he talked back to her in a hard, cold voice, telling her that he had warned her that he would never eat or sleep where Abe had eaten or slept and that she'd known what she was doing when she made her decision.

The window was open a few inches at the bottom, to let fresh air in, and I slipped my hands under it and raised it up. I leaned out so I could see the entrance to the building down below. I concentrated on the five windowsills below mine and the way they jutted out from the wall and got narrower and narrower, but in an even way like an upside-down pyramid, until they reached the first floor. I wondered what would happen if you'd jump—if you would have time to twist around backwards in midair and catch onto one of the sills with your hands, on the fourth or third or second floor, or if you missed, what would be the best way to land on the sidewalk, and if you could survive. In Ripley's *Believe It or Not* there was a drawing of a sixteen-month-old baby from Buffalo, New York, who had fallen eleven floors from a fire escape and had survived, with only a broken wrist and bruises.

I let myself imagine that Abe was holding me upside-down from the roof above, by my ankles, to test how brave I was and how much I trusted him.

"*Davey!*"

My mother grabbed me from behind. She yanked on my right ear with one hand while she tried to turn me around with the other, but I twisted away.

"Are you nuts?" she screamed. "How many times do I gotta tell you not to lean out windows with your feet off the floor? How many times?"

I let her drag me to my grandfather's bed. A few of the old men seemed to be moving toward me. One of them pointed at me and yelled something at my grandfather in Yiddish and he yelled back. Then I saw that the men were moving, not toward me but toward the door, and I realized that a bell had rung while my mother was grabbing me—or that it had rung a few moments before that, while I was looking down at the sidewalk. My grandfather stood.

"It's time to eat," he said.

He started toward the door without saying goodbye. My mother went after him and whispered to him, glanced at me, motioned to me to turn away. I did, but I looked back a second later and saw her hand him something from her purse. Then she called to me.

"Grandpa wants to say goodbye to you. He wants to give you something."

"Here."

My grandfather handed me two quarters.

I took the money and thanked him.

"You can give me a kiss goodbye."

He bent over and I stretched up and kissed him. He moved away again, but my mother held onto his sleeve. She told me to tell him that he should come to the party, that everybody would be disappointed if he didn't. I did what she said, but while I spoke I thought about Tony and I wondered if anybody from his family had come home on the same troopship with Abe—any of his cousins or uncles—and if there would be parties for them. One of Tony's two older brothers was overseas, in the Philippines. Had the government sent him there on purpose, because it didn't trust him? My father had told me that Italian gangsters helped the American Army when we invaded Sicily near the end of the war—Tony knew the story and was proud of it—but I wasn't sure if I'd have the courage to ask Abe the question that still bothered me: How did Italian soldiers fighting for America feel about killing Italian soldiers fighting for Italy?

"Enough already," my grandfather said. "I'm late. The food will all be gone."

He shuffled into the hallway where the men were crowding together at the staircase, then pushed a few men aside so he could get in front of them. If Tony and I could get to be in charge someday, would we be able to make peace between everybody so that when we were old men

our children and grandchildren would visit us and bring us gifts and
thank us? My mother was calling to my grandfather, telling him she
loved him and would visit him again soon. She lied and said that my
father had sent his regards. I let one of the quarters slip out of my hand
and watched it roll across the floor.

"Catch it quick!" my mother yelled. "*Quick*, Davey."

By the time I crawled out from under the iron bed, the hallway outside my grandfather's room was empty.

At the Hoyt Street stop in Brooklyn my mother pulled me to the train
door just before it closed. She was yelling at me, but I couldn't hear
what she was saying because of the roaring inside the subway station.
I'd been playing a game I invented—staring at people's shoes and trying
to imagine, just from the shoes, what the face of the person would be
like. You could tell a lot from shoes—from the color and style and
creases in the leather and from how dull or shiny or scuffed they were,
or from the position they were in—and I usually came pretty close to
knowing the face I'd see when I looked up.

"What's the matter, you can't hear when I tell you something? What's
the matter with you anyway?"

I kept my eyes on the sidewalk, brown and slushy now from people
having walked on the snow all morning. We were outside, across the
street from the Brooklyn Paramount.

"Is this the way you treat me after I give you a day off so you can be
with me? Is this the way you say thanks to your mother?"

She took my chin in her gloved hand and forced me to look up at her.

"See what happens? Do you *see?*"

"Leave me alone," I said. "I didn't do anything."

"Oh shit," she said then, and she cupped her palm over her mouth.
"It serves me right for trying to be the good one, don't it? Just in time
for the party. Am I a genius or what? Listen. We gotta find a drugstore
so I can get something for this or by tonight it'll be spread all over my
mouth."

She started walking fast while she talked to herself.

"Just in honor of my kid brother, right? Well. It serves you right, Evie
—you try to make peace and look what happens. Sol is right. If people
want to eat each other up alive, you shouldn't deny them the pleasure.
Did God give Lillian fever blisters? Did he put a plague on her like he
did on me?"

We crossed another street and I could make out the letters on the
arcade of the Brooklyn Fox now. *The Story of G.I. Joe* was playing, a

new war picture that some of the guys at school said was better than
Objective Burma.

What would you be ready to die for?

I wondered if my uncle would ask me the question at the party. I
hoped not, because I still didn't know how to answer it. If I gave him
the wrong answer, would he still love me?

We passed the IRT Nevins Street stop and entered a Rexall's pharmacy. The prescription counter was in the back, near the crutches and
wheelchairs, and when the pharmacist came out my mother showed
him her lip. The pharmacist was a short, chubby man with a trim black
mustache like Governor Dewey's. He wore a light blue smock. He fur-
rowed his brow while he examined my mother's lip. Then he nodded
and said that it was herpes simplex and my mother began to give him
the whole story, about how Abe was coming home and we were having
the party for him and how she'd tried to get their father to come, how it
had made her nervous stomach act up.

"You got a mirror?" she asked.

The pharmacist went back to the booth where he mixed the drugs and
returned a few seconds later with a small mirror. I concentrated on how
things had looked from six flights up in my grandfather's house, and I
imagined myself letting dart-bombs loose from my Bombs Away game.
Bombs Away was my favorite game. There was a map on a board of
different Nazi bunkers and airfields and aircraft carriers and roads and
bridges and mountains with hidden mortar positions and a box you held
up at eye level that had two holes in it, like those on binoculars. When
you looked into the holes there was a mirror at the other end, set at an
angle that let you see the map below. As soon as you had your target in
sight you pressed a small lever that let two steel-pointed bombs drop out.

"Well, Lillian will sure be happy to see me like this, won't she?"

My mother put the mirror down and touched the back of the pharmacist's hand.

"You got something to make this go away, right?"

"Not exactly, ma'am, but—"

"Listen. You look like the kind of man who don't just give people the
routine. I can tell. I mean, you look like the kind of man who cares, if
you know what I mean." She touched her lip. "Oh yeah—it's not a
terrible disease like cancer or polio, but the trouble is it takes place right
in the middle of your face, yeah?"

She laughed then. The pharmacist looked worried for a second, as if
he were trying to think of a remedy, but he didn't smile. He said that he
thought her herpes was too advanced to be stopped—sometimes, if you
sensed one coming, you could treat it before it blistered—but he asked

if she had ever tried tincture of nicotine. She seemed happy while she was talking to the man about her lip, and when she paid she touched his hand again and then held onto his wrist to show him how much she appreciated what he was doing for her.

"So say something," she said suddenly, turning to me, winking at the pharmacist.

"Is he your son?"

"Oh yeah. This here is my silent one, but I'll tell you one thing. I'm only thankful I never gave these things to him, you know what I mean? When he was a baby I was very careful. They say that's when they're most catching, when your baby is just born and nursing, so I was always careful not to kiss this one—"

She bent down and took me by the cheeks, squeezing so that my lips puffed forward.

"See?" she asked. "Is that a gorgeous mouth or is it a gorgeous mouth?"

"Come *on*," I said. "It's too *hot* in here."

"Listen—he got a voice too," she said. "Didn't I tell you?" She took the brown jar out of the bag and with a Q-tip from her purse she began applying the tincture of nicotine to her lip. I imagined her embarrassing me at Abe's party by telling about what was happening now. And what if Abe asked me what we were doing downtown, I wondered, and why I hadn't been in school? Could I keep from telling him that we'd gone to visit his father? Could I lie to him if I had to, about how much his father hated him?

My mother was telling me to say goodbye to the pharmacist.

"He's a good boy," she said, roughing up my hair. "I can take him anywhere with me and he's never any trouble. He was always this way. At home is another story, if you know what I mean. But look at that mouth and that little nose, would you? Take a good look," she went on, and I knew what was coming next, the way it always did. "See those curls and those tiny little ears—wouldn't you say sometimes that it was a waste on a boy? Give me your honest opinion, mister. Wouldn't you agree about what a beautiful girl he would of made?"

I sat on the floor in front of the wardrobe closet, reading comics, while my father kept at me, demanding that I tell him why he knew he was the smartest man in the world. He had come to Abe's party the night before and now, a day later, Abe was coming to dinner at our house. I tried to see Abe's face, to remember how surprised he was when he said goodbye to me and noticed my folder for the first time. He'd gotten down next to me then, in a deep-knee bend position, and touched my folder very gently, telling me that he didn't want to look at my drawings while there were so many people around.

I saw a picture in my head of Little Benny and Spanish Louie clinking glasses with Tony Cremona's father after they'd frisked him and escorted him into the living room. I saw Tony's father, in his long black overcoat —a messenger—embracing Abe, giving him greetings from Mr. Fasalino, Abe and Tony's father patting each other on the back with both hands as if they were long-lost relatives.

Abe didn't trust any of them, though, and when I saw the others again, in my head—Louie Newman and Monk Solloway and Waxey Shreibman and Avie Gornik and Big Jap Willer and the rest—all the warmth and happiness I'd been feeling about Abe coming to dinner washed out of me. I looked down, almost as if I expected to see warm water come leaking out of my shoes, onto the carpet. I thought of my uncle's cronies walking around his apartment, eating and drinking and laughing, and of how I'd looked hard at each of them, trying to see through their jackets to tell if they had guns or blackjacks or knives underneath. I remembered how raucous they'd all been and how they'd spent so much of their time flattering Abe the way my father did.

"Come on," my father insisted. "Answer the question—do you know how come I know I'm the smartest man in the world?"

He'd asked me the same question dozens of times before and I stayed quiet because I knew that he liked to be the one to give the answer.

"Because I married your mother!" he said. "That's how come!"

My mother waved a hand at him but I could tell that she was pleased. I wanted to get away from them so I could prepare my room for Abe's visit. If I tried to leave while my father was putting on one of his routines about how much he loved my mother, though, I knew he'd get angry with me. My mother was in her panties and brassiere. When she sat down at her vanity table, my father put his arms around her, from behind. I looked away. I didn't want to see my mother smiling at me as if she wished I would give her the kind of affection my father was trying to give her.

"Hey—cut it out. I gotta concentrate."

"What I think," my father said, "is that you're still ten times more beautiful when you got your little things than most women are the rest of the time. Tell your mother, Davey—isn't she as beautiful as a movie star? Couldn't she of been a movie star if she wanted to?"

My mother put her lipstick on, very carefully, and then, with her index finger, some cake makeup, but you could still tell that her upper lip was swollen to almost twice its size, and you could see the tiny rows of blisters through the makeup.

The church bells sounded, through the window, six times.

"Oh shit," my mother said. "Just shit. Sure. They'll be here any minute and I ain't even ready yet. Look at this face, will you? Will you just look at it?"

My father took my mother by the chin and turned her around to make her face him.

"So I'm looking and you still look terrific. That's all I got to say. Do you think I care about a few little pimples? I'll show you how much I care."

He tried to kiss her on the lips. I imagined Abe walking up the staircase, smiling, taking the steps two at a time. All afternoon I'd tried to be alone so I could sort out my drawings and baseball cards and comic books and sports magazines, but my mother kept interrupting me, saying she was too excited about Abe coming, that she needed me to keep her company.

"Jesus," she said, looking at the smear of red on my father's mouth and chin. "I didn't even blot myself yet and look what he's doing. What are you, crazy or something?"

"Yeah. I'm still crazy in love with you. Wouldn't you be crazy in love, Davey, if you were lucky enough to have a wife like I got?"

"But he's gonna be here in a second," I said. "Jesus Christ! What's the matter with you two—don't you got ears? Didn't you hear the bells?"

"Oooh—has that one got a temper," my mother said. "Only don't you curse in my room, mister. You wanna curse, you go into the alleys with your friends." She turned to my father. "Thanks for coming home early like I asked. And for last night. Did I remember to tell you how much that meant to me?"

"Family is still family," he said. "And I'll tell you the truth, Evie. Abe seemed different. I honestly think Abe is gonna be okay. And if Fasalino starts up with him, Abe's the one who can handle things. I mean, did we beat the Germans over there so that the Italians could kill us here?"

My mother never reacted when my father talked about Abe's business. She reached up, as if to wipe the lipstick from his chin, but instead she took the cigarette out of his mouth and put it in her own. The makeup was already cracking, the skin above her lips looking the way dirt did after heavy rains, when the rains had all dried up. She drew in on my father's cigarette, leaning backwards so that her skin, between the top of her panties and her brassiere, stretched flat.

"You really think I'm still beautiful, even when I got these things all over my face?"

"I honestly do, Evie."

"Ah," my mother said, and she smiled now, the way my father liked. "You're really cockeyed, Sol, do you know that?"

"Sure," he said. He took his glasses off, set them down on the night table and began walking around the room, his hands out in front of him, feeling his way like a blind man. "Yeah, me, I'm the original cockeyed wonder, right?"

My mother laughed. With his glasses off, my father could hardly see anything, not even the big lettering on signs in store windows.

The buzzer went off in the kitchen, from downstairs.

"It's him," I said. "He's *here.*"

My mother backed up to the dresser and my father kept walking toward her.

"He's here!" I said. "Didn't you *hear?*"

The buzzer went off a second time.

"*See*—?" I said. "*Now* do you see?"

"Now do I see what?" my father asked. "The trouble is that I *don't* see."

"If we don't let him in he'll go away! Come *on!* Please!"

"So go let him in," my father said. "Who's stopping you?"

I ran to the kitchen and, just as the buzzer sounded a third time, pressed on the button that clicked open the downstairs door. Then I went to our front door and listened for the sound of Abe coming into the lobby. I heard Kate barking, and I heard Abe's voice, and then Kate was quiet. It made me feel warm inside to think of Abe petting her. I looked down the staircase, through the crisscrossing of the banisters, and when I saw the top of Abe's head I pulled back quickly so he wouldn't think I was spying on him.

My Aunt Lillian reached me first. She bent down, grabbed me behind the ears, pulled me up to her. She wore her long fur coat with the fox heads around the collar, a coat Abe had bought her before he went overseas—not a coat my grandfather had made.

"So come on and give your Aunt Lillian a big kiss," she said, "and tell me where your mother's hiding."

"In the bedroom."

"Oh yeah?" She laughed and moved past me, into the apartment, calling out my mother's name. "And give your cousin Sheila a kiss too," she called back. "You're not too old for that yet, are you?"

"Oh come on, Ma," Sheila said. "He's just a baby."

I pressed my back to the wall and didn't look into Sheila's face. Sheila was fifteen years old and until about two years ago she baby-sat for me whenever my parents went out. At night sometimes now, if I was allowed out after supper, I'd see her hanging around in the doorways of the stores on Rogers Avenue with her girlfriends, or with some of the older guys from the neighborhood.

"Wanna kiss me?" she asked.

She smelled like soap and when I peeked upwards I could see that she was wearing bright orange-red lipstick. I kept quiet. She laughed at me the way her mother did and walked off. I didn't feel well. I'd forgotten that Abe wasn't coming by himself.

"Hello Davey."

I looked up into Abe's face then. He was looking down at me with a smile that seemed half happy and half sad. He touched my hair gently and when he did I felt that he knew exactly what I was feeling.

"Hi," I said, and I looked down again.

"It's okay to give me a kiss—or we can just shake. Whatever you want."

I put my hand into his and shook it, trying to give him my best grip, and then he was carrying me into the apartment and lifting me up toward the ceiling so that my head nearly scraped the light fixture. I looked down into his face and laughed with him. His eyes were shining.

"Are you still my boy?" he asked. "Answer me that—are you still my favorite little guy?"

"I hope so."

"Sure you are." He let me down a little so that my face was level with his. He held me in front of him for a second, staring at me—his eyes didn't blink or move sideways—and then he pressed me to him so that our cheeks touched. His skin was smooth and warm.

"Come on, you two guys," my mother said, pulling us apart. She put her arms around Abe's neck but warned him not to kiss her on the mouth. They walked to the living room, their arms around each other's waists. My mother looked back at me. "So come on already. What are you waiting for—a royal invitation?"

After supper we sat in the living room and I was scared Abe might leave without asking to see my drawings. My father stayed close to Abe, patting him on the back a lot and telling him how terrific he looked, and I just stared at my uncle and tried to imagine what he was thinking. I wondered about what he'd thought of on all those dark nights when he was out on patrol and his life could have ended in the next instant. I wondered how he felt to have to be living with Lillian and Sheila again. I wondered if he was worried about Fasalino's men crossing over borders and ambushing Avie or Benny or Spanish Louie or my father, forcing them to betray him.

Abe hardly said a word, and this made me feel that he could tell how two-faced my father was—how quickly my father would change his opinion just so he could get Abe or my mother to like him. I stood with my back against the door to my bedroom, feeling very small, and what I wanted to do was to tear my father's fingers from Abe's shoulder—to shove him up against a wall and force him to tell Abe the truth of how he felt.

But there was nothing I could do, I knew, except to wait and hope. I was almost happy when Sheila interrupted to say she needed to leave to do her homework. Lillian told her that her homework could wait—since when was she such a perfect student?—and then she said that if we were boring her so much she should go into my room with me and we should play something together.

"Oh Ma, he's just a baby," she said, but even while she said it she walked past me, opened the door to my room, and went in. "Come on," she said. "As long as we got to."

I followed her, and Lillian laughed while my mother said what she always did whenever Sheila visited me—about how when I was a baby she used to put Sheila into the bathtub with me, and about how Sheila had liked to help bathe my ducky-wucky.

"Do you wanna play Monopoly?" I asked.

Sheila looked at the magazines on my bed.

"Is all you guys ever think about sports?"

"I don't know."

"You'll be the same as all the rest. Sports, sports, sports—it's the only thing that ever fills up your head." Then she giggled. "Except for one other thing."

"What's that?"

"You're too young."

"I'm past eleven," I said. "I'll be twelve next September."

She went to the window, turned around, leaned backwards and arched her back so that her breasts stood out inside her sweater. Her sweater was a pale yellow-pink, the color of peaches.

"Do you think I'm pretty?"

"I guess so," I said. "I don't know."

"People say I'm gonna look like my mother when I grow up, but I think I got my father's eyes and smile more." She came closer so that her breasts almost touched my chest. She wore the kind of brassiere that made me think of the nose cones on dive-bombers. "My mother was real pretty when my father married her. Not all fat the way she is now, with too much makeup."

I looked into her face quickly and saw that she was right, that she had Abe's soft brown eyes.

"You wanna play something else?" she asked. "I got a new game."

"Okay."

"You ever play 'Radio'?"

"No."

"You wanna learn?"

"I guess so."

"You sit down on the bed," she said, "and I sit next to you."

I sat on the bed and she sat next to me. Then she smiled—her gums showed above her teeth the way Abe's did—and twisted herself around so that she was almost on top of me and I could smell her again, the way I could in the foyer. She closed her eyes. I waited. I heard my mother and Lillian laughing. Sheila opened her eyes and pushed her chest toward me.

"How you play radio is that you turn my knobs and your antenna goes up."

"I don't get it," I said. "What knobs?"

But as soon as I said it, she jiggled herself from side to side so that her breasts rubbed against me, and then she started laughing, forcing herself at first, then lying back on the bed and covering her mouth and getting hysterical and pointing at me and making fun of how red my face was getting.

"You're an idiot," I said, standing. "I don't gotta play with you. You're crazy."

"Oh yeah?" she said, and she clapped her hand over her mouth again, to keep from laughing too loud. "Wanna hear another game?"

I stood by the window, looking out into the courtyard, wondering if Kate and Beau Jack were nice and warm together in their apartment. I heard Sheila come up behind me and when she touched my back I twisted away and shoved past her to the door.

"You leave off me, do you hear? Do you *hear?*"

"What're you scared of? Don't you like girls?"

"I don't like you and your stupid games."

She came closer but she didn't touch me.

"So here's the other game," she said. "It's called 'Crazy,' and in this game I get to put my hands in your pockets, see, and then you ask me if I'm feeling crazy and when I say yes, you say, 'Well, you put your hands in a little bit further and you'll feel nuts!' "

She lay down on my bed again, laughing and rolling from side to side and pointing at me. I wanted to smash her face in, but instead I just went back into the living room.

"Hey," my mother said. "You two sound like you're having one swell time in there."

"My Sheila knows how to have a good time," Lillian said. "She's just like I was. Didn't I always like a good time, Abie? Didn't we have fun?"

"Can we go home *now?*" Sheila asked, coming into the room and smoothing down her hair.

"You stop pouting," Lillian said. She turned to my mother. "Don't she look gorgeous when she's mad?"

"Sheila's a pretty girl," my mother said. "I always said so. She'll hook a guy before you know it."

"Be a good girl, I keep telling her," Lillian said. "And if you can't be good, be careful, right?"

"Stop," Abe said. His voice was hard.

"Yeah, Ma," Sheila said, smiling at her father. "You make me embarrassed."

"Since he's back it's like instead of a sergeant in the Army he's Holy Joe from Holy Cross or something. All he does all day is tell us to stop talking the way we talk." She stopped. Her eyes flickered. "I was good enough for you before the war, so what's the matter with me now? You get used to them high-class French broads or something?"

"You won't talk this way," Abe said.

"Why? You're gonna stop me the way you used to stop everyone, huh? You're gonna have your goons do a job on me too, like—"

Abe slapped her face so quickly that I wasn't sure I saw him do it. Then he sat. We waited. In the silence I could still hear the crack of his palm against Lillian's cheek. I saw the red marks rise on her face. Her eyes and mouth opened wide, but it was my mother who started crying.

"Oh Abe, my baby!" she cried. "What did they do to you over there? Tell me, darling. I was so worried all the time. I was so worried. What did they *do* to you. What did you have to *see*?"

"We should go," Abe said. "Get your coats."

"I think maybe you should put some ice on your cheek," my father said. "I really think so. Do you want me to get you some ice, Lillian?"

"A lot of good that one is," my mother said. "What are you asking for —don't you see how fast she's swelling up? Don't you got eyes?"

"Here we go again," Sheila said.

"She's right," my father said, forcing a smile. "It seems like old times again already, doesn't it?"

"He didn't get enough fighting over there," Lillian said, "so he gotta come home and start in."

My mother put out her arms and Lillian went to her. The two of them kissed and hugged and sniffled. Sheila laughed. My father shrugged. Abe was looking at me, puzzled, a new crease line between his eyes. I imagined one of Tony's brothers machine-gunning him to death in an alleyway. My mother pressed the cold washcloth against Lillian's cheek and talked about the kind of job she wanted to get. My father told her to be quiet, that he didn't like talking business when we were with family for a happy occasion. My mother sat next to Abe and took his hands in hers. I remembered that Little Benny had come to the party late the night before and had gone into the bedroom with Abe. After that, two of Abe's men had taken turns guarding the building downstairs, with

Louie Newman on the roof for lookout. If I knew where Abe was hiding out and Fasalino's men caught me and tortured me—upside-down with a hose in my mouth, or with pliers to tear my nails off, or by making me watch them do cruel things to my mother—would I be strong enough not to rat on him?

"Listen," she said. "I'm not complaining about Sol's job, only I just wanted to say that if you should run across something—a good opportunity, if you know what I mean—you should keep Sol in mind."

Abe went to the foyer, took their coats from the closet. I stared at him hard so that he'd notice me. He looked my way for a few seconds, nodded his head once.

"Yes," he said. He came back into the living room, set the coats down on the couch. "Yes." He smiled. "Can I see your drawings, Davey?"

"But I thought we were *going!*" Sheila said.

"This one here is worse than his father sometimes, the way he won't speak up for himself," my mother said. "If I'm not for myself, who then? That's what Poppa always used to say to us, didn't he, Abe?"

"Can I see your drawings?" Abe repeated, as if he hadn't heard my mother.

"So get your drawings already," my mother said. "Didn't you hear your Uncle Abe? Why do you always gotta be asked twice?"

"If you want to wait until we can have more time, alone, that's all right too," Abe said to me. "It's late and you must be very tired."

"It's okay. I can show them to you now."

"Look," my father said, taking me by the arm and stopping me from going into my room. "We'll do even better than that. Listen. I got an idea. Everybody sit down." He took Abe by the arm. "I mean, my son got a talent—a real gift like you won't believe, Abe. So you sit down here and watch something you'll remember for the rest of your life. Everybody sit."

My father pulled his desk chair out from next to the breakfront—the top drawer of the breakfront opened down on hinges and my father worked there at night sometimes, paying bills and writing letters—and he made Abe sit.

"You go get your paper and pencils, Davey, and then you draw Abe's picture for him the way you know how, okay? I mean you won't believe it, Abe, the way this kid can copy people's faces so it looks just like them. It's a gift from God is what I think, a boy his age."

"Don't go showing him off so much," my mother said. "Maybe Davey don't feel like it. You shouldn't force the boy."

"Who's forcing? The way he worships Abe, you think I gotta force him? He don't want to do it, all he's gotta do is say so."

I took my drawing pad and a few different-number pencils from my room, and the old cutting board from the kitchen that I used for leaning on—I'd sandpapered it down so that the nicks and scratches were gone—and I brought a wooden chair in from my bedroom. I liked to sit on something hard when I drew. I set myself up about five feet from Abe so that I'd be able to see all the details in his face. Lillian and my mother and Sheila went to the kitchen to make more coffee. My father pulled a chair up behind me so he could watch, and he started talking about what a great drawer I was and how he figured that with a gift like mine I could be practically anything—I could go into advertising or commercial art or make comic books or do pictures for medical books or engineering companies. Or maybe I would be an architect, he said, and design new kinds of buildings for the future, like the ones at the World's Fair. Did I remember when he took me to the World's Fair before the war, he asked, and carried me around on his shoulders?

I started near the top of the paper, sketching in my uncle's hairline. It always felt easier for me to start at the top, with the forehead and hair and eyes, because that way I could be sure not to run out of space. When I first started doing portraits I sometimes began with the person's shoulders and neck and lower part of the face but got so lost in the details that by the time I was ready to do the hair I found I'd run out of room on the paper. I didn't like to do what they told you to do in books—to sketch in an outline of the entire head in an oval shape first, and then to section off the bottom, lengthwise, with three light parallel lines where the mouth and eye and nose lines were. I worked best when I worked feature by feature, making each one as real as I could before going on to the next. What I loved most, the way I did now when I saw that I was getting the line of Abe's hair and his forehead right—the gentle way it sloped down toward the little rise above his eyebrows—was the feeling that I was making something where there had been nothing.

I loved seeing the different parts of a person's face come into being slowly, one at a time—the hair and then the forehead and then the right eye and then the left eye and then the nose and then the mouth—each appearing by itself on the white space and making the parts already done seem even more real than they'd been by themselves. To see a single eye staring out from a white space, all shaded in under the eyebrow so that you could feel the way the bone went in backwards, made me happy. When I'd stop and look at the person and then back at my drawing it seemed like a miracle to me that my own hands had been able to imitate reality while at the same time—though I never told this to anyone—it was as if my drawing was somehow *more* real than the person himself. I would get excited too, not just because I was able to draw things so they looked real, but because I'd be a little bit frightened all the time that I was going to mess up—that once I got the left eye I wouldn't get the right eye to look as if it belonged with the left. Still, I liked the way being frightened got me worked up inside, into a kind of trance, yet let me concentrate on doing my best, on getting the reality of the face I could see inside my head, the face that stared up at me from the depth of the white paper.

That seemed magical to me too—how deep the white of a plain piece of paper could be. Before I started drawing, the paper would be flat and blank and ordinary, but the minute I put a single line on it, the way I was doing now—starting to sketch the curls of my uncle's hair lightly with a number 3 pencil—the flat white space would suddenly seem to me to be the deepest thing in the world. It would seem to go down forever and ever, so that to sketch in lines first the way the books said, crisscrossing them across an egg shape like tick-tack-toe boxes, wiped away the depth the paper could hold and made it flat and ordinary again.

It also seemed like cheating—as if *anyone* could draw faces correctly if only they could learn to follow rules—and I liked it when people admired my drawings at school, or at work with my father, and remarked on how incredible it was that a boy my age could draw the way I did, without sketching in an outline of the whole head first. Drawing portraits was something I could do that nobody else my age could do as well.

Abe's hairline was starting to recede at either side of his forehead, and I noticed the faint indentations there, where I imagined hair had been when he was younger. The hairline curved down gracefully from both sides of his head in what my mother said was a perfect widow's peak—though I couldn't figure out then why they used the word "widow" to describe a man's hair. Abe's hair was a deep brown, almost black, with a few wisps of gray at the temples, moving backwards over his head in thick curly waves, a little bit the way you'd see the waves in oceans drawn sometimes, one following the other in a nice easy way, and I left white spaces here and there near the tops of the curls to show the reflections. It made me feel good to see the effect you could get by leaving a bit of white just below the top of the gently rolling crests. Without the white it would look as if you'd traced a two-dimensional outline, like those in coloring books, but with the white highlights, which I added in a few places by blackening the hair first with a number 2B pencil and then erasing, you could feel the hair actually curving, one layer into the other, so that when I looked down at the paper I wanted to dip my fingers right in and press the curls flat and then feel them spring back up at me.

I sketched in the worry lines on his forehead, three of them, lightly, and on the sides of his head I brushed in a few strokes, then rubbed the pencil marks with my index finger so that they blended into gray shadows that showed the shape of the skull curving beneath his skin. Abe had a nice high forehead, with flat planes along the sides. His sideburns ended near the bottoms of his ears, and his hair curled back there, hiding most of his ears so that from the front you saw only the outer rims. I began doing his eyes next—they were always my favorite parts of portraits, and if I got them right the rest usually went well—and as I outlined the left one, and got the folds above and below, and the light smile lines that radiated from the outer corner, like the fine lines you'd see in school books, in drawings of the way a flower's roots spread out under the soil, I got upset for an instant because I knew I'd seen eyes exactly like Abe's somewhere before. At first, because of the smile lines, I thought they reminded me of the way Ted Williams's eyes looked. I'd copied a picture of Williams from *Sport* magazine, in which he was smiling at you, not from his Boston Red Sox uniform, but from the cockpit of a Marine fighter plane in the South Pacific. But there was something else too, and when I shaded in the space along the inner edge of Abe's eye, where the eyebrow began sloping down along the bones of the nose and cheek, I realized that Abe's eyes were steady and penetrating the way Williams's eyes were—Williams had the best eyesight of any player who ever lived, and there was a photo in the article showing him reading the title of a song on a 78 rpm record while the record was still spinning—but that they were also like someone else's eyes: like the eyes Abe's father had, and that Abe was staring at me in the same way his father had stared at my mother the day before, when she mentioned Abe's name.

As I drew in the lines under his eyes, and then went back up and began darkening the middle of the eye, pressing down lightly, yet with enough force so that you could tell that the deep brown of the iris was lighter-colored than his hair, I knew I was nervous. My hand trembled slightly, so I put my left hand on the paper, at the bottom edge, palm down, and leaned my right hand on it for steadiness. Abe's eyes seemed gentle because of the wrinkle lines around them and the soft way they were set into their hollows, but there was something in them that terrified me—something hard and unforgiving that told me there wasn't anything in life, no cruelty that he had not seen.

I kept drawing, though, and by the time my mother and Lillian and Sheila returned to the living room, I was almost done. They came up behind me and made a big fuss about how my picture looked exactly like Abe, and my father kept saying he'd told them so, hadn't he? He'd told them what a terrific gift I had.

The welts on Lillian's cheek were red, as if she had fingers stuffed under her skin. Sheila had put on fresh lipstick. She bent down close to the paper.

"Hey, that's good, Davey," she said. "You really draw good. How'd you do it?"

"I don't know."

"He don't know," my mother laughed. "With a gift like that, he don't know. Oh my Davey!" She started to give me a kiss, to show how proud she was of me, but my father grabbed her hands and warned her about not touching me while I was drawing. "You know what I think the secret is?" she said. "I think the secret comes from how quiet he is all the time. It leaves him lots of time for staring, you know what I mean? I never seen a kid who could stare so much."

I was working on Abe's lips, the final part of the picture, and my mother, seeing where I was, warned Abe not to talk. She said that when he was a kid, Abe was like me. She remembered how he could look at a single page in a magazine for hours. When he wasn't even two years old, people were amazed at him, the way he could stare at records or news-papers or playing cards or the voice from a radio, without moving. Some people thought he was a genius, the way he could concentrate, and before he was a year old he was able to pick out any song from a stack of records, or give you any card you wanted from a deck of cards.

Abe looked at me with affection and I could tell that it pleased him for my mother to remember him this way. His mouth opened slightly and that helped—it was what I'd been waiting for because I was able to draw him with his lips parted and turned up a bit at the ends, and that softened his expression. He had a large lower lip, very full, with a nice deep shadow under it in a crescent. I darkened in his long upper lip with a plain number 2 pencil and put in a highlight along the top edge with my eraser, then shaded the lower lip with a number 3H pencil so it would be lighter. I shaded in the points at either end of his mouth— they were like dimples—and did the same for the cheek lines that came down from beside his nose and curved around his mouth, and then I softened those lines by smudging them sideways slightly with my finger, to give the effect of roundness.

I stopped to see if I needed to touch up anything else. My father was talking about how a man like Abe didn't need to use words in this world, and Lillian was saying back to him about how, in his own quiet way, Abe was going to get things reorganized now that he was back, about how things were going to be different, more high-class.

"Personally, my Abe has no use for rough stuff," she said. "I mean, rough stuff is out of date, right? Behind the times, if you know what I mean."

She looked at Abe, and his mouth set itself in a hard line again.

My father tried to change the subject by talking about Roosevelt and how sad it was that he hadn't lived to see the end of the war, but his words didn't change the expression on Abe's face.

I left the paper behind Abe's head blank, not shading it in with the little crisscross lines I often used—the kind professional artists put behind heads for a background. It seemed right for Abe to have a lot of open space around him, without the background calling attention to the fact that what you were seeing was a drawing made with pencils, and in that open space I imagined Abe's henchmen spinning in long loops, like planets circling the sun, all of them grinning like idiots and waving their hands and telling Abe how great he was.

"I think it's done," I said, and before my mother or father could get to it, I picked it up and turned it around so that Abe could see first.

He looked at the drawing, nodded a few times, and then he swallowed. I watched his Adam's apple slide up and down in his throat, and his eyes, I saw, became moist. He stood and set the picture back down on my drawing board, then bent over and kissed me on the forehead. He let his lips stay there for a few seconds.

"Didn't I tell you the kid was terrific?" my father said. "Didn't I? I mean, is he terrific or is he terrific?"

"So come on, Abe—say something already," Lillian said. "Do you like it or not?"

"Shh," my mother said to both of them, and the soft quality of her voice surprised me. "Shh. Can't you tell how much he likes it?"

I didn't know what time it was or if I'd been sleeping for a few minutes or a few hours, when I realized that my mother was in my room, sitting on the bed.

She caressed my cheek with her hand. "Don't be scared," she said. "It's just me."

Light slipped in through the slats in my venetian blinds. I rubbed my eyes and tried to get used to the dark. She moved closer to me. Through my covers I could feel the warmth of her body. All her makeup was off and the swelling on her lips was pretty much gone. Under her robe she wore a silk nightgown. Her face looked gray and peaceful.

"That was nice of you to give Abe the picture. It meant a lot to him."

She moved her fingers across her face as if she might have been wiping tears away. I took my hand out from under the cover so I could touch her nightgown, and I wondered how long she'd been sitting there, watching me.

"You're a good boy, Davey, did you know that?"

"I suppose."

She didn't laugh at me this time, and I had the feeling, in the silence, that there was something else she wanted to say to me, something about Abe's life, something about what he'd been like before I was born, when they were brother and sister growing up together.

"Your father was real proud of you too. He was worried before we went to sleep that maybe he shouldn't have pushed you so much to do Abe's picture and that maybe you felt forced to give it to him, but I told him I could tell you wanted to, that keeping things like that for yourself don't matter much to a boy like you. One thing you're not is selfish." She touched my cheek again. "You mean a lot to your father, did you know that?"

"I suppose."

"Oh Davey, Davey," she said. "What are we gonna do with a boy like you?"

"Keep me, I guess."

"Sure. You got a sense of humor too. But listen, I didn't want to wake you up. It was just that I couldn't sleep and it relaxes me if I can sit here and watch you when you're sleeping. Do you mind?"

"No."

"You love your uncle a lot, don't you?"

"Yes."

"Well. You're just like I was, I guess." In the faint light from the window her face looked very beautiful to me. "I wish you'd known what he was like when he was young. I mean, who didn't worship him? He was always good to me. He brought me presents all the time. We used to snuggle in bed when we were kids and then, even when we got older and could go out on double dates together, we'd hold hands with each other sometimes. He was very affectionate, Davey. I mean, he was always a big shot wherever he was—in school and in the neighborhood, with sports or with the guys or with women—but most people never knew how much affection he could give you when he was alone. Do you see what I'm saying—what I'm trying to tell you?"

"He's said he's gonna take me to a Dodger game," I offered. "Maybe to a doubleheader on Memorial Day."

She brushed back my curls. "Sure," she said. "If Abe makes a promise he always keeps it. But who can tell what the future's gonna bring— that's what I'm trying to say to you, Davey. Who can tell? Who can ever know?" She put her hands on the sides of my face to make me look straight up into her eyes. "You won't tell your father about me being here, okay? I mean, this is just between you and me, like a private conversation, all right?"

"Sure."

"No matter what you hear or what people say I want you always to remember that your uncle Abe is a good man." Her fingernails suddenly tightened into my cheeks, but I didn't dare let her know she was hurting me. "He's a good man, do you hear? Do you *hear?* No matter what people say I want you always to remember what I'm telling you right now. He did the best he could. He had no choice. If my father—"

She pulled away from me and stuck her fist into her mouth and bit down so hard I got scared she was going to make herself bleed.

"Are you all right?" I asked. "Do you want me to get you a glass of water?"

We heard noises from the other side of the wall that separated my bedroom from my parents' and we both froze. I imagined my father stumbling through the house without his eyeglasses. I wondered again about what he actually *saw* when he looked at the world, because I knew from what I'd read in a drawing book about perspective that with only one good eye he couldn't see in three dimensions. What then, when he looked at my drawings, did he *see?* I'd close one eye lots of times and try to judge distance, but distance wasn't the same as depth, and I knew that I couldn't ever really see the world in the exact way he did.

The noise stopped. My mother breathed out, withdrew her fist from her mouth. I wanted to tell her that I wished she would be like this all the time—I wanted to tell her that in some crazy way I wished that the middle of the night could last forever so she could be the way she was now—for if it would last I felt that maybe after a while I'd have the courage to ask her all the questions I wanted to, that maybe I could find out what she and Abe and their father had been like before I was born. I wanted to tell her that it didn't make sense—the way Abe was, and the way people said he was.

"I'll always be your best friend, Davey," my mother said then, as if she'd prepared the words beforehand. "I want you to know that. No matter who you make friends with in life—no matter what people give you, no matter who you love and who loves you, I want you to remember that you'll never have a friend like me. Do you understand what I'm saying?"

"Not really," I said. "You're my *mother.* I mean, friends are my own age, from school."

She put a finger on my lips.

"No, no. You're not listening to what I'm trying to tell you. You listen and Momma will explain. It's something I learned—Abe and I both learned—from our mother, and I think you're at the right age for me to tell it to you." She shifted so that her body wasn't touching mine anymore. "Lots of people will want to be your friend in this life, lots of them will tell you they're your best friend. And why not, a boy like you. But when it comes down to it you'd be surprised at the way people can turn against you. What I mean is, most people are out for themselves in this life. Sure. They'll be your friend so long as you can do something for them, but a mother will always be her own boy's best friend no matter what, do you see?"

I didn't speak.

"No matter what you do, Davey—even if, God forbid, you should kill somebody and be waiting for the electric chair—I'd still love you as much as always. That's what I mean. If the whole world should turn against you and abandon you, a true mother would never stop loving you. That's how deep my love for you goes and I wanted you to hear it from my own lips, so you'll never forget. Nobody can ever be a best friend to you the way a mother can."

"Not even Uncle Abe?"

"Not even Abe."

3

A WEEK AFTER SCHOOL was out the next summer, my mother began spending her afternoons going from doctor to doctor. When she wasn't making rounds of their offices, she'd lie on the living room couch, a cold washcloth over her eyes. When I'd ask if I could do anything for her, she'd turn her head away from me, into the cushions, and repeat my name over and over again.

By this time my father had been working as a collection man for Abe for more than a year. His route took him along Flatbush Avenue, from Empire Boulevard—across the street from the entrance to the Botanic Gardens, near Ebbets Field—all the way to the Albemarle Theatre, past where the new Macy's was being built. He seemed happier than he'd been during the war, and it helped that my mother was ill, I sensed, because he could do things for her. He cleaned and cooked and shopped and took clothes to the wetwash man and picked them up and hung them out on the line we had on the roof.

On the Friday before July Fourth weekend my mother went into Beth Israel Hospital for tests. She came home two days later and the first thing she told me was that Abe was going to California on business and that he'd invited her to go with him. Would I mind if she went?

My father got excited and talked about how the two of us could cook and clean together, and about us going to ball games and restaurants, and then he made the three of us hold hands and dance around while he sang "California, Here I Come!" the way Al Jolson did, in a raspy voice. When he got down on one knee for the last part, his hands clasped upwards towards my mother as if he were praying, she told him to stop making her laugh, that her stomach hurt where the doctors had tested her. I could see that her eyes were shining, though, and when he put his arms around her she let him kiss her on the lips for a long time.

My mother and Abe left from Grand Central Station eight days later on the Twentieth Century Limited. We went there early in the morning to see them off—Lillian, Sheila, my father and me. Little Benny and Turkish Sammy came too. Turkish Sammy, an enormous man with dusty, potato-colored skin and an oblong-shaped head that seemed too big for his body, was Abe's new bodyguard, and he and Benny shared a compartment next to the one Abe and my mother were in. My mother had on her favorite dress—the chiffon one with the purple irises—and a beautiful wide-brimmed lavender hat she'd bought for the trip, with two long white silk streamers that flowed down along the back of her neck. My father teased her about how she looked like a movie star, asking if she was going to be interviewed on the Twentieth Century Limited radio show, where they spoke with famous people who were taking the train from New York to Chicago.

Abe was dressed in a beautiful cream-colored summer suit, a Panama hat tipped down at a slight angle over his right eye. He looked handsomer than ever, and all the porters and guards along the platform smiled and tipped their hats to him. When one of the policemen said "Good morning, Mr. Litvinov—taking a long trip?" my uncle nodded to the policeman, touched the brim of his hat with two fingers, then winked down at me.

He had champagne and oysters waiting for us inside their compartment, and a big orchid corsage for my mother. Benny and Turkish Sammy stayed in the room with us, eating and drinking and making jokes, and my mother kept asking us, over and over, if it was really true that she was there instead of in the hospital.

I was twelve years old. For the first time in my life my father and I were alone in our apartment together for more than a few days, just the two of us, and I was surprised, not just at how peaceful things seemed with my mother gone, but at how different my father was. He didn't put on any acts or pester me to do things the way he did when my mother was around, and he spent more time with me, playing boxball or hit-the-penny in front of the house, or talking with me about sports, or taking me with him on his route, or just sitting with me in my bedroom and smoking cigarettes while I read or drew or we listened to a Dodger game together on the radio.

I loved going with him on his route. I was big for my age, taller than most of my friends—five-foot-five, only an inch shorter than he was—and he liked to have me walk beside him, on his good side, and to tease me about it only being a matter of months before he'd be looking up to me. He kept seven or eight different composition books in a black briefcase, and at each stop he wrote things down in one of the books. In the afternoons or evenings he worked at the breakfront in the living room, transforming his notes from pencil to ink. He showed me how he had the name of each one of Abe's clients printed out at the top of a different page, along with the person's address and phone number. Below, in neat columns, he wrote in the date of each transaction, how much money the person bet, and if the person won or lost. For cross-reference he kept separate books for each kind of bet people made: one book each for baseball, basketball, football, boxing, horse racing, and the numbers.

He explained to me how the numbers worked—that for a nickel or a dime or a dollar you could bet on any number from 0 to 999. He opened the sports pages in the *Journal-American* and showed me how the number of the day was taken from the pari-mutuel bets at the racetracks. If the winning horses of the first three races paid a total of $347.67, and those of the first five races paid $462.78, and of the first seven $981.64, you'd take the third digit from each total and you'd have your lucky number. My father was very patient while he explained things to me. If you won, you got paid at a 600-to-1 rate—600 dollars for every dollar, 30 dollars for a nickel. When I asked if he'd let me bet some of my own money, instead of answering he replied that a lot of the Negroes and Puerto Ricans and some of the Irish and Italians bet the numbers a lot, and he taught me about odds—how they were 999 to 1 against picking the right number, while the payoff itself was only 600 to 1. In addition, he said, there was no control—no way to use your experience and your knowledge, no way to lower the odds in your favor. Jewish men didn't bet on the numbers much, he stated when he was done explaining, and that ended the discussion.

He also worked with a set of buff-yellow legal-size pads that had crisscrossing brown and green lines, like those on graph paper. He kept the pads in a gray metal box behind the hats in the foyer closet on a shelf above the coats, and once a month, at night, he would put the pads into his briefcase and take them to Abe's apartment.

There were four compartments inside his briefcase, and at every stop, in addition to writing things down in his notebooks, he would collect envelopes. None of the envelopes had money in them. My father said he never knew who collected the money and paid off the winners and that he was just as happy not to know, that he was safer that way. The envelopes were filled with slips of paper on which people wrote things, or sometimes my father wrote things for them, and before he left each place he would lick the flap of the envelope, seal it, glance at his wristwatch, then write the place, date, and time on the outside, sign his initials, and put the envelope into his briefcase. "Now you're all set," he would say, rapping the side of his briefcase with his knuckles. And then —this surprised me the first time he did it—he would put his arm around me, draw me close to him, and add, "And all I can wish for you is that your luck should be as good as mine, right?"

It made me happy to see how much people liked my father. He made stops at forty-three different places on his route—luncheonettes, barber shops, clothing stores, candy stores, service stations, beauty parlors, bowling alleys, hat stores, stationery stores—and in almost every one of them, even if the people had been losing money steadily, they always brightened up when he walked in. They never seemed to hold their bad luck against him and if they had a big win they would sometimes tip him a few dollars.

Our last stop of the day was back at Church Avenue, next to Erasmus Hall High School, to a set of four rooms on the third floor of an office building. The front was the real estate office that Abe ran for Mr. Rothenberg—Mr. Rothenberg owned a few apartment houses, a small construction company and three restaurants—and in the other three rooms there were lots of telephones and blackboards, with men calling out numbers to one another, and even though a few of them stopped their work and made a fuss over me because I was Abe's nephew—they called me the Prince—my father didn't like going there. He didn't like going into the restaurants Mr. Rothenberg owned either. In the restaurants, I knew, after the last customer had gone and the shades were drawn, Abe's men would just keep punching the cash register. This, and paying the construction company for renovations on the apartment houses that never got made, was how they made all the gambling income seem legitimate.

After the first few times we went to Abe's office, my father would have me wait downstairs in front of Bickford's cafeteria. He'd go upstairs by himself, and when he returned, unless they had errands for him—sometimes he'd have to deliver large sealed envelopes to other offices, in Brooklyn or Manhattan—he'd be free for the rest of the day.

Then we'd go out for lunch, and that was my favorite part of the day. Usually we'd eat either at Garfield's—the big cafeteria at the corner of Church and Flatbush, which I always thought of as being the center of our neighborhood, where everybody met—or, more often, at one of the luncheonettes where he was the collection man. Until that time I'd hardly ever eaten in a restaurant, and it made me feel very grown up to sit at a table across from my father, the waitress standing there with a pad in her hand, my father saying to me, the way he always did, "Well, what'll it be today, Davey? I want you to order anything you want, you understand? Anything at all." He liked to tease the waitresses. Sometimes he'd take a waitress's hand just as she was about to leave and ask her if she made home deliveries—he'd explain about my mother being in California—and the waitress would laugh and tell him not to be fresh.

I liked eating in restaurants, yet no matter where we ate I almost always ordered the same thing: a grilled cheese and tomato sandwich with french fries, a vanilla-Coke, and either lemon meringue pie or a hot fudge sundae for dessert. I loved the way the grilled cheese sandwich tasted from being pressed down hard on the grill, the odors of hamburgers and sausage and bacon and onions cooked into the bread, the cheese and tomato melted into one another, and I loved the way my father would always say, "He's some kid, my boy—you offer him the whole menu and he winds up choosing the same thing every time. He's one steady kid, my boy—a guy you can count on, right?"

After we were done eating, if he didn't have any errands we would stay on in the luncheonette for an hour or two and I would make sketches of some of the people—waitresses or cooks or owners or one of the regulars—and when everybody crowded around and patted my father on the back and told him how talented I was, he would glow.

One afternoon when we'd finished lunch early and were walking back home along Church Avenue—my mother and Abe had been gone for more than two weeks and she had written that they might not start back until mid-August, that Abe had to take care of some business for Mr. Rothenberg in Las Vegas—some of my friends called me from inside the Holy Cross schoolyard to come in and play with them. Tony Cremona was there, and for a second, knowing that part of the reason Abe was staying away was because there'd been some threats from Fasalino's organization, I wondered if it would seem disloyal to my uncle to play ball with Tony. But when Tony called to me, my father smiled.

"You go enjoy yourself," he said.

I went in and started shooting with the guys—they were between games—and when we were lining up at the foul line to shoot for new sides, I noticed that my father had entered the schoolyard and was leaning against the fence. His jacket and tie were off, his shirt sleeves rolled up.

"Can an old man get a few shots?" he asked.

"Sure," I said.

He bounced the ball on the concrete a few times, using both hands the way the girls did at school. I cringed. He stood to the side of the basket, about twenty feet away, his cigarette stuck in the corner of his mouth, cocked his head to one side, took a step and a half, and shot the ball with two hands, using an old fashioned set-shot with a lot of backspin, but letting the ball go more from his waist than from his chest. The ball smashed off the backboard without even touching the rim.

"C'mon. C'mon," he said, gesturing impatiently. "I gotta get the right angle."

Tony tossed the ball to him and he lunged for it too soon, so that it hit him in the chin. He bounced it a few times, tilted his head, shot again. The ball zoomed toward the backboard in a straight line and this time it went right through the hoop. I was amazed. He smiled and took two steps backwards. "C'mon, c'mon," he called. "Gimme." I tossed the ball to him. He caught it, shot again, his right foot going up in the air backwards, almost as if he were skipping. The ball rattled the metal backboard and fell through the hoop again. I couldn't believe it.

He started going around in a circle, from the right side to the left, the way we did when we played Around-the-World, and he made eleven shots in a row before he missed, all line drives.

"Not bad for an old man, huh?" he said. "Can I shoot or can I shoot? You answer me that."

Behind his glasses, enormous magnified droplets of sweat dripped down along either side of his nose. Under his armpits his shirt was soaked. He waited a few seconds, listening to my friends tell him how great he was and asking him what teams he'd played for when he was young, but instead of answering he just looked at me, smiled, and repeated what he'd said before. "Can I shoot or can I shoot?" He told me to have a good time but not to come home too late because he had a surprise for me.

When we were done playing, Tony asked me to go to his house with him. He said he had a surprise for me too and that there was still plenty of time until supper. We walked up Church Avenue and then along New York Avenue to the Italian section on the other side of Linden Boulevard, and I felt a little nervous, being in Mr. Fasalino's territory. But I told myself to act the way Abe acted—as if nothing were the matter and we were all at peace with one another. If you acted as if something were so, Abe said, sometimes everyone would believe it was so.

I liked being with Tony. He had straight, sandy-colored hair that fell over his forehead and into his eyes, and just before he asked a question he always gave a flick to his head that made the hair flap back on top of his head. He had small, sharp features and a smile that seemed to slant the same way his hair did, and sometimes he'd tease me about how, because of my dark curls, I looked more like a Wop than he did. While we walked and he asked me things I explained about how my father was blind in one eye since he was a kid and had almost no vision in the other and Tony agreed with me that if my father had had two normal eyes he would probably have been good enough to make it in the pros. Tony said that his priest explained to him how if you were a good person God made up for things—if you lost a leg, God might give you strong hands, or if you had rotten teeth, say, He might give you beautiful hair, or if you lost an eye He could give you good hearing, and when we came to Tony's street we talked about athletes who'd had diseases when they were young or who got wounded in the war, and of how they'd overcome their handicaps. We talked about guys like Monty Stratton, who pitched for the White Sox with a wooden leg, and Lou Brissie, the Athletics pitcher, who had a steel plate in his head from the time he got hit while chucking hand grenades into a Japanese bunker, and Three-Finger Mordecai Brown and his great fork ball, and Ed Head of the Dodgers, who was wounded on the beach at Okinawa and had switched from being a right-handed pitcher before the war to a lefty after the war, and Pete Gray, the one-armed outfielder who'd played for the St. Louis Browns.

When we were done discussing ball players and were at Tony's house —it was a small two-story private house with a porch and a green roof and a big garage and lots of pictures of Jesus and Mary on the walls—I repeated things my father said about President Roosevelt and how he was the greatest president our country ever had even though he'd had polio as a kid, and when I talked about how Roosevelt had worked like a maniac, swimming and exercising, and about how terrible it was that he hadn't lived to see the Japanese and Nazis surrender, I got tears in my eyes the way my father did when he talked about him.

Tony asked if I'd ever drawn a picture of Roosevelt and I said I hadn't. Then he took me to his basement, and from a box under his workbench —Tony was good with tools and could make benches and birdhouses and doorstops and things—he took out a big package and handed it to me. Inside were five packages of different kinds of drawing paper: nice thick creamy white paper made from rags—the kind I'd look at in the art store but couldn't afford to buy.

"I figured a guy who could draw like you should have quality merchandise to work with," he said.

"How'd you get it?"

"I got my ways, you know what I mean?"

"No."

"Ah. C'mon, Davey," he said. "Things fall off trucks sometimes, right? Only you gotta be there at the right time, that's all."

I said I had to get home to see what my father's surprise was and he said that the paper wasn't the real surprise. The real surprise was out in the garage.

"C'mon," he said, and I followed him up from the cellar. The side door of his garage was locked with a combination lock, and when he had rolled the tumblers and opened it and turned the light on inside, he motioned me in.

"Take a gander, Davey. You take a good long gander."

I stepped inside and gasped. The garage was filled with dozens of pinball machines, soda machines, candy machines, and juke boxes, all new and shining.

"Jesus!" I said.

"That ain't all."

He led me past the machines to the back, to a corner where there were still a lot of oil-soaked rags and sawdust and nuts and bolts and pieces of metal. He pushed aside a few window screens, and came up with a little machine that looked something like my mother's meat grinder, except that where you would put the meat in, the opening was narrower, like a slot for letters.

"Watch this," Tony said.

He reached up to one of the rafters, pulled down a sheet of thin metal, fed it into the machine, cranked the handle, and suddenly little round pieces of metal were dropping to the floor. Then he took a quarter out of his pocket, showed me that the slugs of metal were the same size as the quarter.

"Listen," he said. "I ain't shown this to nobody else and if my old man knew he'd kill me, but I figure you're a guy I can trust, right?"

"Sure."

"You got brains, Davey. Everybody knows that. You ain't gonna be like the rest of us. Me, I'll probably wind up like my brothers and my old man, running dirty trips for Fasalino and taking a rap once in a while, but you—I got the feeling, even though your old man works for your uncle—that you ain't gonna wind up as dumb as the rest of us."

"You're not dumb," I said.

"Well, I ain't smart like you." He laughed. "You want proof?"

"Sure. Give me proof."

"The proof is that you're here and I'm showing you all this stuff my old man got stored for Fasalino." He grinned and I grinned with him. "I mean, how dumb can a guy be? See those big cartons over there?"

"Yes."

"Got enough fags in there to keep your old man happy for the rest of his life. They fall out of trucks too, them cigarettes, only they ain't got their tax stickers on them yet. My brother Victor, that's his deal, peddling the cigarettes. Phil, he works the juke boxes and pinball machines. And my old man, what's his racket? He's the doorman, see? He opens and closes the door for his sons. What a drip!"

I moved back a step. "Why are you showing me this, Tony, if it can get you in trouble?"

"I don't know. When I saw your old man, and the way you looked down when he started shooting, I just kind of felt like it. Only he surprised you, didn't he?"

"Yes."

"Yeah. Let's face it, Davey. You and me, we got drips for fathers mostly, only your old man might have been better with two eyes, so you can't blame him completely, and I got these fucking brothers too who like to beat up on me. They found me in here with you, they'd pound the shit out of me till you could hear me in Canarsie. Only what's the fun of having all this stuff, I say to myself, if you can't show it to somebody, you know what I mean? C'mon—you and me are gonna have some fun."

Tony got a paper bag and filled it with the slugs. Then he put the machine back under the screens.

"You're lucky you ain't got brothers," he said when we were walking again, away from his house. "The thing of it is, even if I wanted to be different from them—more like you—they'd fry my ass. They're bigger than me and when I try to say no to them, all the shit they want me to do, my father sticks up for them, and you know why?"

"No."

"Glad you asked," he said, laughing. "Because they pound the shit out of him too, see? They're bigger than he is and it's really something —I wish you could be there to watch, to see the way they slap him around sometimes, him whimpering and begging. Nobody would believe it, the way it is in my house sometimes." He stopped. "Listen. You won't tell on me then, will you—to Abe or your father?"

"No."

"Yeah. Good for you, Cremona." He slapped me on the back. "I figured I could trust you, that you and me could be buddies, no matter what happens in the rest of our lives. I mean, when we're on the same team in the schoolyard, is there any two guys can beat us? It's like when I'm about to make a move toward the basket, you always know it ahead of time and get the ball to me. We're a good team, you and me."

"Sure."

"So that's why I figured I'd choose you to go in partners with me." He jingled the bag of slugs. "What we do, see, is we go somewhere where they got candy and soda machines, and then we put a slug in, and that way we get ourselves a soda for a nickel and twenty cents change too. Got it?"

"But won't your father and brothers get mad when they open the machines and find all the slugs?"

"You think I'm some kind of idiot? I know which machines are theirs and which aren't, and I know which ones are your uncle's. What we do is we work different territories. C'mon."

So Tony and I got on the subway at Church Avenue, rode to Atlantic, and went into the big station there, where people took the trains out to the racetracks and Long Island. Then we started in on the different machines, trying to act as nonchalant as we could. Tony let me put the first slug in. A cup dropped down and filled with Coke, and four nickels came spitting out of the change compartment. I drank the soda and put the nickels in my pocket. Tony put a slug in and the same thing happened for him, and then we did it again—I couldn't believe it—and when we got twenty nickels each we went to a change booth and asked the woman there to give us dollar bills for our nickels, and then we ran out of the station, laughing like crazy and pounding each other on the back and telling each other what a great team we made! We walked a few blocks, went down into another train station—Tony said it was best to use train stations because of the noise and how people were coming and going and not hanging around—and we filled our pockets with change and our mouths with soda and food: Clark bars and Oh Henry bars and Baby Ruths.

"Jesus," I said, banging on my belly. "What if my father wants to take me to a restaurant?"

"Then you stick your finger down your throat first and barf."

"Like the Romans, right?"

"Yeah. Only you come to my house and do it all over my brothers, okay?"

It was still light out when we'd used up all our slugs, so we decided to walk off our eating by heading back along Flatbush Avenue and cutting left at Parkside. It surprised me that Tony could talk so easily about trusting me, about how I was the only guy at school he considered a friend. During recess sometimes he would get one of the Italian girls up against a car fender outside the schoolyard and everybody would yell to come and see, that Tony Cremona had his finger right up somebody's pussy, and we would all come running. It would be true that he was fingering one of the tough Italian girls, but Tony confessed that he only did it because he felt he had to, because it was the kind of thing his brothers bragged about having done when they were his age and that if they didn't hear he was doing it too they would knock him around even more. In the classroom he was quiet in the same way I was, and even though he didn't get the best grades, you could tell from the brightness of his eyes—the way he listened to things—that he was a lot smarter than he let on.

When we got to the corner of Nostrand and Linden—we stopped at his house to pick up my drawing paper—we separated. I told Tony that I'd hide the money and tell my father I found the paper next to a trash can near the art store. Tony said he hoped we could do more things together in the fall when school started. He said we could use the money from the slugs to go downtown to movies at the Paramount or the Fox or the Albee. We could pick up girls together if we wanted and sit in the balcony and neck, or we could go for walks in the park. He figured that if he was with a guy like me he could meet girls with more class. I thanked him again for the paper and for showing me his father's garage.

"Yeah, we're kind of like blood brothers now, I guess, don't you think? I mean, like in the movies when the white guy and the Indian slit their wrists and cross them and mix the blood, except that instead of us cutting our wrists, what's gonna keep our secret bond is that if either of us tells on the other we're gonna *get* our wrists slit, right?"

"I suppose," I said, and when I did he laughed and pounded me on the back and told me that I was all right in his book, he could tell it from the way I didn't hesitate about going to his house, even though we both knew it might make Abe or my father angry if they found out. "You got real courage, Davey," he said then. "That's why I'm glad I was smart enough to choose you to be my friend. I mean, we're in the same boat, you and me—except the boats are separate, right?"

"I suppose."

He took out his roll of dollar bills. "Wow!" he said. "We really did it, you and me, didn't we? We really did it, partner!"

"We really did it."

"You wanna do it again soon, now that you lost your cherry and we got the jitters out of us? My old man, what he does, see, is he goes into the city and sells bags of the stuff in kangarooland to spics and niggers so they can do what we did, but if he found out I was doing it, he'd cream my ass. You watch your own ass, partner. With Abe and Fasalino and my brothers and all, we gotta make like nothing happened, right? Like we hardly know each other, see—like we maybe just like to play ball together sometimes on account of we go to the same school and we're the two best athletes there."

I was scared my father would ask me where I'd been and why I was late and how I'd gotten the new drawing paper, but instead he just smiled when I got home and handed me an envelope. Inside were two box-seat tickets to the Dodger-Giant game that night—Abe had left them for us—and I threw my arms around my father's neck and hugged him.

During the game my father bought me everything I wanted—a program and a yearbook and a pennant and hot dogs and a Dodger hat—and when Jackie Robinson doubled in the bottom of the ninth to drive in the winning run, it made the day seem perfect. It was Jackie's rookie year with the Dodgers and he was playing first base and leading the league in stolen bases. On the way home, for the first time I could remember, my father was willing to go over the game with me, inning by inning. He teased me about how articulate I was when I wanted to be and how I'd make a good lawyer someday—a fine public speaker—if that was my choice, and how he would give my mother a full report so that she'd stop calling me her silent one. We held hands too, which we hadn't done for a long time, and I liked the way his skin felt against mine —soft in the middle, but hard and calloused along the edges from all the years of breaking off twine.

We stopped at Carsten's, on Flatbush Avenue, for ice cream sodas, and when he gave me a small speech about democracy and how terrific he thought it was that the Dodgers were the first team in baseball to hire a black man, I almost told him how proud it made me feel too, that Jackie was a Dodger. But I was afraid that if he knew how much I cared about Jackie—how scared I'd been that Jackie might have a hard time under all the pressure and get sent back to the minors—he might use it against me sometime later on, when things weren't going so well for the two of us and my mother was home again.

The air was nice and cool when we left, and we talked all the way to our block about the Dodgers, with me asking him questions about the crazy players he'd seen play for them in the twenties and thirties—Babe Herman and Casey Stengel and Van Lingle Mungo and Dazzy Vance. In front of our building two men stepped out from behind a parked car. One of them was a thin black man wearing sunglasses and a flowered yellow shirt. The other man was fat and wore a dark double-breasted wool suit.

"Mr. Voloshin?" the fat man asked. "Mr. Solomon Voloshin?"

"That's my name."

"And this is your son David, yes?"

My father didn't answer, and the fat man smiled and reached toward me. I pulled back and stared hard into his face so that I could memorize his features.

"He's a nice-looking boy. Looks a little like his uncle, wouldn't you say? You must care a lot about him, Mr. Voloshin. I got sons too. Three boys. So believe me when I tell you that you yourself don't got a thing to worry about. I ain't here to make no trouble. I'm only here to say that if you get word from your brother-in-law you tell him that maybe he shouldn't come home. That maybe he should consider settling in California." He laughed. "They got no winters in California, I hear, so it should be much better for his health out there. Okay, Mr. Voloshin? I can count on you to deliver the message?"

"Get out of our way," my father said. "Get out of our way, do you *hear* me? You just get out of our way."

The black man stepped forward, but the fat man put a hand on the black man's arm.

"I told you once, Mr. Voloshin. I ain't here to make no trouble. I'm just a messenger making a delivery, yes?" He laughed again. "You make deliveries. I make deliveries. We all make deliveries. So we should understand one another, yes?"

"Come on, Davey," my father said, and he pulled me with him. I held back a bit, trying to see through the black man's sunglasses.

"You'll deliver my message? You'll tell your brother-in-law that Mr. Fasalino wishes him a long and happy life?"

My father tried to get the key to our building out of his pocket, but his hand was shaking so much he couldn't grab onto it. He jerked his hand away angrily and his key ring and coins spilled out. I got down on my knees and started picking up the change. I looked back at the two men and whispered to my father, asked him if he wanted me to ring Beau Jack's bell. My father's hands were shaking so much now that I knew he wouldn't be able to hold onto anything, so when I found the right key I put it into the lock myself.

My father stepped into the lobby and grabbed me, his nails digging into my muscle, above the elbow. Then, with the door still open, he started screaming with all his might.

"If you goons touch a hair on my boy's head I'll kill you, do you hear? Do you *hear* me? *Do* you?"

The black man started toward us and I helped my father shove the door closed. The lock clicked. My father kept screaming, his hands in the air, his fists opening and closing the way they did sometimes when he argued with my mother.

"You're scum of the earth, that's what you are! Do you hear me? You ain't nothing but lousy scum of the earth! You ain't nothing but dumb goons. You ain't nothing but scum of the earth! Scum of the earth is what you are!"

The black man's nose was squashed flat against the glass. I heard doors opening behind us, people shouting at my father.

"Come *on!*" I said.

He stopped screaming. He looked dazed.

"What?"

"Just come on. Don't be a fool, okay? Just come on before they get in after us. All they gotta do is ring and get somebody to buzz the door open."

"Of course."

He let me lead him up the stairs. I opened the door, locked it behind us, took my father with me into the kitchen.

"Should I call the police?" I asked.

"Don't do nothing."

He leaned on the sink with one hand, breathing hard, and I was afraid he was going to faint. His skin was a pale ivory white. He looked as old as some of the men in my grandfather's home.

"I could call Aunt Lillian," I offered. "She'd know what to do. Abe must have left her instructions."

He sat and took off his glasses. Without them he looked young and helpless again, the way he did in the wedding picture my mother kept on her vanity table. I brought him a glass of water and he sipped it, bending over, tilting the glass toward his lips. The skin around his eyes was puffy, as if it had absorbed warm water, and the lid on his bad eye hung down almost all the way, the dead eyeball floating toward the outside corner.

I tried to figure out what I would do if he had a heart attack. I imagined lifting him, laying him out gently on the floor, covering him with blankets, telephoning for help. I thought of how I'd felt, lying on the dirt behind the hedges in front of our building, my eyes closed, while my friends talked about my wounds, about field surgery, about plastic land mines. I thought of how wonderful it was when they caressed my forehead with their cool hands and put an imaginary last cigarette in my mouth. I was glad Mr. Fasalino hadn't used Tony's father as his messenger this time.

My father licked his lips and moaned. He held his eyeglasses in his right hand now. I reached across, flattened his palm, took the glasses away from him. I thought of running upstairs to Stevey Komisarik's apartment and getting his father to come and give my father an injection. Stevey's father was a dentist and Stevey had once shown me the black emergency bag in their hall closet. I saw myself telephoning to California. If my mother answered I would ask her to put Abe on so I could tell him and he could break the news to her. I saw myself racing down the staircase, jumping five or six steps at each landing, swinging around the turns, knocking on Beau Jack's door and taking him back upstairs with me. Beau Jack would know what to do. During the first World War he had been stationed in France with an all-Negro unit, digging up American soldiers and burying them again.

"See?" my father said. "Do you see now? Now do you see?"

"Are you all right?"

He pressed against the inside corners of his eyes with thumb and forefinger. He reached across to me with his other hand.

"Give me my glasses."

He held his glasses up to the light, then stuck the right lens into his mouth, fogged it, wiped it clean with his handkerchief.

"I was scared," I said.

"Sure you were—bums like that—who knows what they wouldn't do? Even for women and children they got no feelings."

"I mean I was scared for you when you were shaking so much. When you got all pale."

"Come," he said.

I followed him to the living room. He took a bottle of whiskey and a shot glass from the side cabinet of the breakfront. He drank the whiskey in one swallow.

"You want a taste?" he said. "You're okay?"

"I'm okay."

The telephone rang.

"Don't answer it. It's those bums. But they won't get nowhere with me."

I tried to smile. "You really screamed at them," I said.

"I screamed at them."

"I mean, I never thought you . . ." I stopped, shrugged. "I don't know."

He cocked his head to the side and sniffed in.

"You mean you didn't think your old man had it in him to stand up to them, right?"

"I guess. I don't know. You were screaming like a maniac."

"I wouldn't say I wasn't scared," he said. "But that don't mean I gotta let bums like that run my life, do you see?" He sat down in his red easy chair, under the window. He stared at me, sucking on the right corner of his lower lip the way he did when he was shooting set shots. His voice was stronger. "So listen. I've been wanting you to know something, okay? That what I used to say about your uncle when he was overseas, I want you to know that I changed my opinion. That first night he got home, didn't I say that the war changed him, that he was different?"

"Yes."

The telephone rang again and we sat there and waited until, after sixteen rings, it stopped. In my head I made up pictures of Abe dying in front of my building, of him saying to me that it was so crazy, wasn't it, to have lived through the war in Europe in order to die in the streets of Brooklyn.

"If not for your uncle Abe, do you see the kind of trash that would take over the neighborhood? Do you see? People don't want to know how bad it would be if Abe surrendered and let them muscle into his territory. They don't know how good they got it."

"Does Abe hurt people?"

"What—?"

"At school sometimes I hear stories that he hurts people."

"Does Abe hurt people."

My father rubbed his chin, pretending that he was trying to figure out my question.

"All right," he said. "Listen. I can honestly say to you that to the best of my knowledge Abe himself has never laid a hand on anybody. Not counting Lillian and Sheila, I mean, and what he had to do in the Army."

"It's okay," I said. "You don't have to answer me. I was just wondering, is all."

"You got a right to know these things, Davey. Only let me ask you a question. Did you get a look at that fat Italian with the *shvoogie* behind him? And the *shvoogie* with a knife or a razor in his pocket probably? Sure." He pointed his cigarette at me. "That's the kind of stuff they use, those types. Rough stuff is all they know. What's so terrible if people make a few bets? Who gets hurt? When the state of New York gyps people at the track, that's legal, but when a hardworking fellow like Abe, who risked his life for his country, gives people honest odds, that's illegal. Why? You answer me that, sonny boy, and you're a genius. And Abe ain't no loan shark either, like he could be if he wanted, do you hear me?"

I told him I heard. I could tell he was pleased now, to have me for an audience, and he kept talking about Abe and how Abe let people have credit when they owed him money and found jobs for them when they couldn't make ends meet. I wondered if the fat Italian was related to Tony's family. I imagined myself asleep, the windows open, a breeze coming through, the sheet to my chin. I reminded myself to put my baseball bat under my bed and I imagined what I would do if somebody tried to crawl into my room from the fire escape. Would I lie still until he was past me, and then attack? What if he had a gun or a knife? What if there was more than one person?

"They won't let you live," my father was saying. "Sure. I don't remember what the Black Hand did, the way Momma and Poppa were frightened so they would hardly leave the house? I don't remember the way those *momzers* used to walk around the neighborhood like they owned us? So what's Abe's big crime—that he saved us from being lamp shades so that now their bums should tell him where he can and can't live?"

"What's the Black Hand?"

"Murderers," he said. "Gangsters. When I was your age, if you got a note in your mailbox with a black hand on it, it meant you were dead."

"Did anyone you know ever get a note?"

"Sure. The Italians and the Jews, we lived near each other then, first on the Lower East Side, then when we came to Brooklyn, in East New York. Like now."

"Did anyone you know get killed?"

"Stop with the questions. Always the questions, this one. You just listen to what I'm saying, do you hear me? People like that with no education, they don't value life the way we do." He tapped the side of his head. "That's why they're so scared of Abe and Mr. Rothenberg. They know Abe don't gotta use rough stuff the way they do. If all you got is muscles and guns, see, then as soon as somebody gets more muscles and guns than you, you're dead. So why did God give us brains?"

My father didn't answer his own question. He walked from one side of the room to the other, as if he didn't know where he was, and when he looked at me again after a while, he seemed surprised to find me there. He bent down, kissed me on the forehead.

"It's late. You should get some sleep. We'll talk more in the morning if you want. Only you don't ever tell your mother about what happened tonight, all right? You just let that be something between the two of us."

My mother came home from California during the last week of August, and from the moment she walked through the door all she could talk about was how wonderful California was. In California she had picked lemons and oranges right off the trees; in California the air was clean and there were no winters; in California Abe had found a job for my father that would enable us to move there and buy a home of our own.

We were in the middle of a broiling heat wave and the air hung on our bodies, so damp and heavy that I felt as if it was falling through my skin and muscles, softening my bones. My mother moved around the bedroom in slow motion, unpacking, putting things away in drawers. She had on nothing but a brassiere and panties—her skin was brown and shiny, glistening with sweat—and each time she passed the open window my father yelled at her that she was giving the neighbors a free show. She yelled that she didn't care, that she couldn't wait to get out of this stinking city, that she couldn't wait to get to California where a human being could breathe. Her lips were tingling already—she hadn't had a herpes once during the six weeks in California, she said—and she began rubbing them with ice cubes and crushed aspirin. I thought of the jars our science teacher kept at school, alcohol and chicken bones in them, and of how soft the bones would get, so that you could bend them.

My father sat on the edge of the bed, hunched over. Gray hairs curled around the nipples of his breasts. Sweat slid down his face and neck, ran along the folds of his stomach. My mother explained to me how easy the job would be, how all my father would have to do would be to stand in a booth all day and give out keys to cars. He would be a parking lot attendant in downtown Los Angeles. In hot weather the booth would be air-conditioned.

"But do I got a brain or do I got a brain?" my father asked. He said that to spend the rest of his life in a booth giving out keys would be like moving into a coffin.

My mother laughed, said we were living in hell already, so what was the difference.

"If it's so wonderful out there, let Abe go first," my father said. "Sure. And if he loses his connections and we get stranded out there, who's gonna get me another job? You answer me that. Your big-shot brother fills your head up with his lousy dreams, but I'm the one who gets left to pay for them."

"And what about the boy? What kind of life is there for him if we stay here? Can you answer that?" My mother turned to me. "You wanna be like him, Davey? Come on and answer me. You wanna grow up to be a nothing like your father, then you just go on and take lessons from him. If Abe didn't take care of him, he wouldn't have a pot to piss in and you wouldn't have clothes on your back, him and all his talk about brains. Where'd his brain ever get us?"

"You're hot and bothered," my father said. "You should of waited to come home until after the heat wave, is what I think. But I'll tell you what—how about a nice movie, where it's air-conditioned, all three of us together? They got a good double feature at the Granada and maybe by the time it's out things'll be cooled off and we'll all feel better."

He stood and tried to put his arms around her. She pushed him away, pulled a stack of postcards from her suitcase, and came toward me.

"Let Momma show you how beautiful it is, Davey! Let Momma show you, so you'll see the new life you can have, with new friends and fresh fruit and palm trees and beaches . . ."

"I gotta go," I said. "I promised the guys I'd meet them downstairs."

"Hey—don't you be walking away from your mother like that!" my father shouted at me. "You get back in here."

"Leave him be, Sol."

"Leave him be? Is that fresh or is that fresh, to walk out on you when you're in the middle of talking to him?"

Downstairs people were sitting on chairs, listening to radios, cooling themselves with paper fans. Rosie sat on a wooden stool, her skirt up over her knees, her feet in a bucket of ice.

On Rogers Avenue the older kids were leaning against cars. I saw Sheila necking with a guy. She wore red shorts and a green halter, and I couldn't understand how she could let a guy's body press against hers in such sticky weather. I turned right on Linden Boulevard, ducked down the alleyway between the first two apartment houses, thinking I might find some of my friends out back in the courtyard. It was usually cooler there at night, where there had been grass and shadows all day long.

"Hey Davey. C'mere a minute—that's you, right?"

Avie Gornik was standing in the doorway to the cellar, holding a bowl.

"You wanna suck on some ice chips? I got plenty."

I reached into the bowl and took some chips.

"Your uncle got back today, yeah?"

"Yes. But I haven't seen him yet."

"Yeah. Me neither. He got lots on his mind these days. Things got out of hand some while he was gone, but you know all about that, right?"

"No."

"I thought you did. I mean, you and the Cremona kid being such buddies. He didn't tell you that we lost two trucks?" He laughed. "I mean, if you think about it, it ain't easy, to lose a truck. You got no idea where we could find what was in the truck?"

"No."

He patted me on the shoulder. "You're okay, Davey. I mean, you're like Abe—you got so much ice water in your veins you don't need old Avie's chips. Only you should be careful who your friends are, get what I mean? You wouldn't want your uncle to get mad on you—to know things you do when he ain't here. You get my drift?"

"No."

Avie leaned toward me and I could make out his features now. He looked as old as his mother—big-nosed and thick-lipped and pasty-skinned, with small, mean eyes set too close together. He wore a sleeve-less undershirt like the kind my father used.

"So tell me—where you going down here at night?"

"Nowhere. Just looking for my friends."

"They ain't here, but listen. I been hoping to meet you sometime, you know what I mean? Not because of the trouble we got, which ain't your fault—just some of our boys seem to trust some of their boys when they should know better—but because I been hearing a lot about you from your friends."

I sucked on the chips, let the freezing water glide down the back of my tongue.

"You know what all your friends say? They say you got a real big cock —that you got the biggest cock of all the guys your age."

"I gotta get going."

"Let me ask you a question first." He held my arm. "When you grow up, what are you gonna be—a big shot like your uncle or a little pip-squeak like your father?"

I turned to walk away—it was too hot for trouble—but he grabbed onto the back of my neck and forced me around. He laughed at me, his teeth yellow like old lamb bones.

"Ah, don't get mad on me, Davey. I didn't mean nothing. Your old man's okay. He don't bother nobody, I guess. Only c'mere a minute with me where nobody can see us, yeah?" I didn't move. "Hey—you ain't scared of me, are you?"

"No."

"Sure. I mean, why should a big kid like you be scared of an old fart like me, works for your uncle? I mean, if I did anything bad to you, I'd be in big trouble, right?"

"I suppose."

"I knew your uncle when he was in diapers, right? I knew his old man and his old lady." He made a sucking noise with his lips. "Ah, the old lady was really a knockout. He ever tell you about her?"

"She died before I was born."

"All the men had the hots for her. All them fancy clothes and fur coats."

He pushed the cellar door open with his shoulder.

"C'mon in with me—it's real nice and cool in here. It's always cooler where it's been dark all day, so you come on inside, yeah?"

He kept pressure on the back of my neck with his thumb and forefinger. I could smell the damp coal dust, the garbage cans full of winter ashes.

"Now listen. If you don't trust old Avie, you just let me know, only I figured from what your friends told me that you got the most courage of them all, right?"

"I don't know."

"This'll only take a couple of minutes, so if you don't want to do it, you say so now."

"Do what?"

"All I want is to see if the guys are right, if your little fire engine is really bigger than theirs. They all showed me theirs—to brag, yeah?— but if you wanna be left out, that's okay by me. Only I figured a big kid like you ain't scared of much." He was unbuttoning my fly. "I mean, anytime you want me to stop, all you gotta do is say the word."

He let go of my neck, but I didn't move.

"Let me ask you something. You do it yourself yet?" He reached inside my shorts and touched my penis very lightly, as if to see if it was there. "Hey, that's nice—I mean, your friends all bragged to me that they do it to themselves already fifteen or sixteen times a day, only between you and me, Davey, they ain't big enough yet. They just wanna impress people, you know what I mean?"

He started stroking my penis and what surprised me was that the huskier his voice got, the more gently he touched me.

"Hey, I think your friends were right, did you know that? For a kid your age you got a terrific pecker, Davey. I mean, how old are you already? You're gonna make the ladies very happy someday, just like your uncle does. So how old did you say you were?"

"Twelve. I'll be thirteen in September, after school starts."

"Oh yeah? Thirteen, huh? I would of figured fourteen or fifteen from your size. See how nice and hard it's getting? That feels good, don't it? I mean, if you don't trust old Avie, you just say the word and I'll stop, yeah? All you gotta do is say the word."

The cellar was pitch black, no light leaking in, and in the blackness he kept rubbing me and talking to me, telling me that if I didn't beat my meat yet I should take a tip from him and not start, because once you started you had to do it all the time, every few hours. In my head I saw myself running away and I saw him falling on top of me before I could get the cellar door open. He was twisting my arms back behind me and spreading my fingers apart and breaking them, cracking them one at a time with his bare hands. I'd seen a photo of an artist once who had so much pain in his hands that he strapped them to boards so that he could keep painting. I thought of the men in my grandfather's home, lying on their beds, the lights out. I wondered if anybody had ever done this to Tony and what his brothers would do to him if they found out. I felt sick. I wanted to go home. Avie scooped up ice chips, moaned, and then started talking again.

"You really like your uncle, don't you, Davey? I mean, he's the big man, yeah? He's the really big man . . . the big man. . . ."

If I wanted a thrill my friends didn't know about I should do what he did, he said—that when I felt the stuff about to explode I should shove ice chips under my little acorns. He opened the door, told me it was best for us to leave separately. He told me my erection would go down by itself in a few minutes and that I shouldn't say anything to my friends about me being the biggest because it would only make them jealous.

"Your uncle was big like you when he was your age." He held me by the shoulder. "Listen. You don't believe old Avie, you ask your uncle sometime about how he did the same thing with me when he was your age. He liked it too."

You're a liar, I wanted to shout. *You're a dirty liar!* I tightened all the muscles in my face and neck and chest, to make sure tears wouldn't come bursting forth, and from the way he forced a laugh I knew it bothered him that I wouldn't show him how angry I was.

"Here," he said, shoving coins into my hand and crunching my fist closed around them. "You go treat yourself to a movie or a malted or something, yeah? You're okay, Davey. I mean, you're a real man now, you know what I mean?"

In the morning, I was the first one awake. There were no sounds in my parents' room or from the courtyard below or from the other buildings. I took out my paper and pencils and drawing board and sat in front of my window and stared at the apartment house across the way. The world was wonderfully quiet and still, and I felt again what I'd often felt when I was younger—that in the room next to mine my parents were lying in the bed, dead. For miles and miles, in every direction, there was no sound because all living things were dead. I was the only person left alive in the whole world, and that feeling—of being able to live inside total silence in a world where nobody would talk to me or want things from me or do things to me, where people could never be mean to one another again—comforted me.

My mother was right. I loved to stare, and the longer I stared, the more I saw. A warm breeze came in across the fire escape. I heard sparrows. I saw pigeons lift silently into the air from the roofs of apartment buildings. If I strained, I could make myself hear cars and trucks in the distance.

Why did I love the face of the building across from mine so much? In my drawing there was no sky, no ground, no sidewalk. There were no birds, no dogs, no cats, no people. Nothing moved, nothing lived. I concentrated on a section of the building that ran from just above the first floor windows to just below the fifth floor windows, so that all you saw on my paper were bricks and windows and fire escapes—squares and rectangles and diagonals—so that from my drawing there was no way of knowing where the building began and where it ended.

What I wanted was for somebody looking at my drawing to feel he could reach into it and rub his hands across its surfaces, along the iron slats of the fire escapes, the smooth glass of the windows, the pocked clay of the bricks. If you looked at my drawing long enough, I wanted you to be able to feel the difference between each brick, to feel the tiny pebbles caught in the mortar, and I was frightened that I would never be able to, that I would never get it right. I was afraid that no matter how long I stared, or how hard I worked, or how well I learned to draw, I would never be able to make people see what I saw when I looked at the world.

I sat perfectly still, waiting for the sun to rise just a little higher so that, coming from behind, it would use our apartment building to cast a long horizontal shadow across the bottom half of the other building—a line that cut straight through the fourth row of bricks between the second and third stories.

The shadow moved up slowly from the middle of the second-story windows. I let my eyes move from window to window, from apartment to apartment, amazed, as always, by all the different things people kept outside on their sills and fire escapes: flower pots and jars and shoes and bread boxes and toasters and cereal boxes and scatter rugs and brooms and mops and chairs and shower caps and egg cartons and telephones and radios and clothespin bags, litter boxes for cats and small iceboxes for milk and juice, and old farmer-cheese boxes to grow radishes and parsley in, and toys and wigs and underwear and lamps and stacks of newspapers and even enema bags. I left most of these things out of my drawing. I put in a few flower pots and wooden boxes and clothespins. But the clothespins held up no clothing and the flower pots contained no flowers and the wooden boxes had nothing growing in them. I liked sketching in the curtains behind the windows, as if through fog, and then layering the reflections from my own building—bricks and ladders and drainpipes—over that.

When the sun was almost up to where I wanted it, I began working, a piece of blank paper under the right edge of my hand so that as I moved along I wouldn't smudge things. I used my kneaded eraser, twisting the putty to a fine point to create highlights along the edges of a clothesline that went out from a window on the third story, looping down from its pulley in two long widening lines of pale gray that were cut off by the right edge of the paper.

The heat hung in the air like thin sheets of damp gauze. It was only when my father burst into my room, making my door crash open against my bookcase, that I realized I'd been hearing noises behind me.

"What's the matter with you, you're deaf or something? How many times do we gotta call you to get out here?"

He stood in the doorway, hands on hips, his face red. He wore only his underpants, a pair of green-and-red flowered boxer shorts, stained at the fly. I slipped my drawing under the cover of my pad and I put the pad on my desk. I moved deliberately. When I started to pick up my pencils, he grabbed my arm and yanked on it.

"When I say to move, you move, do you hear me? When I call you, you listen to me the first time!"

I jerked my arm free and the pencils went flying. They rolled along the linoleum, clicking. I bent down to collect them. I couldn't believe how angry I felt. I was ready to burst, to spring at him, to claw at his face with my hands. Could I hold my anger back, the way Jackie Robinson did?

"You don't touch my drawing," I said. I moved back, my fist clenched around pencils, and I wondered what I would do, really, if he came at me again. I thought of Tony, watching his brothers beat up their father.

"Oh does that one have a temper!" my mother said. "Sol—get in here and leave the boy alone, okay? We got troubles enough as is."

I looked past my father and saw Abe. His skin was very brown and smooth. He looked handsomer than he had when he'd left for California.

"Hi uncle Abe," I said. I felt embarrassed. "I didn't know you were here."

"Did you see Sheila last night?"

"Yes."

I gasped. Abe had pulled me from my room and was holding me up against the living room wall so that my feet were off the floor. "Yes. You say yes to me? That's *all*?" His eyes were blazing. "You talk and you talk fast."

"He's only a kid," my mother said. "So listen, darling. You shouldn't do anything to the boy that you'll be sorry for later. I love my brother and my husband, but if it's only my son who wants to be saved, I'll take the boy. I mean, just because you saved Momma, does that mean I gotta do what you want for the rest of my life? Did I ask you to save her?"

"Shut up."

Abe set me down, told me to tell him what I knew.

"I saw her down on Rogers Avenue, near where she always hangs out, in front of Lee's luncheonette."

"And—"

"I don't know." I swallowed hard, to keep from crying. My mother was smiling at me as if she was glad to see Abe hurt me—as if this would prove that she was right about him. Abe let go of my arm. I could hear myself screaming at him that I didn't know anything, but no words came from my mouth. I wanted to be back in my room. I wanted to be staring at the fire escapes on the apartment building across the way. I wanted to be in the schoolyard with my friends. I wanted to have a different mother and father, to be living some other life than the one that was mine.

"Listen," my father said. "You tell Abe what you know. What happened is people did things to Sheila last night—she's home now and she'll be okay, so you don't gotta be scared—but Abe is trying to find out who the people are. Do you understand me?"

"No."

"See?" my mother said. "The boy's like his mother. He don't understand none of this stuff."

"Because he don't want to understand!" My father came at me, his hand in the air, to slap me. I still had a few pencils in my fist and I let the points press into my thumbs. *If you touch me I'll stab your good eye!* I heard myself say. *If you lay a single finger on me . . .*

"It's too bad we didn't have another child," my mother said. "Because what I was thinking, Sol, was that even if I couldn't save Davey, maybe I could have saved his brother or sister when Abe wasn't looking, one out of two, so at least I wouldn't come out of this life with nothing. What I was thinking was—"

"Shut up," Abe said, softly. "Your father is right. Sheila is home, scared but unharmed. Only there's going to be trouble. Do you understand?"

I started talking. "I saw her when I went downstairs at about nine-thirty. I know it was nine-thirty because Mr. Lipsky had his radio on in front of the house and he was listening to the 'Lux Radio Theater.' I heard the commercial. Then I went around the corner and Sheila was where she usually is at night, in front of Lee's, with her friends. They were leaning against cars and smoking. She had her back against Mr. Waxman's blue Ford and she was letting a guy neck with her. The guy's name is Marty Reiss and he's in a gang called The Flashes and he was there with his friends. He goes to Erasmus with Sheila and he's on the football team. He plays wingback. He hangs out in the Pigtown section usually, by Empire Boulevard, except he and his gang have been coming over to visit Sheila and her friends at night this summer. They come here looking for guys to beat up and girls to make out with. They don't fight much if it's hot. Sometimes they stop you and ask you to loan them money and if you say you don't have any they grab you and say, 'Then all I find I keep.' So I didn't stop to talk with Sheila and they didn't bother me. That's all I know. I came home through the courtyard on Linden Boulevard instead of going back around Rogers Avenue, so I didn't see her again."

"See?" my father said. "Didn't I tell you the boy got a voice when he wants to? Didn't I say so?"

"I'm sending Sheila and Lillian to the country for a while, for a little rest," Abe said. "In the meantime I want the three of you to keep out of sight. I'll have a man posted downstairs. If you need to go to the store, you tell him and he'll get somebody to go with you. No movies, is that clear? You go nowhere where there are crowds. You stay away from open windows."

"In *this* heat?" my mother said. "Thanks a lot. So why did we come back then? Tell me that. Maybe now, my brilliant brother, you'll tell me why did we have to come back to this stinking city. A goddamn oven is all it is, a goddamn stinking oven for us to bake in."

"Be quiet, Evie," Abe said. "I'm not through."

"Sure," my mother said, and she slumped down in my father's chair. "When you're through you send me a telegram, yeah?" She closed her eyes, reached across her chest with her right hand, let it slip inside her housecoat to touch her left breast the way she did when she was drowsy. Was *that* where she was sick?

"If you follow my instructions, you'll be safe."

My mother leaned forward. "But you promised me," she said. "God-damn you, Abe, you *promised* me! No more rough stuff, Evie, you said. I give you my word. No more rough stuff." My mother stood and shook her fists at the air. "I'm begging you, Abe—I'm down on my knees except it's too hot—but in my heart I'm down on my knees and I'm begging you not to start up again. Please. For me, Abe. For Lillian and Sheila. For Davey. Please! Like Poppa used to say—if you touch shit, your own hands smell from it. You're too good for them, darling. You don't—"

"What do you mean, start up again?" my father said. "They're the ones who started, ain't they? If you don't stand up to bums like that, they walk all over you. Didn't Roosevelt do his best to keep peace in the world? But when the Japs and the Nazis went too far, then he stood up to them. So I want you to know I think you should keep your trap shut, because I agree with Abe."

My father turned and grinned, looking for Abe's approval.

"I meant to ask you, Sol," Abe said. "While I was gone, did you have any trouble?"

"Trouble? What kind of trouble should I have?"

"Just answer the question. Did you have any trouble? Did anyone leave messages for you to give to me?"

"No, Abe. None."

"You're sure?"

"Of course I'm sure. Why wouldn't I be sure? You ask Davey here if you don't believe me."

"How many times do I gotta tell you to leave the boy out of it," my mother said. "This ain't none of his business, all this crap. The same goes for you, Abe. Do you got a brain or what to come in here scaring the kid this way? Look at him—look at how pale he is." She came towards me, arms extended. Was my father lying to Abe to protect me —so that Abe wouldn't get after me for not having told him about the message? "My little baby Davey—let Momma hold you, all right? Let Momma—" She stopped, turned on Abe again. I felt dizzy because what drove me craziest of all was not being able to figure out when my mother would be for Abe and when she would be against him, or when my parents would switch around in deciding to protect me. I slipped away from my mother, stood apart from all of them, in front of my bedroom.

"Can't you see what you do to him?" my mother said. "You want I should bang my head against the wall first so then you'll see what it is you're doing? Here!"

My mother turned her back to us and began banging her forehead against the wall. "Now are you satisfied?" she asked. "Is this what you want?" She reached sideways, grabbed onto the moldings around the door—she was facing the narrow width of wall that separated their room from mine—and whacked her forehead against the wall again.

"That's very brilliant, Evie," my father said. "Oh that's really smart. I mean, you're really helping the situation a lot."

There was a small red circle on my mother's forehead, as if she'd been hit by a baseball.

"So why should I wait for somebody else to break my head? You tell me that. Why should I wait for somebody else?"

"You're exaggerating, Evie, the way you always do. If you follow my instructions there'll be no trouble. I'll speak to you at least once a day. If there's a problem, you buzz the downstairs door four times. That will be the signal. I give you my word that I didn't look for trouble."

"Not much. Sure. Tell me another one."

"If I don't take care of things they'll only get worse for us all. They made a mistake, you see, and they have to be shown what the mistake was, so that they don't repeat it. They should not have touched a member of my family."

My father brought in a washcloth and my mother lay down on the sofa. "The problem is that everyone's already dead for you, Abe, don't you see?" she said. "First Momma and Poppa and then your friends in the Army and now Sheila and soon yourself, if you keep going in the same direction. But when they call on the phone to tell me you're dead too, it won't be a big surprise, see? All it will be is a chance for people to say what a big shot you are now, below ground." She lifted the washcloth. There was a tiny piece of white paint stuck to her forehead. "If you were really smart, you wouldn't give them the satisfaction, that's all

I been trying to tell you. Sometimes you win by losing, yeah? Only you're too stubborn to see that. Like always. So why be against California? In California we could start all over. In California we could live without being scared for our lives all the time. Only you're too pigheaded to do it, even though you know I'm right, that it's our only chance. Even though . . ." Nobody spoke. "Don't anybody see that I'm right? Don't anybody care?"

"California," my father said. "That's all she got on her brain since she's back. California. The Promised Land. Sure."

"So tell me something, Abe darling—is there a law that says we can't be happy too while we're still alive?"

Abe didn't answer. Instead he bent down and kissed me on the cheek.

"I'm sorry about before," he said.

"That's okay."

He went into the foyer and opened the door. Turkish Sammy was on the landing, waiting for him.

4

BEAU JACK was the only person who knew how much I loved Jackie Robinson. Whenever I could get out of our apartment—while Abe had our building guarded—I'd go down to Beau Jack's and stay with him and we'd talk about Jackie and speculate on how much greater Jackie might have been if he'd been white, if he hadn't had to wait until the age of twenty-eight to become the first black baseball player in the history of the major leagues.

I'd begun following Jackie's career the year before when he was in the minor leagues with Montreal, where he led the league in batting with a .349 average. Beau Jack kept lots of newspaper clippings, and his favorite told about how, long after the final game was over—Montreal beat Louisville in the Little World Series, with Jackie scoring the winning run—when Jackie was the last player to leave the dressing room, the crowd was still there, waiting for him. They hugged him and kissed him and cheered for him and chased him through the streets of the city. It was probably the first time in history, Beau Jack said, that a black man had run from a white mob, not because it hated him, but because it loved him.

Sometimes Beau Jack would tease me.

"You think just because I'm a colored man and Jackie's a colored man that I care more about him than the other players, don't you?"

"I suppose."

He'd wait a few seconds. "Well," he'd say, a faint smile on his lips. "You know what?"

"What?"

"You're right. I care more about that pigeon-toed black man than any player ever lived!"

I knew everything about Jackie Robinson there was to know. He was born on January 31, 1919, in Cairo, Georgia. His full name was John Roosevelt Robinson and he was the youngest of five children. For many years Jackie told others that his father died a year after he was born, but the truth was that Jackie's father, who worked as a sharecropper for twelve dollars a month, ran off with a neighbor's wife six months after Jackie's birth. The plantation owner blamed Jackie's mother and ordered her off the land, so she sold what possessions they had and took her family across the country to California, where she had a brother, Jackie's uncle Burton. In her new life, washing and ironing for white people, Jackie's mother was up before daylight and home after sundown. Sometimes the family lived on nothing but old bread and sweetwater. During these years, Jackie's mother sustained herself with the dream that all her children might one day be able to go to school.

When Jackie was a boy he belonged to a gang made up of blacks, Japanese, and Mexicans called the Pepper Street Gang. They weren't allowed to swim and play ball where whites could. Instead they roamed the streets, stealing from local stores, getting into trouble with the police. By the time Jackie was in high school he had few friends his own age. He was close to three older men, though: his minister Karl Downs, who took him out of gangs and brought him into church life and athletics; and his two brothers—Mack, who was a great track star and Jackie's coach, and Frank, who was his best friend.

In 1936, despite a heart condition, Mack went to Berlin and came in second to Jesse Owens in the Olympics. Soon after, while starring in football, baseball, basketball and track at Pasadena Junior College, Jackie broke Mack's broad jump record. Dozens of four-year colleges recruited him but he decided to go to U.C.L.A. so that he could be close to home. In the fall of 1938, however, shortly after he enrolled there, Frank was killed in a motorcycle accident. Not long after that Jackie met Rachel Isum. Although he fell in love with her at once—they became especially close during the months following the death of Rachel's father —they did not marry until almost a decade later.

In all the articles I read, Jackie rarely spoke of his feelings. It bothered me that I knew so much about his athletic career and so little about the rest of his life. I wanted to know what he'd felt when he was a boy my age. I wanted to know what he felt during all the years he had to hold back his true feelings—during all the years he had to live, day after day, believing he would never reach the major leagues. But whenever I'd ask Beau Jack about Jackie's childhood, hoping he could fill in the details of what it was like to be a young black boy growing up in America, he would never say much.

Beau Jack had no trouble talking about the facts of Jackie's career, or about the Negro Baseball Leagues and the great players he'd seen, or even about his life as a soldier during World War I. Although he could give me all the details I wanted about what the war had been like— stories of trench warfare and hand-to-hand combat, of cantonment cities and potato-masher grenades and mustard gas and redoubt lines and bolo knives and rolling barrages—he never talked about his life before the First World War. I had the feeling that he didn't want to live through those years—not even in his memory—ever again, and that nothing in his adult life could ever be as painful as an ordinary day of his childhood had been. How helpless and ashamed he must have felt, I thought.

He spoke in a slightly slurred way that made me think he grew up in the South, but I didn't know for sure. He never mentioned any family he had, or friends; he never had visitors or went on trips. And yet I knew this was a large part of what made it so easy for me when I was with him. He seemed to have come from nowhere. He was the only person I knew who needed no other life than the one in which he was living.

It made him happy, too, to have me come down and visit with him, even if we just sat in his kitchen together doing nothing, just being quiet with one another. We'd listen to ball games on the radio, or talk about Jackie, or about different people in the building, or he'd ask me about school, or I'd ask him to tell me about the First World War—but when we weren't talking it never bothered me to just sit with him and sip a Coke and pet Kate and let time drift by.

Sometimes, if he had to go to an apartment to put up a cabinet, or fix a refrigerator or a sink or a toilet, or if somebody's door buzzer was jammed, he'd leave me by myself. I'd take off my sneakers and rest my bare feet on Kate's warm body and I'd feel far away from everything and everyone. Sometimes when he was gone I wondered if Beau Jack was real, or if I'd merely invented him. I thought often of asking him to let me draw his portrait. Sometimes when I stared at him, tracing the bones under his skin with my eyes, I ached to be able to make his face come to life on a piece of blank paper. I loved all the different colors I saw in the brown of his skin. What I couldn't figure out, though, was how to transform those colors into grays and whites. When I thought of trying to get everything I saw into a portrait—all the different hues: the slight redness, like sunburn, at the cheekbones; the purple that seemed to lie beneath the brown like grape-stain; the pitted black pockmarks along his cheeks and chin; the flat orange-brown near his hairline; the marbled tans and pinks around his missing ear; the smooth gleaming chestnut of his neck—I worried that I would just wind up with a dark, confusing mess. I wanted to be able to draw each pore of his skin, each hair, each wrinkle—to see what no painting or photograph could see—and because I didn't see how it would ever be possible, and because I even began to wonder if what I saw inside my head was actually *there*, I chose to do nothing. I knew I could have drawn his features and gotten them right, the same way I copied out pictures of Jackie from magazines— Jackie's full, thick lips, his lamb's wool hair, his broad, flat nose, his dimpled chin, his soft almond eyes—but without shading in the skin I was afraid I would never be able to suggest the way the darker colors underneath shone through to the surface.

After U.C.L.A., where Jackie was an All-American basketball player, the N.C.A.A. broad jump champion, and, in football, the leading ground-gainer in the country with an average of twelve yards a carry, he went to Hawaii and worked for a construction company near Pearl Harbor while playing football for the Honolulu Bears. In the spring of 1942 he was drafted into the Army and sent to Fort Riley, Kansas, where he went to Officer's Candidate School and became a Second Lieutenant, a Morale Officer in charge of an all-black truck battalion. He was transferred from Fort Riley to Fort Hood, in Texas, and then to Camp Breckenridge in Kentucky, where a friend who'd been a member of the Kansas City Monarchs, in the Negro Baseball Leagues, told Jackie that the Monarchs were looking for players.

After Jackie received his honorable discharge in November 1944, he wrote to the Monarchs. They gave him a tryout, then offered him a job at four hundred dollars a month. Jackie was happy. When the season began in 1945, though, and Jackie saw what his future would be like—a fatiguing, humiliating life of traveling from city to city by bus, of never eating or sleeping well, of never getting the rewards and recognition that white players received in their leagues—he became bitter and discouraged. But if he left baseball, where could he go, and what could he do to earn enough money to help his mother, or to be able to marry Rachel?

The answer came in August 1945, when Branch Rickey, the owner of the Brooklyn Dodgers, sent Clyde Sukeforth to see Jackie. Sukeforth, one of Rickey's scouts, told Jackie that Rickey was looking for players for a Negro team to be called the Brooklyn Brown Dodgers and he persuaded Jackie to come to Brooklyn for an interview.

"The truth," Rickey said, the first time he and Jackie met, "is that you are not a candidate for the Brooklyn Brown Dodgers. I've sent for you because I'm interested in you as a candidate for the Brooklyn National League Club. I think you can play in the major leagues."

They talked more and Rickey, an elderly, churchgoing man who didn't smoke or drink or swear and who would not even attend his own team's games on Sunday, told Jackie a story.

In 1910 Rickey was a coach for the Ohio Wesleyan team. The team went to South Bend, Indiana, to play against Notre Dame, and the hotel refused to let one of the team's players, a black named Charley Thomas, register. There were no black hotels in South Bend and Rickey talked the hotel manager into letting Charley Thomas sleep on a cot in Rickey's room. Instead of sleeping, Charley Thomas sat without speaking on the edge of the cot. Then he began to cry and shake, to tear at one hand with the other, as if he were trying to scratch his skin off with his fingernails. Rickey asked him what he was doing.

"It's my hands," Charley Thomas sobbed. "They're black. If only they were white, I'd be as good as anybody then, wouldn't I, Mr. Rickey? If only they were white!"

"Charley," Rickey said. "The day will come when they won't have to be white."

Rickey told Jackie that he would have to play for Montreal in the International League for a year. He told him that he knew Jackie was a fierce competitor. He liked that. But if the great experiment, as he called it, was to work, Jackie would have to control his temper and take a lot of abuse. He would be the object of beanballs and spikings, curses and name-calling.

"Mr. Rickey," Jackie asked angrily, "are you looking for a Negro who is afraid to fight back?"

For the first time, Rickey exploded. "Robinson," he replied, "I'm looking for a ball player with guts enough *not* to fight back."

When, afterwards, Rickey was proven right—when pitchers threw at Jackie's head, when fans called him nigger, when bus drivers made him sit in the backs of buses, when hotels turned him away, when restaurants made him get his meals in paper bags at back doors, when his own teammates wrote petitions to Rickey declaring that they would not play if Jackie did—Jackie kept his part of the bargain: he took all the jeers and taunts and insults, all the hatred and injustice, and he didn't fight back, he didn't show his anger.

Whenever Jackie would come to bat and get a hit, or when he'd make a spectacular play in the field, or steal a base, my heart would swell and inside my head I'd be screaming *Good for you, Jackie! Good for you— you show the bastards!*—and I'd have to fight to hold my tears back, to keep my feelings inside.

I imagined Rachel comforting Jackie at night, his head on her bosom, her stroking his hair and forehead, kissing his eyes. I thought of how she must have wept inside herself because she alone knew how helpless

Jackie felt—how much strength it took for a man of his courage *not* to fight back. Whenever I went to a game with my father or Abe or my friends, I'd look for Rachel and Jack Junior—their first child, born the previous year—in the box seats behind home plate, where the Dodger wives sat. Mostly, though, I'd keep my eye on Jackie and try to bore my thoughts into his skull so that I could feel exactly what he was feeling. When he knocked the dirt from his spikes with the end of the bat and took a practice swing, eyeing the pitcher, did he think of his childhood then? When a pitcher dusted him off or a catcher called him nigger, did he escape then by letting his mind remember those parts of his childhood that he never spoke about? If you'd had a miserable childhood, could you still love it and dwell on parts of it simply because it was yours?

Once, when I was at a Dodger-Cardinal game, I could tell from the way Jackie stared into the Cardinal dugout that they were riding him. Earlier in the season the Cardinals had threatened to go out on strike rather than play against Jackie, but baseball Commissioner Frick warned that he was willing to wreck the entire National League if he had to, in order to protect Jackie's right to play. The Cardinals called off the strike. Now, with Cardinal runners on first and second, I saw that the players had turned their attention to the Dodger shortstop, Pee Wee Reese. I stared at their mouths. They were calling Reese, a southerner from Louisville, a nigger lover. Jackie kicked at the dirt around first base and pounded his glove. Reese called to the umpire for time-out and motioned to Jackie. They walked toward the pitcher's mound and the Cardinal players came out of the dugout, onto the steps, and razzed Reese some more. Reese looked up, smiled at them, and then, as if it were the easiest thing in the world, he reached over and put his arm around Jackie's shoulder, the way any player would. The jeering stopped. Reese slipped his glove down along his wrist, rubbed up the ball for the pitcher, tossed it back to him. Jackie nodded to Reese, retreated to first base. My fists were clenched as tight as I could get them. I didn't tell anybody what I felt.

Beau Jack liked stories about hunting and fishing, and I'd read through his magazines—*National Geographic* and *Argosy* and *Field and Stream* and *The Police Gazette*—and we'd talk about the pictures and the stories. Sometimes he talked about hunting and fishing in the sewers of Brooklyn, about the alligators and crocodiles that supposedly lived below the city, set loose there by people who'd kept them as pets in fish tanks. In one of his magazines there was a story about unwanted babies being dropped into sewers or flushed down toilets—black and Puerto

Rican children born to unwed thirteen- or fourteen-year-old mothers—and Beau Jack believed the stories. He never smiled when he talked about the wild children who might be growing up in sewer tunnels, roaming the city underground like packs of wolves.

Beau Jack also got the *Daily News* and *Daily Mirror* and I'd read through them, starting at the back with the sports pages. I knew Beau Jack didn't like my uncle, so I wasn't surprised when he gave me the *Mirror* one morning folded open to an article on page three about the gang wars my uncle was supposedly involved in. According to the article there were carloads of hired thugs riding around Brooklyn shooting at one another. The article said that residents in several Brooklyn neighborhoods were afraid to go out into the streets. The Brooklyn District Attorney promised that, using whatever means he had to, he was going to gather enough evidence to end the reign of terror that the rival gangs were inflicting on innocent citizens.

Everything was so quiet in Beau Jack's apartment below ground that it was hard for me to believe that in the world outside our building cars were actually rolling along streets in the broiling heat, full of men with loaded guns. When I imagined the cars cruising up and down half-empty streets and when I saw pictures in my head of Little Benny and Avie Gornik and the others staring out of car windows, tommy guns and .45s on their laps, the pictures came to me without sound—as if I were watching a silent movie, as if I were deaf.

When I went upstairs late that afternoon, my mother was in her bedroom, asleep on top of the bedspread, nothing but a washcloth over her eyes, a yellow towel across the middle of her body. I tiptoed into the kitchen and telephoned Tony Cremona.

"What do you want?" He sounded angry.

"Nothing," I said. "Just to talk. I've been cooped up in my building for over a week now. I just wanted to talk to somebody."

"I think you chose the wrong guy. Your uncle finds out, he'll cut your cork off."

"You listen to the Dodger game today?" I asked. "They really creamed the Phillies, eleven to two. I bet they'll win the pennant easy."

"Hey listen, Davey, do you know what I really think?"

"What?"

"I think you're crazy, calling me. That's what I think. I mean, I really think you're nuts. Or else—"

"Or else what?"

"Or else you're trying to trap me somehow. I'll see you around, okay?"

"Nobody told me to call you," I said. "And nobody's listening to me. I just felt like talking to you about the game and things. That's all."

"Bullshit."

"You don't have to believe me, but I'm telling the truth, Tony. I still have some of that good paper you gave me, and I've been making a drawing I think you'll really like. Maybe when I get out of this house again and we're back in school, I'll show it to you. Would you like to see it?"

"Jesus Christ, Davey. Are you for real? If my brothers came in now, you know what they'd *do* to me? Do you? They been after me all week about that creep Gornik and if you ever made me visit him, and I don't think they believe me when I tell them no."

"How about if I write a note and sign it, saying you never did?"

There was a brief silence. Then Tony started laughing and I did too. He told me that I really cracked him up, to say a thing like that, and he left the phone for a few seconds to make sure the doors were all locked so no one could know he was talking to me. After he came back and we kidded around for a while, making jokes about me giving him notes for his father and brothers and Mr. Fasalino to read, and him giving me notes to give to Abe and Little Benny and Spanish Louie and Mr. Rothenberg, we agreed that we were glad all the trouble between them was taking place before school started, because both sides would probably have had guys spying on us there to make sure we never talked to each other. I tried to find out why his brothers were interested in Gornik, but he said he didn't really know, just that he thought Gornik had had some kind of meeting with Mr. Fasalino. I said that my uncle used Gornik as a messenger a lot and that maybe that meant they were close to a peace settlement.

Tony whistled. "Not from what I hear," he said. "I think they got something on Gornik. I think that old bastard got trouble going both ways."

"What kind?"

"I don't know. Trouble, you know? Just trouble. Only one question I got for you, though, Davey—"

"Yes?"

"Did he ever get funny with you?"

"What do you mean, funny?"

"I don't know. *Funny!* I think he gets funny with guys and it don't matter to him if they're from my neighborhood or yours, if they're Italian or Jewish or black or white or yellow or purple. From what I hear, whoever gets him first—your uncle or mine—is gonna have a good time with him."

"Jackie Robinson got three hits today. It puts his average over .300."

"Oh yeah?"

"I bet he wins Rookie of the Year."

"So what?"

"Nothing. When you said black, I thought of him."

"You really dig that spook, don't you?"

"I suppose."

"Victor says that if they ever catch him with his black dingus in a white muff, they're gonna make sure he ain't got balls left to play ball with."

"Don't you think he's a good player?"

"He's okay. I mean, he got courage, I guess. Only that don't change that he got black balls and my brothers hating him. They'd love to put him on one of those trucks that never comes back. But listen—you took a chance calling here only you got lucky that I was the only one home, so don't do it again, yeah? Don't be crazy like me and act like a dumb guinea. It'll make sure we both live long enough to see the World Series this year, right?"

"If I can get tickets, would you go with me?"

"The only place I'm going is off the phone. A car just drove up. Hey Davey, you know what?"

"What?"

"I'm glad you called, you nut. They got me pretty locked in too. When this is all over I'll show you the stuff I been making in the cellar, okay?"

"Sure."

"Don't take no wooden nickels, you hear? No slugs neither. Go fly a kike, okay? Then I'll see you around."

"I'll see you around," I said, but he was gone by the time I said it.

When my father came through the door about an hour later, he looked awful. His good eye was bloodshot, his short-sleeved shirt drenched. My mother wandered into the living room, holding a towel around her, at the hip.

"So?" she asked. "Is he dead yet?"

"Who?"

"Abe. Who else?"

"What kind of smart talk is that?" He looked at me, head tilted. "You should have your head examined, talking like that in front of the boy. It makes me very happy I came home, a greeting like that."

He walked into the bathroom and she followed him.

"Just tell me yes or no, so I can decide if I should go back to sleep or not."

"Abe ain't dead. They don't kill a guy like that so easy."

"I'm glad to hear it. So you'll wake me when it's over, right?"

My father came out of the bathroom, his shirt off. My mother was in the bedroom, singing.

"I saw what it said in the newspaper this morning. About the gangs shooting at each other. Is it true?"

He put his eyeglasses on and the lenses fogged up at once. I almost reached out to touch his face, to feel the heat there. He took his glasses off, wiped them with a handkerchief.

"Your mother been letting you go down there all day with the *shvartze* again, right?"

"I guess."

He grabbed my arm and shook me. "Why all the time with the *shvartze*, huh? Can you answer me that? What's going on down there with you two, huh? What kind of monkey business?"

"Leave me alone," I said, and yanked my arm away.

"I'll leave you alone when I'm dead," he said. He grabbed my arm again, and even though his hand was wet I couldn't get out of his grip. He pulled me to the kitchen. "You get in here with me, sonny boy. Abe wants to speak to you."

He held me with one hand and dialed Abe's number with the other, then handed the phone to me. His voice shifted.

"Be careful," he whispered. "Watch out for his temper."

"Davey?"

"Yes, Uncle Abe."

"All right. I don't have time for anything except the truth, do you understand?"

"Yes."

"The night you saw Sheila, did you notice anything unusual?"

"No."

"*Nothing?*"

"No."

"You saw Avie that night, though, didn't you?"

"Yes."

"All right," he said. "That's what I needed to know."

"Did Avie tell you?"

"I ask the questions, Davey." Then, "Is your mother all right?"

"The same as always. She's lying down now."

"I'm glad you told me the truth, that you didn't hesitate."

"Will Avie get into trouble?"

"None that you made. Listen. You go and take care of your mother now. You be good to her. If things go as planned, you should all be able to leave your building by the end of the week. You tell her I said so."

He hung up without saying goodbye. I turned and saw my mother standing in the doorway, dressed in a flowered housecoat, smiling at me in a crazy way, singing to herself. Her arms were way up over her head, as if she was going to spin around, as if she was dreaming. I told her what Abe told me to tell her, but she didn't act as if she heard my words.

I wondered which way Abe would have hated me more—if I'd done what I'd done and admitted seeing Avie, or if I'd lied. I imagined Abe riding in the back of his black sedan, Little Benny and Spanish Louie on either side of him, the car floating a half-foot above the road, sliding through the heat waves in slow motion, through rainbows of shimmering oil slicks. My mother kept grinning at me, glassy-eyed, and the longer she grinned at me, the more I hated her.

"Listen," she said, and she leaned her cheek on my father's bare shoulder. "Once you make up your mind you can't be happy, there ain't no reason you can't have a pretty good time, right, Solly? Didn't you teach me that way back?"

"I saw the sentence in the newspaper once. Sure. Moe Berg said it, I think, from the time when he was playing catcher for the Yankees."

My mother twirled around, left the kitchen, yelled to us from the living room to come in and join her. I followed my father through the foyer. My mother was pouring two glasses of whiskey. She handed one to my father, then drank the whiskey from her glass in one swallow. She switched on the phonograph and began moving around the room, dancing to the music but singing a song different from the one playing. She took my father's hands and tried to make him dance with her, singing words about being close together dancing cheek-to-cheek. I backed up against the door to my bedroom.

"It's too hot for funny business," my father said, shoving her away. "What's the matter with you, anyway? Are you crazy or something?"

"What's the matter with *you*—ain't you in love with me no more? You don't want to dance with a beautiful lady?" She pushed him aside and came towards me, arms out, eyes half-closed. "Then maybe my handsome son will give his mother a dance. I mean, we may all be dead anyway in a day or two, so why not dance, right, fellas? Why not have a good time? Let's break out the booze! Let's be happy! Strike up the music! Let's live a little!"

My father moved in front of me, to block her. She turned away, drank from the bottle the way I remembered her drinking on the night the war ended, her head way back, her throat stretched to its full length.

"Am I the only one wants to have a good time?"

"I think the heat's getting to you," my father said. "You heard what Abie told the boy, about finishing his business by the end of the week, didn't you? Only I'll tell you the truth, on a day like this, it's the heat that'll kill me before any of their dumb bolagulas do."

"From your lips to God's ears," my mother said, and then she drank some more, laughing and sputtering so that she spat some of the whiskey right back out.

"What's a bolagula?" I asked.

My mother clicked off the phonograph, swayed from side to side to silent music. She licked whiskey from her wrist.

"Oh Solly," she said. "I ain't heard that word since I was a kid. Bolagula! What a memory you got for a blind man! What a brain you got that's melting there in your tiny head. Only you know what—?"

She stopped, set the bottle down on the arm of my father's easy chair, steadied it so that it wouldn't topple over. Then, without finishing her sentence, she walked into her bedroom.

The next morning my mother and father slept late. I dressed, made my own breakfast, knocked on their bedroom door so I could tell them I was going to Stevey Komisarik's apartment to play Monopoly. They didn't answer, and for a second I was frightened, thinking they might have been murdered during the night. I pressed my ear to the door— the keyhole was stuffed with cotton—and I heard my mother giggling, telling my father to stop, asking him if he was crazy or if he was crazy. I yelled in that I'd eaten breakfast and about where I was probably going and before they could shout back anything to stop me, I was gone.

Stevey's mother looked through the peephole in the middle of their door, and when she saw it was me she put the latch on. She told me to go away, that she didn't want trouble.

Beau Jack let me into his apartment, handed me the morning paper. Kate nuzzled my hand. I sat and looked at the photograph on the front page of a beat-up old Ford, from behind, its trunk wide open. A policeman stood at each side of the car, at attention, looking straight into the camera, and on the ground—you almost didn't notice them at first— were two bodies, the heads facing down into the gutter, over the curbstone. According to the caption, the bodies had been found in the car's trunk, the car discovered next to an open lot in Canarsie. The dead men were rumored to be thugs who worked for Mr. Fasalino.

"Jesus!" I exclaimed.

"He ain't gonna be no help now."

I turned to the story on page three, searching for Abe's name. It wasn't there. I told Beau Jack about what Abe had said to me on the phone the night before.

"That man dotes on you. I don't deny it, only if you want to stay down here, Beau Jack do what he can."

"What do you mean?"

"I killed men before, I guess I can do it again, they try to hurt you."

"It's not my uncle's fault, what's happening."

"Didn't say it was."

"Do you believe me?"

"Sure I do. You a boy a man can trust."

"But you don't believe my uncle, do you? You never say his name. I noticed that."

He pointed to the newspaper.

"Those bodies real enough, Davey. I'm scared for you, is the truth. I'm just scared."

"But Abe *loves* me," I said. "I'm his *nephew*. Don't you understand?"

"Oh sure. I understand that. Lots of people gonna love a boy like you. That part's easy."

"Do you have a gun here?"

"Yes."

"From when you were a soldier?"

"Yes."

"And you've already killed with it?"

"That's right."

"Do you think I look like my uncle?"

"Maybe."

"Do you *really?* We have the same color eyes. The same kind of dark curly hair. . . ."

"You know who Beau Jack thinks you look like most?"

"Who?"

"Jackie Robinson."

"Come on," I said. "Be serious. How can I look like Jackie? I'm *white*."

"You sure are," he said, and he brought me a glass full of ice cubes, poured a bottle of Coke over the cubes, let the copper foam rise to the top of the glass, then settle. He poured again. "You drink this and then I give you something to eat, so we bring some color back to that handsome face of yours."

"Do you really think I look like him?"

Beau Jack started making us ham and Swiss cheese sandwiches.

"When I look in your face, Davey, all I see is young Jackie, don't ask me why. You got a look in your eyes like he must of had, he was your age, is what I think."

The next morning there was another front-page photo, this time of two bodies lying on a waterfront pier on Red Hook. "GANGLAND RE-VENGE," the headline said. The bodies had been fished out of the river and I recognized the names of two of my uncle's men, Mel Weiss and Skinny Epstein. An hour after the men's bodies were recovered, the article said, the District Attorney announced that a key member of one of the gangs had been arrested and was turning state's evidence. The man was known, the newspaper said, as Spanish Louie.

"Jesus!" I said.

Beau Jack smiled.

I went upstairs right away, but my father was already gone and my mother was walking from room to room in a bathing suit, cleaning the furniture with a feather duster, singing songs, asking me if I wanted to learn the words, if I wanted her to teach me how to dance.

I stayed in the kitchen so I could be there with her in case she turned on the radio and heard the news. I tried to draw, but I couldn't concentrate and decided to work on my baseball card collection instead. Sometimes my mother and father bragged about my drawing so much to other people—arguing with each other to prove which one of them believed in my talent more—that I felt as if their praise made what I did more theirs than mine. And sometimes, listening to my mother go on and on about how I would wind up running Abe's business someday, I had to agree with her that I could never do that and be an artist at the same time.

Abe came to our apartment that evening with my father, and after she heard the news my mother screamed and begged Abe to do something—to take us all to California, to give us new lives—but Abe stayed calm, even when she started bringing up things about their life from when they were children, from when he'd begun living the life he was leading now.

"If I had a different life, I'd have had a different life," he said to her. "I didn't. Here I am."

"Sure," my father added. "Like we used to say—if my aunt had balls we would of called her uncle."

Abe told us not to worry, that Spanish Louie was a very weak man. He told us that he had posted extra guards around our building and that if trouble increased, he would send us out of the city, to be with Lillian and Sheila.

The next day, before the sun was up, when the apartment house across the way was all in shadow so that the bricks were dusty white as if covered with old chalk dust, I went down to Beau Jack's. He nodded once, handed me the newspaper. He wasn't smiling.

Spanish Louie's photo was on the front page—a police photo from when he was younger that made his dark, milky eyes seem even sadder than they were in real life—and next to his photo there was a picture of the Hotel Mirapol in Coney Island, a circle drawn around a window on the eleventh floor. The article said that Spanish Louie had either jumped or was pushed from the window. It said that the District Attorney had been hoping to use Spanish Louie as his star witness in cleaning up the borough. At the time of his death, Spanish Louie's whereabouts were supposedly top secret. He was being guarded by six New York City detectives. At 1:23 A.M., when he fell, there were two detectives in the room with him, two detectives in the hallway outside his room, and two more in the hotel's lobby. They all claimed to be either in the bathroom or taking naps. The District Attorney was furious. He suspended the six detectives and declared that his investigation would now expand to include possible police corruption.

Less than an hour later my father came banging at the door. He ordered me to come with him, and kept trying to slap my face all the way up the stairs, yelling at me for having snuck away, for being with Beau Jack again.

Abe sat in my father's easy chair. He spoke in the same calm way he had spoken the night before. He told us that we were now free to come and go from the building whenever we wanted. My father could resume his regular route, my mother could get out and do her shopping, I could play with my friends. Sheila and Lillian were on the way in from the country.

"See?" my father said to my mother. "Didn't I tell you they don't got no power against a guy like your brother? Ain't we gonna be one happy family again, eating supper together and things?"

"Sure," my mother said. "Terrific. And what about Spanish Louie, huh? What about the promises in California? What about Davey? What about if they get Mr. Rothenberg and the cops don't fall asleep? What about the next time?"

"Spanish Louie thought he was a bird," Abe said, very flatly, in a voice I'd never heard before, and when he spoke my mother's eyes seemed to shrink, to return to their normal size. All the questions in them—about how she had given up on her brother and her husband, but what about her son—were suddenly gone.

Abe spoke directly to us, yet it was as if he wasn't there—it was as if somebody else was talking for him.

"Spanish Louie thought he was a bird. Only he wasn't. He could sing, you see, but he couldn't fly!"

My father laughed.

"Mr. Fasalino and I are even. We both want peace. Things are arranged now, all right? Come, Davey," he said, without pausing, "I'd like to spend some time with you, now that things are settled." He looked at my mother. "You don't mind if I take the boy with me, Evie?"

My mother bit on her lip and waved her hand at Abe, to show him that he could do whatever he wanted, that it was all the same to her.

"Do you want to come with me, Davey?"

"I suppose."

"Good."

He stood and stared hard at my mother. She turned away. He twisted his Army ring around on his finger so that the top part was on the inside and it looked as if he were wearing a gold wedding band.

"There is one more small piece of business we need to take care of, and you can help us, Davey. Then we'll be all done with the rough stuff."

"You got choices, Abe," my mother said.

"That's right."

"That's really terrific," my father said, forcing a laugh. "I mean, I didn't know you had such a sense of humor. I used to think the war knocked it out of you. He can sing but he can't fly! Do you get it, Evie? See—they thought Spanish Louie would spill the beans and—"

"There's no need," Abe said softly.

Downstairs, the women from our building were already outside sitting on folding chairs, knitting and talking. Next to the curb, in the little squares of dirt around the oak and maple trees, their children were playing with pails and shovels and dixie cups. When the women saw us, they stopped what they were doing and called their children to them. Abe said good morning, tipped his hat.

I said nothing. We walked along Rogers Avenue, then turned up Church Avenue, toward Holy Cross. Abe seemed very far away, even when he asked me what I'd done to pass the time during the previous two weeks. There was more gray in his hair, especially in the sideburns. He was still well tanned, so that the worry lines in his forehead and the smile lines around his eyes seemed deeper. He looked handsomer than ever, but inside, behind his eyes, something was dead. I kept looking at him—while I talked about reading sports books, and sketching, and listening to Dodger games—and thinking that he was really somebody else disguised as my uncle.

"I'm sorry," I offered.

He ruffled my hair the way he liked to. "You have nothing to be sorry for. Everything's settled. I told you."

"I mean, I'm sorry your men got killed. I'm sorry you lost your friends."

"I have no friends."

"Not even me?"

"You're my nephew."

We crossed Bedford Avenue, near the entrance to Erasmus Hall High School—I'd be going there in another year—and Abe was silent again. I thought of him on night watch in a forest somewhere near France, peering out from under his G.I. helmet, looking through field glasses.

All his men were sleeping in their foxholes. Abe never spoke about his war experiences to me. He'd given me some souvenirs—a compass in a leather case, a few ribbons and medals, old machine gun shells—but he never spoke about what it was like to be in charge of a platoon, of four squads of a dozen men each. What had he felt when some of them were killed? Had he written to their mothers and wives afterwards?

I told him that I was reading in one of Beau Jack's magazines that hunting was actually good for certain animals like deer and foxes and bears and wolves—that by killing members of the species who weren't quick enough or healthy enough or smart enough to get away, the hunters made the entire species stronger. I asked him if he felt that way about his own men. Would his organization be stronger now that the weaker men were gone?

"Something like that," he said.

We were across the street from the art store, near the firehouse and the post office. I wanted him to talk to me. I knew what to say.

"What was your mother like?"

He stumbled, but caught himself quickly, brushing my arm with his hand, for balance.

"*What—?*"

"Nothing," I said. I'd saved the question for a long time.

"I heard you."

"What was your mother like, is all I asked. My mother says sometimes that you used to worship her for all she did raising you, but that when you got older, if the two of you were in a room together there were always sparks. Until she died, I mean." I shrugged. "I don't understand."

"Neither do I," Abe said, and he almost smiled. "Listen. I thought about it a lot when I was overseas, when the war was over and I was waiting to be shipped back home. They didn't kill only the weakest, Davey. They killed all they could find—the strongest, the smartest, the bravest. The weakest got away sometimes because they were weak, or because they were cowards, or because they were rich."

He shook his head sideways, talked more, and I realized how much I liked listening to him, how much I loved simply walking close to him so that I could feel the heat coming off his body. He asked me if I knew about the ovens and the gas chambers, and I said that everybody did. I'd seen a newsreel with my father, of American and British soldiers wearing gas masks while they loaded bodies onto trucks. Most of the bodies were covered with lye, decomposing. I saw bulldozers pushing mountains of Jews. I saw pictures of empty barracks and hills made of eyeglasses and false teeth and hair and crutches and children's shoes.

We were almost to the corner of Flatbush and Church avenues. Abe seemed more relaxed. Bundles of newspapers came flying toward us from a passing truck. The deaf newsdealers signaled to one another with their stubby fingers.

"You think I'm a brave man, don't you?"

"Yes."

"I'm not a coward. That's true." He nodded. "If I really had guts, though, do you know where I'd be now?"

"In California?"

"In Palestine. That's where I'd be if I had the guts. Like Mickey Marcus. I'd be fighting the Arabs and the British, so that Jews could be free, so we could have a place of our own—a home, Davey, a real *home!* —so nobody would ever again try what Hitler tried. Can you understand that?"

"Not really," I said. "I didn't know you cared so much that we were Jewish. I didn't think you were religious."

He sighed and looked around, as if suddenly aware that we were outside in the street, walking.

"Forget it. Just forget the whole thing, okay?"

He put his arm around my shoulder and told me that he wasn't religious and that he never saw the camps, but that he did see some of the people from the camps afterwards, when they were in hospitals. He said it made him wonder how and why it was that some people survived— why some were chosen to live and others to die. It made him ask himself lots of questions. The will to survive, he decided, wasn't everything. The sources of survival weren't only in us, in individuals. He said he would tell me a quick story, the kind he and his Army buddies heard again and again. A woman he was friends with told him that when the Nazis took her two sons away she begged for their lives, and when the boys were on the truck and she was running after it, an officer stopped the truck and brought her two boys to the tailgate and lifted them up by their necks, one to either side, like chickens, and said to the woman that he would show her he was human. She could choose one. I asked which one she chose, and Abe grabbed my arm angrily, accused me of not having listened to him, and walked off.

"I'm sorry," I called, and I ran after him.

"Don't you understand *anything* I was saying to you? Don't you even listen to me?"

"I always listen to you," I said.

Abe blinked. "Sure you do. Let's go, okay? We're late." He took my hand and we walked in front of a mounted policeman who was coming in our direction. Abe didn't seem to notice him. I watched the policeman's gun and holster bob up and down on the side of the saddle. The policeman waved at my uncle in a friendly way. "Sometimes I forget that you're still a kid, that you're only a boy."

"Me too," I said.

He smiled now, in the way I loved. I had said the right thing. He warned me not to dwell too much on the story he had just told me. Evil, he stated, was not personal. What was it then? We were on Flatbush Avenue. He led me into the Bickford's building, up three flights of stairs to his offices. We fooled ourselves in very sentimental ways, he said, whenever we decided to personalize evil. There were evil people in the world, it was true, just as there were good and brave people. But when I'd heard enough stories, he added, I would come to see that the mother's choice had been one of the easy choices. A choice that made little difference. Like the choices Abe himself had made. His hand on the doorknob, he turned and looked at me again. His eyes were brown holes. They looked exactly like his father's eyes.

I heard voices coming from the other side of the door.

"Come," he said.

He closed the door to the back room, a room I'd never been in. At the far end Avie Gornik sat on a wooden chair by himself, bent over, head in his hands. He looked up at me, groaned. The room was large and bare, about fifteen by twenty feet, but with no phones, no rugs, no windows, nothing on the walls. There was a long metal table in the center, like the kind doctors gave examinations on. Four of Abe's men were there: Little Benny, Turkish Sammy, Louie Newman, Big Jap Willer.

Little Benny put his hand on my uncle's arm, whispered.

"There are no secrets while my nephew is here," Abe said, pulling away. "He'll always know anything I know."

"Sure, Abe. Whatever you say. Only I just wanted you to know that everything's set, the way you ordered it."

I didn't trust any of the men who worked for my uncle. They talked and walked as if they were actors trying to get parts in movies, as if they were imitating the guys who played henchmen for George Raft or Edward G. Robinson. I'd heard them talk about movies sometimes, *The Blue Dahlia* or *Double Indemnity* or *Key Largo* or *The Big Sleep*, and it always seemed strange to me that they talked about the movies as if the actors' lives on the screen were more real than their own.

Louie Newman said something to Abe about Spanish Louie, but Abe didn't react. Louie was a fat man, about my father's height, shaped like an eggplant—like the Penguin in *Batman* comics. We'd make fun of him behind his back for the way he walked around our neighborhood, waddling from side to side, carrying a little black doctor's satchel in which, according to Tony, he kept the usual: a rope, a knife, a gun, an ice pick, and false identity papers. The store owners were afraid of him and gave him whatever he wanted.

Big Jap Willer smiled at me, but I didn't smile back. He had a jaundiced complexion, greasy flat black hair, slanty eyes. During the day, whenever he saw me with my friends he'd make me tell them that he was a Jew, not a Jap—that there were lots of Jews from Russia who looked like him. Sometimes he'd show up at our house with a package of steaks or lamb chops wrapped in butcher paper, and if my father was gone he'd hang around talking to my mother and telling dirty jokes. Afterwards my mother would say that the easiest thing to do with Big Jap was to humor him because he sometimes became mean toward women who didn't laugh when he expected them to.

"Everything's been taken care of," Benny said. "All we been waiting for is you and the kid here."

Gornik moaned. Turkish Sammy went to the door. Benny went around telling everybody that Turkish Sammy had served time in jail because, when he worked in a traveling circus, he broke a man's back with his bare hands by holding the man across the small of his own back and stretching him until the man's spine cracked.

"Avie."

When Abe said his name, Avie looked up at once.

"Please, Abe," Avie said. "For old time's sake, huh? Don't do it. What for? We been through a lot together."

"We want to help you," Abe said. His voice was smooth and silky. It soothed me the way petting Kate soothed me. "I warned you years ago, Avie. You've been doing things that can get us all into the kinds of trouble we don't need."

"Jesus, Abe," Avie said, reaching towards Abe. The thumb and index finger of his right hand were stained yellow from nicotine, the way my father's were. "Have a heart, huh? I never hurt none of them. I didn't know—"

"You know my nephew."

"Sure. He's a good kid. He's a good little ball player. All the other kids look up to him. Davey Voloshin."

"Now listen carefully," Abe said to me. "We had a meeting here before—a kind of trial—and we found out that Avie's been acting in a way that can bring harm to everyone. He put his small needs above the good of the organization, you see. Mr. Fasalino never wants to speak to Avie again. So that we have to clean up our own house. Do you understand?"

"No."

Benny reached under his jacket, to hitch up his pants. I saw the leather harness, the black butt of his .38.

"You want me to draw him a picture?" Benny asked, and he laughed.

"Nah," Big Jap said. "You don't gotta draw pictures for this kid. You ever seen the pictures he can draw? Even when he was a little pisher he used to draw these terrific war pictures. His mother always showed me."

"Sometimes we have to perform acts that may seem cruel, Davey, but I hope you'll come to see that they're not. It's why I brought you here." He got into a deep-knee bend position so that his eyes were level with mine, and he spoke to me as if we were alone, as if we were the last two people left on earth. "All right. This is what I was thinking before, the conclusion I came to: that I'm your uncle and that there is no way, from now on, that you are ever going to be free of that fact. It's nobody's fault, but it's so. Do you see? Therefore, we have to give up false hope and begin thinking of the future and of the life you're actually going to have. We have to begin to show you things, the way they are, do you understand?"

"No."

"Because he don't want to," Benny said.

"Sure," Louie said. "I mean, it won't be too long now and maybe he'll be working for his uncle and we'll have to take orders from him, right?"

"You might even have to take Abe's place someday," Benny said, and then as if he'd said the wrong thing, he added: "If he's gotta be gone to Havana or Vegas or somewhere to look after other things. I mean, a guy with your uncle's brain ain't gonna rot the rest of his lifetime in Flatbush, is he?"

I turned to Abe and tried to ask him with my eyes if what they were saying was true. He showed nothing.

"All right, Benny."

Benny talked to me about the things Avie did, taking boys into alleys and cellars, and even into his own apartment when his mother was asleep. Benny laughed. He said Avie was what they called a switch-hitter, that he did things with women too. But he had gone over the borderline this time, had fallen for some dumb young guinea, had let himself be set up, had given away information about trucks. At their meeting they had decided that Avie's fate would rest in my hands.

"Yeah," Louie said, laughing. "I mean that's fair, right, since Avie had the kid's future in his hands, you know what I mean?"

"Jesus, Abe," Avie began. "Don't put the kid on the spot like this. I give you my word, I'll do *anything*. I mean, didn't I take a chance, setting up the council with you and Fasalino, after what happened? Didn't we get ours back? Didn't I show you something?"

Avie sounded like my father when my father was in the middle of begging my mother to forgive him.

"Please, kid. Give me a break, huh? Don't you know what they're gonna do to me? Don't you got any idea?"

I said nothing. Had men really been killed, I wondered, because of a

few trucks full of cigarettes and slot machines and juke boxes? I wanted
to be able to ask Abe questions, but I was embarrassed in front of his
men, and I was afraid he wouldn't answer me truthfully or fully, that he
would just say what he'd said before: that it wasn't the money or the
territory that made men act the way they did. It wasn't power either, but
the *idea* of power—of controlling others, of never having enough—and
that I wouldn't understand that idea until I was older, had lived more.
Benny kept on talking, telling me to tell them exactly what Avie had
done to me that night in the cellar. I told them. I felt as if I were in a
trance. I left nothing out. Avie whimpered, protested that I was only
repeating words that Benny had put into my mouth.

"Nobody puts words into my mouth," I said. "I'm telling the truth,
the way it really happened."

"Anything else?" Abe asked.

"He said he did the same thing to you when you were a boy."

Benny whipped his pistol from his holster and went for Avie, but Abe
stopped him. Avie covered his face with his hands.

"Oh Jesus, Abe," Avie said. "Jesus H. Christ. Oh Jesus . . ."

"I figured out that he was only trying to scare me. I figured he was
telling me that so that I would never tell you."

"Sure," Benny said. "The kid's got a real brain, just like you, Abe, see?
He got ice water in his veins, too."

"I ain't your enemy," Avie said. He spoke quickly, frantically. "It's
Fasalino and those guys are your enemies, Abe. It's them we need to
take care of. They're only suckering you, with the deal on territory.
They're waiting until they feel stronger and then they'll try to carve you
up good. They're scared of you, the way you reacted so fast. Now's the
time to move in, don't you see? Now's the time, Abe—"

"All right then," Abe said to Benny, and he nodded once. "Yes."

Benny left the room and returned a few seconds later, pushing a
young man in front of him. The young man was blindfolded. He was
tall and thin, with curly strawberry-blond hair. He wore a doctor's white
coat, open in the front.

"This is Dr. Feinberg," Benny said, removing the blindfold. "We
talked him into volunteering to help us out for our little job."

"I'm not a doctor. I told you before. I'm only a medical student. I still
have a year to go before—"

"Yeah, yeah. We know all about it. He'll do just fine." Benny patted
Feinberg on the back. "You don't worry about anything, doc—you just
do your job and leave the worrying to us."

"Jesus H. Christ," Avie said. "Have a heart, Abe. I mean, have a
heart, for Christ's sake." Avie stood up, but Turkish Sammy stopped
him from moving toward my uncle.

"Sometimes, Davey," Abe was saying to me, "we have to cut out an unhealthy part of the body—an infected organ, a cancer—in order to save the entire body. Do you understand?"

"No."

"Sometimes when I was overseas we'd have to cut off a soldier's leg or arm or finger in order to save—" He stopped, blinked, then wiped his eyes with the back of his wrist, as if he were sweating. He wasn't. "Avie should not have touched you. Everybody needs to know what happens to the one individual who endangers us all." He spoke to Benny. "Did you get everything the young man needs? I don't want any complications."

Benny flashed Abe a grin that made me feel ill. He motioned to Louie and Louie reached under the metal table and brought out a carton, took a cloth package from the carton—something wrapped in a sheet—and put it on the table. Benny told Feinberg to check things out, to make sure everything was there.

"Listen," Feinberg said to Abe. "You seem different from the others and I feel I can reason with you. You seem like a very intelligent man. I don't really understand what's going on and I don't think I want to, but—"

"That's right, doc—" Benny said.

"But I'm not allowed to do this kind of thing. You know that. I don't know your name yet and I don't want to, but should anything go wrong—"

"Hey kid, your hands are trembling, you know that?" Benny said. He took Feinberg's two hands in his own, as if he were thinking of bending the fingers back and cracking them, one at a time. "You want a shot of whiskey or something before you get started?"

"Yeah," Louie said. "You guys remember that movie with Brian Donlevy where he has to operate on a guy in a submarine, only he's an old drunk and the Nazis are firing torpedoes at them and they ain't got much air left?"

"It was William Bendix," Big Jap said. "You ask the kid here. It was William Bendix in the movie."

"All right," Abe said. "Begin. The longer we wait, the harder it will seem, for everybody."

Turkish Sammy stood next to Feinberg. Feinberg swallowed hard. Soft golden hairs curled out on his chin next to two birthmarks. Turkish Sammy lifted Avie from his chair. Avie called for his mother. He screamed for her to come and help him, and then he began crying out for God to save him. Nobody told him to be quiet. Big Jap helped Turkish Sammy drag Avie across the floor. I thought of the story Beau Jack told me about a friend of his whose face was chewed up by a

German attack dog so that you couldn't tell who he was afterwards. I saw a dark stain on the floor, trailing behind Avie.

Louie Newman held his nose.

"Jesus, Avie," he said. "Don't be a fucking baby, huh? You seen a lot worse."

"Ain't it true, Abe," Big Jap said, "that when they think they're gonna die in the war they always call for God and their mommies?"

Avie lay on the table, his body heaving, his forearm across his eyes. For an instant I saw my mother on her couch, the washcloth over her eyes.

"There should be as little pain as possible," Abe said. "I hope you understand that I'm not interested in hurting him." He touched my arm. "Your imagination can often make things more horrible than they actually are. This is a simple procedure, isn't it, Mr. Feinberg?"

"At the hospital, yes," Feinberg said. "I suppose it would be relatively routine there, but here—?" He almost smiled, winced instead. " 'There are no minor surgical procedures,' my professor says, 'only minor surgeons.' "

Benny told Feinberg to stop talking and get started. He reminded him of their conversation, of what would happen to Feinberg if he refused to help. He asked him if there were many great surgeons who could work with broken hands.

"Infection is the major cause for concern. I'll need to wash up, to clean him where he lost control of his functions."

"You know what I really think?" Benny said. "I think you're too good to guys like these, Abe. And then they crap all over you. You ask me, you should of let us do it the old way, just tie a string tight around his balls and slice."

"Nah," Louie said. "You don't even gotta slice. You just leave the string there, way up high and tight, so that the balls turn black and hard in a day or so. Then you let the poor sucker drag his ass into a hospital somewhere and they do the rest of the job for you, nice and safe. That's the way I seen it done in the old days. Remember what we did to Crapanzano? Hey, didn't you do it to him yourself, Avie—?"

Avie wept. I wondered if he had ever done things with Tony. Tony said that guys in the war who jacked off all the time were the first to get killed because they were always dozing off. He said that the guys who saved it lived the longest.

"Yeah," Benny said. "Abe likes to run things modern, though. Only the best for Abe's boys, right?"

Feinberg washed up with soap and water and alcohol. He put on thin rubber gloves and unrolled the emergency kit. It was the kind used for minor procedures, like draining abscesses, Feinberg said. There were scalpels and hemostats and Kelly clamps. There were strange-shaped silver scissors with pointy ends that looked like the snouts on baby alligators.

As soon as Feinberg started on Avie, his nervousness disappeared. His hands were steady. He pulled down Avie's pants, pushed up his shirt and undershirt. Avie's penis was almost gone, drawn back inside his scrotum like a turtle's head. Feinberg looked at Benny, who patted his gun. Feinberg looked at my uncle. Abe nodded, and then Feinberg did not look at any of us again until he was done. I'd never seen such concentration. I'd never seen anybody be so patient and steady and careful. Feinberg took a hypodermic syringe that had a long needle, like the kind I imagined they used for horses, and he gave Avie a few injections of novocaine, along his thighs. Avie screamed. Turkish Sammy and Big Jap held his arms down. Louie stayed at the end of the table, palms on Avie's head. Feinberg explained each step as he went along, as if he were talking to himself, as if he were repeating things that had been taught to him. While the novocaine took effect, he washed Avie. Feinberg said that there was one large artery running to each testicle, and that there might be a great deal of blood after the incision. Sometimes incisions were made in the groin, above the genitals, and the testes were drawn up—that was the safest and neatest way, but to do that one needed hospital facilities. The procedure he was following was one he had seen used for cancer of the testes. Normally they would give the patient a spinal, especially if they went in from the top, but Feinberg believed that the novocaine would be sufficient.

He draped cloth around Avie's groin—over his stomach and legs, above the knees, in a lopsided open rectangle, so that all you could see underneath was hairy pink skin. I stepped closer. Benny joked about putting a mirror on the ceiling so Avie could watch also, and Abe told him to be quiet, that there was no need. I imagined that Abe had seen scenes like this, only worse, in field hospitals. I imagined the night sky lit up outside the tent, rockets and bombs and howitzers and flares. Was there somebody special in his unit—a young farm boy from Minnesota —whom Abe had loved? Had he once watched a boy like that die on the operating table? I thought of Spanish Louie's blackjack, hanging out of his back pocket, how he would always call it his *yarmulke*. If Spanish Louie were alive, I knew, Abe would be in jail, in danger of dying. Dead. I remembered Avie and Spanish Louie and Little Benny warning me and Tony not to tell my uncle what we saw them do on the night the war ended. Spanish Louie was dead. Avie was on the table. Only Little Benny was left unharmed, the way he'd been.

Feinberg checked Avie's pulse. He acted as if there was nobody else in the room with him. He picked up a scalpel and the smooth steel, reflecting the light from the fixture above our heads, flashed in my eyes, gleaming like the frozen surface of a clear pond. Feinberg bent over, hesitated. Then, with a slight and definite downward motion of his wrist, he made a slit in the scrotum. He reached inside and, cupping his fingers around Avie's testicle, as if he were scooping out seeds from the inside of a cantaloupe, he separated the testicle from the lining, pulled it down. Blood flowed onto the towels, brown and thick, splattering the white sheet. Feinberg sopped up the blood, dropped the towels and gauze to the floor. He reached inside again. He pulled down the vessels leading to the testicle, sliced them neatly, applied pressure to the severed tubes, tied them off with thin white strings that looked like dental floss. I'd never seen anybody work so deftly, so delicately.

He lifted the testicle, set it on top of the white cloth. It looked very small, like the kind of egg my mother sometimes found inside her chickens—*ayelas*, she called them—except that it was threaded pink with veins. Did doctors remove patients' eyes in the same way? How far forward could you pull an eye from its socket without detaching it while you operated behind it, inside the skull?

Feinberg worked on the left testicle. For a split-second I wondered if I was really human, to be able to watch what was happening and not to find it horrible. Why didn't it make me feel sick? Why did it all fascinate me so?

I remembered my friends telling each other that the way the Japanese tortured American flyers who were shot down over the Philippines or Tokyo or Saipan was to tie them to stakes and to dance beautiful naked women in front of them. When the soldiers got erections, the Japanese commander would come along with his curved sword and chop their dicks off. I'd always gotten sweaty and cold along my thighs when the guys talked about that. Why had that frightened me, when what I was watching now didn't—when it seemed magical, almost beautiful? I felt as if I could have watched Feinberg's hands forever. With the fingers of one hand, he was tying small knots.

Abe touched the back of my neck. His fingertips were warm. He moved away from me, stroked Avie's forehead. He told him that he'd be able to lead a more normal life, that now he would live to be an old man. Avie wept like a baby, but quietly, and he didn't seem to feel pain, to know when things were happening to him. Benny said he would spread the story, for a warning to others. Avie told Abe that he was sorry for the trouble he'd caused, for making Abe do this to him. He held Abe's hand against his wet cheek.

Feinberg worked on, carefully wiping things with the corner of a towel, blotting things with gauze. Benny said that in the old days they sometimes got veterinarians to do the job. Feinberg sprinkled sulfa powder into Avie's scrotum. He said that he wasn't going to sew Avie up permanently because he wanted to be sure no infection set in. He said that Avie should walk into an emergency ward the next day—but not to Kings County—and that they would take care of the rest. He gave Avie another injection and told Abe that Avie would be in some pain when the novocaine wore off, that Abe should get a strong painkiller for him —Demerol, if he could. Feinberg looked at my uncle for the first time since he'd begun the operation and when he spoke there was something proud and defiant in his voice. He declared that he himself could not write out a prescription because he was not yet an M.D.

I watched Feinberg remove his gloves, one finger at a time. I saw how clean his nails were, how soft his palms. I saw sweat roll down his forehead and cheeks. He seemed exhausted suddenly. I had forgotten how young he was. He stepped away from the table. Abe covered Avie with a sheet, a thin gray blanket. Avie's eyes were closed. Was he asleep? If you could watch long enough and hard enough, without falling asleep or looking away, I wondered if you would be able to see cells begin to grow back toward one another, if you would be able to see the body heal itself, the new skin grow.

"Here you go, kid," Benny said, and he peeled a few bills from his money roll, handed them to Feinberg.

Feinberg slapped Benny's hand, knocking the bills to the floor.

"I don't want your dirty money."

"Now you be careful there, kid," Benny said. "You did a good job for us, but if you get fresh you'll maybe have to look for another profession, like I warned you before. You need real good hands for your work."

Feinberg turned to my uncle. "All right," he said, breathing hard. "You got what you wanted from me, but I don't have to take your dirty money, do you hear?"

"I have ears," Abe said.

"Pick it up, kid," Benny said. "You be a good boy and bend down and pick up your money. We ain't welchers."

"Never," Feinberg said.

"Money is never dirty, Mr. Feinberg," Abe stated. "If you were ever poor, you would know that. Money is never dirty. Money gives people the freedom to live the way they want. The world exists to protect the people who earn money and have money. That's reality. You've earned your fee and I want you to have it."

"You think you're such a big shot, don't you?" Feinberg said. "All that double-talk about helping the man, while you let the child here watch —all that nonsense about being good to him when you're nothing but

. . . but a monster with a brain. Did you know that? I don't care how intelligent or rich or powerful you are, or how many lackeys you have around you to bow down to you and do your dirty work."

"Abe?" Benny asked.

"Let him talk," Abe said.

The muscles in Feinberg's long neck were stretched tight. He looked like a bird in its nest, opening its beak, straining upwards to get food from its mother.

"You're Jewish too, aren't you?"

"Yes."

"Then you bring shame on us all."

"Do I?"

"Oh, you cover it up with a veneer of respectability. I know more than you think. More than I said before, when my life was threatened. I've heard all about you, Mr. Litvinov. In this neighborhood your reputation precedes you, as they say, and it visits shame upon us all."

"Hey Abe," Louie said. "Do we really gotta listen to this crap? Why don't we see if we can get this bird a job working for the BMT, yeah?"

"The men who shipped us into the camps in boxcars and shoved us into the ovens—my own aunts and uncles, do you hear me?—and tore out our fillings and shoveled our ashes out the other end—many of them were kind to their families too. Did you know that, Mr. Litvinov? They were good to their own children, to their wives and parents and nieces and nephews. They—"

"I think you've said enough."

Abe touched his ring with one finger. Silence. It was almost, I thought, as if Feinberg had been there in the street with us, listening. Feinberg looked around the room, his eyes wild, as if he suddenly realized where he was, as if he suddenly realized that my uncle's men could cripple him as easily as he had sliced Avie's scrotum.

"You didn't have to do it," Abe said, and I was surprised that what Feinberg accused him of did not seem to bother him. When Abe spoke now, he spoke calmly and precisely, as if to a child: "You had a choice, you see, Mr. Feinberg. You didn't have to do it. Life always presents us with choices, big ones and little ones, and there are always consequences and many of them are unpleasant. But you did have a choice, you see, and you chose. Take the money, please."

Abe nodded to Turkish Sammy. Turkish Sammy picked up the money, stuck it into the hip pocket of Feinberg's white coat. Abe glanced at Benny. Benny took Feinberg by the elbow, guided him to the door.

5

My father was waiting for me in the lobby, hiding behind the staircase. I was dead tired, drenched from walking home in the rain, and when he came toward me, smiling—he'd been squatting in the small alcove where the mailman left his shoulder bags each morning—I felt nothing, not even irritation.

"Hey—you were terrific tonight, Davey. Really terrific. Twenty-three points and you hardly played most of the last quarter."

"Thanks."

I started up the stairs. My arms and legs felt waterlogged. All I wanted to do was sleep.

"Stevey Komisarik said you were shooting the eyes out of the basket." He laughed. "I thought it was a terrific way of putting it to a man like me, to shoot the eyes out of the basket."

"Sure, Dad."

"Davey?"

I stopped.

"I waited for you. I wanted to talk with you."

"Sure."

I shivered. I was sixteen years old, in the middle of my junior year at Erasmus, the leading scorer and rebounder on the team. During practices and games the guys would sometimes talk to me as if I were someone ordinary, just another player. I'd even gone to Garfield's with them after the first home game. We sat in the back room, and as each player walked in, some with their girlfriends, everybody cheered. They'd cheered for me too, but when I said I had to get home early, I sensed that they were relieved. The instant I was gone I heard them laugh in a way they didn't while I was with them. Some of Abe's men were at a table near the back room and they called out to me, raised their coffee cups, said they'd heard what a star I was.

My father held on to my sleeve. He talked to me about how, if I kept up my scoring average and my good grades, I was certain to get a scholarship to any college I wanted, Harvard or Princeton or Yale or Columbia. I should make sure not to get injured and I should stay out of trouble. The Ivy League liked clean-cut types. He seemed to be losing his balance, to be falling sideways on the wet staircase.

"I'm tired," I said. "Thanks for coming to the game, okay? I meant to say that before."

He laughed. "Did you hear that or did you hear that? I got a boy with a terrific gift like he got and he thanks *me* for coming to his games!" He clucked inside his mouth. "You're really a terrific kid, Davey, did you know that? I mean, I never known anybody like you. Only I want you to promise me one thing, yeah?"

"Look, Dad. I said I'm tired. What did you want to talk to me about?"

"What did I want to talk to you about." He let go of my arm. "Sure. It's why I was waiting for you, right?"

"Tell me."

"Not too loud," he whispered. "But listen. All right. This is why I waited for you. I mean, you're a smart boy, Davey, so maybe you can tell me what you think I can do to make Momma happy. I want to make her happy, only I don't know how, see?" I moved away from him, up the staircase. In the dim light of the stairwell, his face seemed very pasty, a flat dull-orange. When he touched me I wanted to pull back, to strike him across the cheek so that he'd tumble down the stairs. I thought of the guys in the back room at Garfield's. I thought of their girlfriends holding their hands and stroking their fingers, one at a time. I thought of the girls' sweaters, the soft pastel colors: powder-blue and powder-pink, beige and peach and lavender and yellow. "I figured a smart boy like you, maybe you could give your old man a good suggestion so that every time I come home I don't gotta feel like poison."

I looked away and tried to remember the game, to fix my mind upon some moment—upon the faces of my teammates, the sound of the crowd, the flight of the ball as it settled into the net and swished through. Had I really been running back and forth and soaring through the air only an hour before, playing my heart out? I tried to see Tony, feeding me a pass under the basket, slapping my ass as we ran back upcourt. I tried to think of something—*anything*—that would get my father's voice out of my head, and what I began to see was a photo of Jackie, the way he looked two months before, smiling down at Rachel from the back page of the *New York Post*. Rachel was in the hospital with their new child, Sharon. In another month Jackie would head South for spring training, to begin his fifth season with the Dodgers, and if Rachel and their two children went with him they would stay in the team's camp with the wives and families of the other players. They wouldn't board with a black family the way they had during Jackie's first season. There were dozens of black players in the league now, and as I stared at Jackie's face he looked so happy that I wondered if, in that moment, he had any room inside him for memories of the hard times that had come before. Could one moment of pure happiness wash away years of pain and bitterness? Jackie—who'd led the Dodgers to two World Series; who was voted Rookie of the Year; who was an All-Star second baseman, the league's Most Valuable Player—could fight back now. When pitchers or infielders got in his way on the base paths, he aimed his spikes for their shins, he rolled over them.

"With you gone so much now at school, and then with Abe the rest of the time—it's only that your Momma don't feel *needed* the way she used to, do you see what I mean?" He tried to laugh. I thought of Tony's girlfriend Regina, waiting for him after games in the darkness under the Bedford Avenue arch. I remembered the starched white blouses the Catholic girls would wear on the days they got out of school early for Religious Instruction, and how I'd always felt less shy with them, less frightened—how I'd felt they wouldn't want to own me the way Jewish girls did. The lips of Catholic girls felt less sticky to me when we necked —firmer, cooler.

"Sure, sure. All that running up and down the court, and the way those big *shvartzes* were banging you around under the basket. . . ." He tapped on the side of his head with his knuckles. "I should have my head examined, to try having a conversation like this tonight. Only"— he laughed—"only I guess I was just afraid to go home by myself." He shrugged. "I didn't want Momma to yell at me no more."

We walked upstairs together. All the lights were out in the apartment. I thought of Stevey Komisarik, next to my father, clapping like mad when the coach took me out of the game. Once, when I was thirteen and Abe asked why I didn't play more with the boys from the neighborhood, my mother said that it was Stevey's mother who kept him from playing with me. Two days later all of Mr. Komisarik's dental equipment was destroyed. Everybody in the building went to the office on Bedford Avenue—Mr. Komisarik was renting it while they saved up enough money to buy their own house, where he could have his office and laboratory in the front part and they could live in the rest—to stare at the damage: the piles of twisted wiring and drills and springs, the ripped-

out fixtures, the broken glass and porcelain, the smashed sets of false
teeth. The next day Stevey knocked on my door, his mother behind
him, and asked if I wanted to come to his apartment to play with him.

In my bedroom, my mother's old tan coffee mug was on my desk. My
mother spent a lot of her time sitting in my room while I was away. She
sat there and she worried, she said. Or she sat there and tried to remember what a sweet child I'd once been. She said she liked sitting in my
room because it was neat and uncluttered. She said she felt peaceful
when she was in my room because it wasn't like her room, or like the
room she and Abe shared when they were children.

Senator Kefauver's hearings were on television every day now, inves-
tigating organized crime—they'd started four weeks before at the beginning of February, and they were making all the big shots like Frank
Costello and Meyer Lansky and Joey Adonis and Mickey Cohen testify
—but we had no television set, and my mother never asked me if I talked
with Abe about things like that. The most she would do would be to look
out a window and go through her old routines about how someday she
would get a call from the hospital and they would ask her if she was
David Voloshin's mother. They would tell her that my arm was crushed
or my head was split or my neck was snapped in two. That was all the
good Abe or sports would ever do for me.

From behind the wall, I heard my father and mother whispering.
Maybe, I thought, it had relaxed him to talk with me about her. Maybe,
when I was out of school in another year and a half, they could actually
move to California. I'd visit them during college vacations and I'd take
early morning walks by myself along deserted beaches. I'd be there before the sun rose, and the beaches would be quiet and clean, and one
morning I'd see a girl coming toward me. She would have long honey-
colored hair and large pearl-gray eyes and she would be carrying her
sandals in one hand. I'd smile at her and she'd smile back shyly, but her
eyes wouldn't waver. We'd stop and stare into one another's eyes, and
then, without saying anything, I'd put out my hand and she would take
it and we would walk together. When she kissed me she would hold my
face between her hands so gently and sweetly that I'd want the kiss to
never end. We wouldn't tell one another our names, or where we were
from, and we'd never meet anywhere except on the beach, and each
time we parted we would say nothing about meeting again. And when
vacation was over and I was back at my college, working out with the
team or walking across campus, I'd think of her, searching for me,
hoping I would return. She would be there every day, waiting, watching
the ocean, and it would give me a wonderfully painful kind of pleasure
to see tears slide down her cheeks, to know how much she missed me.

I took off my sweat shirt and my T-shirt, looked at myself in the mirror. I was six-foot-three now—two inches taller than Abe—and I had what our coach called a perfect swimmer's body: long waist, high broad chest, wide shoulders, strong neck, long muscular arms. It always surprised me, in a mirror, to see the face that was so familiar to me sitting on top of a body I hardly recognized. I put my hands on my chest, palms flat, fingertips almost touching, and I rubbed slowly. During the school year, from the time football practice started in the fall until the baseball season was over in the spring, I worked out in my bedroom, using weights, skipping rope, doing sit-ups and push-ups. Sometimes, early in the morning, when Beau Jack was putting out the garbage pails and sweeping the walks and mopping the corridors, to build up my wind I'd go up and down the four flights of our building as fast as I could, five or six times in a row, until my lungs felt as if they would burst. Afterwards I'd sit out in front of the building with Beau Jack and drink water from the nozzle of his hose.

I loved playing ball. I loved the feeling of slipping and crashing through other bodies and then of being free—suspended in air, the ball in my hands, nobody touching me, everybody straining to reach me. And I loved to win. When I didn't win I'd be furious, enraged—I'd go over every second of the game, every move I'd made, vowing to do better next time, vowing to make up for my teammates' deficiencies. I played end on the football team, first base on the baseball team, forward in basketball. I was good in all sports, but I was best at basketball. Like Tony, I was never the favorite of the coaches—they were especially wary now because of the fixes, because gangsters like Abe and Fasalino were allegedly behind the bribing of college players—but they would use me as an example in practice, to show the others how, even with my immense natural abilities I never gave up, I never stopped trying.

My mother's voice, shouting at my father to stop bothering her, sounded as if it had sand in it. Couldn't my father tell she was getting another migraine? Didn't he have *any* sense? I unzipped my gym bag, put my sneakers on the windowsill, unlaced them to the bottom so they would air out. I took my sweat socks and T-shirt and underpants, picked up my mother's coffee mug. The mug was on top of the old drawing I'd done of the apartment building across the way—I'd take the drawing out now and then to look at it, to make myself wonder how long it would be before I'd either give up the dream of someday being an artist or do something in a sustained way that might make the dream possible—and the mug had stained the drawing, had left a dark circle in the lower right-hand corner.

I sucked an enormous amount of air into my lungs, then left my room. My father rushed by me, a glass of water in one hand and a bottle of aspirins in the other. The pink ice bag, with its round silver cap, hung from his mouth. Through clenched teeth he explained that he didn't have three hands.

"Davey, is that you? Are you home? Are you all right?"

My mother came into the kitchen. She rested her head on my back for a few seconds. I put the coffee mug into the kitchen sink, but I didn't turn around. If I turned and looked at her she might ask if I thought she looked older. She might whisper to me about her secret bank account—she kept the passbook in Mr. Lipsky's freezer—and how she thought that in five years, by saving from what she got every Friday from my father, she would have enough money for her to take me with her to California.

"I had a little headache, so I went to sleep," she said. "You must be hungry. You never eat before your games, so let Momma make you something, all right? Would you like a nice grilled cheese sandwich?"

"I wish you wouldn't go into my room while I'm gone."

"But I like to sit there, Davey. What else do I have, with both my men working for my brother? Listen. You don't think I go in there to spy on you, do you?"

"You ruined one of my drawings. You left your coffee mug standing on it and it left a ring."

"But you don't draw anymore," she said.

"It's a shame," my father said, coming into the kitchen. "A real waste."

"I mean, I could understand you being upset if you still showed that you cared about drawing." She sighed. "Your father's right about that—God gave you such a gift and you never use it anymore. I'm really sorry, darling, but this is what happened: the phone rang and it was Lillian asking me to come over and watch TV with her—the hearings, with Mr. Rothenberg getting ready to go on—and by the time I was off the phone I forgot all about my coffee. That woman turns my head sometimes! But you bring me the drawing, sweetheart, and I'll see if I can get rid of the ring, all right?"

"He could still draw if he wanted to," my father said. "A gift like that just don't disappear overnight. If he started again he could pick up where he left off."

I went into the bathroom. My jaw ached on the right side and I peered into the mirror to see if my gums were bleeding. In my head I saw my mother laughing with Mr. Lipsky, telling him that he was going to make her wet her pants from all his jokes. When I was a boy she would leave me alone in his shop sometimes while he took her into the freezer to show her special cuts of beef. In the summer, if he saw me on the street he would ask if I wanted to sit in his freezer to cool off. I should watch out that no sides of beef fell on me, he said. I should always sit with my hands on my lap. That way, he laughed, I wouldn't get cold-cocked.

My mother called and said my snack was ready. I put on a clean sweatshirt, walked into the kitchen, looked at the bowl and spoon.

"I asked for a grilled cheese sandwich."

"No darling," my mother corrected. "I asked *you* if you'd like a grilled cheese sandwich, only I needed to use up some nice cold borscht first. You don't mind, do you?"

I heard knocking, went to the front door, opened it. Tony and Regina stood there, grinning.

"Hey—where was the fire?" Tony asked.

"How'd you get into my building without ringing from downstairs?"

"I got my ways," Tony said. "But how come the big rush home?"

"Would you like to do something with us?" Regina asked. "That's what we came by to say. When we didn't find you in Garfield's, Tony thought you might like to go out and celebrate with us."

"Yeah. We were thinking of taking the train down to Coney Island— hit the boardwalk and Nathan's and some of the games. Fun by the ocean with Davey Voloshin, right?"

"I could call one of my friends if you want a date," Regina said.

"Hey," Tony whispered. "I think Roberta Pegorara got the hots for you. Only—"

"Oh Tony, just be quiet will you?" Regina looked past me. "Hello, Mrs. Voloshin," she said.

"Listen, Davey, if you really want a grilled cheese sandwich, I'll make you a grilled cheese sandwich. What I think is, you're overtired."

"Now you hold on a minute, Evie," my father said. "Here you are fighting a migraine and you get out of bed—" He stopped, cocked his head to the side. "What's *he* doing here?"

"I'm going out." I took my jacket from the foyer closet.

"It's the Cremona kid," my father said.

"You think I'm blind too?" My mother laughed, caressed my father's chin with the back of her hand. "Listen, Sol. Do you remember those straw-tipped Melachrinos I used to smoke before the war?"

"If Abe asks, you weren't here—is that clear?" my father said to Tony.

"Take it easy, Sol. It just happens all over again sometimes, see? Like with Momma and Abe, the way they used to argue. All over again, Sol, is the way the world works. Can you see the temper he still got, that he's saving up inside him? It's why he acts so cold to us."

"It was only an idea," Regina said, backing away. "We were just passing by—"

"Listen, Mrs. Voloshin," Tony said. "Between me and your son ain't

like it is between the others. You don't gotta believe me, but I want you
to know, from my heart, that it's true. It's just that Davey did so good
tonight me and Regina figured he was entitled to somebody giving him
a celebration. I mean, you know your son better than anyone, but don't
you think he needs to get out more and have a good time so he can get
rid of all the energy he keeps bottled up? Ain't he entitled too?"

"Ah Tony," my mother said, and to my surprise she actually reached
over and touched his forehead, brushed his hair to the side. "You really
understand my little Davey, don't you? Sure. You take him down to the
beach. You fix him up with one of your friends." Her head dipped to
one side. She seemed happy. "Remember when we were on the boardwalk in Sea Gate, Sol, the summer after our honeymoon and that handsome man with the little stringy dog stopped me and said I looked just
like Claudette Colbert?"

"Davey looks a lot like you," Regina said.

I told my parents not to wait up for me and I left.

Roberta was standing in the entranceway downstairs, outside the front
door, and when I saw her and Tony put a hand over his mouth and said
what a coincidence it was that she just happened to be there, we all
laughed. Then we walked along Church Avenue to the BMT, to get the
Brighton line, and headed for Coney Island, with Tony talking a lot
about the play-offs and about what a great team the two of us made and
teasing me and Roberta when we held hands. It stopped raining by the
time we got to the end of the subway line. We walked around, playing
games and riding the Go-Karts and eating hot dogs and french fries, and
walking on the boardwalk.

We got back to our section of Brooklyn past midnight, took the girls
home, and then Tony put his arm around me and teased me about the
way Roberta and I had been necking on the bench next to him and
Regina. When we got to my block he began talking more seriously,
though, about how much he liked Regina and how he was scared because her parents didn't like the idea of her going with him on account
of his uncle and his father and his brothers.

He talked more quickly then—almost pleading with me—about how
much he wanted to have a family of his own someday, and about how
he was scared because of the family he came from, that he never would.
He said that he and Regina talked about running away together when
they got to the right age, but he was worried that she might not wait for
him that long, that the pressure from her parents was too great. We sat
down on the steps in front of my building—the air had warmed up and
the sidewalk smelled good, the way it always did after a rain—and I
found myself telling Tony about how I sometimes dreamt of having a
family of my own too. I didn't tell him about the girl on the beach, but

we talked about how many kids we each wanted to have and if we'd feel differently about having boys or girls and about where it would be better to bring your kids up—in the city or the country—and about what the best way to treat a wife would be: how we'd want to be in charge of a family the way our fathers weren't—wasn't this the reason our mothers were always so unhappy and trying to make us do things for them that our fathers didn't?—but about how we would also know how to be very gentle and thoughtful, so that our wives would never doubt our love.

By the time Tony got up to leave, it was past two in the morning. We laughed about how the time had flown by, and Tony confided in me that Regina wasn't like the other girls he'd gone with—she wasn't one of those Hail-Mary-and-let's-neck types—and that what had surprised him most of all was that when he was with her he didn't feel the need to talk a lot or to show off. That showed, he said as he walked off, what the love of a good woman could do, even for a guy like him.

My father died two weeks after that, on Tuesday afternoon, March 13, 1951, while taking my mother home from a doctor's appointment. Our team was working out in the gym, getting ready for our play-off game against Jefferson for the Brooklyn-Queens championship, the first game we would play in Madison Square Garden, when our coach, Mr. Goldstein, returned from taking a phone call in his office, stopped the practice, asked me to come with him.

The gym was quiet, and I felt myself tense because I knew the guys were figuring the same thing I was: that Mr. Goldstein was going to speak to me again about my uncle and the basketball fixes, that he was going to ask me again if I didn't want to just sit out the rest of the season, until the D.A.'s office and the F.B.I. finished their investigation.

But when, in his office, he put his hand on my shoulder and told me that he had bad news for me, that my father had had a heart attack, that they'd rushed him from the subway to Kings County Hospital but that he had died before they got him there, all the rage I was feeling washed out of me. I said nothing. I did what he told me to do: I went to the locker room, I got out of my uniform, I showered and I dressed and I packed up my books and gym bag.

Mr. Goldstein walked with me from the school, along Bedford Avenue. He talked about how he had felt when his father died, three years before. He talked on and on, telling me the story of his father's life. His father had been born in a small village in Russia, had come to America in 1888 and had worked fifteen hours a day in the dark, candling eggs, in order to save up enough money to bring his wife and his younger sisters and brothers here. Mr. Goldstein talked about how happy his father was on his eighty-third birthday, his children and grandchildren and brothers and sisters and nephews and nieces around him, and of how his father called it a miracle, that he had lived to see such a day. A second Bar Mitzvah. Seventy plus thirteen. In the synagogue Mr. Goldstein's father was called to the Torah to recite the same prayers he had recited in Russia seventy years before. Everything after seventy was a gift, Mr. Goldstein said. That was what his father believed.

I tried not to hear his words. I tried instead to fix my mind upon some picture of my father that might make me feel close to him, that might cause tears to come into my eyes. Mr. Goldstein asked me if I wanted him to walk home with me. I told him I would walk home alone.

"Look Davey," he said. "Jefferson's the class team in the city this year. Even with you in there, and you're as good a player as there is, it would take a miracle for us to win. What I'm trying to say is that you should go and be with your mother and take care of her at a time like this. Nobody will hold it against you that you couldn't be there for the play-off. These things happen."

He probably believed that he was being straight with me, I realized. I could play or not play. The choice was mine. That was what he'd been saying all along. There were others—league officials, alumni, school administrators—who'd been urging him to suspend me, to ask me to sit out the season, but since nobody could prove I'd done wrong, he refused to listen to them. Sure, I thought. And won't it be convenient for him that my father died two days before the game in the Garden?

I said nothing. I crossed Church Avenue, and as words began to fill up inside my head again—the words I wanted to hold there, ready to fire at Goldstein and all the others who hoped my father's death would do their dirty work for them—I realized that I was feeling less weary, less drained. Anger did that for me. It was as if I could look down inside my chest and see flames there, bright and steady, warming me, giving me energy, keeping me alive. I'd show the bastards. I'd show them all.

In the Holy Cross schoolyard, children were lined up in double rows, holding hands, and the nuns, their black capes and gowns swirling close to the ground, pulled them here and there. Know who your real enemies are, Abe had taught me, because your true friends will take care of themselves. But Abe's words were flat and unconvincing. I wanted to hear my father's voice, to see his face. Was he really gone? I squeezed my eyes shut, then opened them and gazed ahead until I could see him walking toward me.

I was eleven years old and I was leading him by the hand. He had a white patch over his good eye. They had called me to the principal's office at school and told me that I was to take the subway to the Lower East Side, where he was waiting for me at Gordon's. While he was tying packages, a piece of twine had whipped up and scratched his good eye. My mother telephoned to say she was too ill to travel. The principal gave me a nickel for the subway, asked if I felt brave enough to make the journey myself.

My father sat on a stool in a corner of the store, near racks of dark winter coats. When I spoke to him he beamed. He touched my face with his fingertips so that, in front of the other men, I felt embarrassed. I wrapped his eyeglasses in tissue, then in brown wrapping paper. On the subway platform I was terrified that he would fall over the edge in front of an oncoming train. In the train I was terrified that I would get through the doors and that they would snap closed behind me with him still in the subway car, grinning, feeling the door with blind fingers. On the street I kept urging him to stay close to me, to hold my hand, and I was afraid he would trip and fall, that I would fall with him and smash his glasses. Yet all the while I led him home he was quiet and obedient. With a son like mine, he said to the men at Gordon's, who needs eyes?

In our apartment my mother kissed me and laughed at my father, at the way he groped and stumbled from room to room. Was there a difference, she wanted to know? Was there a difference between when he was blind and when he could see?

He kept the patch on his eye for twelve days. He learned to dress himself and to wash himself and to make himself sandwiches. He learned to shave himself while I told him where he had missed spots, where he had nicked himself.

"Hey Davey—wait up."

It was Tony. He put his arm around my shoulder and I didn't shrug it off.

"I'm sorry."

"Thanks."

"Are you okay?"

"I'm okay."

"Goldstein was a real asshole, giving us all that Holy Joe shit about you and your father. You know what I think?"

"What?"

"I think he's glad. I think he's glad he got an excuse to bump you off the team."

"He can't."

"I know. You're gonna play, right?"

"Right."

He pounded me on the back and we walked together without saying anything to each other for a while.

"What are you going to do about college?" I asked.

"Nothing."

"I heard you got an offer."

"Oh yeah, they been sucking around my ass—these small Catholic places in Upstate New York, and one in Pennsylvania—but I don't know. I mean, I don't *know*."

"You should go to college."

"Tell you what—you help me see that my old man follows yours, so we'll be even, and then you and me, we make a deal, right? We tell these colleges we're a team—Mr. Outside and Mr. Inside, like Davis and Blanchard were for Army, remember?—and that they got to give us a package deal. The Kids from Brooklyn, right? The Gold-Dust Twins, like Reese and Reiser. Shit, they'll pack in the fans and please all the Wops and Hebes and get two aces for the price of one."

I smiled.

"There you go, hey! I was waiting for that, to make sure you were still alive inside that ice chest you got on your shoulders."

"I'm alive."

"I'm glad you're gonna play in the game. Life goes on. I mean, that's what I think, don't you? That life goes on, no matter what."

"I suppose."

"Does it hurt, though, that he's gone?"

"Some."

"Where does it hurt most, can you tell?"

"No."

"You really think I should go to college? That I got the brains?"

"Yes."

We were at the corner of Rogers and Church, where the trolley conductors and switchmen and supervisors were huddled together in front of Dominick's Barber Shop, going over their bets.

"I've been trying to imagine what it would be like to lose my old man," Tony said, "and I came to the conclusion that the difference is I don't really give a shit about mine, and I think you loved yours. Your old man ain't *mean* the way mine is. That makes a difference, even with drips. About college, though, I don't know. If I went off somewhere instead of following in my famous brothers' footsteps, he wouldn't think twice about getting out a small contract on me."

"You should go to college."

"Are you angry with me for following you, for talking so much?"

"Not really."

"Your uncle say anything to you about us going down to Coney?"

"Maybe."

"Yeah. They gave me a hard time too. But don't you think if things were different with our old men—our families—that I'd want to hang out with you more the way we did in the old days? Don't you know I'd do it if I thought it wouldn't get us into worse trouble than we're in already?"

"I suppose."

"I suppose. Yeah. Only it takes two to be enemies the same way it takes two for friends is the way I look at it. You've always been free to be my friend too."

"Why don't you just get lost for a while, okay?"

"Nah. I figure you need somebody like me to get mad at now. It'll do you good. Death *should* piss you off. Hey listen—you want Regina to fix you up with somebody else tonight? Hey Davey, the broad'll ask— how'd the day go? Get it? How'd the Da-go?"

"Get lost, Tony. I mean it. I'm not in the mood."

"Ah, if you're so pissed at me, how come I see you starting to smile?"

"Fuck off."

"Listen, though: what I wanted to say was that I figured the only hope for me, if I do what you say and go to college someday, is to take on some new name like all the college players do for the summer up in the Catskills, playing for hotels. Grow a mustache maybe. Put on some weight. Tell people I'm a Jew, that you and me are cousins or that I ain't got no mother and father, that I grew up in an orphanage, raised by rabbis. I mean, I got the nose, right? I got—"

"I think I want to be alone. Really."

"Sure thing," he said, and he was moving away even as he said it, past the London Hut, up Church Avenue toward Nostrand. He called back to me: "You stick to it, Davey. You stick to it and play if you want and don't let anybody tell you different, you hear? And you know what else?"

"What?"

"I'll see you in the Garden on Thursday. We'll cream those guys, you and me, Mr. Inside and Mr. Outside. Impress the hell out of all the scouts too."

He waved and moved off. I walked along Rogers Avenue, realized that pictures were coming more swiftly, easily. I saw my father going down the staircase by himself. I saw him walking along the street, tapping a cane to the left and right in a semicircle. He said hello to people, guessed their names from their voices. The patch was gone. The sun was bright. We were in the courtyard together having a catch. I was eleven years old. He held my hand and showed me how to throw a curve ball, how to snap my wrist down and out at the last instant.

My father was leaving the apartment, wearing his good black coat, his air-raid warden's hat. I crouched beside the kitchen window, my ear to the wall. I lifted the black window shade and watched until I saw him walking by himself along our street three stories below. If German Messerschmitts and Stukas got through our radar and attacked New York, would he get back before we were hit?

I saw us on my bed playing blackjack for pennies. I saw him sitting in my room, hour after hour, smoking and daydreaming while I worked on my drawings. I saw him waiting for me outside the gym, and how surprised I was, walking home with him, to realize that I often thought of myself as being older than him, of him being my younger brother.

I felt less angry. Would Tony be angry with me, though, because I hadn't wanted to talk with him, to let him be with me?

With a son like mine who needs eyes.

Abe's black Buick Roadmaster was parked in front of my building, Turkish Sammy in the driver's seat, working at his teeth with a silver toothpick. Waxey Shreibman and Lefty Kolatch huddled under the arcade. When they spotted me, they started pacing back and forth, flapping their arms against their sides to keep warm. Lefty held the door open for me.

"Sorry, kid," he said. "I liked your old man a lot."

"Yeah," Waxey said. "He was a terrific little guy."

I waited in the lobby. I didn't want to be angry when I entered the apartment. Could I know what my mother was feeling now? Could I ever know all that she and my father had been through, all that they had truly felt for one another? I walked up the stairs. I wondered if Beau Jack knew about my father. I opened the door and the warm air hit me as if it were a wall. The living room was already packed with people, but I tried not to see them. I stood just inside the door, closed it softly. My mother was moving across the living room, eyes red, cheeks flushed, and the instant I saw her she looked my way. I set down my gym bag and moved toward her.

"Oh David!"

She came to me and I felt almost happy suddenly, to feel warm air swell inside me, to feel tears beginning to well in my eyes.

"Oh mother!" I said. "I'm so sorry. I'm just so sorry. . . ."

I wanted to take her to me, to comfort her and to be comforted, to kiss her and to feel her kisses and tears all over my face, to shut out the rest of the world and to talk for hours about him, about how we would miss him, about all the things we remembered! She smiled at me, her eyes shining, so happy to see me that it made my heart lurch. And then, as she came to me and as I put my arms out for her, she suddenly changed her mind. She shot out her right hand, toward my chest, and pushed me back.

"Not now," she said. "I've already cried enough already today, believe me. Not now. But come. I want you to meet people. We've been waiting for you."

I stood there and stared at her hand—I imagined a policeman's gloved hand holding up traffic for schoolchildren—and I could actually feel the tears recede, drain down the back of my throat. She led me to the kitchen. Lillian and Sheila were setting out fruit and nuts and crackers and pretzels in bowls. They kissed me. Sheila held to me for a long time. She said that my father was her favorite uncle, that on the day that Abe went overseas he came to their apartment and said to her that as long as Abe was gone he would try to be a second father to her. She said he was a man who never hurt anybody in his entire life. Lillian said that my father was always ready with a smile and a joke, that he had a good sense of humor and a sunny disposition.

They left. My mother stood close to me, drew in on a cigarette.

"Listen. What I wanted you to know before we go into the other room is that Sol's brothers are here already, see? God bless Abe for taking care of things, but Sol's brothers—listen—you don't trust them for a second, do you hear? They'll try to get you alone and work on your guilt and make you change all the plans. I know them." She blew smoke toward the ceiling. "You know what they wanted me to do, first thing? They wanted me to call the hospital and have your father's body shipped back here so they could wash it and clean it on the kitchen table. Can you believe it? And here"—she took a small brown box from the top of the refrigerator—"do you know what's inside this? *Do* you?"

"No."

"Dirt! That's what! The first thing they do when they get here is they hand me a box of dirt. No kiss, no hello, no I'm sorry, no nothing—just barge in and hand me a box of dirt. From the Holy Land, they say. From Israel! And I shouldn't forget to bury the dirt with Sol."

"Are you all right?"

"How should I know? I mean, do I know what I'm doing? Do I know what I'm feeling?"

I tried again to put my arms around her, but she moved away, set the box back on the refrigerator, extinguished her cigarette under the faucet. She held up the wet stub.

"So you tell me why I'm smoking these crappy Chesterfields. Because I want to smell like your father, so he won't go away so fast?" She laughed and then, her mouth wide open—I thought of the car trunk, the bodies on the ground—she shoved the back of her hand in. "Oh Davey! I lost my best friend, did you know that? I lost my best friend!" She came close again. "But just you be smart and promise me not to get into any arguments with his brothers, yeah? I don't want no trouble.

You just agree with whatever they say and let Abe take care of the rest. Orthodox Jews are all nuts. Listen. Abe insisted I call. A brother's a brother, he said. Death is death. Who can tell?"

"But are you all *right*, mother? You seem so—"

"Whenever Abe gets near them—you watch—it makes me want to laugh the way they kind of slide around the room to get away from him. Come."

In the living room, people crowded around me, told me how sorry they were, what a wonderful man my father was. Stevey Komisarik shook my hand, recited words I didn't hear. Was he thinking of the game, wondering if I'd play, hoping I wouldn't? Was Tony at home, having to take shit from his brothers, or was he with Regina? Everyone was eating or smoking or talking. How had they arrived so soon? And why did they act as if they were at a party? My mother introduced me to Sol's brothers and gave me their names. Manny and Harry. They looked like twins. They wore black coats and black hats and had thick dark beards that covered their throats in wild curls. My mother said she hadn't seen them since she got married but whose fault was that? Avie Gornik cupped his hand to my ear and whispered: "The original Smith Brothers, right, kid? Like on the cough drops."

I shrugged him off. I stared at my uncles, trying to figure out how it could be that these two small men had played with my father when he was a boy, had slept in the same bed with him. In the wintertime, my father had told me, when they took him sledding, they smeared goose fat on his ears. They wore thick rimless glasses. Behind the glasses their eyes were small, like black beads covered with gray film. Their cheeks were pink, as if rouged. They held little black books in their hands, index fingers wedged inside, and they looked at me as if they were appraising merchandise.

Manny nodded. "You're Sol's boy," he said.

"Yes."

"He's Sol's boy," Harry said, and he sucked in on his lower lip, as if to keep from crying. Eyes closed, he rocked back and forth, heel to toe. Was he praying? Sometimes, I knew, when my father had taken his satchel and stayed away for a few nights, he stayed with them and they tried to talk him into divorcing my mother.

Manny tugged at my jacket, asked me how old I was.

"Sixteen. Sixteen-and-a-half, actually. I'll be seventeen next fall."

"Were you Bar Mitzvah?"

"No."

Harry pushed his book into my face, held it open.

"Can you read Hebrew?"

"No."

"So tell me how do you expect to say Kaddish for your father? Can you answer me that, sonny boy?"

"I don't know."

"Are you a Jew or are you a Jew?" Manny asked.

"He's a bright boy," Harry stated. "Sol always said so. We can teach him the words, from memory. We can write them out with English spelling."

"Will you say it for him? He wanted you to say Kaddish for him. Believe me when I tell you this. To us he always called you his little *Kaddishel*. My little *Kaddishel* Davey, he called you. That means you were the one who would live after him and remember him by saying Kaddish. You say it every day for one year. We'll come get you every morning before school and take you with us. It's no trouble. We can teach you to put on *tephillin*."

"Where we pray nobody will make fun of you for not knowing."

"Your father said Kaddish for his father, yes? And his father said it for his father, *olev hashalom*, for our grandfather. You should say Kaddish for your father."

They moved away from me, eyes downcast.

"Hello Davey."

Abe's eyes were as dry as mine. Did he feel anything? He smiled slowly, almost as if he were happy. He opened his arms to me. We embraced.

"Are you all right?"

"I suppose."

We stepped back from one another. He looked well tanned, rested. He wore a soft gray pinstriped suit, a white shirt, a beautiful blue silk paisley tie. Manny and Harry whispered to one another in the corner, next to my room, and I imagined them in the kitchen, washing down my father's body with soapy hands, snipping hairs inside his nose.

"We'll do whatever you want, whatever you choose," Abe said. "Okay? But not now. When everyone's gone—later—you and your mother talk things over and then you decide."

I pressed my eyes closed, but when I opened them everyone was still there, Abe was still smiling at me. I wondered if it occurred to him to think of his own father at a time like this, and if my mother would call him or visit him at the home, to give him the news, to have him come to the funeral. And why, I wondered, if I was taller than everyone else in the room, did I feel so small?

My mother had my hand in hers and was taking me around the room, introducing me to cousins and aunts. Neighbors kissed me. Avie and Benny sat on the couch together, under the window, Avie's mother between them. I couldn't recall the last time I'd seen her outside their apartment. Avie introduced me to his mother. She said she knew who I was, that she was honored to meet me. She set her wool and knitting needles in her lap.

"You know what I can't get over?" she said. She pointed to Abe's men. "That once upon a time they were little boys and we changed their diapers, and now they're all grown up and they kill people."

Avie told her to be quiet, but she laughed at him. My mother said we had private business to talk over and took me with her to the bedroom. She told me to stand by the door, to guard it. She got down on her hands and knees, and from under the bed she took out my father's gray metal box, the one he'd kept his important papers in. She cursed my father for not having given her the combination to the lock. She took a hammer and screwdriver from under her pillow, then got on her knees again and started beating on the lock with the hammer. She'd warned my father, hadn't she? She'd told him something like this might happen someday.

If you lived and then died, there should be a difference in the world, I thought. There should be a reason for your life. I wondered if Abe thought the same way, if he ever compared his life now, in Brooklyn, to his life during the war, and if, like me, he felt somehow ashamed of the difference. My mother took one of my father's slippers from under the bed, put it on top of the lock to muffle the sound, and smashed down. The lock stayed closed. She talked about my father's life insurance policies, how she'd made him take out a special policy from the Jewish Guild for the Blind that would have paid a hundred dollars a month for the rest of their lives had he gone blind before he died. She tried to pry the lid of the box open with the screwdriver. I told her to stop, that what she was doing was crazy.

"Crazy? Listen. At a time like this you gotta be thinking overtime or people will steal you blind. The police brought me home but I was having fits because I didn't know if they were police who were Abe's friends or police who were Abe's enemies, but they didn't try any funny stuff, so the minute they were gone, before I even called you or Abe, I ran to the bank and took all our money out of the accounts and got my diamonds and jewels out of the safe-deposit box. You call that crazy? And if I left it here for the courts to seal over for a few years?"

She moved to the wardrobe closet, reached in and took out a shoe box. She showed me the cash and jewelry.

"What do you think, that I'm doing this for myself? Is that what you think?"

"No."

"Good." She held the handle of the screwdriver with her left hand, the blade against the lock, then banged down on the screwdriver's handle with the hammer. "Do I even know what kind of report I'm gonna get from the doctor? Sure. I'm the sick one but your father goes and dies. The operation was a success but we lost the patient. Oh Sol. Sol. That was just like you, wasn't it—to have your heart attack *after* we left the doctor's office."

"I think I can open the lock," I said. "I think I know the combination."

She dropped the tools.

"So why didn't you say so before?"

Sweat dripped along her forehead and cheeks. She unbuttoned the top two buttons of her blouse, blew downwards to cool herself. She put the box on the bed, and when I went to it she backed up and stood by the door.

"Just hurry, yeah? We gotta see what else he left in there, in case he had another policy for me—for a surprise—only if you think I dragged you in here so I could find out how rich I'm gonna be, you're wrong. It's for you, Davey. For you. You were the real light of his life. That's what this is all about."

I turned the lock, listened to the tumblers click. I'd watched my father open and close the lock a thousand times.

"Oh Davey, Davey," she said. "Things were just so awful between us sometimes. Do you forgive me? Do you think you'll ever be able to forgive me for what we did to you, all those years, watching the way we were with each other, night and day and day and night?"

"Yes."

"I mean really. You shouldn't answer so quickly. I want you to think about it, that the last thing we wanted was to make you unhappy. But it was terrible between us sometimes. Didn't I know it? Abe said that—"

She backed away. The lock opened. I stood. She wiped her eyes with the back of her hand.

"What did Abe say?" I asked.

"Not now." She pointed to the box. "There's a surprise for you in there and I want to make sure you get it before the courts take charge. The surprise is that your father once said that when he died there would be something special in here for you that he put away."

She took out account books, business envelopes, booklets of check stubs. She held up a large manila envelope, read the writing on the outside. Her right hand moved to her chest. On the outside of the envelope, I recognized my father's handwriting:

> *For my only son, David Voloshin*
> *To be opened in the event of my death*

He had not signed his name.

My mother's hand rested on my wrist with such gentle pressure that it was as if she didn't even know she was touching me. "Your father was a sweet man. Before we were married he used to write poems to me, did you know that? He had beautiful penmanship, like on the envelope here. He won prizes in grade school when he was a boy. Who could believe?"

She touched the envelope as if she were touching him. She seemed puzzled.

"It's so thin," she said.

"Can I open it?"

I pressed the metal tabs together, straightening them. I slipped my index finger under the flap, at the corner, and slid it along slowly, so that the flap gave way where it was glued, where he had licked it closed. We said nothing. I reached inside and felt a single sheet of glossy paper. I slid it out. It was a reproduction of President Roosevelt's portrait, the unfinished portrait that he was sitting for in Warm Springs, Georgia, when he had a brain hemorrhage. The picture seemed pale, the green, brown and pink watercolor washes, under the ink sketch, faded. My mother grabbed the envelope and looked inside.

"Is that *all?*" she asked. "This is the big deal?"

Later, when everybody had gone, she came into my room and sat on my bed. I opened my eyes so she would know I was awake. She touched my forehead, thanked me for being there, for having been polite to all the visitors. She said she didn't know what she would have done had I not been there, had she not had me to lean on, to live for. We agreed that the easiest thing would be to let my father's brothers bury my father in their cemetery the next day. A Jew was supposed to be buried within twenty-four hours of his death and she figured that was a good thing. Why prolong the suffering for the living? There would be enough hard times to come. Whatever his brothers wanted was fine with her. Sol was dead. Now we were two. What else mattered?

She didn't say anything else for a long time. She had brushed her hair so that in the dim half-light the gray wisps looked like silver threads. I felt peaceful. I was drifting off to sleep—seeing myself on the beach, telling the girl with the long hair about my father's death—when I felt my mother's lips on my forehead.

"You get a good night's sleep. Tomorrow won't be easy. Tomorrow we say goodbye to him, yeah?"

"I suppose."

"I love you, Davey."

"Mother?"

"Yes?"

"Why wouldn't you let me kiss you when I first came home?"

"Sure," she said, but I could tell she wasn't listening to me. "You're a good boy, Davey. I always said so. So listen—I wanted you to know something else I been thinking about. I wanted you to know that no matter what impression he gave, that your father was always able to satisfy me."

"What?"

"Shh. You rest now. You don't gotta say anything, but I wanted you to know. Oh it was crazy sometimes, believe me, life with your father— but he did satisfy me and I wanted you to know." She kissed me. "You get some sleep now. You're a good boy. Like Lillian said and I have to agree, you got your father's sweetness sometimes, so I never worry about you really, did you know that?" I didn't reply and she kept talking. "Oh I worry the way a mother worries sometimes, and I know you still got a temper that scares me. For example, if you should find a girl you like someday I worry what you might do to her if she ever got you angry. Because this is what I've been thinking—that maybe God will be good to us from now on. Maybe He took your father early so that He'll take you late. Who can tell about things like that?" She laughed. "Abe," she said. "I love him like a brother, don't I?" She kissed me on the forehead, went to the door. Was there something else she wanted to say?

6

Mr. Goldstein was telling us what he'd been telling us all game long: to take our time, to move slowly, to get the ball to me every time we could. We were ahead 57 to 56 and I had 29 of our points and most of our rebounds. There were two minutes left in the game and I didn't sit down during our time-out because I was afraid that if I did I might never get up again. My arms were sore and heavy, my feet felt as if they were being pumped full of warm water—and all I wanted was for the game to be over. I wanted to die, to float weightlessly above the court the way I did in dreams.

The guys patted me on the back and rear end, told me that I was playing like a madman. I felt hammers banging against my skull, from inside. Everything went black. I pressed my eyes shut, opened them, saw my teammates' hands in the circle, and I bent over, put my hands there too. The buzzer sounded. I looked at the stack of hands and I couldn't tell, at first, which fingers belonged to me.

The noise from the stands broke over me like waves. The guys were staring at me, and for an instant I felt that they were trying to understand why it was I was playing so hard, why it meant so much for me to win. Three of them, to my surprise—Tony Cremona, Julie Bender, Jerry Friedland—had even shown up at the funeral. Tony had come with Regina, and I figured he'd caught hell after. The guys started out onto the court, but Mr. Goldstein held onto my wrist. Did he want to apologize to me again? The referee blew the whistle, pointed to me. I pulled away. It was our ball, in back court.

I thought of how angry Manny and Harry were that I wouldn't sit and mourn with them for seven days. I'd let them bury him the way they wanted, hadn't I? I'd let their rabbi slit the collar of my good suit with a razor blade. I'd made a fool of myself at the cemetery, trying to recite the Kaddish with them, unable to pronounce the words correctly. What more did they want?

I heard voices again, calling to me, and I did what I should not have done. I looked up, past Mr. Goldstein—past our bench, past the scorer's table, past rows of wooden benches, up to the first tier of box seats. I glared, believing for an instant that if I stared at them hard enough they would leave me be. But they only smiled and waved. Louie Newman cupped his hands around his mouth and called to me, so everybody could hear: "Hey Davey baby—you go sink a hoop for me and all the boys back on Flatbush Avenue!" Avie Gornik and Big Jap Willer laughed like idiots, swiveled their heads from side to side to show all the dead-beats that they knew me.

The whistle blew. The ball was in play. Did Abe know his men were here? Would he have let them come if they'd asked permission—or was it possible he'd sent them to show the D.A. that he had nothing to hide? I faked left, moved right, and the ball came to me, open, just above the foul circle. There were three men around me at once. I heard them grunting, breathing, talking to me. One of them—Jackson, number 24 —needled me again the way he'd done from the opening whistle, asking me how much my uncle was paying me to throw the game. I swung from side to side, elbows out, to get free. I heard Jackson groan. With three men on me, somebody had to be free behind, closer to the basket, but all I could do was stay hunched over the ball, protecting it, moving from one side to the other, trying to keep the ball from the hands that were moving in on me, grasping. The whistle blew. I stopped moving. The referee called a jump ball.

Julie Bender had his arm around my shoulder. What good did words ever do? What could I say to anybody to make them know how much I'd loved him? What good were words if my father was cold in the ground? I rose in the air and my timing was perfect. I slammed the ball toward Julie and he was there, taking it in full stride, being hacked at the last second as he went in for the lay-up. The ball rolled around and out.

I was under the basket, Julie at the foul line. I was standing on the court where all my old heroes had stood, yet the only faces I could see were the faces of Gornik and Newman and Willer. Less than a year before, the C.C.N.Y. stars—Eddie Warner, Eddie Roman, Herb Cohen, Al Roth, Floyd Lane—had been where I was now, a full house cheering its lungs out for them, streamers and confetti and programs and paper cups raining down on them. They'd done what no other college team in history had done. They'd won both national championships in a single year, the N.C.A.A. and the N.I.T. And now where were they? They'd all been fixing games, rigging scores. They'd all confessed to the D.A. They were all banned from college, waiting to be sentenced.

I saw Turkish Sammy and Louie Newman and the others sitting in the black cars that ringed us on the other side of the gravestones while we buried my father. We stood under a green canopy. Abe said nothing, but I'd seen enough movies to know that gangsters liked to pick each other off at times like this. Did Turkish Sammy have a tommy gun on his lap? Did Abe wear a bullet-proof vest under his good suit? As the casket slipped down on cloth straps, I even wondered whether my father's body was inside the pine box. I'd never see him again. The rabbi had forbidden it. I was supposed to remember my father in life, he said to me. Not in death.

Julie made the first shot. I recalled pictures I'd drawn of the Knick players: Harry Gallatin, Vince Boryla, Max Zaslofsky, Ernie Vande-weghe. My father showed them to everyone on this route. The Jefferson fans were booing and hissing, stamping their feet. I looked at the banners that hung down above us, for college and pro teams that had won championships. Julie's second shot bounced off the rim and Jefferson was moving downcourt. I ran back, my feet throbbing, my heart pounding inside my ears as if there were kettle drums there. Tin blades with ragged edges turned around inside my chest, faster and faster. I waited under the basket, glanced up at the clock, moved out and waved my hands when the ball came into my zone. Then it was in the far corner, away from me, and Willie Benz, Jefferson's redheaded sharpshooter— All-City two years in a row and headed for North Carolina, even though he was only five-ten—let go with a jump shot. I screamed cross-court, but too late. Benz shot his jumpers like line drives, without arc, and the instant the ball left his hand I knew it was in. I started back up court.

The score was tied. There was a little over a minute left. Would I ever play so well again? I imagined the still, flat surface of a lake. I saw enormous white water lilies. I saw a stone fall, disappear soundlessly through the black water. I was sitting on the grass beside the lake, knees up, arms locked around them. The girl sat next to me, her head against my shoulder, her hair dusting my arm. When she touched my cheek with her fingertips, I shivered. Why did she love me so much? Why did she stay with me when she knew I would only bring trouble into her life?

Tony moved by. "You okay?" he asked.

"Yeah."

"You look dead."

"I'm okay."

"You want a time-out? We got one left—"

"I said I'm okay."

I moved from left to right, under the backboard. Goldstein was shouting at us to work for the last shot, to take the tie if we had to, not to give the ball away. I drifted from one side to the other, shoving past defenders, following the ball. My head was thick, as if clogged with damp towels. I looked up, saw the roof of the Garden. What went on way up high, in the darkness above the canvas cloths and tarps? Before the war, Abe took me to the circus each November, got me everything I wanted —programs, peanuts, cotton candy, hot dogs, soda, souvenirs. The roof had seemed higher then and I'd wondered how they rigged up so many ropes and wires and platforms, how the workers got up there to connect everything. Whenever the high-wire performers worked without nets, I was terrified. I wanted to talk with them in the dressing rooms afterwards, to ask if they were scared too, if they imagined what it would feel like to miss, to plunge, to know in those few seconds that there was nothing in the world that could keep them from breaking, from shattering against the ground.

I felt someone pressing on me from behind. I pushed back, saw the referee's eyes, shot my hands out and felt the ball come to me. Two other players collapsed on me at once and instead of going up for the shot—if they fouled me and I missed one, they would have the ball with a chance to score two and go ahead—I looped the ball right back outside, to Tony. The whistle blew. I turned to the referee. He pointed to the man who was leaning on me. I had one shot at the foul line. Damn!

"Why didn't you shoot?" Tony asked. "Jesus Christ, Davey, they're knocking shit out of you and the refs don't call nothing. Why the hell didn't you *shoot?*"

The crowd was applauding. The man who fouled me had five personals and was leaving the game. He shook my hand, told me how great I was. I breathed in, bounced the ball twice, looked at the basket, let the ball slip off my fingertips. Swish! We were one point ahead, but they had the ball.

"Tighten up! Tighten up!" Goldstein yelled. "No fouls!"

Louie Newman was screaming like a maniac, cursing the referee and yelling at us to foul, to get the ball back, to call a time-out. Had he bet on me? I felt as if I were deep underwater, near the bottom of a lake where all things were cold and dark. I wanted to sleep. The ball went left to Benz, streaking across the key and, in mid-flight, with the slightest movement of his head and shoulders, he sent Tony high into the air, Tony's hand outstretched to slap down the jumper, then slipped under him, off-balance, and drilled the ball through the basket. The Jefferson fans went crazy, shaking their fists in the air, yelling at us to eat it. They were ahead for the first time since the second quarter, and there was nothing in the world I could do about it.

"Jesus fucking Christ," Tony muttered as we hustled back the other way. "Oh Jesus fucking Christ. What am I gonna do now?" He braked to a stop, turned, took the ball past half-court. "C'mon, c'mon," he called to us. "Number eight. Number eight."

Nobody called a time-out. Goldstein didn't like us to call time-outs when there was less than half a minute left and we had the ball because he believed that gave the other team time to set up their defense. He preferred to let us use the momentum, to take our chances.

"Get it to Davey!" he yelled. "Get it to Davey—!"

I made my moves, waited for Morty Zisk to pick for me so I could take the ball at a low post and go up for a bank shot, left side off the boards. The cheerleaders waved megaphones in the air, led our fans in a chant, a deafening crescendo, the way they'd done all season when I was hot. "Vo-lo-shiiiin . . . Vo-lo-shiiiin . . . Vo-lo-shiiiin . . ." There were nine seconds left. If I got the ball and made the shot, the crescendo would become a whistle and the whistle would end in a loud "Boom!"

"Hey fixer," Jackson whispered. "How much your uncle gonna give you for letting us beat your ass?" I didn't react. "We all know you ain't gonna make no last shot." I moved out to the foul line, slid backwards, kept my distance so as not to get fouled. One foul shot wouldn't help. They didn't collapse on me now because they needed to defend against the short pop-shot from outside, where Tony was deadly. Seven seconds. I saw Al Roth's face, smiling at me, telling me that someday I would be better than he was. I had the size and the moves. I blinked, tried to turn his face around. Was he somewhere in the Garden, watching me?

Six seconds. "Come on, fixer," Jackson said. "Do your uncle's work now, baby." Roth had been All-City at Erasmus four years before. He'd been the playmaker on C.C.N.Y.'s Cinderella team. I could see his photo, signed, on the wall of Goldstein's office. I blinked again, but all I could see when I got rid of Roth's face were other photos of old Erasmus stars: Waite Hoyt, Sid Luckman, Jerry Fleishmann, Lou Kusserow, Johnny Rucker.

Three seconds. I shoved off, almost tripped where the floor was slick from sweat, and I prayed that the ball would come to me. If I scored, we won. If I missed, we lost. And it seemed unfair, suddenly, that I was only one person, that I had only one body, one mind, one life. I wanted to be everywhere, to be doing everything! I wanted to be passing the ball and stealing the ball and shooting the ball and taking the ball off the boards. I wanted to be inside the bodies of the other guys on our team, making every play for them so that there would never be any mistakes, so that we would never lose.

Two seconds. Tony was driving the baseline. I tried to stop seeing faces, to concentrate on the game. Roth was leaning forward, biting his nails, rooting for me. Tony moved out past the foul line, dribbling right. I was being clobbered, held, but there was no whistle. The floor vibrated from the stamping. I heard girls' voices, wild and shrill. I saw my mother, on her knees, hammering away at the metal box. Tony started to go up with the ball to shoot, and the instant he did my man moved out, tried to get to him to stab at the ball, and Tony slipped the ball past him to me, perfectly. Tony crashed toward the basket, through a wall of Jefferson players, a broad grin on his face. I was exactly where I was supposed to be, about eight feet away, on the left side. I turned right, went up, my feet light as feathers, and my man was too late getting back. I was high in the air for the easy shot off the boards and there was nobody up there with me. There seemed to be no sound, no voices. The ball slid from my fingers. I heard the other players gasp, stop breathing, their backs to me, their arms high. I floated down, watched the ball hit the backboard and angle down for the basket. The buzzer sounded. My feet touched the ground. The ball hit the front rim, hung there, fell off.

I was hardly surprised. The guys on the Jefferson team were running around the court, leaping up and down and shouting like crazy men, their friends pounding them and hugging them, their girlfriends shrieking and jumping, kissing them. I didn't wait for anyone to say anything. Goldstein looked right at me and I stared back. He could think what he wanted. They all could. I picked up my jacket and warm-up pants. Three of the guys sat on the bench, their heads in their hands.

Benz was next to me, grabbing my hand, pumping it up and down, telling me how great I was. "Tough luck," he said.

Jackson shook my hand. "Hey—you're okay, Voloshin. No hard feelings, huh?"

Then they were gone. One of the Jefferson cheerleaders, a tall girl with a blond ponytail who'd been eyeing me all game, grabbed my arm and leaned up toward me. "I think you're real cute," she said, her lips brushing my ear. "Wanna come to a party later—?"

"Suck off," I said, and pulled away from her.

"Oooh—and you're mean too," she said, prancing off, laughing at me.

I walked down the ramp toward the locker rooms, and it was only after I'd stooped down and made my way along the arcade, shoving through the crowd, that I realized Gornik and Newman and Willer were not there waiting for me. Nobody would be waiting for me. I'd go home by myself on the subway, my mother would ask me about the game, and I'd lose either way, wouldn't I? If I showed that I was sad because we lost she'd laugh at me for taking the game so seriously, and if I said nothing or showed I didn't care she'd try to make a big deal of it, asking me why I kept things from her.

My father would not be there. I made a fist, lifted it, wanted to drive it through the brick wall. But there were too many people around. I didn't want them gawking at me afterwards—calling for a doctor, trying to help, whispering to each other about what I'd done and why.

Where was my father? The question did not seem strange. And what, of my father, would live on? Who, after a few weeks, would remember that he'd ever lived? Even before we'd gone to the cemetery, my mother had emptied out the closets and dressers, putting his clothes in boxes, telling me to take them downstairs to Beau Jack. Beau Jack was much taller than my father, but maybe he could get the clothes altered, maybe he could trade them in somewhere, at a tailor's or a rummage shop. While she went through my father's clothes, she talked to him, chided him for not treating himself well. If he'd liked himself a little more and her a little less, she said, things might have been better. Didn't she know it was no good the way he worshipped her? But what could she do? Abe said to marry him, so she married him. Abe said he wouldn't be like the others, that he'd treat her right, that he'd be good to her.

I imagined my father sitting in the stands after everyone was gone. Beau Jack was next to him, wearing one of my father's old ties. Dull orange, with brown stripes. Beau Jack told my father not to worry, that everyone had bad luck sometimes, that I was young, that I was a winner.

High school kids shoved by, telling me what a great game I'd played, telling me we'd do better next year. Sure. Someone asked me what college I was going to play for. I pushed him aside and entered the locker room. I was the first one there. There had been lots of scouts and coaches at the game, I knew, but none of them introduced themselves to me and none would be talking to me now. That was for sure. They were all scared because of the scandals. The hope that I'd nurtured for a few years, the one dream I shared with my father, of being able to get out of Brooklyn, to a good out-of-town college—that dream was now dead.

What college would give Abe Litvinov's nephew a scholarship? Even if Abe was never convicted or named by the D.A., I knew I didn't have a chance. Sure. They were all cowards and liars. Abe was right about that too. The only difference between men in his business and men in so-called legitimate businesses, he said, was that the men in his business were honest with themselves. They were free of illusion, of self-deception, of hypocrisy.

The 50th Street platform was jammed, the Jefferson students celebrating as if it were New Year's Eve. Some of them were necking in the
middle of the crowd to show how free and happy they were. I wedged
my gym bag tighter between my feet, closed my eyes, let my head rest
against a steel girder.

"You won't hurt yourself, will you?"

I opened my eyes.

"What?"

She smiled up at me. She had large hazel eyes and soft, wavy brown
hair that spilled out along one side of her forehead from under a black
beret.

"Hi," she said. "I hope you don't mind, but I've been watching you
ever since the game ended—I've been watching your eyes—and I have
the distinct impression that if somebody says the wrong thing to you,
you might do something you'd be sorry for later." She seemed to speak
without taking breaths. "Not to them, but to yourself."

She stared at me intently, her lips pressed tight, her eyebrows fur-
rowed, as if, I realized, she were imitating the way I glared at the world
when I was angry. I recognized her. Her name was Gail Kogan and she
was a senior at Erasmus—a girl with a reputation for being brilliant and
Bohemian, for hanging around with the brainy kids and going out with
guys from Ivy League colleges. There had been an article about her the
year before in *The Dutchman*, the school newspaper, about how she
was trying to organize a repertory company modeled after the All-City
Chorus—a group of high school students from the five boroughs who
would put on a series of plays that they did everything for: sets, lighting,
directing, music, acting.

"Look. If you don't mind, could you just leave me alone?"

"No," she said. "Of course not. I'm too worried about you. We have
to go home most of the way on the same train anyway, so I'll just keep
you company. That won't be so terrible, will it?"

She had a large, full mouth—no makeup—and when she smiled the
right half of her mouth seemed to smile by itself, with the left side
following, as if it wasn't sure of itself. She sighed. "I'm not usually like
this," she said softly. "But I figured that at a time like this . . ." She
stopped. "What did I figure? Can you tell me?"

A downtown local came into the station—I'd already let two go by—
and I picked up my gym bag. Maybe if I got on the train quickly, if I
shoved myself in there would be no room for her. But as the train slowed
down I saw that it was as packed as the others. I set my bag down again
and looked at her. She cocked her head slightly to the side and to my
surprise I found that when she smiled at me, warmly, I almost smiled
back. For a brief instant I imagined that she was somebody I knew well

—a sister or a cousin—and I couldn't figure out what I wanted to do more: to let all the anger and frustration I was feeling out on somebody like her, somebody who cared about me enough to take it—or simply to let her comfort me and tease me for a while, so I could get my mind off the game.

"Look," she said. "I have an idea. How would it be if you took me out for an ice cream soda? Would you like to do that?"

I felt warm, slightly dizzy. I unzipped my team jacket. She was looking at me with such eagerness that I had the strange sensation, for a moment, that were I to say no to her she might do what she'd said I would do, something to hurt *herself.*

"I don't mean to be rude, but all I really want is to be alone, okay?"

"He vants to be alone," she intoned, mock-dramatically. I moved away, but she touched my hand and spoke again, quickly. "Only you really shouldn't be alone at a time like this. Listen—if you took me out for an ice cream soda, by the time we finished and came back the rush hour would be over and the trains would be empty. *Then* I'd leave you alone, all right? You must be hungry. You played so hard. I never . . . Just come with me, please? You won't be sorry if you do."

"Some other time."

"What other time?" I tried to look away, toward the tracks, but she moved into my line of vision and stood on tiptoes. "I warn you. I'm very persistent. I thought you should know that."

"You have a sister who's blind, don't you?"

"I have a sister who's blind." She looked bewildered, as if I'd wounded her somehow. "That's what I'm most famous for. You're famous for your basketball skills and your uncle's profession and I'm famous for my beautiful blind sister. We have a lot in common, then, don't you see?"

"No."

"Listen. How old are you?"

"Sixteen."

"Me too. When's your birthday?"

"September twenty-second."

"Mine is September nineteenth. Which means I'm older. How do you feel about that?"

"About what?"

"About being seen with an older woman? I skipped grades when I was young, that's why I'm a year ahead of you. My parents pushed me. My mother is two-and-a-half years older than my father. She helped put him through medical school by working as a teacher. My parents want me to be a doctor, like my older brother Peter. I like you."

"What did you say?"

"I *like* you." She smiled broadly, so that her gums showed. "Oh I knew I'd get a rise out of you if I kept at it. Persistence is my most salient quality. What I said was 'I like you.' Do you mind?"

"I don't know." I started to smile, and when I did it was as if tiny flashlight bulbs went on behind her eyes. "Do I mind that you like me, or that you *said* you did?"

Her smile broadened. "Listen," she said. "It doesn't create any obligations on your part. The truth is, I've never had the courage to approach you at school. I must feel safe talking like this in a crowd. I don't mean to be so clever or arch, but I *am* nervous—and when I saw the way you were glowering, I said to myself that it was time to act. It's only that I thought you might kill somebody, from the way you looked." She reached towards me, and when she touched me I didn't draw back. "I thought you might break your hands."

I said nothing. I wondered if Tony would be coming soon, with Regina. I imagined the four of us walking along the boardwalk together, Gail and Tony making jokes to cheer me up, and I thought too of how good it would be simply to have somebody holding my hand, laughing with me, being affectionate. A train roared into the station. I didn't pick up my bag. I didn't look down at my hands. I didn't want to recall the way I'd felt after the game. I saw some of the Jefferson players come through the turnstile now, holding their gym bags high. People cheered. I thought of Al Roth walking along Broadway under the arcades of movie theaters, hands in his pockets, walking and walking, all the way down to Union Square. I saw him going into a bar, sitting by himself, watching TV with a bunch of drunks. I saw him getting on the train late at night, when it was empty, and riding into Brooklyn, old newspapers under his shoes. The Jefferson players would change at 42nd Street for the New Lots Express, and I would change there for the Flatbush Express, but I didn't want to ride with them for even one stop. And if they stayed on until Nevins or Franklin before they changed? If they noticed me and said things to me? If their girlfriends tried to flirt with me?

Gail let out a long breath of air. "This is positively my last offer then. I'll take *you* out for an ice cream soda, all right?"

I saw the Jefferson players coming toward us. Light from the incoming train sprayed through Gail's hair, making the dark curls seem suddenly silver. Gail smiled at me, but her smile broke slightly and I could see how scared she was that I might reject her.

"All right," I said.

"Do you *mean* it?"

"I suppose."

"I don't believe it," she said. "Oh Jesus."

We pushed our way toward the back of the platform. I kept my head twisted to the right, looking away from where the Jefferson players were.

Someone set off a firecracker. Gail reached back and took my hand, pulled me along through the turnstile and then up the stairs and out into the street.

"I think of your hands," she said.

"What?"

"Your face too, but it was your hands I noticed first. I think of them a lot. You won't resent me later, will you? For pushing you so much? I'm really quite shy when you get to know me. The real me is shy and modest, is what I mean. I can be demure and domestic too, if I have to." She shrugged, pulled her coat closer for warmth. "It's just that I've taught myself to compensate for my natural shyness and insecurity by covering them up with this way I have of being terribly forward and direct. It alarms people sometimes. My mother disapproves. Are you alarmed, David? Do I alarm you?"

"I'm just tired, I think."

We walked along Broadway, then turned up 48th Street, toward Seventh Avenue. It was raining again, a thin cool drizzle. I saw myself in a soft V-neck sweater, rust-colored, returning to Erasmus after I'd become a star for a college team. I was presenting Mr. Goldstein with an inscribed photo to put on his wall. I saw the faded brown pictures there, of men in old-fashioned uniforms, in business suits and Army uniforms and judges' robes. Mr. Goldstein was shaking my hand and introducing me to a kid sitting in his office and telling the kid about the time I'd played my heart out after my father died, and for an instant I felt wonderful, imagining the look in that young boy's eyes. Goldstein gazed at the photo and his smile vanished. He looked up, puzzled. I followed his eyes and saw that inside the black frame was a drawing, not a photo, and that it was not my own face staring up at me, but Abe's.

"Did you know that my father was blind in one eye?"

"Yes. You mentioned it the day we came to your class, when my sister showed how splendid she is at reading Braille. It's one reason I always thought I had a chance."

"A chance?"

"With you." She shivered. "Is my sister still blind. Sure. If she wasn't blind, who would she be? I mean, she has a large investment in being a beautiful, altruistic blind woman. Everyone admires Ellen. Ellen Kogan, fair of mien, blessed of the Gods, eyeless in Gaza. . . ."

"You're jealous of her."

"You're perceptive." She tugged at her beret, poked her hair under it. "Sure I'm jealous. But sometimes I'm not above using her affliction. As I did with you. If I didn't have a beautiful blind sister, would you have remembered me?"

"Once, when I was a kid, my father scratched his good eye and was blind for a few weeks and I. . . ."

"And you what? What were you going to say?"

I shrugged. "And I was happy. That was what I was going to say. He was too, I think. He was very proud of how much he could do without his eyes."

"I *am* sorry about your father's death, David, only I don't know what to say, or if I should say anything at all. I used to see him on Flatbush Avenue sometimes, with his little briefcase and his hand over his good eye." She stopped, pointed to a luncheonette. "Do you miss him yet? I've never lost anyone close to me that way. My four grandparents are still alive. My mother and father are here. My brother and sister are too much with us, late and soon." I started to open the door, but she held back. "Only I don't really put much stock in words. Can you believe me? If I could be sure you'd know what I was thinking and feeling, I'd. . . ." She closed her eyes and came to me suddenly, placed her head lightly upon my chest. I didn't move. I wanted to put my arms around her, but I was afraid to do anything more than let her head rest where it was. Her arms stayed at her sides, unmoving. "There," she said, a few seconds later. "Wasn't that better? What good are words for what we truly feel, after all? Can we ever know the difference—between a feeling and the name we give to a feeling?"

We found a booth in the back and I helped her off with her coat, took off my jacket. She wore a gorgeous Scandinavian sweater, a pale peach-colored scarf at her throat. She took off her beret, leaned back, brushed her hair lightly from underneath. Her hair was dark and thick and the rain had made it frizz slightly. I thought of lamb's wool, of the Persian lamb coat my grandfather had given my mother during the war, of the stories my mother told me about watching her father work on the coats when she was a girl. Gail said that during the game the students talked about my father's death, about how brave I was to play. She said she didn't agree with them, that she figured his death had made things easier for me. Was she right?

In the bright steamy light of the luncheonette, I was surprised at the difference—at how, from a distance, her skin had seemed soft and smooth, but how, close up, you could see all the little scars and pock marks. I imagined her, at thirteen or fourteen, trying to scrub the acne away, trying to cover the pimples with makeup and Clearasil, healing the sores and scabs with creams and ointments.

When the waitress came I ordered a hot chocolate and a grilled cheese sandwich. Gail asked if I minded her staring at me, and then, before I could react, she asked if I minded being teased. She said that I looked so sad sometimes, at school, that she had the feeling I spent my life

believing people were about to make fun of me or accuse me of awful
things. From the way I was smiling, though—my eyes first, crinkling at
the corners—she figured that I didn't mind being teased. The colors in
her sweater were wonderfully soft and bright—greens, reds, ochres and
browns in diamond-shaped designs that ran in a crescent across the top
half. The background was beige, muted. I tried to imagine the colors on
paper, in blacks and grays. Were I to draw her face, would I put in all
the imperfections, all the tiny pitted marks that made her cheeks seem
perforated? She leaned forward, elbows on the table, her face resting in
her hands.

"I like giving you a hard time," she said. "And I do like looking at you.
You have gorgeous eyes. They're like your uncle's eyes. But listen. Do
you like *my* eyes? I think they're my best feature. My mother claims
they're too large for my face and my father says we have to *keep* an eye
on me—bulging eyes can be the early sign of some kind of hyperthyroid
condition that troubled young ladies with antic dispositions can often
have. Do you like them?"

"They're hazel."

"Well, that's true." She laughed. "I'm sorry. I'm embarrassing you.
Do you have enough money? I can pay for us if you want."

"It's okay. I have enough."

"Tell me then—do you think you could learn to like a girl like me?"

"I hadn't thought about it. I suppose—"

"I suppose," she said, and then she leaned back, crossed her arms
against her chest and grinned. "What's not to like, right?"

"I guess." I smiled. "My father used to use that expression."

She put her hands back on the table, and for a second I was afraid she
was going to reach across and want to hold hands with me. She hadn't
said anything about what I'd said about my father, and yet I felt she had
taken it in and wasn't commenting because she knew that if she reacted
too much she might scare me away.

"Listen," she offered. "Why don't we just make believe we're two high
school students who happen to meet in the subway after a play-off game
and decide to go and have something to eat together until the rush hour
is over, all right? Just to keep one another company, since they recognize each other and go to the same school. Would that make you feel
more comfortable about being with me?"

"It's okay," I said. Her gaze was so intense—she seemed to care so
much, to sense what I was feeling—that I looked away. "I mean, I'm
feeling okay. It's just that I never had anybody to talk to me the way you
do. I'm distracted, is all. My head seems too full, with all that's been
happening. I'm sorry. I don't mean not to pay attention to you."

"You're the one who lost the game and the father and all I think about is whether or not I'm making a good impression on you. God! Would Ellen think of herself in a situation like this?"

Gail looked down, tore at her napkin, rolled small bits of it into tiny pellets. The waitress brought our food. For a while we ate in silence. I thought of Tony and Regina, walking along the dark streets, Regina telling him that it was all right that we'd lost, that it wasn't his fault. I thought of Abe, in his front office, getting a call from one of his men. Would he care if I lost? Would he be happier if I won? Gail sipped her hot chocolate quickly, bending down so that she wouldn't have to pick up the cup. She licked marshmallow foam from her upper lip and asked me if I had a girlfriend. She said the girls at school couldn't figure me out. Big athletic star. Strong, silent type. Handsome young man with brooding Semitic features. Some of them wondered if my uncle supplied me with women.

"Being mysterious is the most attractive quality a person can have," she said. "Don't you agree?"

"I don't know."

"To know so much about a person, and still to want to know more—the way you feel at the end of a wonderful book. That's the way I feel about you."

I thought of saying that she hadn't read me yet, but I was afraid that if I did she might become self-conscious and stop talking to me the way she was—saying the things she'd waited so long to say—and so I said nothing.

"Do you know what I wish sometimes, David? I wish I could learn to keep quiet so that other people would think I was more mysterious, that there were things about me that were unknown and unfathomable, strange and deep. Do you like poetry?"

"Some."

She pressed her eyes closed and recited: " 'Below the surface-stream, shallow and light/Of what we say we feel—below the stream/As light, of what we think we feel—there flows/The noiseless current strong, obscure and deep,/The central stream of what we feel indeed.' " She opened her eyes. "Do you like that?"

"Yes."

"I wish I knew how to be more patient. That's my biggest problem. Gail Kogan, long on persistence, short on patience. What it is, is that I keep being afraid, when the situation is at hand, that if I remain quiet nobody will pay attention to me. My psychiatrist says that—"

She clapped her hand over her mouth, coughed, gagged, raised her arms. I pushed her glass of water toward her. She gestured backwards. I stood, reached across, pounded her on the back. She coughed more, let her hands down.

"You can sit now," she said, wiping her eyes. "Thanks—"

"Are you all right?"

She grinned. "Were you worried?"

"Yes."

She drank, took a long breath. "I see a psychiatrist two times a week. Do you mind? It won't make you frightened of me?" She made a fist, looked straight at me, as if she were very angry, very determined. "Oh David, isn't that the most scary thing of all—to be afraid that other people won't like you, that you won't be able to like them and trust them? Isn't that what it's all about?"

She waited, but I didn't say anything. "Do I make sense to you? Do you know what I mean?"

"Yes." I smiled. "Did you write the poem?"

"No. I like to memorize poetry, but I don't like to write it. It seems too much trouble, in prospect, to school myself in all the meters and rhyme schemes and forms. It's easier to memorize. Like studying for a test. I'm fine when somebody gives me a deadline, an exam, something specific to work toward, but if I have to do it on my own . . . it's like wanting to get to the top of a staircase without going up the steps, to play the piano without practicing scales."

"Wouldn't practicing scales be like studying?"

"My mother says I'm two ends against the middle and that the middle is me. She's very psychological. She's taking courses at Teachers College now. She wants to be able to help other young girls like me, right? Yet when I do know what I want, I get so single-minded that it's almost physically painful. I get so far ahead of myself, wanting the things I want, as I do now, with you, that . . ." She sat back, exhausted. "I should try to take things more slowly, shouldn't I? Well. We've finished eating. You don't have to sit next to me on the train going home. We could pretend we never met, that the past hour never occurred. There are lots of options. Louis Braille was only fifteen when he invented the Braille alphabet. What have we done that's comparable? Whatever you want to do is okay with me, David Voloshin. You decide. I'm pooped. The effort has been tremendous, folks. Did she ever expect to get this far with the young man of her dreams? Could he tell how surprised she was when he agreed to depart from the subway station with her?"

"Yes. He could."

She leaned toward me. "What were you thinking just then—when you said yes? Would you tell me?"

"I was wondering if this is real. It all seems so crazy, as if I'm somewhere else dreaming that I'm here. I mean, with my father yesterday and then losing the game—"

"I'm impatient because I'm afraid of being imperfect—that's the way I'd put it, were you to ask. I was thinking that I was afraid you'd dislike me later on when you were alone, not for anything I've said or done, but for having let yourself share things with me. People are that way, I think. They become frightened of the people they've trusted. They feel tricked and betrayed. Why?"

"I don't know."

"I was being rhetorical. But listen: what I was thinking most was that it was your silence itself I've been after—what drew me to you—because whenever I see you or think of you I keep thinking that you're silent and distant not because of what everybody thinks—your uncle and all—but because underneath you're really like me. I keep thinking your silence and my brashness are there for the same reason: to cover up fears." She breathed out. "Okay," she said, and then—I had to blink, the shift in her manner was so abrupt—she cocked her head to the side, winked. "So tell me: what do you think?"

We had already gone past her house four times, but each time we approached it she asked if I wanted to keep walking, and each time I said yes. Three more times, she said, and the walls of her house would cave in.

Her neighborhood was peaceful, quiet. There were no apartment houses, no stores, no garbage cans lining the sidewalks. The private homes were set well back from the road, surrounded by lawns, fancy hedges, large shade trees. The wealthier students from Erasmus lived here, closer to the Midwood High School section, a few blocks from Brooklyn College. It was a neighborhood in which I'd never walked with my father and in which, as far as I knew, Abe had no influence.

"Do I still make you nervous?"

"No. Not really."

"Then you must trust me a little. You must not be afraid of me."

"Was I afraid of you?"

"Are you kidding? When I first went up to you—I'd been rehearsing my line from the time the game ended—I was afraid you were going to bolt away like a frightened colt, you looked so startled."

"I played like one. Like a horse. Damn! Why didn't the last shot go in?"

"Fate. But you can look at the bright side, too, David Voloshin. Think of it this way: if you'd won the game, you might have lost me. How does it go—unlucky in cards, lucky in love? I mean, if you'd won the game, would I have been brave enough to approach you?"

She took my hand, rubbed my thumb with hers, gently. We were passing her school again, the elementary school she'd gone to from kindergarten through sixth grade. She led me toward the gate.

"Come. I won't bite. A journey to the scene of Gail Kogan's child-hood. A small detour, folks, on the highway of life."

I followed her toward the school building, away from the lights. I thought of Al Roth. I'd seen him at the Holy Cross schoolyard a few weeks before, standing near the entrance in his street clothes, leaning against the fence, watching us play. He'd taken me under his wing when I was a kid, had given me pointers, encouraged me. Now he was living at home with his parents, growing fat and pasty-faced. I recalled how frightened I'd been near the end of the game, seeing his face suddenly. Would he come to the schoolyard again? In a few years, would I be like him? Nobody asked him about the fixes. Nobody asked him what he was going to do now that he could never play college ball again, now that he'd never get the chance to play pro ball.

"Are you all right? If you'd rather not—"

"I'm sorry. What were you saying?"

"I wasn't saying anything. We were just walking, but you were looking so sad, it made my heart hurt. What is it, David? Tell me! What do you think about when you get the dark look—when those grim, bruised clouds pass over you?"

"Nothing."

"Nothing." She tightened her grip on my fingers. "Oh you do need somebody to keep an eye on you. It was the first thing I ever felt toward you. Don't you agree that you need someone to watch out for you?"

"So that I won't hurt myself?"

"Yes. If you get the urge, you can think of me, all right?"

"So that I can hurt you instead?"

Her arms were around me, her head against my chest. "Of course not. I'm not like that. I don't believe in martyrdom. It's just that I want you to *like* yourself more, that's all. Why? Because then you'll be able to like me. That's one of Gail Kogan's theories: that people can't give of themselves to others often because they're afraid they have nothing of value to give. If people liked themselves more, they'd feel that when they liked another, they were giving a precious gift to that person, see? Q.E.D. Am I logical?"

I touched the back of her head, ran my hand over her dark curls. We were hidden from the street, standing over a large iron grating in an alcove at the side of the building.

"We used to come here on our lunch hours in the sixth grade. To do things," she said. "And at night later on, when we were in junior high. Until our parents formed patrols to check on us."

"To do what things?"

"Smoke. Neck. Pet. We were a most progressive bunch. We stole cigarettes and pills from our parents. We found the sexy passages in books and read them to each other by flashlight. Would you like to kiss me?"

"What?"

"I thought I'd ask, in case you were interested but too shy to begin."

I thought of things falling through the grating—pennies and nickels and dimes, pens and pencils and erasers, bobby pins and baseball cards and candy and marbles and tie clips and jackknives. I thought of Beau Jack's stories, about the children who lived below the city, and I was glad I hadn't given him my father's old clothes, that I'd simply stuffed them in the garbage. I hadn't seen Beau Jack since my father's death. Was he afraid to be with me? Was he too shy to say anything, afraid he might say the wrong thing? Gail put her hands to my face, touched my eyes, traced their shapes with her index finger, then brushed my mouth lightly with her fingertips. I pulled her closer and wondered if, through her coat, she could feel how hard I was below.

"I—"

"Yes?"

"I don't think your eyes bulge so much. Not at all right now."

"Yes. Because I'm calm. See how good you are for me?"

"I'm not poison then?"

She drew back, baffled. "Why should you think such a thing? Why should you use such a word?"

"I don't know. I just feel sometimes that there's this vial of the stuff inside me, ready to leak out onto anyone who touches me, who becomes involved with me."

She took my face between her hands, drew me down to her. We kissed and her mouth opened to me at once. I was so surprised that I almost pulled back. For a split-second, my brain whirled. I saw Jackie Robinson, his teeth gleaming like stars in a black night. Was I crazy? Why was I seeing Jackie when I was kissing Gail? I tried to push his face from my mind. Gail's lips were large and warm—"nigger lips" the guys would have called them. I imagined Rachel rubbing Jackie's back at night, telling him that everything would be all right. I thought of Beau Jack, digging up bodies in France, burying them again. When Jackie married Rachel, Karl Downs, his minister, paid his own way to Los Angeles, to officiate. A few days later, Karl Downs, forced to wait in the corridor of a segregated hospital for an operation he needed and never received, died. Jackie knew that Karl Downs would not have died had his skin been white. Gail pressed against me, moving her head in small circles, varying the pressure, stroking my face, the back of my head, flicking my tongue with hers. I couldn't tell how long we held to that first kiss. When we parted, she backed away, smiled, leaned up and kissed me quickly on the nose, then hugged me.

"Wow!" she said.

"Wow?"

"Wow."

She didn't speak for a while. I reached down, lifted her chin, kissed her again. I loved the feel of her lips against mine—I couldn't believe how much I liked feeling them, how astonished I was at their softness and warmth, how wild I felt when she touched the inside of my mouth with her tongue, when she nibbled at my lips, my chin, my ears.

"Oh I should probably act very cool at a time like this," she said, her head on my chest, her fingers moving across my lips as if she were reading them. "And not let you know how I feel, how incredible this all is, but I can't *not* tell you, David. Is that all right?" We kissed again. "Only I'm worried that you won't desire me if I don't play hard to get. That you'll throw me over for some shapely young blonde with ponytail and Ipana smile."

"And what about the college guys you go out with? Don't you go to their colleges for those fancy weekends? What about all the actors you work with—?"

"You *care?*"

"I suppose. I don't know. I'm just saying back to you what you said to me. I mean, I never imagined kissing you before tonight. I never imagined what it would make me feel."

I pushed against her, so that her back was pressed to the brick wall. I thought of the times I'd necked with girls on Rogers Avenue, in the doorways of Mr. Lipsky's butcher shop and Lee's luncheonette, and of how the taste of cigarettes in their mouths always excited me. *Don't you trust me?* I'd say it again and again. *Trust me. Trust me.* Gail slipped her lips by mine, to my ear.

"Hey—"

"Shh."

She pushed me away for a second, to unbutton her coat. I ran my hands around her back, felt heat coming off her body through her sweater. We kissed again. I felt the shapes of her breasts against my chest.

"Do you mind?"

"Mind?"

"If I kind of take the lead sometimes. I mean, most boys believe they have to be the ones to think of everything, to be in charge—"

I stopped her mouth with another kiss. It was the only thing I wanted to do—to keep kissing her, to never stop, to feel her lips against my own.

I thought of the way I would move the hands of the girls on Rogers Avenue down to my fly when we necked, and how they would play with me, protesting the whole time and asking me what kind of girl I thought they were, but being sure I had my handkerchief ready in time so they didn't stain their clothes. Did I want Gail to touch me there? Or was I frightened somehow that if I tried to move her hand she might resist, she might get angry with me, that it might ruin everything. But I was aching and throbbing so terribly it was almost as if I could hear my heartbeat thumping away in my groin. Slowly, tentatively, I pressed in, rubbed myself against her. She hummed with pleasure. She held to me fiercely, reached up, tugged on my ears, half-laughed and half-moaned, then moved against me.

"I know I'm not as pretty as a lot of girls, in the popular sense." We were walking again, on the street. "But I am pretty *inside*. Still, if you were to visit a museum, say, and look at great-beauties-through-the-ages, you would see at once that the current ideal of a woman's body in the United States of America is a dreadful anomaly. Do you go to museums much? If you did you would notice that as far back as the Greeks and Romans, most artists have preferred to sculpt and paint women who were built like me. Ample. I thought I would mention the fact, in case you feel cheated. You know what I mean? Handsomest boy gets prettiest girl. Smartest boy gets smartest girl. Star athlete gets—"

"I used to go to museums a lot."

"Yes?"

"I liked to draw when I was younger. I even used to think that I might want to become an artist someday. When I grew up."

"When you grew up. Can we go to museums together, do you think? When you grow up?"

"Sure."

"What else can we do?"

"This," I said, and I kissed her.

"Ummm. Good. How about the *the-a*-ter then? Do you like the *the-a*-ter David? Hey—" She stopped. "You're like the main character in *Golden Boy* then, aren't you?"

"*Golden Boy?*"

"He was dark, too, the way you are. Italian, though. It was a play by Clifford Odets my mother took me to see in the Village last year. She and my father saw it together on one of their first dates, during the Depression. It's about a young boy who grows up to be both a great boxer *and* a concert violinist, if you can believe that. And he has to choose one or the other, you see—"

"Is that one of the plays your group put on?"

"My group?"

"That all-city theater thing you organized."

"*Dis*-organized would be more like it." She laughed. "Oh, we may yet get a production mounted before the end of the year—the Brooklyn Academy of Music will let us use their stage and equipment—but *you* try creating a working ensemble out of several dozen teenagers drunk on Stanislavsky. Mostly, see, I've been concentrating on designing a crest for us—a coat of arms that we can put on jackets and blazers—like your team jacket, right? Narcissism rampant on a field of ego . . ."

We kissed again, and I opened my eyes this time. She did too, and when she saw that mine were open, we both laughed.

"In Paris, young lovers kiss on the street all the time and people hardly notice. Our family went there last summer."

She looked at me very intently, very steadily. Neither of us moved. There were no questions in her eyes.

"I like you too," I said.

"You *do?*"

"Is it all right for me to say so?"

"Oh David!"

She hugged me, kissed me once on each eye, tenderly, then on my nose, my cheeks, my mouth, my chin. She was smiling at me so happily that I had the urge to swear to her that we would be friends forever, that I would never do anything to cause her unhappiness, to take away what she was feeling right then. But I said nothing. I thought of how my mother's lips would curl in disgust when my father tried to kiss her. I pulled Gail to me, to kiss her again—it was the only thing I wanted to do, the only thing that could stop the pictures and questions and voices from flooding my mind.

"Don't be so rough," she said.

"I'm sorry. I—"

"It's okay. It happens. It's just that, with the cold air and all, my lips are beginning to get a little raw. No wonder, right?"

"I suppose."

She leaned back against a tree.

"Come here," she said softly. I moved to her. "Did I hurt your feelings?"

"A little."

"Will you forgive me?"

"Sure."

"I do love kissing you."

She touched her lips to mine in the gentlest way then, so that I could hardly feel them, so that, holding to each other that way for as long as we could, I ached with pleasure—so that, tickling one another with our tongues and lips and then with our fingers, it was as if we showed the depth of our passion for one another by the way in which we could restrain it.

When we walked again, she carried my gym bag, swinging it at her side as if it were a pail of berries.

"Can we be together a lot, do you think?"

"Sure."

"Sure." She paused. "I'm asking because you *are* in mourning. I'm trying to remember that. Will you have to go back to sitting *shiva* tomorrow, for example, or could we meet after school?"

"I'm not religious. We don't do any of that stuff."

"You seem angry with me for asking. Are you? I see those dark, bruised clouds—"

"Stop."

I thought of the time my father locked me in the bathroom with him when he'd lost five envelopes and one of his account books, having left them somewhere along his route. He sat on the closed toilet seat and screamed at me to beat him up. *C'mon, c'mon. Hit your stupid father and get it over with. Do your uncle's dirty work and then he can finish the job. C'mon already. Beat me up so maybe I'll learn to have some sense in my dumb head.* I refused. He wept. I was thirteen years old.

Somebody was trying to do him in, my father said. But why? Somebody was setting him up so that Abe would do a job on him. Abe would kill him, poke out his good eye, so why shouldn't I get started first? He took off his belt, handed it to me. I dropped it. He flushed his cigarette down the toilet, closed the lid, sat again. Each time I tried to leave he grabbed my wrists, pleaded with me to beat him up.

"It's just that I keep seeing pictures of my father," I said. "He didn't leave much. I mean, when I die I want people to feel I did more than take up space."

"What pictures do you see, David? How do you remember him?"

I shrugged. "You don't know much about me," I said.

"I know enough."

"No you don't. I won't be good for you. You're making a mistake."

"Look," she said, pressing close. "I know about your uncle and about what your father's job was. You're not your uncle and you're not your father. I know what my parents will think about my being with you, all right? But I also know *you*. I know that you're a good person, no matter what you think. I—"

"What's the matter?"

"I don't know. I'm just getting sloppy all of a sudden. I do that sometimes. I'm just so damned happy to be with you is all, and I guess I don't want to think about anything else—your family or mine or what other people will think of us or any of that Romeo and Juliet stuff, even if it's the script we seem to be living in." She sniffed, kept talking. "And I guess for a second I had my doubts too. When you talked of your father I could see mine, puffing on his damned pipe in our living room, and how much pleasure I'd get standing up to him and my mother about seeing you, and how they would take it as a typical act of rebellion on my part, of how I need to oppose their *values*, and of how I'll have to go into a whole song-and-dance with my therapist, and oh God, David, but it all seems so lousy and boring in prospect that all I want to do is cry."

And she did. I didn't know what to say or do, so I just let her nuzzle her wet face against me. I led her to a dark spot, under a different tree, away from the streetlights.

Maybe Abe would go easier on him, my father said, if he found out I'd beaten him up first. But when Abe came, my father let me out of the bathroom without any fuss. Abe was gentle. He told my father he wouldn't do anything to him for losing the envelopes and the book. He told my father to unlock the door and come out so that they could talk together reasonably. If I hadn't met Gail, I wondered, would I be angrier with Abe? Would I have spent the evening hating him? It wasn't his fault that other men were cowards. Sure. But what was I going to do about the fact that for the rest of my life the only basketball I would ever play would probably be in the schoolyard? What happened to people over a lifetime if they couldn't do the things they loved? Because I agreed with what Abe had once said to me, that he was my uncle and that there was no way I would ever be free of that fact—that it was nobody's fault, but it was so—did that mean that I would be able to give up my hopes and my dreams? Would I ever be able to think only of the life I would actually have, of things the way they were? The questions tumbled through my head, one after the other, and I wanted to give them to Gail —to voice them—to have her comfort me and tell me that it was all right to be confused and frightened, that it was all right for me to hope and to dream and to wonder.

"Thanks," she said, when I handed her my handkerchief. "We can be good friends too, don't you think? If—"

"If what?"

"I don't know. I'm just talking. I'm just very upset."

I kissed her eyes, her mouth. I licked salt from her cheeks. We walked to her home without saying anything else. At her door she said she wouldn't invite me in because she didn't want to ruin things. I wouldn't think she was ashamed of me, would I? It was just that she wanted what had been ours to remain ours. She didn't want it smothered under a bunch of introductions and false small-talk.

"It's okay," I said. "Really. I'd do the same, if you were walking me to my door."

She laughed, kissed her fingertips, touched them to my lips. I heard a clicking sound and turned sideways, imagined that Ellen was walking along the street, tapping a long white cane in front of her. I closed my eyes, tried to recall what she had looked like. The clicking faded, stopped.

"What is it?"

"I was thinking of your sister—wondering what I'd feel if we met now. Do you mind?"

"You're lovely, David." She held to me. "Do I mind? Sure I mind. But I'm glad you told me. Only listen. Would you promise me something?"

"Yes."

"Would you promise to try never thinking that there's poison inside you?"

"I'll try."

"And could you do one other thing for me?"

"Yes."

"Would you call me in the morning, before school?"

"If you want."

"Just so I'll be sure this all happened. I won't keep you on long. All you have to do is say hello. It would be important to me."

"I'll call."

We heard sounds, from behind the door. Ellen? Gail grabbed me and kissed me very quickly, very hard, then shoved me away.

"Go now. Hurry—"

7

WHEN I CAME into the kitchen the next morning Abe was already there, sitting at the table, my mother's hand on top of his, the two of them laughing together so easily and happily that I wanted, at first, to disappear. A copy of *The Brooklyn Eagle* lay next to the toaster, open to the sports section.

"Sorry about the game," Abe said.

My mother kissed me, touched my lower lip with her finger.

"Did somebody hit you there? Your lips look all bruised—"

"I heard that during the game people made some nasty remarks," Abe said. "You shouldn't listen to other people. You know that, don't you?"

"Yes."

I sat. My mother put a glass of orange juice in front of me. Abe wore the same double-breasted gray pinstripe suit he'd worn to my father's funeral.

"I thought it might be good for you to get away from things for a day," he said. "I have to get out of town and I stopped by to see if you wanted to come along."

"Sure."

"It'll be nice," my mother said. "My two favorite men going off by themselves together."

"You don't mind being left alone?"

She kissed me, said something to Abe about how thoughtful and sweet I was, then went back to the stove to make me bacon and eggs, to fry my toast in the bacon grease, the way I liked. The phone rang. My mother answered, raised her eyebrows, said it was for me.

"It's a girl."

My heart bounced.

"Davey?"

"Yes."

"This is Regina. I'm sorry to call you like this and I hope it don't make trouble, but Tony was afraid to call himself, in case the wrong person answered. He asked me to call you and find out if you're okay, after yesterday."

"I'm okay. What do you want?"

"Just to give you Tony's message. He said if you'd like to get together, just the two of you—away from everybody—that I should arrange things, for where you two could meet."

"Forget it. I'm going with my uncle today."

"All right. I'll tell him. And Davey?"

"Yes?"

"As long as I got you on the phone I wanted to tell you, for myself, that I'm real sorry about your father. I know how it feels, with my mother dying last year and my father sick a lot with his lungs. I mean, I'm sorry."

"Sure."

"Also that I'm glad you keep telling Tony he should go to college someday. I tell him the same thing all the time and he tells me I'm crazy. But he listens to you, I think."

"Sure."

"I get the feeling you can't talk. Your uncle must be there."

"Yes."

"I'm sorry, Davey. I really am. About the game and your father and things. Don't hold things against Tony, though, okay? I mean, he tries as hard as he can. I think he'd like to be your friend still, no matter what."

"Sure," I said, and hung up.

My mother rolled her eyes. I was wary, tight. I tried not to think of Gail. I tried not to remember how I'd felt the night before. What good would that do me now? My mother liked to joke about how the girls were all after me but that I was their silent one too, she supposed. Abe said nothing. Could he guess that the call was from Tony? Would he grill me about it later on? Abe and Fasalino had been at peace for years, but none of us believed it would last forever. The only thing Fasalino understands is motion, Abe had said. He thinks motion is progress. When his organization stops moving he thinks it's dying. My mother caressed my cheek with the back of her hand, said that it would do all of us good for me to be away for a day, that she had been saying to Abe that what she wanted most of all, after the last few days, was just to be left alone.

"Sometimes I dream about getting away all by myself," she said, setting down my bacon and eggs and toast. "Do you know what I mean? I dream about going to some faraway place—not California, I gave up on that a long time back—but just somewhere where the sun shines all the time and it's like I still got my whole life ahead of me."

"It can be arranged," Abe said.

"Do you think your mother's crazy to have a dream like that?"

"No."

"If we don't have dreams, then what do we got?"

"I told you before, Evie, I'd like to treat you and Davey to a real vacation if you'd let me. You deserve it."

"Nah." She waved his offer away. "I know you mean well, but what I'm talking about ain't some hotel in Miami or Havana. What I want is to be like on a beautiful ocean liner where nobody knows you and nobody knows nothing about you and everything in your life is brand new—that it can all still happen. Where nobody can phone you or send you letters or be ringing your doorbell." She touched my hand. "Your father, with his brain, he used to talk about these giant ships that would go back and forth across the ocean someday, that would take maybe ten or twenty thousand people at a time, and I don't mean rich people or poor people or immigrants but just plain people like us. He talked about how there would be these enormous cafeterias and giant movie theaters and lots of classrooms—they could let schoolteachers go for free, see, if they gave classes for an hour a day—and sleeping rooms like dormitories in colleges. He worked out all the arithmetic, about how big the ship would have to be and how many people they'd have to carry and how many years it would take for the companies to make a profit. I kept telling him to write it down in a letter to one of the big shipping outfits. He had a terrific brain when he wanted to, your father."

"I thought I'd take Davey to meet Mr. Rothenberg," Abe stated. "It's where I'm going today."

"No!"

My mother stood, backed up against the refrigerator, hands crossed at her throat, pulling her robe tight.

"Mr. Rothenberg sends his condolences and asked if he could meet Sol's son, if he could meet Momma's grandson."

"No, Abe. Please! We should leave the children out of these things. I mean, did they ask to be born?"

"No, Evie. But they were, and if you're born into this world, like it or not, there seems to be an admission price."

"Listen, Davey." My mother turned to me. Her voice was soft and sweet, but her eyes were large and crazy. "Just make believe Abe never said nothing, okay? Listen to your mother for once, because this is the way it all starts, see? Listen to your mother. Maybe there's an admission price. Sure. But if you pay once, why should you keep paying your whole life long?"

"Mr. Rothenberg is an old man."

"Oh he ain't a bad man, Davey," my mother said, taking my hands in hers. "I ain't saying that. Nobody was good to us like he was good to us once upon a time, only don't get started, all right? Stay home with Momma today. You stay with Momma and keep the neighbors away— tell them I got one of my migraines so we can be alone here together, just the two of us. Please, darling?"

"You're still upset because of Sol," Abe said. "The boy said he wants to come with me. Right, Davey?"

"Yes."

My mother drew back from me. "Sure," she said. "Sure. Only I'll tell you something else I've been thinking about that I didn't want to say, but maybe with the phone call he got before, maybe it's time I said what's on my mind, because do you know who I pity most of all? I pity any girl who gets stuck on him, that's who. You know what this one will do if he ever catches her with another guy. He'll kill her."

"You're talking crazy," Abe said. "Stop."

"Sure. Go off with your uncle and let Mr. Rothenberg suck you in the same way he did Abe, and when you got money spilling from your pockets and a bunch of floozies reaching in with their dirty hands—"

"I said to stop."

"Who's gonna make me, huh? You, big shot? Or one of your goons? So why shouldn't the boy get started with the killing and the rest of it? The truth is that all you were waiting for was till Sol was gone. Didn't I know it? Didn't I know all along you'd start up with Davey even more once Sol was out of the way?"

Abe grabbed her wrist. She pulled away. "Only what am I made of, after all these years—stone? What do you want from me, Abe, huh? What do you want from my life? Can you answer me that?"

"I want you to be happy."

She laughed. "Tell me another one. Sure. Tell me another one." She walked in circles, from the window to the sink, from the sink to the window. "Am I made of stone or am I made of stone? First they take away Momma and now they take away Sol and in between Poppa's dead for you and you're dead for him and for twenty years guess who's in the middle? Little Evie. So how do you think I felt the whole war, waiting every day for a telegram from the President telling me they took you away too and I could put my star in the window if I wanted to. . . ."

I imagined Gail entering our apartment, watching my mother. Would she laugh? Would she cry? Would she embrace my mother? What would she feel towards me? I thought of calling Regina, of apologizing to her for how severe I'd been.

"So if the telegram didn't come, maybe the phone call will, right? When the phone rings, do I know if it's the police or if it's one of your goons so he can tell me you got caught in a bad accident like Spanish Louie or Avie? Ha! You think I don't know all about that, that everyone in the neighborhood don't know. Sure. I know where it all begins, Abe —only where does it end, can you answer me that? Where does it end?"

She put the telephone receiver to her ear.

"Hello? . . . Yes, this is Eva Voloshin. . . . What? You got news for me about my big-shot brother Abe Litvinov, but you need somebody to identify the body down at the morgue? . . . Listen, as soon as I put on some makeup I'll be there, only as long as I got you on the line, maybe you can tell me how many years you think I got left with my son Davey . . . ?"

Abe took the phone from her hand, put it back in its cradle.

"You made your point, Evie. Now cut it out."

"Why? I didn't cry enough already?"

"You cried enough," I said.

"Wise guy. Now we'll get our two cents from the peanut gallery, yeah? On how I did the wrong thing after his father died, that I didn't cry with him. You think I don't know you hold a grudge against me for that? You think I don't know how you can't wait to get out of this house—with Abe today, and then in another year it'll be thanks a lot, Momma, but goodbye and good luck and I'm off to college. And in between if some nice little tramp should come along and open her fuzzy little purse for you—"

"Leave the boy alone."

"What's the matter, he can't fight his own battles?"

Abe grabbed her by the chin, forced her to look at him.

"When we needed help, Mr. Rothenberg was the only one, and don't you forget it. Don't forget what they would have done to Momma if not for him. You remember that and then you think twice before you open your mouth to the boy."

"Whatever you say." She glanced at me. "Whatever he wants." She pushed him away. "You want to be with your uncle, darling? You go with your uncle. You want to get killed now when you're young? You go get killed now. It will save us grief later. You want to know if I care anymore, if I'll be here after you're both gone, you send me a telegram, yeah? You want me not to open my mouth no more, I won't open my mouth."

She left the kitchen.

"Was she always like this?" I asked a few seconds later. "I mean, when you were growing up together, was she like this then?"

"No."

I heard her grunting, behind me. I turned. She stood in the doorway, the bottom half of her face covered with adhesive tape. Abe tried to laugh. My mother went to the phone, wrote a message on the note pad: "I CAN'T OPEN MY MOUTH. NOW ARE YOU HAPPY?"

Abe stood up and I was scared for a second that he was going to tear the tape from her face, but instead he just put his arm around her and kissed her cheek, told her that she'd made her point, that she could say anything she wanted to us, that we both loved her. She cocked her head to the side. Did she know how much he loved her, that he still loved her like nobody else did, like when they were kids?

We were on the highway outside the city, heading upstate, before I remembered that I'd forgotten to telephone Gail. I tried to imagine the inside of her house—carpeted rooms, expensive furniture, bookcases, porcelain vases, thick draperies, painting and prints on the walls—and Gail walking around, getting ready for school, eating breakfast, watching the phone. Why hadn't I kept my promise? I imagined us in the rain, her hair rubbing against my chin. We kissed. I told her how sorry I was that I'd forgotten to call. She smiled. Was it really possible that two people could make one another so happy, so soon, merely by being together, by touching?

"Will we be back late tonight?"

"Why? Got a date?"

"No. Not really."

"Got a girl?"

"Sort of. I don't know. How could you tell? I mean, the call wasn't from her this morning."

"I know."

"I met somebody I like, though. That's true."

"Is she worthy of you?"

"Is she what?"

We laughed. I looked out the window, at trees, houses, barns, and I felt easy suddenly, as if I could ask him all the questions I'd always wanted to ask him, as if—it had been the same with Gail the night before—there was nothing that two people who liked each other could not say to one another.

"Did you have a girlfriend when you were my age?"

"Me? Sure. I always liked the women, Davey."

"With your hat down that way, you look like Robert Taylor a little bit, except that your mouth is larger." I stopped. I thought of the picture I'd drawn of him and wondered if he still had it. His lips were full the way Gail's were. Could I draw her picture and give it to her for her birthday? Would I be able to do her portrait from memory? "Why did you marry aunt Lillian? Can I ask that?"

"Sure." He laughed. "That's an easy one, Davey, because the short answer is that when I was young I was what your mother said you're going to be: a sucker for women." He touched his hair. "Sure. I liked skirts, and in my business that was a liability. The way I looked at it was this, see: you have a choice with women—you can get to know what they're all like by knowing lots of them a little bit, or by knowing one of them well. Does that answer your question?"

"But you don't love Lillian, do you?"

"No."

"Did you ever love her. I mean the way—"

"—the way your father loved your mother, for example? I doubt it. It's too far back to remember. Lillian is good for me, though. She protects me. By sticking with her and getting to know her well, life is safer. She enabled me to develop a distaste for other women. She cured me."

"But that's terrible."

"Why?"

"I don't know. It just seems a waste—somebody like you not to have somebody to love, to love you back your whole life."

"Love isn't everything. I had enough to last me a few more years." He reached over, touched my hair. "You're a sweet kid, Davey. A real romantic. Your mother would be happy if she could hear you talking like this." He nodded. "But I'm glad you have a girlfriend. It's good to have somebody at your age, somebody you can stick it into when you get the urge."

"It's not like that."

"It never is at first."

We were quiet. Was he being this way on purpose, trying to protect me by making me hate him?

"You said that just to hurt me, didn't you?" I moved closer to him. He turned his Army ring so that sunlight bounced off the red stone. "Why is it you have to get so cold and mean sometimes? My mother says it's not your fault, that you weren't always this way, that you had no choice."

"Not true," he said quickly. "We always have choices." He licked his lips, waited, and when he spoke again it was as if he'd said the same words to himself, over and over, a thousand times: "The rich have more choices than the poor, and the strong have more choices than the weak, and the powerful have more choices than those without power. But we all have choices. Always."

"That's not true," I said. "I didn't choose to have you for an uncle."

To my surprise Abe showed no anger. Instead he smiled, reached across, ruffled my hair. We turned off the highway onto a two-lane road.

"You're a smart boy, Davey. Sure. They'll try to visit the sins of the uncles on the nephews, right? For a while—a year maybe—the scouts won't come sniffing at your door, but don't worry about it. One way or the other, you'll have your chance."

"How?"

"When things blow over. When the investigations end without them pinning anything on me or Mr. Rothenberg. We're clean, Davey. We have better things to do with our time than hang around locker rooms."

Could I believe him? Did I *want* to believe him? He tipped his hat back, touched his left jacket pocket with his right hand, as if to feel for a gun. But there was no gun there, I knew. He seemed very happy, and I wondered for an instant if this wasn't so because he was already thinking about the strings he could pull in order to get me into college—because he was already imagining talking with Mr. Rothenberg about me and what deals they could make to fix things.

"We'll be at Mr. Rothenberg's in about twenty-five minutes. You'll like his house."

"Do you mind my asking questions?"

"You have more?"

"Lots."

"Such as—?"

"What things were like when you and my mother were kids. What you feel about the colleges not talking to me because of you—because of the scandals. Why you always turn your ring around on your finger when you get upset. Why you won't speak to your father. Why he hates you the way you hate him. What Mr. Rothenberg did for you and Mom. What he stopped people from doing to your mother . . ."

In my head, Gail was smiling at me, encouraging me to go on, telling me that life was too short *not* to say the things we wanted to the people we cared about. I gazed out the window. In front of a small run-down gas station a young boy, sitting in a wheelbarrow, waved to me.

"I want to know things," I said. "Sometimes I want to know everything, Uncle Abe! I want to know why things happened, why you're the way you are, how you got to have the life you have. Sometimes I think you don't want anyone to know what you feel, though. That you want to shut everybody out."

"Sometimes I do."

"But it matters to me—what you feel. When you were overseas I used to wonder a lot about what you were thinking and feeling. Were you scared?"

"Sometimes."

"Are you ever afraid now—since the war ended, I mean?"

"Not much, though I don't like pain. I've always been frightened of physical pain if you want the truth, and yet when it's come it hasn't bothered me much. Strange. It's always been as if I could simply close a valve to the part of my brain the pain was in. Then I'd be there, as alert as I could be, and it would be as if what was happening was happening to somebody else. Does that make any sense?"

"My mother says that your father used to beat you a lot. Did he?"

"Probably."

"Probably?"

"It wasn't the pain that hurt, Davey. It was being humiliated. Degraded. All I ask for, see, is a little notice, a mild amount of respect. I thought about that a lot when I was overseas and I decided that my one wish, really, was simply to know ahead of time. I didn't want to die in my sleep or in a coma or on my knees, and I didn't want to die with a bullet in the back of my head either."

"Did you ever *want* to die?"

"No."

"I'm glad. Do you ever want to now?"

"There's not much that gives pleasure in life, Davey. Still, I figure I'll stick around. To see how you turn out, right?" He touched my shoulder. "The truth is, I was pretty happy when I was over there and could kill a few Krauts. I felt good when I was able to save some of my boys. I was sorry the war didn't last longer. I still write to some of them."

"To the guys in your platoon?"

"No. Why would I do a thing like that? I write to the women who lost sons or husbands or brothers."

"But why? Why does that mean so much to you, when nothing else—"

"Because I couldn't save them all."

"But how could you? I mean, why would you think you were supposed to? I don't understand."

"Sometimes I don't either."

"Do you think of me that way too sometimes? As if you're responsible for my life, as if you don't know whether or not you'll be able to save me?"

"They were going to throw acid in Momma's face. That's the answer to your question. They were going to throw acid in Momma's face. They were going to teach our father a lesson, but a guy warned me and I went to see Mr. Rothenberg and asked for help and he told me that he would take care of things and he kept his word and it never happened. All right?"

"That's the whole story? That's all I get?"

"You are persistent, aren't you?"

"Sure." I thought of Gail. "I want to know, Uncle Abe. I want to know everything I don't know."

To my surprise, Abe was smiling at me as if he was pleased to see this side of me—how much I could talk, how much I cared about his life. I tried to look at him as easily and lovingly as I could, so that he wouldn't change his mind, so that he wouldn't become frightened. I waited. I wished we weren't so close to Mr. Rothenberg's house because I felt that if only we could keep on driving—just the two of us, away from the city, away from our apartment and families and our other lives—he would have felt free to tell me everything.

He touched his jacket pocket again, nervously. When I'd asked him once about why he didn't carry a gun, I remembered, he had answered by saying that there were many stupid people in the world who thought that if they killed him, they could sit in his seat and have his power and live his life. I'm the only one who can lead my life, he said.

"Your mother was a very beautiful woman, wasn't she," I offered.

"My mother was a very beautiful woman," he said. "Sure, Davey. Sure she was." He touched my hair again, as if to reassure himself that I was actually in the car with him. "She was so beautiful that men and women used to come to our house from all over the city—rich men and women—just to see her face. Can you imagine?" He smiled at me in a way that told me he was happy to be answering my question, to be talking about her. "When your mother and I were kids growing up on the Lower East Side, our father had a small fur store on Howard Street where people would come to buy their coats. We lived in back of the store, in two small rooms—plus there was the room our father worked in, where he did all his work—the sewing and cleaning and tipping and dyeing and pointing and repairs—and we had half the cellar downstairs too, which the landlord rented to my father for storage.

"There was a gorgeous silk curtain from China I loved to stare at— blues and reds and silver and gold threads, with birds and flowers and mountain peaks covered with snow—and it hung between our apartment and the storefront. Momma and Poppa slept in the kitchen near the stove, see, and Evie and I slept in the one bedroom, which had no windows, and downstairs Poppa had this enormous kind of icebox— bigger than our whole apartment—where he kept coats stored for customers in the summer. Cold storage. That's what they called it. People would bring him their coats in the spring, or he'd go around and pick them up and he'd keep them there through the summer, then take them out in the fall and get them ready for the winter. He built the room himself out of sheets of tin and wooden slats, with chambers between the inner and outer walls for the slabs of ice and sawdust, and with drains to let the melted water run off. He could make a fur coat from scratch—scraping and soaking and fleshing and tanning and stretching and drumming and dressing and bleaching and the hundred other operations the skins had to go through before they became coats. When I was a kid he'd show me the whole process, his part of it, let me use his knives and emery wheels, let me try to get the thin membrane of flesh away from the pelt without cutting into the fur, let me pluck the top hairs of the beavers and seals so we could get at the soft underfur. Sure. In the summertime Evie and I would go down and stay inside the room, sucking on ice chips—I'd knock them off with a screwdriver—and we'd put the chips in paper cups and pour blackberry syrup on them, and speculate on how much money you had to have to be able to afford the sables and ermines and minks, the astrakhans and sealskins and the different kinds of foxes.

"Evie would model the coats for me the way Momma modeled them for customers—that was what she did, see—and I'd act as if I was some rich guy from Park Avenue, tapping on the floor with a cane, and I'd keep making her take off one coat and put on another, and sometimes she would sit next to me and act like one of the ladies who was buying the coats. A lot of rich German Jews bought their coats from our father, and I hated them most because they acted as if they thought their crap didn't stink. Mostly we'd make fun of them. I'd mimic the way Poppa would whisper to us, as if revealing state secrets. 'Now children, I want you to remember that these are *very* wealthy people.' And when he'd come to the word 'very,' he'd always close his eyes, and suck in his cheeks.

"I liked being down below with the furs when it was real hot, so I could cool off, pet the coats, run my hands over the silk linings, run my fingers across the monograms on the inside labels. He worked hard on those because he said it was the mark of ownership that mattered most to his customers. Evie and I would talk about what it would be like to be able to buy whatever you wanted, to have servants, to be able to go wherever you wanted in the world if you suddenly just felt like it. The world exists for money. Sure. Wasn't that what all of us believed then? Me and Evie and Momma and Poppa and everyone in our neighborhood? That the world existed to serve and protect the people with money? When there was trouble on the street, between a guy dressed fancy and a bum, who did the cop grab first?

"Upstairs, whenever the customers would come, Poppa would seat them next to the front window so that the neighbors could see, and he would get them something to drink, tea or wine or sherry or Turkish coffee. He had special engraved silver trays and little demitasse cups and saucers edged in gold, and sometimes if we were dressed right he'd let me and Evie serve them. He taught us to bow and curtsey and how to answer questions politely and how not to look goggle-eyed at their clothes and jewels. He would have long conversations with his customers before he showed them coats, see—making fun of how poor and stupid everyone in the neighborhood was, telling them about the other wealthy people who'd been in and what they were buying. He had these fancy leather-bound books with photographs of models in coats, and he'd open them and, while he showed them the photos, he'd ask about trips they'd taken and about their houses and then—"

Abe stopped and blinked, as if surprised to find that he'd come to this part of his story. His eyes seemed to frost over, to go dead.

"He was just teasing them, though, because what they were there for, see, was for the moment when he'd stand, put his cup or glass down on the tray, and clap his hands sharply so that Momma would come out of the back room for the first time, wearing one of the fur coats. She'd push the curtain aside very tentatively, clutch the silk almost as if she needed it for balance, then let it slide between her fingers slowly so that the creases disappeared, and step forward toward the customers. And the crazy thing was that she loved it all. Why, Davey? Why did she love it so much? Can you tell me that?"

I didn't try to answer his question, and I knew he didn't expect me to. I imagined Abe letting me off in front of the house later and instead of going upstairs I was going to the corner candy store, calling Gail. I imagined us walking together along Bedford Avenue, near Brooklyn College, and I was telling her the story Abe was now telling me. I was feeling her press my hand when I came to the sad parts, and I was hearing her tell me that what we had to remember most of all was that it wasn't just a story, that it was their *lives*, that these things had actually happened, that here was a difference between a person's life and the story of that life.

"Momma would sit in the kitchen by the stove, not doing anything at all except getting the tea and stuff ready for him and chewing at her fingernails until she heard him clap for her. Then she'd light up." He laughed. "I'd forgotten," he said, turning toward me. "The way she'd hold her nails up to the lamp to see through them. She didn't really chew at them, just kind of nibbled at the air around them, clicking her teeth lightly while she did. Evie and I teased her about this way she had of biting her nails and not biting them. But she doted on him and did whatever he wanted, mostly. Except for his customers she rarely got dressed up fancy. He bought all her clothes for her—he'd bring them home in big boxes and take them out of the tissue paper very carefully and she would make a big fuss over how good he was to her. She only wore the clothes when she modeled for customers, though. It was crazy. You're like a diamond in the mud, he would say to her, and they'd both laugh. He had one extraordinary Russian Crown sable—it was the most expensive coat there was, a deep blue-black like you've never seen— that he would have her model only once in a while and that he never sold. It was hers, and he would promise each customer that if he ever found another like it, that customer would have first chance to pur-chase. Momma only wore the coat in the house.

"We weren't at all poor, see—he did well enough to move us out of the neighborhood into a snazzy place uptown if he'd wanted to, but he knew it was better for his business to stay where we were. He was shrewd, all right. He knew what kind of image gave the rich people their kicks. The thing that seemed crazy to me, though, was that he himself used to dress like the rich men who bought from him—in silk shirts and derbies and fancy underwear and gaiters and this incredible black broad-cloth coat he had, fur-lined with nutria. Until the middle of the nine-teenth century, see, all the fur coats had the fur on the inside, and even after they discovered a way to remove the coarse guard hairs so the furs would look beautiful on the outside, the men's coats kept the fur on the inside. Close to the vest, right? 'My own Beau Brummell,' Momma used to call him, because he was the one, not Momma, who spent hours getting dressed, fixing himself in front of mirrors with tweezers and creams and lotions and pomades and colognes and all kinds of crap. And she'd smile and help him. Jesus, it made me sick, Davey, the way he carried on, the way he treated her—the way she worshipped him and did everything for him, and then he went and . . ." His voice trailed off, his knuckles tightened on the steering wheel. "All I'd dream about some-times would be the day I'd be big enough to take him, okay? To bash his perfumed head against the stove, to knock his shiny teeth through the back of his throat, to break his manicured fingers one at a time, to—" He laughed suddenly, sharply. "But he wasn't the one, was he?"

"The one?"

"The one I got my chance on." Abe licked his lips. "Okay. You asked me, right? So I'm telling you. He wasn't the one I had to do my first job on. Sure." He shrugged slightly, seemed to relax. "Anyway, it all seemed very real back then—how small the rooms were and how much I hated him and how beautiful Momma was. She was a tiny woman. Even before she got sick at the end and went down to under sixty pounds, she was tiny—she never weighed more than ninety, ninety-five pounds. About Little Benny's size, if you think about it, only she had these giant brown eyes with long dark lashes, and a sweet set of lips—what we called a bow mouth in those days—and when she'd wrap herself up in one of those elegant minks or sables or silver foxes, or, best of all, in one of the beautiful black capes or long evening coats, she'd take your breath away. Like glowing coals, my father would say to his clients when they remarked on Momma's eyes. Like glowing coals.

"If Evie and I were around after school or on weekends, we'd wait with Momma in the kitchen, and then when Poppa came in and told her which coat to put on we'd take off down the cellar, out the back door, into the alley and back around to the front so we could be there at the window when Momma made her entrance. She was terrific, Davey. When she'd come out of the back, pushing the curtain aside like some timid schoolgirl wearing store-bought clothes for the first time, and turn and pose and look back over her shoulder shyly and smile for the clients, it was incredible. Magic. And when she'd glance over at Poppa and get a wink from him, to show her she was doing fine, her face would glow. I never saw anything like it. I—"

He looked at me, as if puzzled.

"Tell me Davey—is there anything else in the world like the smile of a beautiful woman? Is there anything else in the world like a smile that says just to you that you're the most important guy in the whole world, that you're the only thing that matters, that all the love and tenderness behind that smile is for you, that—"

I said nothing because I didn't really think he wanted an answer. I tried to see Gail's face, smiling at me, but instead I saw my mother, sitting on my bed while I slept, staring down at me. *Do you know what my trouble is, Davey? My trouble is that I love you too much. It's no good to love somebody too much. . . .*

"She smiled like that for Poppa, and when he wanted her to she did it for his customers, and afterwards when me and Evie would go back around and in again through the cellar and she'd come into the kitchen and ask us, 'How was I?' and we'd tell her that she was wonderful, she'd hug us and kiss us and smile at us in the same way, and give us each a piece of her special chocolate, the ones with sweet, dark cherries inside that she kept hidden and would eat whenever she knew she'd helped Poppa sell a coat. She'd let us sit on her lap, and when she held me— this was when I was really little—I tried to touch her hair and curl it around my fingers and tug on it so that she'd make believe she wanted to bite my fingers. Her hair was dark and curly, like yours and mine— like the astrakhans, only softer. She liked to tell me about the softest and most fragile of the lamb pelts—the ones from a newborn or one-day old Caracul lamb or sometimes from those born prematurely, that came in a watered silk pattern—what we called *moiré* then—and it was nice

to sit on her lap and let my hand go back and forth from the fur of a
coat to the softness of her hair and then back again.

"She didn't always smile right away, of course. Sometimes she'd take
on this cold, sophisticated I-don't-give-a-damn look—she and Poppa
had a set of signals for how she performed—and once in a while she'd
go through a whole showing without smiling at all. Evie and I tried to
figure out their signals and what he made her save the special smiles for,
but who knows? She looked like some of those gorgeous movie stars
from the silent films, like Janet Gaynor if you could have seen her then,
only darker and more fragile, I guess. She wanted to be an actress too,
did you know that? Did Evie ever tell you that?"

"No. But my father used to say that she should have been one—*my*
mother, I mean. Like this morning, with the tape over her mouth—"

"Sure. Because if she had—" He stopped. "Anyway, that was what
she wanted. To be an actress up on the stage, with a bouquet of flowers
in her arms and hundreds of people clapping for her, and sometimes if
she got too upset about how my father wouldn't let her—he'd pull the
shades on the store window and give her a coat and gesture to the
showroom as if he was Jacob Astor himself, and say, 'Here, my darling
—here is the only theater you will ever need! Here is where your star
will shine!' But even in the old country, see—in Odessa, where they
came from—she wanted to be an actress. She'd recite lots of poems and
parts to us in Russian. Who knows why? Who knows where these things
get started, Davey? Sometimes I used to think that if I could have known
her when *she* was a girl, the way I knew Evie—the way I knew you—if I
could have spent a day or two with her when she was growing up—if I
could have been there invisibly—that I could have understood everything. Do you ever think that way? That all you need is a few minutes
or hours in somebody's home—to see how things were when they were
growing up—and you'd understand them forever after?"

He didn't wait for my answer. "I still think that way sometimes," he
said. "Whenever I need to figure out some guy I'm dealing with, what I
do is imagine the way he was when he was five years old, say, or eight or
nine. I imagine that—I send the guy back in time to what he was like
hanging around some small apartment, and what his face looked like
when he watched his mother and father speaking to him, what he felt,
and when I do that it helps me to know how to act. I saw it all overseas
too—saw it proved—when guys were dying, when they came back in on
stretchers, when the shit was running down their legs. Because the two
words that came out were always the same: 'God' or 'Momma.' Momma
most of all. Please Momma, save me. Please Mommy. Mommy.
Mommy. Please." He glanced at me. "It's a good thing to remember,
Davey—no matter who somebody is, no matter how rich and powerful,

that once upon a time they were just little boys who weighed maybe forty or fifty pounds and who wanted their mothers to smile at them and to hold them." He shrugged. "Though I have to admit that in my business I've come across a few characters, through the years, who might be different."

He laughed, as if he'd told himself a joke. "Oh yeah, Davey, I have come across a few who might not be like the rest of us. Pretty scary. To look in a guy's eyes and feel he could just as easily never have had a mother or father. Turkish Sammy is that way. It makes him useful to me for the work he might be called on to perform one day soon." Abe clicked his teeth together, lightly. Was Abe taking me to Mr. Rothenberg because they were expecting trouble from Fasalino? The word around the neighborhood was that the Italians had not had anything to do with the basketball fixes—Italians don't love sports the way you crazy Jews do, Tony said to me—but that men like Abe and Mr. Rothenberg and Harry Gross were trying to finger them for it with the D.A. Why? "Anyway," Abe went on, "Momma dreamt of being an actress—that's the story I started out to tell you—but in those days for a Jewish girl to be an actress was like her wanting to be a prostitute. I never got the whole story straight, but the best I could figure was that in Odessa he made some kind of deal with her father to marry her so that she wouldn't run away and join a traveling show. Crazy, huh? To try to imagine all that. Her father managed forests for a rich Gentile, and she was his youngest daughter, his favorite—they had eleven altogether, and three more who died young—and from the time she was born, when her old man was in his sixties, everyone doted on her for her beauty. Her father made out okay for himself, managing the land, and he had a good business going on the side, selling liquor to the peasants who lived there. And sometimes he'd go around banging on trees with a hammer.

"Jesus! I hadn't remembered that for a long time! That was the story she'd tell about going around with him when she was a girl, and do you know why he banged on trees? Because the violin-makers would come to the forests to pick out trees for their instruments, and he had the knack of knowing which ones would be best just from banging on them with hammers and putting his ear to the bark and listening to them vibrate. Sure. She told me and Evie lots of stories about her father, about all the things he could do—how he played the fiddle and sang like an opera star and rode a horse like a Cossack and danced like a prince and how all the women followed him around and left letters for him in tree trunks. Her own mother died when she was eight and he never married again, and she met Poppa when she was fourteen years old and married him two months later. So what chance did she ever have? Can you tell me that?

"All he really was, see, was a small-time gangster who supplied her father with some of the liquor he needed and who also went into the forests to get furs from the peasants. Which wasn't legal either. You ask your mother for details—she's closer to him than I ever used to be. She made her choice too, right? The two of them probably liked each other and went to the same whore houses together, for all I know. Sure. They were the kind of men I always classify as the ones who are born wanting to be big shots. That's the way it is, if you ask me—that some men are born wanting more than anything to grow up so that everybody else in the world thinks they're important. It's what drives them, right? So Momma tried to run off one last time, and when they dragged her back, the story is that she was shouting out words in the street—from *Uncle Vanya*, that she'd been secretly memorizing—and she didn't make it out of Odessa and Poppa offered to marry her to keep her from such a life and her father agreed and it happened. Okay?

"And then they came to America. He took a lot of money off the old man from what I can figure. The old man adored her—who wouldn't? —and he wanted most of all to protect her from harm. He figured Poppa was the guy for the job and in some ways he wasn't all wrong. Poppa spent his life protecting her from harm, and from everything else too, pretty much. There were a lot of gangsters in Odessa then, and Poppa came to the old man one day after they were married and said he was in bad trouble with a guy who was bigger than either of them, that they'd caught him in some kind of double-cross having to do with the liquor— the old man could pay them off and they wouldn't touch *him*, but that if Poppa didn't leave they would kill him and my mother. The old man believed him, and who knows, maybe he was even telling the truth. All I know is they got on a ship and came to America, and Poppa picked up right where he left off.

"Most of the coats he sold, see, were stolen goods. At night I'd watch him at work—he didn't seem to mind—removing labels from coats and putting his own labels in, or dyeing the skins, or bleaching them, or feathering in new colors with a turkey feather, or pointing the pelts by adding hairs, or changing the styles completely so the owners would never recognize them—making them longer or shorter, or putting more padding in the shoulders, or taking out padding, or changing the collars or the sleeves or the linings. On the mink and the sable and the marten and lynx and most of the stuff he dealt in, the pelts were so tiny, and you needed so many of them to make a coat, and the insides were hidden with silk and taffeta and satin, that nobody knew how to trace the stuff once he'd worked it over. He'd take mink coats and slash the pelts into narrow diagonal strips and resew them into longer shapes, into what they called let-out mink in those days. And sometimes, if he got worried, he'd just ship the stuff out of town—he took less money that way, but it was safer. An artist, Momma called him, and she'd sit next to him for hours, him passing her furs, her stitching or brushing or feathering, or putting the furs on horsehide cushions and tapping them with little canes to soften them up, and her telling us that no matter how long she lived or how many times he showed her what he did, she would never have his gift.

"He had a good racket, all right, and after a while he didn't even wait for the coats to come in but just gave guys addresses of his clients. Sometimes he'd sell the same coat, in different incarnations, three or four times over, even sell the same skins back to the original owner. That gave him his biggest charge. When a coat would come back a third or fourth time he would stroke it and put it over his forearm and say that this was the true cat with nine lives.

"He played around with the women here too. If he got the itch, at nine in the morning even—I could always tell by how he would drink his coffee more quickly, by how much time he spent in front of the mirror, and by how, if Momma tried to touch him, to give him affection, he'd get angry with her—but if he needed it, he'd say he was going off to see a client for a few hours, and when he'd come back later he'd stink of wine and perfume and cigar smoke, and then Momma would stand up to him and they'd go at each other for a while. Once she threw boiling water at him, but it missed his face and only did in one of his shirts and scalded his arm some. Another time she got her nails into his cheeks and I felt pretty good about that. But he was too strong for her mostly and whatever it was he had, she seemed to want it too much.

"Sometimes I used to think that maybe he only felt important and loved her when he saw the way *other* people looked at her. Some things aren't worth much to people until somebody else wants it, I guess, because what happened was this: Momma finally fell in love with this little Irish guy who came to the store all the time delivering the stolen coats to Poppa. His name was Dennis Mooney, and Poppa used to make jokes about him because that was what he'd do all the time around Momma—he'd moon around and try to steal glances at her.

"He looked like a little jockey, or a prizefighter, only too pretty—a short, wiry guy with a shock of strawberry blond hair, fair skin and a broken nose that made him handsomer than he would have been without it—and he was no more than twenty-one or twenty-two. Momma was almost forty by then. I was nineteen, a little younger than Dennis, and Evie was twenty and working uptown as a secretary for a shirt company, where Poppa got her the job, so we weren't home as much as we used to be. I hung around with guys from the neighborhood who liked to live it up—the other Jews cursed us and prayed we wouldn't cast eyes on their daughters, right?—and their daughters spent most of their time dreaming about when we would. I liked the high life then, Davey. I liked skirts. I liked fancy clothes and fancy women. I made my money by working for Poppa's friends—driving trucks and picking up stuff and running things here and there. Prohibition was over, but there was still a lot of stuff, out of bond, that needed trafficking and nobody got hurt most of the time. Did I think of doing anything else with my life? Who knows? Momma thought I should go to some kind of school, to get something safe, but I never did well in school, even though the teachers said I had the brains. I always watched the skirts too much. I liked to get bashed on good bourbon and roll around in silk sheets and wake up the next morning and have my buddies brag to me about the crazy things I did. I had a reputation.

"Anyway, while I was dipping my stick uptown, Dennis was having a good time with Momma downtown, only we didn't know about it for a while. It turned out he wanted to be an actor and singer in vaudeville, see, and he'd get down on one knee, with Momma sitting on a chair, her hands in her lap, and he'd sing these Irish songs for her, like John McCormack, and come with scripts in his coat pocket and they'd act out the parts together and Poppa thought it was all a gas. He even had Dennis come around once or twice for his clients, and he dressed him up in a tuxedo and had him sing for them while they sipped tea. It was crazy, believe me.

"Until he caught them at it one day when he got home, before he was supposed to—Evie and I weren't there either—and he beat the guy up so bad that no woman would ever want to kiss him again, he told Momma. Afterwards he took his knives, from working on the furs—the ones he used for making let-out minks—and said that next time he'd use them on the guy's pretty face. The cops came, but Poppa had them pretty much in his pocket and they just took Dennis away to get him stitched up, and for a day or two—except for the effect on Momma—I guess we figured that was the end of it. She'd had her fling. She was heartbroken. My own idea was that she'd gotten even with him in her way, even though he caught her. Did she *want* him to catch her? Did she want him to know after all those years that she could still experience love, that she could still give herself to someone else the way she'd first given herself to him?

"He tried to cover up the way he felt by bragging to everybody about the job he did on Dennis, but he didn't fool me, and when he wasn't around I gave a lot of attention to Momma, not pushing her, but encouraging her, telling her that I could set her up in her own place, that I'd even get her together with Dennis if that was what she wanted. What did I care that she was twice his age? I never minded if things worked out crazy in this life, Davey, if the combinations went against the odds, because who ever said anything good followed the rules? Sometimes, I guess, I even figured the stranger and crazier the combination, the more likely it could make you happy. But Momma didn't want to hear me. She just sat around crying a lot and not making a move to do anything else.

"It mixed *your* mother up pretty good too. She always had a thing for Poppa, and now he went to town on her. He got her a bunch of new clothes, gave her one of his silver fox coats—a gorgeous smokey-blue one that was worth a small fortune—and took her out to restaurants a lot, giving her a sob story about how much he loved Momma, about how he'd never get over the hurt she did to him, about how he was going to change, and she lapped it up. Well. She wasn't so unlike her brother, was she? I mean, she liked the fancy clothes and I guess she liked pants the way I liked skirts.

"She and I didn't talk much then—she was ashamed of me too, I guess, because the old man made her think I was involved with Dennis, that I'd fixed the whole thing up to start with. I couldn't get through most of what was going on, to figure out what he said to her that I had to make up stories to cover, but the real truth is that there wasn't time either, because a guy I drove for, a fat Irishman named Dunn who took a shine to me, took me aside a few days later and told me that Mooney was the nephew of a big shot named O'Shea, who was Dunn's boss, and that O'Shea had hired some guys to take care of Poppa.

" 'Good,' I said. 'It'll save me the trouble.' Then—would you believe it?—this big guy put his hand on his heart and got tears in his eyes and told me they were going to get Momma, that O'Shea heard how beautiful she was and decided to teach Dennis a lesson too. O'Shea said that if Momma wasn't beautiful anymore, then she would never give any man trouble again, so he hired a guy to throw acid in Momma's face.

"That was the main story, then and now, and I didn't waste time. I went straight to Rothenberg and almost got myself killed barging in on him where he lived with all his bodyguards, but I'll get to the crucial part, which is that when he heard about what was going to happen— he'd bought coats for himself and his wife from us—he didn't hesitate. 'I like you and your mother very much, Abe,' he said, 'and I will see to it that such an atrocity does not take place.' That was all he said at first, except that he could see how shaken I was. So he put his arm around me and took me into his sitting room—he lived near where Belmont's mansion used to be then, on Fifth Avenue and 18th Street—and he asked me if I realized exactly what I was doing by putting myself in his debt. He was pleased to do me a favor, and—it might never happen, but I should be prepared—he might need to call upon me to return the favor one day. I said I understood.

"How can I explain it all to you, Davey? If Dennis hadn't hung around Momma, maybe I'd have a different life today, but he did and what happened happened, and here I am. I try never to think of the life I don't have, right? Mr. Rothenberg and I talked a long time that afternoon and we discovered that we liked each other, that we thought the same way about most things. He asked me why I free-lanced so much for the Irish and the Italians and some of the Jews who ran our section —Shapiro and Ribalow mostly—and would I consider becoming associated with him at some future date. I said I'd consider it but that I wasn't eager, and he liked that—that I deferred things, that I didn't jump at his invitation.

"Nothing happened to Momma. Two of O'Shea's men met with a bad accident in the East River, though. I didn't hear from Mr. Rothenberg for eight months, and then I got a message one day that he wanted to see me. I went. He asked me if I owned a gun. I said I didn't. He gave me a Smith and Wesson .38 and instructed me in its use. He explained very carefully how he worked and why, how he tried never to use force unless he had to because he believed that no matter how many guns you had someone would always come along with more guns and bigger guns, and how force itself didn't create power or influence.

"Could you beat everybody up? Could you kill them all? There was always somebody who could come along who was stronger. What you had to do was to be able to offer people something they couldn't get anywhere else. The brain that knew how *not* to use guns or force or threats, the brain that had a talent for persuasion, for organization— that, he said, was the most powerful weapon a man possessed. That and the imagination to think of possibilities others hadn't thought of yet. Mr. Rothenberg was big on imagination. He himself had been blessed with the brain and the imagination, he said, and he sensed that I had also. Alas, though, neither of us were named Rockefeller or Harriman or Vanderbilt or Morgan. We weren't rich German Jews like Rothschild or Belmont or Lehman. We couldn't count on the police or the Army or the politicians to advance or protect our business interests the way they could.

"He talked for a long time that day and in all the years since he never repeated what he said to me then. He was a very intelligent man—not what he is today, what's left of him—and if he hadn't been born the way he was, and a Jew, he could have gone to the top of anything, in business or government. He was mostly into gambling then, into the numbers and the horses. He had this little guy named Abbadabba Berman working for him—The Human Adding Machine, we called him—and he kept him in a back room with lots of paper, pencils, and gumdrops. Berman would go through the thousands of policy slips the runners brought in and by the time the first seven races were run he'd figure out the number on which the most money had been bet, the one they couldn't let win. Then Mr. Rothenberg would relay the information to a guy at the track where we were taking our daily number from, and the guy would make whatever adjustment was needed in the pari-mutuel handle.

Abe laughed. "I hadn't thought of him for a long time—Berman. I loved that guy. Did your father ever tell you about him?"

"No."

"He died young—younger than your father. Rothenberg kept him in this bare room where he was all scrunched over, wearing a hat, a bunch of pencils in his left hand like a quiver of arrows. Lepke had him killed a few years later, when Abbadabba had gone to work for Dutch Schultz. They shot him in the bathroom of the Palace Chop House in Newark while he was on the pot.

"But that all happened later on. And what did Mr. Rothenberg do wrong? Sell liquor to people when everyone was doing the same? Sure. Why was it legal when the state took your bet at the track but illegal when someone else did it away from the track? 'I am only an American businessman in a land of opportunity,' he would say to me, and I believed he was right, Davey. Except that the difference between him and the heads of the big banks and corporations was that he never took money out of poor people's mouths and he never ran sweatshops and he never busted unions and he never had good people knocked off and he never lied to himself.

"Hypocrisy was the great enemy in life, he taught me. He took me for who I was, and not for somebody else. He *understood* me, Davey—the way I thought and worked." Abe squeezed my shoulder, hard. "All right then. I'll tell you the rest—to the end—because I want to, not just because you asked. All right?"

"Yes."

"Mr. Rothenberg told me I was not to concern myself about who the person was. I was to take his word that the man was at least as worthless as my own father. There were times in a man's life when certain choices were put upon him, he said, and when none of them were good—when, no matter which way he chose, he lost. I was caught in such a situation, and I'd come to him, which was, he said, the smartest thing I could have done.

"He was very old-fashioned, he added, because he still believed in good and evil, and in free will—that we were responsible for the consequences of choices and actions freely made—and he tried to impress upon me his belief that when certain individuals vanished from the face of the earth, nothing was lost. So I took the gun and I went to the guy's apartment—he had a suite in the Hotel Saint George, near the Brooklyn Bridge—and I followed instructions and said I was there with a message from O'Shea, that my name was Jack Healy, and when he opened the door I shot him twice in the chest and, while he was falling, once in the head.

"He wore an undershirt with black-and-red-striped suspenders over it. I had a silencer on the gun. He never had time to say a word or to scream. He'd never seen me before. I pushed him back into the room so I could close the door and I stood over him for a few seconds and thought how thin the line was—how he was there a second ago, with everything he'd done and thought, all his ideas and memories and habits —and now he was gone and would never come back. But it was no problem to him, I told myself, because he wasn't there. I thought how easy it was to kill a man, to make no life where life had been before, and from too many movies, I guess, I expected for a second to see some girl in a silk slip start screaming from the bed behind him. But nobody else was there.

"The next day there was a big story in the papers, with photos of the guy dead and of the guy when he was alive. His name was Harold Bernstein and he was a lawyer. He had a wife and two kids living in Newark, but the papers said he hadn't lived with them for five years and they couldn't get much more information from anyone, except that he had worked for Mr. Rothenberg briefly and for others with worse reputations—Lepke and Schultz—and that he was rumored to be a stool pigeon, to have been one of Dewey's key informers, when Dewey was a special D.A.

"Dewey was hot shit back then, see, and had all the boys scared, even Lansky and Luciano and Costello. He put Waxey Gordon behind bars and got Schultz knocked off and sent Lepke to the electric chair. 'Well,' Mr. Rothenberg said when we read that headline, 'Abbadabba would be pleased. He would have said that Mr. Dewey had Lepke's number, yes?'

"I went to work for Mr. Rothenberg after that. Momma never knew anything about it all, the acid or O'Shea or what happened to Dennis. She got sick about a year later and died within a few months. She was only forty-one, the same age your mother is now. But the word did get back to Poppa and Evie somehow. Who knows? Maybe it was Mr. Rothenberg himself who made sure they knew so he could keep his hold on me. We liked each other, but in our line of work that didn't mean there was trust. We never made an association without making sure we had something we could hold over the other guy. Just in case. Mostly what you learned was that you couldn't trust anybody in this life—ever—though there were a few you could trust more than others."

Abe touched his ring. He seemed angry suddenly. Was he sorry he'd answered my questions? Did he resent having told me why all the years had been the way they were?

"So now that you know, kid," he said, "are you happy?"

8

My MOTHER was telling me about Sam Lipsky and Harry Kanoff and the other men who'd been pursuing her, but I thought only of Gail and of the first moment in which we would see one another again. I imagined her next to the information booth in Penn Station, wearing her navy-blue pea coat, her yellow-and-blue plaid scarf. Suitcase in one hand, she was turning slowly in circles, as if lost. How was it possible, I wondered, that merely by existing I could make another human being so happy? I saw her racing toward me. I imagined the softness of her lips against mine. I touched the backs of my first two fingers to my mouth, pressed light against the soft folds of the skin at the knuckles. I let my fingers trail cross my lips to my cheek, and I stared at my mother as if I were paying attention to her.

What did I think? Sam Lipsky said he couldn't wait much longer for an answer. He had taken her into the vault with him at the Lincoln Savings Bank. There he had opened his safe deposit box, shown her his dead wife's jewelry, and promised that if she married him the jewels would be hers. If she didn't say yes soon, though, he would have to divide the jewelry among his four daughters. My mother wanted me to be truthful with her. Would I feel, a little more than a year since my father died, that she was somehow betraying his memory, that she was letting me down? She talked about which men were liars and which were only out for a good time, and I said little except, as usual, to tell her that she was free to do what she wanted. In a few weeks I would be graduating from high school, she said. By the fall I might be gone and what would she do then? She offered me the money she'd been saving for her trip to California—she had decided she was too old to start out there all over again, on her own—because if I went to college at least I would get away from working for Abe. If I went to college I would get my student deferment so that I wouldn't be shipped off to Korea to be killed. She would be grateful for little things.

"But I do get lonesome. Do you know what? I get lonesome for you before you're even gone. Is that crazy? I mean, do you have a crazy mother or do you have a crazy mother?"

I put my dishes in the sink. "I don't know," I said. "One or the other, I guess."

"*What?*" She was startled. Then she began to laugh. "You got your father's sense of humor, yeah? The way you like to tease me. Only I was always that way, Davey—from as far back as I can remember. Even when I first brought you home from the hospital I remember thinking that someday you'd be all grown up and gone away to have your own family, and what would I do then?" She reached toward me. "Come and sit, yeah? So you'll be late for school for once in your life. Come and sit and talk with your mother for a few minutes."

I sat and I tried not to hear what she was saying about how much she loved me. I imagined Abe, later in the day, waiting for me at the office on Flatbush Avenue. Would he be angry? He had telephoned the night before to say that he would be leaving for Florida, that I should come to the office after school. There was no crisis, he said—simply the opportunity for me to be in charge of things on a daily basis, for his men to get used to taking orders from me.

My mother was saying that she had never expected her life to be like this, without my father, without me, without Abe. The gray in her hair softened her features. Smile lines radiated from the corners of her eyes, the skin webbed with tiny tracings, like the fine lines in cracked ice. Did I think she was capable of living alone? I imagined myself in Penn Station, staring up at the vaulted ceiling, the great steel-ribbed spaces through which the light poured down on polished marble. If you spent your whole life hoping to have a family, how could you ever be happy living by yourself? Through the grilled roof, through the domes and arches of glass and steel, I imagined that I could see a million stars sprinkled across the night sky like silver shavings. In the waiting room soldiers and sailors were sitting on duffel bags, smoking cigarettes.

"Still my silent one, huh?" Her voice was gentle again. "I don't mind, really. You're a good boy, Davey. I don't mind your not saying to me what you think about if I should say yes or no to Sam. At least I got you for a sounding board. I mean, I'm a big girl now, right?"

"When I was a kid Sam used to let me sit inside his freezer with him, in the summertime."

"So?"

"That's all. It was something I remembered. We'd sit inside there eating Eskimo Pies and he'd tell me jokes."

"Sam's got a terrific sense of humor, like your father did. He don't got Harry's money, but when he kisses me things happen inside that don't happen with Harry." She pointed to her forehead. "You give your mother a kiss, yeah? And then you go to school. Kiss me up here because with all that's been going on I got a nervous stomach and you shouldn't be kissing me near the mouth."

I kissed her on the forehead, went to the foyer, took my jacket from the closet.

"Abe used to call them lie blisters. He could be mean sometimes. When we were kids and I'd get one of my herpes he'd run around the school yard yelling to everybody that his sister got a lie blister. Ain't it too warm for a jacket?" She laughed. "I mean, it's May already."

"I'm sorry," I said. The picture I'd had in my head, of Gail, was of how she had looked the last time she'd come in from college. "And listen. I might be home late. Some of the guys are thinking of cutting out early and going to Ebbets Field. The Dodgers are playing the Phillies. Maybe after we'll go out for pizza and bowling and stuff, so don't expect me early."

"You're telling me the truth?"

My heart stopped. "Sure."

"You ain't really going to be with Abe, to get sucked in more?"

"I'm not going to be with Abe today," I said. "Only if he calls, don't tell him I said so."

"And you won't forget the signal?"

"I won't forget the signal."

I expected her to joke about the signal—when I rang the downstairs buzzer, if she buzzed back once it meant the coast was clear; if she buzzed back twice it meant she had a visitor—but instead I saw that she was looking at me in such a sad, forlorn way that for an instant it made me think she knew exactly where I was going and why.

"Are you okay?" I asked. "You'll be all right here by yourself?"

"Oh Davey," she cried, throwing her arms around me. "I get so scared about what's gonna be. I just get so scared sometimes—"

"Sure," I said, and I stroked her hair. "Sure, Mom. But things will be all right. You'll see. They'll work out fine."

"I just get so scared about all the years ahead—about you and Abe and what will happen if I lose you. It's been so nice this morning, talking to you like this, did you know? I mean, Sam or Harry—big deal. What do I give a shit about them, if you want the truth. But I smile and get dolled up and put on an act and I figure I better get set up with somebody before too many years go by and the men stop looking at me. But what's it all about, Davey? I mean, can you tell me that? What's it all about? And what about poor Sol? I mean, I think about him more than anyone thinks, how the last years I should of been kinder to him."

"He loved you the way you were."

"That's true enough," she said, rubbing her nose against my shirt front. "Go on now. You get going before the waterworks start in."

"If you get lonesome or scared, call down to Beau Jack. Have him come up here and stay with you."

"Beau Jack." She wiped her eyes with the backs of her wrists. "He'll miss you too. He doesn't say much, but I know he misses that you don't spend time with him the way you used to."

"I'll try harder. With him and with you. You'll see."

"When? When you're halfway across America playing basketball?"

"Maybe I won't be that far away."

I reminded her that I hadn't played basketball the past season—my senior year—that because of the fixes, because of Abe, there were no scholarships coming my way. My words stopped her for a second, long enough for me to kiss her, for me to tell her that she shouldn't worry about what happened with Sam and Harry or any of the others.

I went out the door. I winked. "You're only young once, Mother," I said, and when I laughed she laughed with me.

We changed trains at the 30th Street Station in Philadelphia. The train out of Penn Station had been delayed in the tunnel for forty minutes and was so packed we'd hardly been able to speak to one another. The new train, only four cars long, was less than half full, and I found seats at the far end of the last car. I put Gail's two suitcases on the seat across from us and asked if she wanted to rest. I said that if she wanted to stretch out I could put the luggage on the overhead rack, but that I'd left them on the seats so that we could be alone. Was that all right?

She slumped down next to me, put her arm through mine, leaned her head against my shoulder. I asked if I could get her anything from the suitcases before the train left the station. If she wanted to sleep, I said, I wouldn't mind. I realized she'd been up half the night, sneaking out of her dormitory, taking the four o'clock milk train down from Northampton. I was sorry she was so exhausted. I was sorry about lots of things, I supposed. She smiled, squeezed my arm. Buy why did she need two suitcases when we were only going to be away for a day? I asked if she was comfortable. Was she hungry? Was she thirsty?

"I'm happy," she said, burrowing closer. "But lordy, the guy I'm in love with is so nervous I hardly know him. Are *you* going to be all right, David?"

She reached up and cupped my chin in her hand. I jerked my head away, pressed my forehead against the window. I watched the platform begin to slide backwards, as if, I thought, it were moving into the past.

"Please don't pull away from me when I'm trying to be affectionate. It's the one time I hate you. I know this has been difficult for you, but let me touch you, all right?"

"Just give me a few minutes," I said. "I need time to get over my nervousness, to get used to being with you again."

The Philadelphia high-rise apartment buildings we were passing looked as run-down as those near the Brooklyn waterfront. Did Abe and Mr. Rothenberg have connections in Philadelphia? In every large city in America where Jews lived, were there men like Abe, in charge of things? Had Abe ever been to Shibe Park to see the Phillies play? In Jackie's first year the Phillies' manager, Sam Chapman, had tried to get his team to go on strike against the Dodgers. He'd razzed Jackie so much that the commissioner had called him in and threatened to suspend him.

"Don't forget," she said. "If anybody asks, just say I'm going to visit a girlfriend at Goucher and that you're my cousin and you're going to Hopkins, all right?"

"Then why do we have tickets to Elkton instead of to Baltimore?"

"Because Elkton is where you have to go if you want to get married first, stupid. Everybody knows *that*."

She moved closer again, let her head rest on my shoulder. I looked through the window, at our images—flecked with dust, suspended in the air like ghosts. "I'm sorry about the way I was before," I said. "I keep being afraid we're being followed."

"Who would follow us?"

"Abe. He might have somebody follow me in order to protect me."

"David?"

"What?"

"When I'm up there without you I get scared sometimes that you *have* been taken from me, but not by your uncle or his enemies." She pointed to the window, to our reflection. "Sometimes, in my room, I try to see your face and all I get is your eyes or your mouth—like a half-drawn picture, and I get scared—panicked, really—that I won't be able to remember the rest of you. And then because I get worried that I can't see the person I love most in the world, things get all mixed up and crazy inside me. I get scared you'll stop loving me. I don't ever want to lose you. David?"

"What?"

"Are you sorry?"

"Sorry?"

"When you get quiet this way, whenever that dark look comes across your face—when those bruised clouds pass over you—I get scared. Nothing makes sense to me then, and I begin to feel, not that you don't love me, but just that you're sorry somehow that I *exist*."

"I get scared too," I said. "But I'm not sorry. The truth is that I never really thought much about what my life might be like before it happened," I said. "I never had dreams the way you do. I never imagined what it would be like to meet someone like you. I never imagined what it would be like to feel what you make me feel."

I put my arm around her. Time passed. We slept. The train slowed down and we heard the conductor's voice, from the other end of the car, announcing that we were approaching Chester, Pennsylvania. *Was I sorry?* Could I tell her the truth—if I even knew the truth? Or was the truth something that had never occurred to me before: that perhaps there were times when you did lie to the person you loved, and that there was nothing wrong with lying. I looked out the window, through the film of brown dust, and saw that about fifty yards from the station two boys were coming out of the woods with a dead animal trussed upside down, hanging from a pole by the legs. They carried the pole across their shoulders.

"Is it a deer?" Gail asked.

"No. It's too small for a deer. It's just a dog."

Gail leaned across me, trying to see, but the train had started and the boys grew smaller and smaller, walking away from us.

"The poor thing. Was it dead?"

"I guess."

"When we were camping in New Hampshire the summer before last, we lost our way and my father turned off onto this country road and just as he stopped to turn the car back around I saw a deer and her fawn staring out of the woods at us. You couldn't see them at first—they were all dappled and camouflaged by the bark and shadows and it was almost as if, I've thought since, I saw them because they'd been staring at *me* so hard."

I couldn't see the two boys anymore. I smiled, imagining Tony's face when Gail and I returned with our news.

"I keep wondering if life is like that," Gail said. "If sometimes when you least expect it, beautiful things happen."

"Was Ellen there?"

"Was Ellen where?"

"In the car with you when you saw the deer?"

"Sure. Why do you ask?"

"I was thinking about how she couldn't see what you saw. I was wondering what things are like for her, without eyes."

"She has eyes—very beautiful gray eyes, as a matter of fact. They just don't work."

Little hairs fanned out in the middle of Gail's left eyebrow, going the wrong way, and I reached across and smoothed them down. The train stopped, brakes hissing, releasing steam. A black man pushed a flat of mailsacks along the platform. I tried to imagine Beau Jack in his World War I uniform, traveling across France in an old train. Our train was moving again, the conductor calling out that the next stop would be Wilmington, Delaware. Gail lifted my hand and put it on her stomach, and I was surprised at how warm she was. I thought of bread, rising under a towel, and of the way my mother would let me peek underneath when I was a boy, of how I would watch for as long as I could, waiting to see the dough expand.

"How are you feeling?" I asked. "I'm sorry I didn't ask before. I mean, how are you *feeling?*"

"I'm a little tired, that's all. Otherwise I'm okay. So is junior."

"The red plague didn't come?"

"No. Don't you think I would have called you so if it had?"

"I suppose. I'm sorry I asked."

"But you were hoping it would come."

"Sure. Weren't you?"

She looked away. "I don't know. Sometimes yes, sometimes no." She held my wrist. "I mean, it's *ours*, David. It's you and me growing inside me, creating new life from our lives, from our love."

"Terrific."

"In medieval times," she said coldly, "children born out of wedlock—bastards—were believed to be exceptionally vital and dynamic beings, begotten, as they were, in the intensity of passion rather than between the dull, obligatory sheets of marriage. To bear the child of the man you loved was, according to the tenets of courtly love, the truest way of bringing the love to its consummation."

"We don't live in medieval times."

"I didn't want to take the pills, David." Her voice was harsh, insistent. "If I took the pills and they didn't work I would have had to have myself scraped out. *You* go get yourself scraped out first and see how you like it. Then—"

"I never said you should take pills. That was your idea. I said this was okay, didn't I? I'm here, aren't I?"

She picked at the skin around her thumbnail. "Even if you didn't agree to marry me—if you didn't propose—I would have had the child.

I decided that before I came to you and told you. I've seen what happens to the girls in the dorm who try to take care of it themselves. There was one girl before Christmas we found passed out in the bathroom, blood glopped all over the shower and the toilet. They use crochet hooks and knitting needles and wire hangers and take quinine tablets and scorching hot baths and ice-cold showers. And then—if they're successful—they can call the hospital to finish the job. Then—"

"Shut up!" I grabbed her arm. "I said to shut up. Did you *hear* me?"

She tried to pry my hand from her arm. "You're hurting me, David. Christ. *Stop!*"

"Then you just shut up. I never asked you to do anything like that and I don't like it when you accuse me of wanting to—"

"Of wanting to what?"

"Forget it." I let go of her arm.

"No. Of wanting to what? Tell me."

"Of wanting to hurt you, okay?" I looked away, so that she wouldn't see my eyes.

"I know you didn't want to hurt me. It's just that—"

"But first you wanted me to hear how I *might* have hurt you. Sure. You wanted to slip all that in first—to stick the pictures into my head."

"Not at all, David. Not at all. Oh shit. Hey, are you all right?"

The train was moving again, clattering and rocking. I kept my eyes fixed on the platform.

"I'm all right."

She wiped my tears with a fingertip. "I love you," she said.

I nodded. I wanted to tell her it was okay, that I loved her too, but I didn't dare try. Was love enough? Love is sweet, my father used to say, but tastes best with bread. I took a deep breath.

"You're not angry with me then, are you," she stated, as if talking to herself.

"Why should I be angry?"

"Because it was my fault. Because I didn't count right." She put her finger to my lips. "It's what I've been frightened of most—that you'd feel I'd tricked you. We Freudians believe there are never any real accidents."

"I never didn't believe you," I said. I let her take my hand, move it in slow circles on her stomach. "Until you brought it up it never occurred to me not to believe you. Why wouldn't I believe you?"

"Can I show you all the things I've brought? Can we talk about the quotidian for a while? First of all I brought lunch." She opened the smaller suitcase, began taking things out, explaining why she had brought each item. There were peanut butter and grape jelly sandwiches, bags of peanuts, Hershey bars, boxes of Cracker Jacks; a small bottle of sweet Malaga wine for the ceremony and a large bottle of French champagne and a can of smoked oysters and a box of crackers for the hotel afterwards; there was toothpaste, two toothbrushes, dental floss, shaving cream, a razor, talcum, perfume, shampoo.

I laughed, and she asked me not to make fun of her, but I could tell from her smile that she was pleased. Was that what mattered most of all to me—to be able to please the woman I loved in ordinary ways, to somehow become the father I never had? She showed me the shirt and tie she'd bought for me, the new cream-colored nightgown she'd bought for herself, the rose sachet that gave a lovely scent to everything. There were a few advantages to being a Jewish American Princess with a sizable savings account, she said. Hoping to keep her at Smith so that they could keep us apart, her parents had been excessively generous during the past year. Wasn't I pleased to know she came with a dowry?

I imagined Little Benny slapping me on the back, calling me the Prince, asking me when I was going to take over the kingdom. When there were no more armies, I'd say, and he'd laugh at me, tell me I had my father's sense of humor. Gail showed me a small package in fancy white paper that contained a wedding gift for me, a plain brown Woolworth's bag with rings in it—a gold band for each of us, a fake diamond engagement ring for her. There was lots of clothing—a bathrobe, slippers, a new plaid sportshirt for me, a change of clothes for her. She'd bought new underwear and socks for me, and one of her brother's old sweaters in case the evenings were cool. She'd brought along some books in case we became bored with one another, and she had also packed her clock-radio, wrapped in a towel the way the champagne was, so that we could listen to music, and her old Brownie camera so we could take pictures. It was the camera she had received from Ellen for her Bat Mitzvah, and she wondered what I made of that, of Ellen giving her a machine for the seeing.

She took a manila envelope from the bottom of the second suitcase, showed me her birth certificate, the results of the blood test, the list of necessary addresses: justice of the peace, hotel, town hall. I gave her my birth certificate, the paper with the result of my blood test, and she assured me again that she'd been over the whole thing with one of the older girls at Smith, a girl who had transferred from Goucher. Everyone knew about Elkton. It was the Reno of the Eastern Seaboard. What postage stamps were to the Republic of San Marino, early weddings were to Elkton, Maryland.

In a corner of the larger suitcase, carefully wrapped and stuffed with newspapers, was a plain drinking glass. When the ceremony was over, she said, she would wrap the glass in a handkerchief, set it on the floor, and I was to stamp on it. Her eyes were radiant now, imagining the look we would get from the justice of the peace and his wife. She explained the purpose of the glass to me, its symbolism in Jewish wedding ceremonies as a reminder of the destruction of the Temple in Jerusalem, of the seriousness and sadness—the history—that were present at all times in our lives, that would mingle always with our happiness. She knew I hadn't been brought up to believe in such stuff, but we were both Jewish, after all, and she wondered if, after we returned and announced the great event to our families, I would mind having a second ceremony performed by a rabbi. She wanted my blessing most of all, but just to be safe—because she wasn't sure if she believed or disbelieved—could we get God's blessing too?

Was there anything she'd forgotten? She took a small brown stuffed animal from the suitcase—brown doggie, she called him—and told me not to be jealous, and she placed brown doggie on my lap with the bag of sandwiches. I wondered what my father would have thought. Would he have liked Gail? For the first time in a while I saw his face clearly. He stood to one side, by himself, shading his good eye, while a rabbi married us. Tears ran down both his cheeks. Was it possible? Could his bad eye weep? When the ceremony was over and I'd kissed Gail and crushed the glass, he took my face between his hands and kissed me on the lips and told me I made him happy and that he was sorry he had given away the gas mask. He should have told them it was lost. He should have paid the penalty and given it to me. Could I forgive him?

"When I was younger," Gail was saying, "I'd stay home some days just so I could watch 'Bride and Groom.' My mother couldn't figure it out because I seemed so—unorthodox is the word, I suppose—in other ways. They worried about me because of the way I didn't want to be like the other girls at school. But I always liked dolls and stuffed animals and I always loved weddings. Why? When I sat on the living room rug and watched the couples get married on TV, I even used to cry. Can you believe it?" She laughed. "I used to fantasize about being on the show, about the gown I'd wear, the veil, the long flowing train behind me, about Ellen being my maid of honor, about the music I wanted, about how clear and smooth and fair my skin would be." She lifted brown doggie and kissed its nose, offered it to me. She shrugged. "Well. Maybe in my next life I'll get to do it that way."

The last thing we talked about before Gail fell asleep was Jackie Robinson, and it seemed crazy to me, but in a wonderful way, that in the middle of our wedding night I'd sat on the edge of the bed in our hotel room, and stroked her forehead, and told her the story of Jackie Robinson's life. And when I gave her the news I'd been saving—that Jackie's third child, born the week before, was a boy, and that Jackie and Rachel had named the boy David—she filled our glasses with more champagne, and we toasted the new David and wished him long life and happiness.

She lay there listening to me, her eyes closed, and said that Ellen was probably right—that I did have the gentlest voice of any man she had ever known. *Probably?* I asked. She smiled, said that she thought a lot about my voice when we were apart. *Gentilesse.* That was the name she had given me. Did I mind? The word was used in tales of courtly love, in Chaucer's work, and described men—knights usually—who possessed in rare combinations the qualities of gentleness, courtesy and good breeding. Gentilesse David, she said, trailing her fingers lightly down the planes of my face. Nor should I think that being gentle meant that I was weak. Gentleness could be allied with power, with strength. . . .

Now she was fast asleep. I watched her, wondered if it were possible that we were there alone, just the two of us, far from everything and everyone we had ever known. I was seventeen years old. I was happy in a way I'd never believed possible. But how could one feel so full of peace and love and not, at the same time, be afraid that such feelings would, in the next instant, be taken away?

I felt as if I were adrift on a clear, still lake—without cares or worries, without either a past or a future. I had no idea of time, or how long I'd been sitting there in the chair, staring at her, studying her face, drawing her picture. I'd taken the gift wrapping from the present she'd given me —her own copy of *The Diary of Anne Frank*, her favorite passages marked lightly in the margins, in pencil—and turned the paper over and used that. When she was twelve she had read *The Diary of Anne Frank* for the first time. Since then she had read it once a year, and she had asked me if we could read it to one another once a year for the rest of our lives. Long before she'd worked up the courage to approach me, she said, she'd thought of me as Peter, of herself as Anne.

I set my drawing on the bed, opened the book to the passage she'd asked me to read aloud to her. *I think a lot, but I don't say much. I am happy if I see him and if the sun shines when I'm with him. I was very excited yesterday; while I was washing my hair, I knew that he was sitting in the room next to ours. I couldn't do anything about it; the more quiet and serious I feel inside, the more noisy I became outwardly.*

Which parts of Anne Frank were like me? Which like her? If Anne Frank had survived, Gail wondered, what then? Had she lived, would we read her book in the same way? Why had she perished only a few days before Auschwitz was liberated?

Gail's dark curls were spread out against the pillow, brown doggie peeking out next to her bare shoulder. How was it possible, I wondered, that she was so still now and had been so wildly passionate only a few hours before? The back of her wrist was across her eyes, her hand toward me, cupped slightly, slack. Did I dare to lift it so that I could see her eyes better, so that I could finish drawing them? I set *The Diary of Anne Frank* on the bed, next to the drawing. I wanted to run my tongue along her forearm, her wrist, the shadow of her palm.

I went to the window. I thought of Anne Frank in her family's secret apartment, looking out at the roofs of Amsterdam, at the horizon that was so pale there seemed to be no dividing line between earth and sky. As long as that world existed, she wrote—the city, the sunshine, the cloudless skies, the heavens—and as long as she was alive to see it, she believed that she could not be unhappy. I reached behind the lace curtain, pulled the shade sideways and looked into the street. We were on the third floor. It was just beginning to be light out. A Borden's milk truck was parked across the street in front of the Elkton Fancy Diner. The milkman came out of the diner dressed in white, looking as if he were an orderly in a hospital. Behind the diner was an open field, tall grass mostly, with several large climbing rocks and, near the far end, a flatter section. Boards and tires were set up for a backstop, a large area cleared of grass and stones for an infield, and beyond the backstop a high wall of slate-colored rock and scrubby trees. A single four-storey apartment house sat on top of the small rise, and the television antennas crowded together on the rooftop, like bright silver framing for box kites, caught the morning light and shimmered.

"David?"

I turned.

"What are you doing?"

"Nothing. Just staring."

"No. I mean what are you doing here, with this?"

She sat up, pulling the sheet with her. She held the piece of paper in the air.

"Oh that."

"It's me."

"I was just sketching a little, to pass the time. I couldn't sleep."

"You were just sketching a little to pass the time. You mean you drew this while I was sleeping? I'm not dreaming?"

"I didn't mean for you to see it yet."

"You didn't mean for me to see it yet. Are you *serious?*" She came to me. "You did something like this for me and you weren't going to let me see it?"

"I don't know. Maybe when I was done."

She pulled the shade up halfway so that the daylight could shine on the paper without hurting her eyes. I'd drawn her in profile, just a few curving lines near the bottom to capture the way her head rested in the pillow. I loved the shape of her head, the hard, perfect oval of her skull. I was pleased that I'd been able to suggest that shape—its weight—with just a few strokes.

"Oh, I do like it, David. I do. Only—"

"Only what?"

"Only somehow you seem to have left out all my imperfections. The moonlike craters in my cheeks. Here." She touched the paper. Her nipples grazed my forearm. "You shaded in the space around my eyes and under my lip, but you left my cheeks white and smooth—embossed in egg-shell white, I'll grant—but smooth. Did you do it to flatter me? Were you afraid of hurting my feelings?"

"I was drawing you in profile. Haven't you ever seen the way—?"

She cut me off by kissing me. She began pushing me backwards, toward the bed, but without taking her lips from mine. She reached down, slid her hand inside my underpants. I felt her falling, stumbling —our teeth clicked—and I realized that, our eyes closed, we'd forgotten about the chair I'd been sitting on. We laughed. I pushed her onto the bed, pinned her wrists, spread her legs apart. I was breathing hard, and all I wanted was to be inside her again, to feel the wonderful moist tongues there gripping me. Her eyes opened and closed, almost as if she were in pain. She whimpered slightly. Could she, when she started to go wild this way, even remember having done it before with me? I sometimes found myself hesitating for an instant when she was like this, wondering if it mattered that it was me on top of her, or if *any* body would have served. She was lifting my shirt, moving her hands across my stomach, straining toward me. I knew what she wanted and I kissed her breasts, her throat, her mouth. Her hands moved along my sides, over my breasts, up into my armpits. She grabbed me there, thumbs pressing in, tongue going wild around mine.

"Careful. The paper. My drawing—"

"What?"

I moved sideways so that I could reach across, push the drawing from us. It fell from the bed. I stretched, lifted the drawing from the floor, placed it on the night table. Her head flopped backwards and she lay there, eyes closed, fists opening and closing. She pushed me sideways, rolled on top, licked my stomach, sucked on my breasts, then sat up straight suddenly—her back arched, her hands behind her on the bed, bent at the wrists for balance.

"David?"

"What?"

"Do you think we'll ever be able to just neck anymore?"

"What do you mean? We—"

"I mean, now that we're free and legal, do you think that in the future, every time we start to kiss we'll feel obligated to go all the way?"

"How should I know?"

I tried to pull her down, to get my legs out from between hers, but she pressed down hard on me, leaned forward, arms extended, palms braced against my chest.

"David?"

"Jesus! What *now?*"

"Do you like the way I kiss? I mean, do you *really* like the way I kiss? Do you think I'm talented at kissing? In the eighth grade, when we passed slam-books around and everybody filled things in, I was never selected by anyone as Prettiest or Sexiest, but when we gathered in the bathroom to open the folded pages and look at the results I was surprised to learn that I was frequently selected by the guys as Best Kisser. And David?"

I sighed. "Yes?"

"Would you mind very much if we didn't do it again? I want to—I know I started it this time—but I think I'm getting a little raw inside. I don't know if . . ."

"Terrific." I covered my eyes with my hand. "That's really terrific."

"I can make him come again if you want." She slid backwards, reached down and gripped me. "What small attentions can I pay to you, sweetheart? It *is* different for women, you know. I'm very happy. Would you like me to turn over? They say it's easier that way when you're pregnant, that the muscles are more relaxed there. Just tell me what you'd like me to do, all right?"

"How the hell should I know? *Jesus!*"

"Shh," she said. "Here." She climbed off, pulled down my underpants, slipped them over my feet, tossed them to the floor, then bent over me sideways, on her knees, and began sucking, her thumb and forefinger holding me tight at the root.

I looked down, to watch her move up and down on me, but all I could see was a moon of black curls floating on my stomach. I asked her if there was something I could do for her, but she just told me to relax and enjoy myself. She said she loved to feel me swell, to feel the skin stretch. The one thing I might do for her, though, since I'd asked, was to kiss her again. Sometimes she thought she could be happy just kissing me, hour after hour. She'd worried about that at times. Was it some strange kind of perversion, to like kissing me more, at times, than having me inside her? Did I mind if she told me things like that?

She nibbled along the insides of my legs, but each time she came near my penis, she slid back down. She said she loved to see the small rushes of goose flesh move up and down my legs and thighs. She let her head rest on my chest.

"God! Your heart is beating so fast, David. Look—you can even see it —you can actually see it going thump thump. Thump thump thump . . ."

She licked downwards along my breastbone and across my stomach, and this time she took so much of me into her mouth that I gulped myself, afraid she would choke. I groaned, felt the shiver begin somewhere near the bottom of my spine and pulse through me, explode slowly. I pushed down on her so that she wouldn't take her mouth away. I wanted her to squeeze and suck on me forever, to draw the long, shuddering thrill out of me and into her and never, never to stop. The spasm went on and on—I couldn't believe it—and she pressed up now with her index finger, from below, and then she sucked more slowly, drawing the fluid from me.

I heard my own voice, strangely high-pitched, telling her how wonderful it felt, and for a brief second I also recalled the sound of Avie Gornik's voice, pleading with Abe. But the memory drifted off. Numbness sifted through me, spreading like warm water. Her head was over my heart again, and I put my hand there, spread my fingers as wide as I could, pressed down.

"Here—where it surges—is that the part the guys call the power vein?"

"I suppose."

"I love making you happy. I love watching your face when you come. Doesn't it stun you, David, that we can do anything we want? I mean, isn't it an extraordinary idea, to be able to do *anything* you want, and not to feel embarrassed or guilty? Tumescence. Listen: did you know that in Japan and other Eastern cultures it's considered the height of pleasure for a man *not* to come, for him to have the frustration drawn out indefinitely. 'Karazza'—that's the word for it. Tumescence and karazza. Great words. Don't say anything. Shh. You doze off if you want. Don't worry about me. I like looking at you. How many times did we do it together tonight? Five? Six?"

"I wasn't counting."

"Neither was I, but I think it was six."

She talked. I dozed, slept, woke, listened to her. She wondered if what people said was true, if it wouldn't be as thrilling for us now that the act was no longer forbidden. She said that according to literary critics nobody had ever written a good novel about family happiness, about married love, not even Tolstoy. In the Western tradition, romantic love was always portrayed as existing outside marriage—as illicit or tragic or stolen or star-crossed. I felt myself slipping into dreams, into long tunnels where gleaming black tiles lined the walls, where light speckled toward me.

I heard Gail talk about Ellen and it was as if I was sliding along a smooth, enamelled tunnel into the very *sound* of her voice. She was talking about books and I heard myself ask her if she'd read about the things we did in books, if that was where she'd learned so much.

"When I was sweet sixteen," she said. "I went through a period where I read all the dirty books I could find—*The Story of O* and the *Kama Sutra* and *Lady Chatterly's Lover* and lots of Henry Miller's books and some books that were, as they say, totally without redeeming social value. Ellen hadn't read any of them, even though she was older, and she startled me by asking me to read *Lady Chatterly's Lover* to her, by pressing me for details. So for once, you see, I had her where I wanted her.

"What I'd do was to read aloud to her and then stop suddenly just when we were coming to the really hot parts. She'd go nuts. She'd swear and threaten and try to whack me. But what could she do, really? Tell our parents? All I ever had to do to quiet her down was to warn her that if she told on me she'd never hear another word from the books she herself could never read. There was no smut industry in the world of Braille as yet."

Her words came to me as if filtered through gauze. I saw steam, rising from cold water. I saw myself on a pier on Red Hook. I was with Abe and we were watching large derricks, cranes dipping down to pick up crates. There were guns and ammunition inside the crates, wrapped carefully in straw and raffia. The longshoremen joked with Abe. *Guns for the Arabs, sneakers for the Jews*, they said. *Not anymore*, Abe replied. *Never again.* They laughed at him, winked at me, made jokes about Jews. Abe paid them off with enormous rolls of bills and he laughed with them. But his eyes were ice cold. The guns were going to Palestine, he told me afterwards, smuggled there to help the Jews fight against the British and the Arabs. I imagined myself on the pier without Abe. I was talking to Tony. Tony had his hands in his jacket pockets. He was inviting me to come to his house for dinner, to meet his children. Would Gail and Regina like one another? Would Tony and I watch a Knicks game on TV together? Would we pretend we were happy? Family happiness. Sure.

Gail and I lay there, holding one another, and she was so still that I wondered how I would feel were she to die in my arms. I wondered what was going to happen next, and about exactly what Abe would say to me when I returned. Then daylight was pouring in through the window—I must have slept—and Gail lay beside me, smiling.

I heard cars, below our window, honking, and I winced slightly, pulled Gail closer. I remembered one longshoreman calling Abe a prick, a circumcised prick—and Abe answering back—it was the first time I heard the line and I used it afterwards, with my friends—*That's true, Gino, but without us pricks where would you cocksuckers be?* I leaned over and picked up the drawing.

"If I had a good eraser I could have done your hair better. I couldn't lift off some of the pencil—the shading—once I'd put it down." I stopped. "You really like it?"

"I love it."

"I feel kind of dizzy. Do you feel dizzy?"

"No. And the morning sickness is gone too. It only lasted two weeks."

"Everything's kind of hazy and spinning," I said, my eyes closed. "Lots of tiny white dots. Circling. Remember the Lone Ranger rings you used to look into, shaped like little silver atomic bombs and when you took off the tailpiece and went into a closet and stared into it you saw thousands of tiny white specks, as if you were seeing an atomic explosion or the end of the world?"

"I'm hungry. Are you hungry?"

"I made the drawing for you." I kissed her hair. I sensed that both of us were afraid to leave, afraid that if we went into the world all that we'd been feeling would be shattered. "It was supposed to be your wedding gift. When you woke up I was going to—"

"Oh David." Tears ran down her cheeks, slid into my mouth. "Forgive me, but I think Gail Kogan awoke from a dream and didn't know if she were a happy woman who had just dreamt she was Gail Kogan, or Gail Kogan dreaming she was a happy woman."

"I didn't know if I could still draw, though. I was frightened to try again."

"I could take in washing," Gail offered. "We could send you to art school. I type seventy-five words a minute. I take shorthand, Gregg-Pittman method. Or I could transcribe books into Braille—I have specialized training. I can use a Braille typewriter. I'm bright and young and efficient—"

"—and pregnant."

"Well, just a little bit," she laughed. "Or maybe we could *make* books together—stories that I'd write and you'd illustrate." She stopped. "I *know* I'm pregnant, David, but that will only be for six more months, and then . . ." She faltered, found no words, pulled me closer to her and held me so tightly that I gasped. "I *am* frightened too, David. I'm very frightened sometimes."

"I know."

"We haven't talked about practical things at all, about whether or not

I'll leave college or if you'll go to college or how we'll pay for things or where we'll live or what hospital we'll use. If my parents offer us money, or if your family does, should we accept? I wouldn't mind working, really, while you went to school. I know I'm very bright, but that's not uncommon—"

"Forget it. Okay? Let's just forget it and change the subject, if you don't mind. What I think is that you worship me too much. Lots of people can draw well. I've seen drawings in books and museums. I've seen the sketches real artists did long before they got to my age. I'm not so terrific."

"You won't know that unless you try."

"I *haven't* tried. That's the whole point!"

"But it wasn't easy in your home, David! It—"

"It's never easy. So do me a favor and don't try to cheer me up. I admit that I wonder sometimes how good I might have been if I'd stuck with it, but so what? I didn't. Sure. We only know that we're here, the way we are, not—"

"But you can be as good as you want! We're *young*. The talent is still there. It hasn't leaked out of you, don't you see? It's never too late to start, if only—"

"No," I said, cutting her off. "Sometimes it is too late."

Which did I want more, a girl or a boy? I said I didn't care, that all I wanted was a healthy baby, but she insisted that I answer the question, and the answer—to my surprise—was that if I had to choose, I preferred a girl. Why? Because it would make things easier for me. Because I'd think of it more as being *her* child? Partly. But also because of me, because I wouldn't worry so much about the bad influence I might have on a girl. I wouldn't worry so much about my temper, about the way I imagined I might get frustrated with a boy if he didn't do things the way I wanted him to. Was I afraid, Gail asked, of having a son look up to me too much?

What she thought we should do next, she said—feeding me a piece of sausage from her plate—was to send telegrams to her parents and to my mother, congratulating them on the marriage of their children. I told her she was nuts. She agreed, but claimed she was being practical, that the telegrams would serve a real purpose: by the time we got home they would have had time to get used to the idea. The best defense, she declared, was a good offense.

We were almost finished with breakfast. From where I was sitting I could see our hotel, and while Gail talked I tried to figure out which window it was that I'd been looking out. I felt restless, eager to get away, to get back to Brooklyn. I remembered a movie I'd seen not long after Abe got home—*Pride of the Marines*—a true story of a blind Marine, where John Garfield played the blind guy and Dane Clark played his buddy. Abe looked a lot like John Garfield, and I'd bragged about it to my friends, told them that Garfield had grown up fighting in Jewish gangs on the Lower East Side. I could hear Garfield's rough voice, see his slanted smile.

Gail asked if I wanted to stay for another day so that we could catch up on our sleep all afternoon and play again all night. Under the table, her foot was in my lap—her shoe off—and she was wiggling her toes along the inside of my thighs. She asked why I didn't look at her and I said I was looking at the window of our hotel room. Did I expect to see somebody looking down at us—a spy? a ghost?

A young couple entered the diner, and Gail, following my eyes, turned to watch them. The guy wore a navy-blue blazer with silver buttons, a fancy crest on the breast pocket. The girl was strikingly beautiful—small, sharp features, pale-pink lips, luminous sky-blue eyes, a dimpled chin, light-blond hair that was almost white. They passed us without looking our way, sat down in a booth.

"Oh dear," Gail said, raising her eyebrows. "I wonder what brings *them* to Elkton?"

"Stop. They'll hear."

"Never. Their ears are too sophisticated. Did you notice how they seemed to refuse to notice us? Yet I saw the girl glance at you while pretending to look past you. She liked what she saw and even in her prissy little mind she must be wondering what the difference is, between the night she just spent with her betrothed and the pleasures I must have tasted with a man like you, with—"

"I said to cut it *out*—"

"They won't hear a thing." Gail leaned back. "They hear the way they speak. Very softly and discreetly. Notice, if you will, in a minute, how little their jaws move when they talk and eat. Wired at birth is what I've heard. They do that to your jaw if you're born to an upper-class Protestant family. It's their equivalent of circumcision, a surgical procedure ensuring that you won't ever show much emotion should the temptation arise."

"Listen, Gail—"

"The groom, wearing his Princeton blazer and tie, will attend the Wharton School of Business next fall. The bride, a senior at Dana Hall Academy and an Aryan from Darien, wearing matching skirt and sweater from Peck and Peck in this spring's new heather tones, was knocked up by her fiancé in the back seat of an Austin-Healy during halftime of the Princeton-Yale game, and—"

I grabbed her wrist. "I said to cut it out." Her jaw went rigid, her eyes wide with rage. "What's gotten into you?"

"Nothing." She looked down. "Okay. I'll be quiet. Let go, though."

I let go. "What gets into you sometimes? I mean, what did they do to you?"

"Nothing." She picked at the skin around her thumbnail. "But you'd like a girl like that, wouldn't you? You'd like some nice cool, clean young thing like that, with long ironed hair and ivory thighs and authenticated pedigree from the Junior League."

"No."

"Do you know why I think it is that Jewish boys like you lust after these silent *shiksas* so much? Do you? My brother was the same before he settled for Janet. Do you know why? I'll tell you. So they can have it both ways."

"Here we go again."

"Really, David. Do you think I'm blind, that I didn't see the way you looked at her? Her boyfriend had the lean look and you had the hungry look, right?" She leaned towards me, her hands tight around her water glass. "I've thought about it, though, and the answer is that it's the challenge and the lack of challenge—that they promise a life of privacy and of peace, without nagging, an image of a woman totally unlike the women you've grown up with, who've smothered you, and yet that's the challenge, isn't it? To try to smash that calm, cool exterior, to see if you can get someone as beautiful and self-contained as that to do every little hot and dirty thing you want, until they're begging for more—until they worship you more than your mothers ever did—"

I grabbed for her wrist, but she was too quick. She pulled back, and as she did she knocked her water glass over. She set the glass back up, smiled at me triumphantly. With exaggerated calm, she took paper napkins and began mopping up the water.

"But why are you so upset, Mr. Voloshin? You seem quite vexed. Would you like to talk about it?"

"Don't pull your psychological shit on me. You're jealous is all. You don't fool me one bit."

"You would like a girl like that, though," she said quietly, tears in her eyes. "I can tell. You'd really like a nice, modest little girl who won't make demands on you, and someday you'll get tired of me and my mouth and my brain and go out and get one—the line forms to the left, ladies—and you'll justify running away because you'll say I trapped you, that I cheated you out of some other life you never lived."

"I like the life I'm living in. I don't think about the lives I don't have."

"You're just saying that because you feel sorry for me."

"I feel sorry for me more."

"For *you*—?"

"I'm the one who has to listen to you." I took her left hand, kissed the wedding ring, then her palm. "I love you." I thought of Abe, in his car, turning his Army ring, the stone pressed tight into his fist.

"I used to imagine I was a girl like that—a young Wasp from some snazzy little girl's school, with fair skin and flaxen hair, who reads *The Diary of Anne Frank* and dreams of being a girl like *me*: of being a dark, intelligent, brooding, Semitic city girl."

She stuffed a napkin into the corner of her mouth and bit down. Her lips were slightly puffy and bruised—plum-colored—and I reached across, touched them. Outside I watched an old prewar Chrysler with New York plates move slowly up the hill, stop in front of our hotel. Gail looked away.

"Do you think I'm *very* crazy, David? Is it very crazy to have wanted to be one of them wanting to be me wanting to be a girl like Anne? I mean, what if Anne Frank had been less altruistic? What if she'd survived because she was selfish and shrewd and calculating?"

I kept my eye on the car across the street. Two men sat in the front seat, someone else in the back. The waitress poured us more coffee.

"Would you let me fix the drawing later, before we leave?" I asked.

"I think I have a pencil with a good eraser." She put her purse on the table. "You asked me before—"

I wondered what it would be like if we didn't go back, if we simply decided to stay on in a small town like this, to get jobs, to start new lives with new names. I smiled. I took the pencil from Gail, then spotted something glistening under her fingers and before she could stop me I pushed her hand aside, reached down into her purse, pulled out a pack of Camel cigarettes.

"You *smoke?*"

"Once in a while. Sure. When I'm studying."

She tried to take the pack from me. "Nine out of ten doctors prefer Camels," she said. "The tenth takes a taxi, right? Give it to me, please."

"But *why?*"

"Because they're soothing to my T-zone, okay? And because I get horny sometimes, away from you week after week, and because as we well know I'm very oral, a quality in me of which you reap the benefits."

I squeezed the pack of cigarettes, listened to the crinkling sound the cellophane made. She snapped her purse shut. "Listen. Can we just forget about it? I told you on the phone how horny I was feeling and you even joked and told me to put something in my mouth, remember? So stop looking at me that way."

Across the street a man in a business suit helped an elderly couple from the car. The woman wore a hat with a veil.

"Tell me the truth—do you ever worry about losing me?"

"Yes."

"*Really?*"

"Why should you ever think that you're less than other girls?"

"And why should you think there's a vial of poison inside you?" She pressed her lips to my hands. "Don't you think that's the worst thing in life, David? That we sometimes hate ourselves because of the very goodness inside us?"

"You said yesterday that guys were after you a lot, at Smith. Did you ever accept dates with any of them?"

"Once or twice—sure—but it didn't mean anything. There were these mixers with Amherst College you were sort of required to attend. I mean, I did it as much to be with some of the girls, really—not to feel so left out all the time—as for anything else." I let the heat flow through me, fill me. I watched the fear enter her eyes. "It didn't mean a thing, David. Believe me."

"And when your nice young boys tried to hold your hand, and when they walked you back to your dorm and tried to kiss you good night, what happened then?"

"Oh Jesus."

"Don't oh-Jesus me. Just answer the question."

"You are being an idiot." She folded her arms across her breasts. Tobacco, curling from the end of one of her loose cigarettes, looked like pencil shavings.

"You look awful, did you know that? You look terrifically ugly, as a matter of fact. Your ears are bright red and your mouth is thin and hard —a slit—and the vein in your forehead is throbbing. Can you just calm down, please?"

My ears were ringing—a high-pitched buzzing sound—as if there were mosquitos there. I touched a finger to my forehead—the vein felt like a thin, warm rubber band. If I got angry enough, would it burst? Would she comfort me then? Would she cry?

"Jealousy," Gail stated, "is the illusion of possession."

"I don't want your fancy theories. Just answer the question."

"I don't have to and I won't."

She had her purse and was out of her seat before I could move. I started after her, realized that I hadn't paid for breakfast, and froze. I stood there and watched her go out the door, run across the street. I was aware that other people in the diner were looking at me. Were they laughing? I swallowed hard, closed my eyes, imagined her in the hotel room, taking the pencil and lying on the bed and spreading her legs and trying to do to herself the awful things she said that others had done in order to get rid of their babies. Something slammed into my chest. I looked around, but no one was near me. I stood there in the aisle, immobile, my right hand on my chest, feeling my heart hammering to get out. I took a deep breath, glanced backwards, spotted the check on the table, looked past our booth to the other couple. They sat there as if nothing had happened, sipping their coffee, looking neither at me nor at one another.

By the time I'd paid the bill and walked across the street, I felt calmer. I glanced up at our window, wondered if Gail was already there, watching me. The sunlight, reflecting from the hotel's windows, made them look like rectangles of blue silver. Behind me I heard the sounds of boys playing baseball in the field. It was Saturday. There was no school.

Gail was at the check-in desk, talking to the clerk, and when she saw me she smiled easily, as if she knew what I was going through, as if she knew everything I'd been thinking and feeling.

"I'm sorry," I said.

I took her hand and we walked to where the racks of newspapers and paperbacks were, near the cigar counter. I saw a headline about Korea, about cease-fire violations. There were photos of President Truman and General Ridgway, the two of them laughing. I remembered the stack of newspapers in our cellar bin in Brooklyn—my father's collection of papers that headlined great events: Lindbergh's flight to Paris, Roosevelt's four elections to the Presidency, Germany invading Poland, Japan bombing Pearl Harbor, the Normandy invasion, V-E Day and V-J Day, Roosevelt's death and Truman's election. My old baby carriage, mosquito netting over it, was nearby. After my father died, without telling me, my mother had burned the newspapers, had given the carriage away to the junkman.

Gail let her head rest against my chest, but without putting her arms around me.

"I didn't want to hurt you, David. Maybe I made a mistake, not telling you, but it meant so little and I was just afraid that—"

"You don't have to apologize. I get a little crazy sometimes too. You're not the only one—"

"It helps, though, doesn't it—to say you're sorry?" She lifted her head, smiled. "I love you."

"I love you too," I said. Then, "Did you pay the bill?"

"Uh-uh." She led me toward the staircase. The lobby smelled of lavender and ammonia. "I sent the telegrams, though."

"You're teasing me, right?"

"No."

"You really did it?"

"I sent one to my parents and one to your mother. Do you want me to send one to your uncle too? I'll need the address—"

"You're out of your mind," I said, but I was beginning to laugh, to feel the tension drain down from my neck and shoulders. "You are absolutely out of your mind."

"I know. Aren't you glad? And I told them we'd be home tomorrow."

"Tomorrow? I thought—"

She was two steps ahead of me. She turned and looked down. "I signed us up for another night. I figured, since we'd just had our first marital tiff, that we should give ourselves some time to make up. Wasn't that a good idea? Aren't I truly intelligent sometimes? I figured that we were entitled to another whole day and night together, you and me."

9

My MOTHER was leaning way out over the edge of the roof, waving at us, shouting down to get our attention. She yelled that she had a surprise waiting for me in the apartment, but that we should come up to the roof first. Gail leaned backwards, her right hand braced against her hip for balance. My mother told her that she looked wonderful, that she should come up and have some ice-cold lemonade, that she must be dying from the heat.

Going up the five flights of stairs I stayed a step below Gail, my hand in the small of her back, as if pushing her uphill. She was pregnant again, and this time there had been no problems. The baby was due the first week in October—it was now the third week in August—and whenever I'd show that I was nervous about becoming a father she would tease me by declaring that I was stuck with her for good, that I'd had my chance to get away the year before and had chosen not to. *You had your chance.* I thought of how cool Beau Jack's apartment would be. I reminded myself that the real reason we were there was that he had telephoned and asked us to stop by, had told me that he had, at last, found what he was looking for, what he wanted to give us. Although he'd never said anything, I sensed that he had been frightened that my mother and Gail's parents might be able to use the miscarriage to force us into separating, and that he hadn't wanted to jinx things by giving us something until he was certain things would be all right with us.

I pushed open the iron door and stepped out, walked around the brick encasement. I felt my shoes sink into the roof's soft, gravelly surface. I told Gail to be careful, to stay close to me, to watch out for vents, bricks, pipes, guy wires. I took her hand, moved around a chimney, stopped. The three women—my mother, Lillian, Sheila—were lying side by side, sunbathing on an enormous yellow blanket. Their bodies, coated with lotions and creams and oils, shimmered in the afternoon heat. Sheila lay face down between the other two, the top of her bathing suit unhooked, her body evenly tanned. My mother and Lillian lay on their backs, their heads on small plastic pillows. Lillian's nose was covered with a triangle of cardboard. She held a tinfoil reflector, like a bib, under her chin.

Gail leaned against me with one hand, gripped the shaft of a television antenna with the other. The back of my throat ached. I tried to imagine that I was far away, that I was floating high up in the sky on a jet stream, where the air was wonderfully cool and thin, and that I was looking down at the three women, three small plastic dolls embedded in tar.

My mother came toward us, apologizing for having made us climb the five flights, telling Gail to save the kisses unless Gail wanted Noxzema all over her. Sheila sat up, asked Gail how she felt, reached behind and fastened the top of her bathing suit. My mother led Gail away, lifted a jug from a red-and-white-striped ice chest, poured two glasses of lemonade, opened a beach umbrella and pushed it into a roof vent she'd stuffed with a towel. Gail sat in the shade of the umbrella, the glass on her stomach, her feet straight out in front of her. Her ankles were swollen. My mother smoothed Gail's hair, lifted it at the nape of her neck, pinned it up. Gail patted the blanket next to her, handed me my glass. I drank. I imagined a bird swooping down over still water, spreading its wings above its head, the tips touching, so that the wings looked like a black iridescent canopy.

The black heron. Gail had shown me a picture in a book, a photograph of a diorama from a museum in Washington, D.C. The black heron made a circle of shade on the water with its wings so that fish below, thinking it was night, were lured to the surface. I'd told Gail about going to the Museum of Natural History when I was a boy, about wanting to draw the dioramas there, about watching a young man painting the background of one of them once, touching up prairie grass.

Lillian told my mother that Sheila's boyfriend would be coming soon, to take them out for supper. Sheila looked straight at me, asked if Abe had sent me to check up on her. She asked me why, if there was no trouble between Abe and the others, I didn't see my friend Tony anymore.

"Listen Gail," my mother said. "You're a smart girl. Maybe you can tell me what to do, yeah? I finally let Sam take me down to his vault, only after he gets me in there he tells me he already gave away the good

stuff to his daughters. So I walked out on him and now he's calling me
a dozen times a day, saying that if I'd said yes a year ago I could have
had everything, and do you know what I said back to him?"

Gail pressed the frosted glass to her cheek. "What?"

"I said to him, 'Sam, if you ask me, you're coming into this marriage
bare-assed.' "

I walked to the edge of the roof, sat on the ledge sideways. I could feel
the blood rush to my face. I could hear it in my ears. Gail had asked me
once if I'd like a job at a museum, painting dioramas, helping to prepare
exhibits. I'd never had courses in painting or sculpture, I replied. I didn't
know how to use charcoal or watercolors or clay or oil paints. Two days
later she brought home a book about the artist who had made the very
first paintings and sculptures of prehistoric animals. He had begun by
drawing live animals, learning their musculature and movements. Then
he consulted with scientists, worked with fossils, made small clay
models. Only after that had he dared to paint what he'd originally hoped
to paint, conjuring up creatures no artist had ever seen: dinosaurs, mas-
todons, giant sloths.

A man waved to me from the street, yelled up to ask if Sheila was with
me. He was glad I was there, he said. I was just the guy he wanted to
see.

I gripped the ledge, but said nothing. I felt the heat move through my
skin and into my bones. Winston Churchill's hobby, all through the
Second World War, Abe had told me, was bricklaying. Whenever he
wanted to relax and think things through, he would go into his backyard
and lay bricks. Abe liked that. You could trust bricks to be bricks, he
said.

"Is Vincent here already?" Sheila asked.

I remembered Tony, in the schoolyard, making a joke about how so
many Italians had broken dicks because they'd been laying so many
bricks. I'd seen Tony hanging around the bars on Nostrand Avenue with
Vincent. I'd seen Tony riding in a van with his brother Phil. Sometimes
I tried to believe that Tony was letting himself get sucked in because of
Regina—because he was so bitter that her family had sent her away to
Saint Joseph's, up near Hartford, and not to the college in Brooklyn.
Was he trying to punish himself so that she would feel sorry for him?
Sometimes I tried to imagine how he felt, knowing that I'd done with
Gail what he had talked about doing with Regina. But since I saw no
way to keep myself from being drawn in further—from having a family
and a job and raising a child in the world Abe had made for me, in the
world Tony and I had dreamt of escaping—I had to wonder which one
of us had been smarter.

My mother went on talking about Sam, about the way he worshipped her, about how the insurance my father left her was almost gone, about how it had never been enough to set her free so that we could move to California. But now that I was married and she was alone—and with a clean bill of health from the doctors—she didn't know what to do. Could she just leave me and Gail and her grandchild here, to live out her life and her brother's life all over again. Should she say yes to Sam anyway? What did we think?

"I think you should shut up."

The four women stared at me, as if from behind glass, as if frozen in time. None of them blinked. None of them moved. Lillian was bent over, stuffing a pear into her shopping bag. My mother's hand was at her mouth, backwards, the palm toward me. Sheila had one hand at her waist, where she had been buttoning shorts she was slipping on over her bathing suit. The air, hot and unmoving, weighed on my ears. The sun, an enormous globe of lava—salmon-colored in the haze, a filmy orange-red—seemed to be falling through space, to be dripping its heat on me. What would it be like, I wondered, to go through life without ever hearing anything? The heat that penetrated your ears and spiraled toward your brain—would you feel it in a different way? From sports magazines and Beau Jack's copies of *The Police Gazette* I remembered photos of Gene "Silent" Hairston, a black boxer who was deaf, and I remembered wondering, when I was a kid, what it had been like for him, to feel the punches, but never to hear them.

Slowly, eyes closed and body limp, Gail moved her head to the left and then to the right. The scene melted. Sheila sneered. Lillian put the pear into the bag. My mother gestured to Gail with her hands to show how helpless she felt. Elephants, Gail had once told me, flapped their ears in hot weather to cool themselves, to lower the temperature of their blood as it passed through their ears. I thought of Gail sitting up in bed, moaning, pointing to the blood on the sheets. I thought of us in her hospital room, the doctor explaining to us that the miscarriage had been normal—nature's way of getting rid of something that wasn't meant to live—and that there was no reason in the world we wouldn't be able to conceive again and have a healthy baby. Did we believe him? Did Gail believe me when I told her that it wasn't guilt that made me stay with her, love her? Now you have the chance you've been waiting for, she said. So take it.

Lillian said that when I was angry I sounded just like Abe. My mother talked about how she felt sorry for me, how she had hoped that the prospect of a new baby might change me. I turned away, stared out at the trees, the sky, the rooftops of other buildings. I lowered my gaze to the houses across the street, small two-storey wooden homes, gray and white and brown. Who lived in them? It had puzzled me, when I was younger, that there was a long row of private homes, without alleyways or driveways between them, and that I never knew any of the people—mostly elderly couples, German Catholics—who lived in them. Sometimes I saw them in the deli on Rogers Avenue, carrying out food in little white containers, and sometimes I saw them in front of their houses, clipping hedges, raking leaves. Behind their closed doors and drawn curtains, did they scream and shout at each other the way we did?

I looked up again. Two blocks away birds swirled lazily, drifting downwards on warm currents of air, settling into the tower of Holy Cross Church, into the dark vaulted space next to the clock. Twenty past four.

Gail's hand was on my shoulder. I controlled the impulse to shrug it off. "I'll be okay," I said. "Don't worry about me so much, all right? And don't tell me again that I'm not my father."

"Do you want to hear the craziest thing, though?" my mother said. "The craziest thing is this call I had from Mr. Rothenberg the other day, inviting me to come out and have tea with him on his estate one day. So what do you make of it?"

"I make nothing of it," Lillian said. She had a small mirror propped up on the edge of the roof and was putting on makeup, painting her eyelids silver-blue. "In fact, I'd make believe it never happened because all he is, if you ask me, is an old man with most of his marbles gone. Including the ones in his pants. I hear they got him in a wheelchair with a big black guy who does everything for him. And I mean *everything*."

"What I said to Sam, see, was that if the only thing I cared about in this life was money, then all I'd have to do was to be nice to Mr. Rothenberg the way a woman still knows how. But I told Sam that I just happen to be the kind of girl who's not like that. Only listen, Davey. He told me he'd been dreaming about snow. Can you believe it? He talked about how his dreams were full of clean snow and in the middle of the snow was my mother in a black sable coat. She was the most beautiful woman he had ever known, he said, and—get this—before he died, since he couldn't see her face again and since he had no pictures, he wondered if I could visit him. He said he remembered how much we resembled one another. So what should I do?"

The roof door swung open. Lillian put a finger to her lips, in warning. Sheila tried to kiss Vincent, to put her arms around his neck. Vincent pushed her aside, grinned, came toward me, his hand extended. Light flashed from a dark tiger's-eye pinky ring. "Hey Davey, how you been? How's tricks? I just saw you up on the roof, did you know that?" He laughed, told Sheila that it was too hot for smooching. He wore canary yellow slacks, a navy-blue sport shirt open at the neck, a gold medallion hanging there on a heavy chain. He was about five-foot-six, Sheila's height—stocky and broad, with a football player's build, perfect for what coaches called a watch-charm guard. He stopped a few feet from me, feet spread, saw that I was not going to shake his hand. "I hear good things about you, Davey. I hear you and your beautiful wife is expecting." He turned to the others, moved his hand to his head. He was balding. I figured him to be eight to ten years older than me, pushing thirty. "Gonna make one beautiful kid, two good-looking parents like this, don't you think, ladies? All that dark hair, right?"

He put an arm around Lillian, asked if she could talk her husband into coming to the wedding, then laughed when Lillian and Sheila started arguing with each other about whether or not it was a free country, about who would have to live with Abe afterwards.

"Hey hey hey," Vincent said, one arm around each of them. "Calm down—just calm down, ladies. Let's not get all excited for nothing. *Piano piano*, right Davey?"

I stared right through him. Vincent D'Agostino owed Abe over twelve thousand dollars in gambling debts. Vincent D'Agostino was a punk, a born loser, an Italian butterfly—even his own kind didn't want him, Abe said. Still, we had to be wary. If Vincent got too deep in debt, or—worse still—if he got so deep in debt that he had nothing left to lose, he would do whatever he had to in order to stay alive. Abe did not believe for a second that Vincent was making a move on Sheila merely so that Abe would erase his debts. Things were rarely that simple. Abe believed that they were trying to set him up. Why had Vincent come to us with his bets in the first place? Why had Benny taken the bets when Vincent was not in our territory? Our family life should have taught us that, at least, Abe said to me—that sometimes when people agreed to marriage, what they really wanted was war and death.

Vincent put a hand on my arm.

"Don't touch me."

"Ah come on, Davey—don't be so goddamned sensitive. What do you think I am, some kind of faggot?" He laughed. "Hey listen, ladies, speaking of faggots, did you hear the one about the guy who gets in bed with his wife on their wedding night and just before they're about to you-know-what, he says to her that he got this confession to make, see, that he used to be a homo when he was younger." He paused, for effect. "So the poor girl, see, she didn't know which way to turn—" Sheila laughed. Vincent followed me, whispered: "Did it ever hurt a guy to listen? You got nothing to lose, believe me." He turned to the others. "Hey—I got a terrific idea. How about we all go out to eat at the Chink's. My treat."

"With whose money?" I asked.

"Ah come on, Davey," he said, and I was angry at once for having spoken. "I told Little Benny this morning—I'm gonna take care of all that in the next ten days. Cross my heart."

Gail touched my hand. "I don't feel well," she said. "Can we go? I'd like to lie down."

Before I knew it, my mother was helping Gail across the roof, telling me to get the umbrella and ice chest. Vincent pulled the umbrella from its socket, pressed down on the struts. I bent over, picked up the ice chest. The women were gone.

"Look—I know what's on your mind, Davey," Vincent said. "Only think of it this way: if I married your cousin and if Abe gave his blessing it would be like in the olden days, right? The way kings and queens used to make deals with their countries by marrying their children off to each other. It stopped a lot of wars that didn't have to be."

"Save it."

"You want me to spell it out for you? Okay then, I'll spell it out for you. You want me to say what we both know anyway, but without words? Okay. I'll do that too." His voice was hard in a way that surprised me. "Listen hey—you think I like being in the middle of all this? Not on your life. All I know is what they tell me, and what they tell me is that they got nothing against you. Absolutely nothing and you should know that. They don't really got nothing against your uncle either. All they want is peace, do you follow? All they want is for him to listen to reason. Only, like you know, your uncle can be a very stubborn guy. Him and Rothenberg."

I watched the words pouring from his mouth and tried to do what Abe had taught me to do, to imagine him as he'd been when he was a kid. Vincent talked about his debt, about being on the level with Sheila, about territory and borders. Everything could be straightened out easily enough if only people were willing to sit down and talk things out reasonably. That was the message. They wanted to be generous to my uncle. They liked the fact that there had been peace between our organizations for so many years now. They wanted to keep that peace. They respected my uncle. They wanted his goodwill. He was a good business-man, a fine organizer.

Vincent was jiggling coins from hand to hand. I thought of the metal slugs Tony and I had used, the change that poured from the vending machines. Vincent slipped the coins into his side pocket, told me that all they wanted was to keep things clean and legitimate—maybe to con-solidate a bit—but that if my uncle wouldn't talk with them, they would be very interested in talking with me because they figured that I was his heir, right?

I had him against the wall before he could take his hand from his

pocket, my knee wedged hard against his crotch to keep him from moving, my fist at his throat, yanking up on his gold chain. His eyes rolled.
I smelled whiskey and after-shave lotion. I pulled him toward me as if to
smash him backwards, to crack his head against the bricks that housed
the staircase. He was whimpering, begging me not to hurt him, and I
was seeing a small, fat, dark-haired boy sitting at a kitchen table, picking
his nose. His older brothers were laughing at him. His mother served
him soup, rapped him on the side of the head with the ladle, warned
him that the next time she caught him with his finger in his nose she'd
break his head.

Vincent kept begging me not to hurt him. If I spoke I knew that the
only sound that would come from my mouth would be air, like the
sound from a leaking tire. I shoved him against the wall again, then let
go. He bent over, his face in his hands, tried to catch his breath. He
looked up at me slowly and smiled. He had stopped whimpering. His
eyes showed no fear. Why not? I stared at the hole in his face—at his
mouth—and I remembered Little Benny sitting on my uncle's desk,
telling the guys about someone who had once tried to welch on a bet,
who had asked if Benny wanted him to suck his cock. Benny had shoved
the barrel of his gun into the guy's mouth. "This is my cock," he said,
and he'd pulled the trigger.

Had he been bragging? Was he trying to impress me? To scare me?
Vincent brushed the back of his hair down with his hand.

"But I delivered the message, right? You're my witness. You got the
message."

Sheila was screaming at Vincent to hurry. I moved toward him, but
he held up a hand, cautioned me to come no closer. "Here. I want to
show you something first, okay? Let me show you something else."

He reached down, lifted his cuff as if to straighten his socks, and then
a small black pistol was in his hand, aimed at my chest. "You'd be
surprised at my speed," he said, and before I could react, the gun was
gone, and he was holding the beach umbrella in his hand. He walked
toward the staircase, opened the roof door, turned back to me. "No
kidding, Davey—like I said, I got nothing against you. In fact, I been
trying to talk Mr. Fasalino into waiting on things till after your kid
comes. I mean, you know how we Wops are—what suckers we are for
women and kids." I said nothing. "You ask your old pal Tony. A smart
guy like you ain't cut out for this kind of stuff, which is why you should
take my advice and go have a talk with them, private, or you should talk
your uncle into one. Believe me, they ain't playing potsie." He started
down the stairs.

I didn't move. I wanted to tear his tongue from his mouth, to jam it
onto an iron stake.

"I could have done something real bad to you, kid, like I hope you realize, but I figure you're under a lot of stress, right? I mean with your uncle's troubles and the baby coming, and who likes the fucking city in August? I'll tell you something else though—with me and Sheila, it's the real thing, just like with you and Gail."

"*Vin-cent!*" Sheila screamed.

"Times are changing, Davey." He mopped his forehead and neck with a handkerchief. "Who needs this lousy heat, but maybe the sun is better for some people than others. Your uncle, he should consider going someplace like California or Arizona, where he can have sunshine all year round. That's what you're supposed to tell him. He should come and talk with my family and then he should take a long voyage and live a happy life."

"*Vincent!*"

"I'm coming, I'm coming," he called. He winked at me. "Women! Who ain't a sucker for a beautiful face, right?" He picked up the umbrella and the towels. "But she got a good heart, Sheila. When we're alone, just the two of us—I mean, you'd be surprised. . . ." He gave me a quick glance, his eyes watering. "No hard feelings, okay, Davey?"

Gail was asleep on the living room couch, her hands straight at her sides, an electric fan set on a chair, directed at her face. The room was dark, the venetian blinds drawn. My mother took my hand, led me toward my bedroom, told me that she loved Gail as if Gail were her own daughter. She put a finger to her lips.

"Shh. Come. You come with me first, so you can see the surprise I got waiting for you in your old room. And Davey?"

"Yes."

"I been scared to do this and all I ask is that you promise me first not to tell Abe, okay?" She held her hand in front of her. "See how I'm shaking, an old woman like me? Would you promise me that—that you'll let me tell Abe when I'm ready?"

"I promise."

She opened the door and the cold air rushed at me, as if a wall of it had given way. "Sam got it for me because of the heat wave."

I entered the room. At the far end, between the two windows, a man was sitting in a wooden chair, his back to us, his head tilted so that the air conditioner blew on his face. The door closed. Nothing was the same. Everything, except for the mirror, had been rearranged. Where were my books and magazines? My desk? My mother spoke into the man's ear.

"Poppa, listen—it's me, Evie. I got Davey here. He wants to see you. Come—"

She helped him to turn so that I could see his face. I stayed where I was, watched motes of dust spin around in the late afternoon sunlight, drift down upon him. Despite the soft white light, his face was all sharp angles. How long had it been since I'd seen him—three years? Four? There were purple crescents under his eyes, like raised scars. There were patches of dark stubble along his cheek and neck and chin. I stared at the shape of his skull, the gray skin stretched over it, stained here and there with brown liver spots, the dome of his head veined with pale-blue threads.

"He's been here since last weekend. Nobody knows except Beau Jack, who helped me get Poppa here from New York." She stopped, as if she wanted to cry. "Tell me I did the right thing, Davey, please? I mean, he's my own flesh and blood just like you and Abe—"

Her father looked up. "What?" he asked. "What did you say?"

She kissed the top of his head, cupped his narrow chin in her hand and lifted his face, pointed him toward me. "I said that Davey is here, Poppa. He came to visit you. You remember Davey, don't you?"

He spoke, but I couldn't understand him. The words gurgled from him as if from a hole in his throat.

"He thinks I understand Russian." My mother laughed, nervously. "Sometimes he even thinks I'm Momma. But who knows what we'll be like when we get to his age, yeah? I mean, think of where he started, of all he's seen, of the whole life he had that we don't know nothing about."

Her father looked at me and his eyes cleared, his neck straightened. "Davey's a good boy. I always said so." He took my hand, pressed a quarter into it. His fingers were cold and bony. "Here. This is from me to you. Now show me your wife."

"She's sleeping, Poppa," my mother said. "Remember how I told you she's going to have a baby—her and Davey—so she needs to sleep."

"I want to see your wife. Why is she hiding from me? What did I do to her?"

His eyelids dropped and his chin fell to his chest. Mouth open, he began wheezing.

"Sometimes he does that. In the middle of anything, he just falls asleep."

"Can we eat soon? We promised Gail's parents we would stop by later."

"Listen. I got some nice cold chicken salad I made before you got here, but I wanted you to know that Sam already agreed it's okay by him if Poppa comes to live with us. Are you surprised? Did I do the right thing? I mean, like you see, he ain't no trouble really, and I got the extra room now. . . . ." She pressed my arm, at the elbow. "You won't tell Abe? He'll never come visit me if he finds out, but I got this crazy dream, see —you know me—that maybe if I arrange things right—if I hope enough!—that maybe they can still forgive one another, that maybe they can still remember that they're a father and a son."

"Where are all my things?"

"Your things?"

In the mirror I saw the door open. Gail stepped into the room. She closed her eyes, drew the cold air in through her nostrils. "Wonderful!" she said. "Oh my God, but that feels wonderful!"

"I would have let you in here before, to lie down," my mother said, "but I felt it was only right to show Davey first." Gail looked at me, puzzled. "It's my father. I brought him here to live with me now that you and Davey got your own place."

My grandfather lifted his head, put out his hand. "Hello," he said. "You must be Davey's wife. *Da.* Come closer so I can look at you. My eyes aren't so good anymore."

Gail moved to him, let him take her hands.

"Good," he said. "Listen. I'm glad you married our Davey. He's a good boy. You should be happy together for many years. I give you my blessing."

"Oh Poppa—!"

"She's a beautiful woman. I know a beautiful woman when I see one. You're a lucky boy. Would you give me a kiss?"

Gail kissed him on the forehead.

"No." He took her hand, pointed to his mouth. "The right way. Here."

Gail kissed him on the mouth.

"I'm not sick," he said. "I'm just old, but I know what's happening. You'll come visit me, you and Davey? Good. Don't be strangers. Family is family." He took my mother's hand, kissed it. "This is my best daughter."

"You have another daughter?" Gail asked.

"No." He smiled. "But she's my best."

His head sagged, his mouth fell open.

We left. In the kitchen, my mother said that she had taken my things to the bin in the cellar, that I could pick them up when I wanted. I heard footsteps. The bathroom door opened and closed. My mother was telling Gail that if she ever needed to take a water stain out of wood—if somebody left a wet glass on furniture—she should mix ashes with mayonnaise and rub it in, but not in hot weather. She asked if Gail's friends or family were going to make her a baby shower. Had Gail's parents mentioned providing her with a layette? She said she had picked up some beautiful hand-knit sweaters at the Muscular Dystrophy Rummage Shop on Nostrand Avenue.

She left us, came back a few minutes later with a stack of clothing, soft layers of pink and blue and white. She showed us each item, asked what we thought. Did we realize how much these things would cost if she'd bought them new? She banged an ice tray on the kitchen counter. She told us she wasn't looking for thanks. Abe was right about that. Did I remember what he used to tell people? That if what you wanted in life was gratitude, you should get a dog.

My grandfather came into the kitchen dressed in a double-breasted blue jacket, a clean white shirt, a maroon tie. He had shaved and there were small pieces of toilet paper stuck to his neck and cheeks. My mother told him how handsome he looked. He sat and told Gail that she looked beautiful. Women always did when they were pregnant, he said. The eyes looked inward, drew men toward them. He spoke in Russian, then translated: If a woman had something in the oven—he patted his stomach—you could know it by the radiant fire in her cheeks, by the silver smoke in her eyes.

I looked to the window, recalled pulling a black shade down during an air raid drill. I imagined my father groping his way toward the cellar to get his helmet and gas mask from the bin. Would he stumble and fall? Gail reached for the bowl of chicken salad, but my grandfather grabbed her wrist. He drew a black silk cap from his pocket and placed it upon his head. First, he said, we should say a prayer. We should never begin a meal without saying a prayer. We were still Jews, weren't we?

I carried the shopping bag, filled with baby clothes, down the stairs. The cellar smelled of chalk dust. I stared in through the slats of our bin but I couldn't make out much except for lamps and chairs, the dark shapes of cartons. Beau Jack's door opened. He tipped his baseball cap to Gail. We entered. He asked if we wanted tea. Tea was the best thing for you in hot weather, he said. Gail was surprised at how cool his apartment was. Was it air-conditioned? Beau Jack smiled, said that it couldn't be air-conditioned because he had no windows, but he explained to her about the vents in the ceiling, the ducts that carried warm air all the way up and out through the roof, five stories above, that sucked coolness from the earth below ground. He asked her if she had ever heard of the Nubians, and of how, in Egypt, they cooled their desert homes. Even modern engineers could not imitate with electricity what the Nubians did without it. He showed Gail pictures of Nubian homes, in a book I had looked at often—white mud-brick windowless

buildings, some with barrel-vaulted roofs, others connected to one another the way Pueblo dwellings were, beams jutting out near the tops
where the air-slits were. The inner chambers were high-ceilinged and
dark, the floors made of earth, the walls white, decorated above the
doors with dinner plates.

If things got as bad as I figured they might, could I hide Gail and our
child out here? Did Beau Jack have some secret chamber, behind or
below his rooms? Would he be willing to help Abe, if only for my sake?

Beau Jack poured tea for us, took milk and lemon from the refrigerator. He set a plate of Lorna Doones and Oreo cookies on the table, and
while we sat there for a while, sipping tea and eating, I surprised myself
by beginning to talk, telling Gail about all the hours Beau Jack and I had
sat in the room together and listened to baseball games. I remembered
making scorecards—drawing lines on blank paper with pencil and ruler,
writing in the names of the players, putting in the play-by-play, inning
by inning. I remembered listening to Red Barber's voice, to the teletype
machine that clicked away behind him. Beau Jack and I had agreed that
that would be a hard job: to sit in a room by yourself somewhere in
Brooklyn, a microphone in front of you, and try to make a game real
and exciting when all you had to work with was a long, thin strip of
paper that typed words out in front of you, giving you only the bare
essentials—balls and strikes, runs and hits and errors—of a game that
was taking place in a city thousands of miles away. I remembered how
much I loved to lean back, to rest my feet on Kate's silky fur.

I looked around. "Is Kate in the bedroom?"

Beau Jack leaned toward me. "Didn't your Momma tell you?"

"Tell me what?"

"Kate's gone, honey. She died the beginning of June. I thought you
knew."

"I'm sorry," I said. I felt my heart catch. "I'm so sorry—"

"Oh me too, Davey. Me too." He ran his finger around the rim of his
cup. "But she died nice and easy, so I'm glad for that. She just went to
sleep one morning and didn't wake up."

"How old was she?" Gail asked.

"Sixteen. That means she would have been more than a hundred in
human years."

I kept my eyes on Beau Jack's face, tried to imagine what he was
feeling, what he'd felt when he touched Kate for the last time. I wished
that I'd spent more time with him during the past few years. I wondered:
what I felt toward him now, and what I thought I'd felt for him through
all the years—did those feelings come, really, only from me, from my
own needs and desires and not from who he was, from what *he* thought
and felt? In what ways did we *know* one another, and what did it mean,

after all, to truly know another human being. Had I merely used him somehow, stuck my feelings onto him the way I'd stuck pictures of my sports heroes on my bedroom wall? I wondered how often Tony thought about Regina and if, when she was in from college, he tried to see her. How could he *not* think about her all the time? If you truly loved somebody else—if you were in the middle of *being* in love when the other person suddenly stopped loving you, how could you ever stop hoping? How could you ever stop wanting to get the other person's love back?

"Do you mind being alone now?"

He touched the spot on the side of his head where the bud of his missing ear was, and when he looked at me, his eyes moist, I knew I'd said the right thing.

"Oh sure, honey. Who wouldn't mind being alone? It's always good to have someone near you, Davey, don't I know that much? The hard thing is to not have someone to be taking care of."

"Yes," Gail said. "But what happens to them? The dead animals, I mean. I used to wonder about that all the time. Where are all the dead squirrels and rabbits and pigeons and sparrows and chipmunks? I used to walk the streets and sneak into my neighbors' gardens, but I almost never found a dead one."

"I buried Kate out in the courtyard. I sit there sometimes now, where you and I used to have catches together, Davey, and I think about her, about how much we loved each other. Does that make old Beau Jack sound like a fool?"

"No."

"I mean, it's not so much not to be loved. The bad thing, it's when you got nobody *to* love. Your Momma, she been coming down to visit me lots since Kate's gone. She got a good heart. I guess you know now how I helped out with her father. I'm glad she done that, only I'm scared for what your uncle Abe do when *he* finds out. That's what Beau Jack worries about. That man still scares me."

"Me too," Gail said.

Silence.

Beau Jack reached across and touched my hand, told me not to worry about him, that he was taking good care of himself. He had his radio so he could listen to the games, and he was thinking of getting a small television set so he could watch Jackie. Weren't we right about that man, about how great he was going to be? Beau Jack said he was in a television store last week, on Flatbush Avenue, watching a Dodger game, and he liked the way they used a split-screen to show how Jackie worried the pitchers when he got to first base.

"Roy, though, he's in a bad slump this year," Beau Jack said. "I worry about him, the way he never stops smiling but always goes up and down and up and down. Not behind the plate. He's the best man there I ever saw, but he gets in awful slumps *at* the plate, and our Dodgers, without him blasting away and with big Newk still off in the service, I don't think they're gonna make it this year." He winked at Gail. "I guess by getting married you saved our boy from going over to Korea like big Newk. I'm glad for that."

"Who's big Newk?" Gail asked.

"Don Newcombe," I said. "He won twenty games year before last, before he got called up. He led the league in strikeouts."

I stood, as if to go.

"Were *you* ever married?" Gail asked. I glared at her. Hadn't I told her that I needed to be home soon, in case there was a message from Abe?

"Oh no," Beau Jack said. "I was never married. Ain't that too bad?"

"Yes," Gail said.

"Wasn't because I didn't want to. I was in love, for sure. It was the woman I loved who gave me my name, over in France. She called me Beau Jack—that meant Handsome Jack in French, like the boxer's name, only my Christian name, it was John. Oh sure."

He closed his eyes, let his head bob up and down a few times. When Gail broke the silence a minute later her voice was so soft and low that I hardly recognized it.

"What was her name?"

"Marcelle. She had hair a lot like yours, didn't you know that? Everybody loved her hair, you always be wanting to touch it." Beau Jack touched Gail's hair in the exact way I'd seen him touch Kate a thousand times. "Oh how that girl loved her hair. It was so soft and silk-like after she washed it, and in the summer, she'd pin it up the way you do."

"David's mother pinned mine up for me."

"Marcelle, she had a mother too, which was where we got our first troubles, only you children don't want to hear the whole story. You got to be getting on home, so—"

"We'd love to hear the story," Gail said.

"Well, I'll tell you this, that we met each other when they sent me down to rest up after they fixed my ear, down to a place they called Savoy, which was the same as the name of the famous dance place up in Harlem then. We all liked that. They sent soldiers there from all over France, you see, away from where the fighting was to where they had beautiful mountains and lakes and these special places to take baths, all stone and marble, where the Romans once did the same. You even saw giant mountains with snow on them that they drove us out to see, where Hannibal crossed over the Alps, only those mountains look like nobody ever walked on them, they so high and clean."

I thought of Tony and me, talking about how nice it would be to live out in the country someday, each of us in our own private homes, with our families, surrounded by beautiful green mountains. Without a wife, could Tony just take off one afternoon and never see his father or his brothers again? And if Abe was right about the trouble that was coming, even though Tony and I weren't friends anymore, would we somehow be able to avoid being enemies? I looked at Beau Jack, as if to give him permission to continue. He smiled. Gail had said that according to the laws of quantum physics, disorganization always increased within a closed system. Salt and pepper, in layers in a shaker, became gray when mixed and, no matter how much you kept shaking, would never again return to separate layers of black and white. I'd given her theory to Abe and he had said that men like Rothenberg and Fasalino didn't need to go to college to discover such things, to believe that the moment you stopped expanding you were already dead.

"I was stationed up in Saint Nazaire till then mostly, unloading ships —we had more than fifty thousand colored soldiers there working as stevedores, and they tried to make things nice for us too. We had canteens and women come over on ships from the States to set up Y.M.C.A. buildings and Hostess Houses and Honey Bee Clubs for us to spend our free time in. To give us the gentle and civilizing influence of women, is the words they used. And they brought in colored French women too, from their colonies in Africa, for our dances. But you don't want to hear all about Beau Jack in the Army, do you?"

"But I do," Gail said.

"Well, you just like Davey then, didn't you know that? When he was a boy, he couldn't get enough of Beau Jack's stories. Oh I seen terrible things, Gail—Davey can tell you—I seen such terrible things when I was young then. I seen men when they be clutching their stomachs from being shot and then they got their fingers blowed off their hands. I seen men with their eyes wide open and their whole jaws hanging half off. I seen brains spill out the backs of heads and I seen them string up poor colored boys in their pretty uniforms—they made us come out and watch, all in lines—'cause they say they raped the French girls. War was more personal then, like they say, and Davey, he had a way to make me tell him about all that bad stuff. He loved to hear about all the fighting I seen, only you know how I knew he still had a good heart?"

"Tell me."

"Because one day when I was telling him about what the trenches were like and what mustard gas did to you, how you got to look right at the people you were killing and they got to look at you, and how they trucked us out afterwards in gangs for burying all those poor white boys, and when I say to Davey that he just like all these smart kids who think war is fine till they get over there themselves, when I ask if he wants to be a soldier when he grows up, like me and his uncle Abe, he answers me no. Just like that. Oh no, he says. Oh no, Beau Jack. I like to *play* soldier, but I wouldn't want to ever have to really kill somebody. I wouldn't ever want to hurt anybody. So that I see he knows the difference."

"I hope so," Gail said. She took my hand. I settled back in my chair, knowing there was no way we would leave without hearing the rest of Beau Jack's story. That was fine with me. Gail said her father wanted to talk with me privately and I wasn't looking forward to that. As for reporting to Abe about Vincent, I figured that could wait until we got home. If anything urgent was up, Abe would get a message to me, probably by hand, since he was convinced that Fasalino had had a drop on our telephone lines for the past few weeks. I listened to Beau Jack's voice and wondered the way I'd always wondered when I was with him, about how the world beyond his voice and his room could be as real as I knew it was. Who could tell? Maybe Vincent was on the level and loved Sheila and was going to pay Abe back. Maybe Fasalino really wanted peace. Maybe I could telephone Tony—in my mind I saw him smiling and brushing his hair back, happy to hear me talk to him the way he had always talked to me—and suggest that he get back together with Regina, knock her up good and then marry her so that the two of us could go down to the schoolyard together and, while we played one-on-one, talk about solving the problems we had in common.

"Oh, he still does," Beau Jack said to Gail. "Which is why tonight I'll just skip the war story and give you the love story. The love story, though, it got the same bad ending the war stories have, except it only happened to two people and nobody died from it.

"The French, they had their colored soldiers in separate units like we did, and the French people, they the same as people all over and they have funny ideas about us, that all we ever think about is gambling and making love with their daughters and stealing from them. Some of them think we got tails like monkeys too, and they get nasty with us. So we keep to our own pretty much, except in this place they send us to rest, where they liked us better because of a legend they have there.

"In this little town, see, near where they have the baths, they would take us in groups to see a church—I showed Davey the photo from the newspaper—and up front in the church they have a statue on the altar of a little black child in Mary's arms, and that child wearing robes of gold and diamonds, and the people in the towns all around, they come there to get themselves healed. They call it the Church of the Black Madonna, and there be crutches and canes and eyepatches and the like around, from people who come there to be blessed. Lots of our boys done the same with their prayers, and didn't it work sometimes too?

"Now the story they tell to us was that the town this church was in, Aix-les-Bains, it got destroyed by a mountain-slide hundreds of years before, with only the church left standing and all the families from the village inside the church, praying to God to be saved. This pretty girl be our guide, and she was telling us the story in English and some of our boys were starting in to pray, and I see something in that girl's eyes that draw me right down inside her—you know how I mean?—and I say to her, I say, does she think that if I pray hard enough I'll get my ear grown back? Now I didn't say that with the other boys around but when she all finished with her speech and we were left alone to wander around and light candles if we wanted, and you know what she do when I ask my question?"

"What?" Gail asked.

"She just start in laughing and laughing, and she reaches right up and lifts my bandage and peeks under and then she laughs some more. Her laugh kind of gurgles from down low, and when she looks at me all I want is to be nearer and nearer to her. You know how that feels? She had hazel-brown eyes with these flecks in them like gold slivers, and even though I was scared, I can't help but want to be nearer to her and look in those eyes and make her laugh some more. So when she was done laughing we got to talking. She asked me questions about myself and how I lost my ear, and then she says, 'Come on, brown soldier boy,' just like that, and she takes me for a walk, holding my hand, and before you know it I was getting out of the hospital every chance I could and I was telling her that the real miracle, it was the two of us meeting one another. How you explain that, I ask her, that out of all the world to wander in, we happen to be in the same place on the same day? How you explain it, that if I don't lose my ear and she don't be so good in English at school that they make her a guide, that we might never know each other existed? I lost my ear, but I found you, I say to her. You *hear* that? That's the way I talk to her, to make her laugh and to cry, and oh sure, how I got my name is one day out at the lake she just start in calling me her Beau Jack so that my name be half-French and half-American. She liked to take my bandage off and touch my ear and make me promise not to take no more chances, especially not to gamble no more, 'cause if somebody take my other ear off, then how I gone to hear her laugh?"

"You lost your ear *gambling?*" Gail asked.

"Maybe."

"*Maybe?*"

"Oh child, we got to leave some mysteries for you, didn't you know that? If you and Davey know *everything* about Beau Jack, what gone to make you come back for more stories? Marcelle and me, we talk about that, how it was the same being in love, that you know you're in love when you still always wanting to know more about the other person even when you think you never been closer to anyone.

"But we were awful scared, from the first. Her mother be warning her all the time about colored soldiers, and our officers warning us about staying away from white women, and maybe being scared made our love a little more special too—we admit that to each other—and what happened finally is that we made up to meet at this band concert they have every Sunday afternoon in these gardens in town, to show we not hiding, and when she gets there to meet me, her Momma's there too—her father be dead from the time she was eleven—Marcelle, she's wearing a yellow kerchief on her head. I can see it now, 'cause it wasn't gold like that child's robe and it wasn't bright like the sun. It was just flat yellow like grass without rain.

"Now when her mother sees me, her standing there with all her family and neighbors too, she calls my name out and then she rips the kerchief off Marcelle's hair and I see that Marcelle's hair is gone. They chopped those black curls off and must of shaved the rest so that you see these little ugly red nicks, and they spitting French words at me too and all I thinking is how I wish I could cover that head and put that hair back. I seen death a thousand times over by then—good friends too—but nothing seem so terrible as that poor head. And Marcelle, while the rest all cursing me, she walks straight up to me and she kisses me hard one time on each cheek and she says to me, 'Well, Beau Jack, we were wrong, yes? There are no miracles.'

"She was one brave girl, I tell you that. She turn back on her family and she says to them what she say to me before, when we by ourselves, that if I was good enough to stop a German bullet to help save them all, how come I'm not good enough to stop her heart and make her life happy? That's what she said, and what I think ever since is that it takes more courage to do that—to say those words—than most things I ever saw soldiers do, and I saw some brave men too.

"Poor Beau Jack, he didn't know what to do, so he stand there for a while and let them curse him, and then he just turn and run. When I got back to my place in the hospital, I tried hard to think about what choices we had, about us maybe going off together to start a new life, but it didn't take much thinking to see the foolishness it all was. You got to look at facts too sometimes, and how you gone to live when the world won't let you. So I figure the best thing for her life, it be to leave. Those French, they know how to be mean when they want, I tell you that.

They mean to be mean, like they say. So I never seen Marcelle again, children, and that's the end of the story."

We were quiet for a while. Then Gail spoke. "That's *all?*" she asked. Beau Jack nodded. I looked at Beau Jack's face—tried to read his eyes— and I recalled him telling me about the green pigeons, in France, that would fly over them and die from fright at the sound of gunfire—about how soldiers would shoot their guns into the air just so they could see the pigeons die and fall. Was it true? Had he made the story up?

"Will you get another dog?" I asked.

"No," Beau Jack said. "It's too late and you got to think about who's gone to take care of who and what happens to some dog if something happens to me. Beau Jack's not getting younger." He laughed to himself. "Now you take in a hungry dog from the street, you know, and you feed him and give him lots of love and get him to obey you, see, and he won't bite you." Beau Jack stood, went to the sink and set his cup down. He turned to us. "That's the main difference between a dog and a man, you ask me."

"Did you make that up?" Gail asked.

"Oh no. I read that on a calendar one time from something Mark Twain wrote. But here." He reached into his locker, brought out a small package wrapped in white paper, tied with a silver ribbon. "Here's what I got for you, why I asked you to stop by today. I thought a long time until I found what I wanted for you children. But you don't open it now, all right, 'cause it only make me upset if you do. You open it before you go to sleep, and then, when I'm getting ready to go to sleep, I'll know you be thinking of Beau Jack."

I sat in Mr. Kogan's study, trying to pay attention to him, to what he was offering me, but all I could think of was Gail and of how happy she was when Ellen came to her in the foyer and asked permission to touch her stomach, to press her ear there.

"All right then. I'll put it as simply and frankly as I can." Mr. Kogan tapped his pipe on an ashtray. "I'm certain you're aware that I didn't like it when you and Gail were dating, that I was not in favor of the marriage —and certainly Hannah was as upset as I was—but I do see how happy Gail is with you, and that's what matters most to me. I accept you, David. I like you, in fact."

I stared at him, gave away nothing. I thought of Gail in a room above me, lying on Ellen's bed. I looked at the photos on Mr. Kogan's desk. To one side of the large green blotter was a head-and-shoulders picture of him in an Army officer's uniform, and tucked into a corner of the frame was a smaller photo of a group of soldiers, arms around one

another. I wondered why it was that in old photos of soldiers or ballplay-
ers or coal miners, the men always appeared to be so much older than
they actually were.

"We've always worried a bit about Gail, as you know, yet I find, in
truth, since she's with you—since I've come to know you somewhat—
that I don't worry anymore."

"So?"

We sat in black leather armchairs, facing each other across an oval
table inlaid with a checkerboard pattern of wood veneers. Mr. Kogan's
study was warm and dark, filled with books and sculptures, photos and
plaques and tennis trophies, framed certificates that thanked him for
service he'd given to hospitals and charities.

"So now that Gail and you are about to have a child, Hannah and I
would like you to have something from us to help you get a start in your
new life. We'd like to give you a gift."

"You already gave us a gift."

He looked out the picture window, at their backyard. He and Ellen
gardened there together. Ellen could tell flowers by their scents, by the
feel of leaf and blossom and stem and bud. She had won prizes at the
Brooklyn Botanic Garden for plants she'd raised, for her flower arrange-
ments.

"You don't make things easy for me, do you? Well, I don't mind
admitting that I'm nervous with you, David, nervous in the same way
I'm often nervous before I have to talk to a patient about what I'm going
to do. We won't press the analogy, though, all right?" He smiled at me.
"I suppose it is true that I spend a good part of my life telling people
about the terrible things I must do to them—invasive procedures, we
call them—while trying, always, not to make them fearful."

I didn't react. He said that when the baby was older he wanted to help
Gail complete her college education. He would help put me through
college also, if I wanted that. He would help me get started in a good job
or a business. Would I at least promise to *think* about giving him the
chance to do these things for us?

I told him that I already had a job.

What he wanted, he said, was for me to think not about the life I had,
but about the life Gail and I and our child *might* have—about the kind
of life I wanted to give them. He *was* happy that we had stayed together,
that Gail had been strong enough to resist his pressure. He had told her
so. He had apologized to her already. But the offer he was presenting to
me now was something she did not know about.

"I tell her everything," I said. "We have no secrets from one another."

"Really? Everything your uncle tells you, you tell Gail?"

I gripped the arms of the chair, saw him glance at my hands.

"All you really want," I said, "is for me to stop working for my uncle so that I can work for you, so that Gail and I can lead the kind of life *you* want us to have."

"Not at all," he said calmly. "You're a bright boy, David—I could see that at once, just looking at your eyes. Did Gail ever tell you that I have that knack—for reading a person's intelligence—that I used to be able to guess her friends' I.Q.s within five or ten points, just from being with them for a while and watching the light come and go in their eyes? So I know how bright you are, approximately. And how much you love my daughter, not approximately."

I looked toward the sliding glass doors that led to the garden and was surprised, in the reflection, to see that I was hunched over slightly, that I looked smaller than Mr. Kogan. I sat up straight. I tried to think of what Abe would do were he in my place.

Mr. Kogan was telling me that my uncle was a bright man too—that he had spoken with him. Was I surprised? Was it perhaps possible that my uncle didn't tell *me* everything? And as much as he appreciated the efforts Abe was making to protect me and to keep things legitimate, he was still in a bad and dangerous business. Now that I was his son-in-law, Mr. Kogan wanted me out of that business. His motive was as simple and normal as that: to protect the people he cared for. I thought of trying to answer him, but the only arguments that came into my head were my father's, and when I heard my father's voice giving them to me, they sounded strangely feeble. I stood. I told Mr. Kogan that I thought our conversation had come to an end.

"You really believe your uncle is a good man then, don't you?"

I said nothing.

"I thought so. It's why I feel sorry for you." He walked to the door and, his hand on the doorknob, turned and faced me. "And I feel even sorrier for Gail, because she *won't* feel sorry for you. She loves you too much. Don't you think I've seen some of the victims of your uncle's goodness come into the hospital, David? Don't you think I know about his back room and his secret trials? Don't you think I know about the black market babies—what doctor in Brooklyn doesn't?—about the way your uncle provides infants for couples who are not as fortunate as you and Gail?"

Suddenly the garden was full of light. I turned away, shielded my eyes. It was as if it was the middle of the day. I heard a strong humming sound and realized it came from floodlights. I looked through the window again, and despite the fact that I was looking at beautiful flowers, a lush green lawn, a stone birdbath, I thought of prison courtyards. I saw high stone walls, turrets, machine guns, uniformed guards pacing back and forth along ramparts.

"Sure," I said. I spoke quickly, so that I could say what I wanted before Gail or Ellen came by. "And he does it for half the price your doctor friends charge. My uncle gives good value, Mr. Kogan. He never deals in defective goods. He doesn't put his arm around a helpless woman in his office, drop her cash in his drawer and then give her whatever he can get that's coming out of the gutter. The only thing your doctor friends are unhappy about is that my uncle cut in on their monopoly."

Mr. Kogan studied my face. "I know you don't want medical advice from me, but if I were you I'd go lie down for a while. Your blood pressure is way up." He gestured to the garden. "Or walk it off in the garden. When you've calmed down, I trust you'll speak with Gail about my offer and that you'll give me an answer. I won't press you. As for your uncle, you're free to believe whatever you want about him."

He turned away from me. I wanted to grab his shoulder, to whirl him around, to smash the smugness from his face.

"Do you think I don't know everything my uncle does?" I began, and saw myself heading toward the questions I'd been saving. "Do you really think I'm dumb enough to believe that he's just some kind of Jewish Robin Hood?" I shook my head sideways, laughed. I felt better. I gave him the questions: "Let me ask you this, Mr. Kogan: in your business, don't you sometimes have to cut off a finger to save a hand, or a hand to save an arm, or a foot to save a leg? Don't you sometimes have to cut away a diseased part—a tumor, an organ—to save the body?"

"Of course. If I must—if there's no alternative."

"Then you understand what my uncle's life is like," I said. "It's the same for him."

"You're talking nonsense," he shot back, and he smiled at me in a way that made me want to ram my fist through his teeth. "But at least you're talking, yes?"

I was alone in the garden with Ellen, and I was frightened. I wanted to be with Gail, somewhere where it was cool and peaceful, where I wouldn't have to listen to the sound of my own voice inside my head, but Gail had fallen asleep on Ellen's bed. Did I want to go in and wake her, or did I have a few more minutes, so that Ellen could show me the section of her garden she loved especially? I said that I had a few minutes. She laughed, told me I shouldn't be shy about saying no to her. She wasn't above using people's unwillingness to refuse things to a blind girl, of course, but if I really didn't want to be there, she didn't want to keep me. Gail had told her all about our day—about Vincent, about Sheila, about meeting my grandfather, about my mother, about visiting

Beau Jack. She knew how exhausted I must be, how divided I must feel.
She knew how much I didn't like being around her father, having to talk
with him.

"But come with me first, all right?"

She took my hand, led me past evergreens to a stone bench, asked me
to sit down beside her. I breathed in and smelled something very sweet,
but I couldn't tell if the scent were coming from the flowers or from
Ellen. I started to withdraw my hand from hers, but she held me firmly,
drew my hand to her lips and kissed my knuckles. She seemed to stare
straight ahead then, her eyes wide open.

"Can I tell you how happy I am that Gail found you?" she asked.
"Would that embarrass you?"

"I suppose. I don't know—"

"Of course it would embarrass you. We're alike in that way, aren't we,
Gail and I? We tend to surprise others by our frankness, by saying what's
on our minds, what we're feeling. Why do you suppose that is?"

"I don't know."

"We're quite unalike in other ways, as you well know by now. I've
thought about it frequently, you see, and I've come to the conclusion
that I don't have the same need to be different that Gail has, precisely
because I *am* different. We've always wanted what the other had. I
wanted sight and she wanted to be wounded in some way, and I often
think the only reason we've come to accept what we *don't* have is because what we do have is what the other desires. Do I make sense?"

"No. You sound like her."

"See what I mean?" She laughed, touched my hand, let one finger
come to rest on my wrist. "Ellen's the flower, she used to say, and here's
Gail, folks, your erstwhile garden slug. So that I would imagine she does
wonder sometimes if you're not too handsome and talented—too *good*
for her. If she doesn't require some *disability* to deserve your love. Her
great fear, of course, is that someday you'll wake up and feel that she
tricked you into marriage, that you'll feel you can do better elsewhere.
She's terribly afraid you're going to be disappointed in her."

"I'll never leave her."

"I know that," Ellen said quickly. She faced me. Her eyes were moving in their sockets as if on a dark rolling sea, as if searching for light.
"I'm glad we're here together this way—it's the place I come to when I
want to get away from the world. My strongest visual memories are
attached to this spot, to these few square feet of grass and trees and
stone. Except for some violets and lily of the valley, there are no flowers
here. Too much shade. I had some vision until the age of four. I remember what the world looks like. You knew that, didn't you?"

"Yes. Gail told me."

"May I touch your face?"

I felt my heart lurch sideways. I stood. Ellen moved toward me, hands stretched upwards. She touched my face, found my cheeks.

"I've been taking a sculpture course at the Brooklyn Museum. Mother had me enrolled at the Lighthouse in Manhattan, but it was mostly elderly people there, for therapy, not for—" She stopped, moved her fingertips backwards along my cheekbones until she came to my ears. "I'd like to do your head sometime. Would you mind? You wouldn't have to pose—this will be enough, if you'll give me a few minutes. My fingers will remember your face."

She closed her eyes, as if by doing so she would see me better, and I was relieved not to have to look at them. I thought of oversized marbles —the kind we'd called "killers"—rolling around in a shoe box. Unlike Gail, Ellen was strikingly beautiful—she had a smooth, fair complexion, a broad face that, except for her dark-brown hair, I thought of as being Swedish: high cheekbones, wide forehead, strong, straight nose with long, flaring nostrils, large mouth, dimpled chin. She had a wonderfully erect and proud way of carrying herself. She moved her fingers over my face very gently, let the tips float along my hairline, then glide along the ridges of my cheekbones, across my eyes. I tried to relax, to remember the stories Gail told me of how, when Ellen would walk around the house with a dictionary on her head, improving her carriage, Gail would tiptoe ahead of her in socked feet, moving furniture into her path.

"You have a beautiful mouth—full like Gail's. Especially your lower lip. You two must look very much alike to people. They say that's often the case with married people, increasingly with each year. I used to wish I had Gail's mouth when I was younger. I used to think my own was too thin and hard, that boys wouldn't want to kiss me, that they would be frightened I'd *snap* at them."

She traced the outline of my lips with both index fingers. She moved closer, her sandals touching the tips of my shoes. I closed my eyes, took a deep breath. Her fingers trailed across my chin, along the curve of my jawbone, back to my ears. She was smiling broadly, her lips like satin. Tiny golden bubbles of perspiration were caught in the white hairs above her upper lip.

"Do you mind my telling you that you have a beautiful mouth? I'm certain that Gail has said so a thousand times. She *is* happy with you, David—happier than I've ever known her to be. That first night you met, she came home and—she so rarely shared that kind of thing with me that I didn't know how to respond, really."

You had your chance.

Ellen put her fingers to my lips. Had I ever seen Charlie Chaplin's *City Lights*, Gail had asked one time, a movie where Chaplin falls in love with a beautiful blind flower girl? I hadn't. Well, Gail said, I'm probably the only human being in the world who was *un*happy when the flower girl regained her sight.

"I wish there were more things in bloom now. August is the hardest month for the garden. In September we'll have chrysanthemums and asters and autumn crocus—to show their contrariness they produce their leaves in the spring, their flowers in the fall—but with the heat and humidity and lack of rain it's terribly difficult to get *anything* to want to bloom now. This is the time of year I always wish that we didn't live in the city. Do you ever think of moving out, David? Of just leaving all this and taking Gail and your child and going somewhere else, of starting all over again?"

"Sometimes."

"Gail tells me that your mother may remarry. That must upset you, given how much you loved your father. It's awfully soon, isn't it?"

"It's okay." I shrugged. "I mean, who believes in grief these days?"

She laughed.

"There. I *can* get you to relax, can't I? Gail has assured us all that you do have a sense of humor. Only wouldn't it be easier to relax somewhere else than in Brooklyn?" Her hand held me above the wrist, her tanned fingers a pale bracelet around the short dark curls of my forearm. I wondered if she'd talked with her father, if they had set me up, but I was afraid to challenge her, for if I were wrong, if I showed that I didn't trust her. . . . "I've always wished I could wake up each morning and make my way down to a barn, by myself, and drink in the stillness that pervades the air before the world begins to make its noise. When I was younger I went to a special camp for the blind. They had lots of animals —goats and lambs and rabbits and pigs—and the wonderful thing about the animals was that they were always glad to see you, and that they were always happy when you touched them. People aren't like that."

She moved her fingers to my shoulders, then along my neck and into my hair, grasping the back of my head with both hands, feeling the shape of my skull with her palms, pressing in with her fingertips and thumbs.

I felt myself drifting off, swaying a bit. I imagined her eyes being lifted from her head—she was on a table, a white sheet across her body, to her chin, and the eyes were being placed in a small silk-lined box. They were being taken downstairs, to be put in cold storage. The whites were parched, pebbled with hundreds of tiny imperfections. Ellen stopped, as if she heard someone approaching.

"If you think of other people in the world as walking around with large wet cloths draped over their faces, then you'll understand a bit how they appear to me. Can you imagine that? That everyone in the world has his or her head covered with a thin brown wet cloth—like armies of beekeepers, yes?—and when the cloths cling to their faces you can make out their features? Can you see what I mean?"

"No."

"Because you don't want to." Her voice was hard. "I think of the cloths as being brown. I recall the color brown most of all: my father's hair, a mug of coffee my mother once left on my dresser, the sandbox after rain, a Hershey bar that melted on my windowsill, my father's overcoat from the Army, the leather handle of his tennis racket, the oak banister in the front hall after the maid polished it, the beauty mark on my right thigh that I once tried to scrape off with the edge of a scissor. . . ." She drew back, let her hands slip downwards. "I dream in colors, so that keeps the memories alive, you see. As if"—she tapped on the side of her head—"there are tubes of paint in here and the dreams squeeze the colors out into the waking part of my brain."

She took my hand and led me away from the stone bench. I looked toward the house. Gail and her father were there, standing at the window of his study. When Gail saw me she waved.

"You can come visit us whenever you want," I said. "You can stay with us after the baby comes."

"I was nervous before," Ellen offered. "Could you tell?"

"No."

"Your presence reminds me that what I don't want is to end my days living here with mother and father, or settling for somebody—one of the nice lawyers or doctors or teachers that come calling—who can't give me what you and Gail give to one another." Mr. Kogan opened the sliding door. "I've loved having Gail confide in me the way she has ever since she met you. That's meant more to me—our becoming friends—than I ever suspected it could, and if I lost that . . ."

Gail came to us, kissed me, told me that she felt better, that the nap had helped. She said that she'd dreamt about us walking in Ellen's garden, and that then—in the dream—the garden was suddenly ours and we were living in an enormous old colonial home—white with black shutters—on a hill in a small New England town, and that on every day of the year we put a fresh vase of flowers in each room.

"You dreamt about three hundred and sixty-five *different* days?" Ellen asked.

"No. I dreamt that I knew we did it every day." She burrowed against my neck. "So tell me what you think: can we have a house and garden like that someday, David?"

Mr. Kogan laughed and told her to go easy on me. He told me that this was a childish habit of Gail's that he and Hannah had never been able to break, this way she had of parading her private hopes and desires around in front of other people, as if daring her parents to reject her, to refuse her her wishes. He apologized for not having cured her of the habit before she married me.

"You have my sympathy," he said.

"Mine too," Gail said. She squeezed my arm, and when she did, and when I saw the way Mr. Kogan smiled at me as he took Ellen by the elbow, to walk with her back to the house, it occurred to me that his offer had been sincere, that he was not being devious with me, that he might really be the good and honest man Gail claimed he was.

I wedged the fan between the sill and the raised window, turned it on exhaust to draw the hot air out of the apartment. I washed my face at the kitchen sink, took a Coke from the refrigerator, and went to the living room. It was almost midnight. The street was quiet. Nothing was moving, not even the leaves on the trees. Gail kissed the back of my neck, said that she was going to take a shower before we went to sleep. Would I wait up for her so that we could talk?

We were living in an enormous five-room apartment on Albemarle Road, near Ocean Avenue, about halfway between my mother's apartment and Gail's house. It was one of Abe's buildings—he owned five of his own now, in addition to those he managed for Mr. Rothenberg—a beautiful six-story red brick prewar apartment building with marble fireplaces in all the living rooms, doctors' and dentists' offices on the first floor, a garden in the courtyard, a doorman on duty twenty-four hours a day, and a lobby in which, in the central fountain, there were live goldfish.

"Do you know what I used to do to cool off when I was a kid?" I asked.

"Tell me, what did you used to do to cool off when you were a kid?"

"When there was a heat wave I'd get the winter blankets out of my closet and crawl under them, and I'd stay there until I absolutely couldn't stand it anymore. Then, when the sweat was pouring off me and I could barely breathe, I'd throw the covers off, spread-eagle myself on the sheet face up and sigh with relief."

"What did Vincent say to you today?"

"Nothing."

"You're not telling the truth. What did he *tell* you?"

Instead of answering, I pulled my chair to the window so that I could let the cooler air move past me. I closed my eyes. When I opened them Gail was standing beside me. She had both hands on her stomach, as if she were going to lift it like a watermelon, hand it to me.

"This is your child in here too, David, can you understand that? Can you get that through your thick skull? And this woman standing here like a perfect idiot is your wife, in case you hadn't heard, and your wife and your child-to-be have a right to know what's going on. We have a *right*."

"It's nothing to worry about," I said. I let my head rest against her stomach. "Believe me, okay? Vincent is just a two-bit punk and Sheila's just trying to get even with her father for a lot of old stuff. That's all."

"There's more. I know it. I know it and I don't like it."

I looked up. "I don't like it either," I said. "Just give me a little more time to think things through, all right? I'm trying. I am trying. Only things keep happening too damned fast and then all I want to do, like today, is just get away from everyone and everything, to crawl down into some dark place and to shoot anybody who tries to come in after me."

"I love you."

"I know." I held to her more tightly. "I can hear a heartbeat. Is it yours or the baby's?"

She moved away, put her hand over her heart. "My heart was still up here, last time I looked. But David—"

"Yes?"

"Do you think I'm *very* ugly when I'm pregnant?"

"I think you're very beautiful."

"Then why don't you want to touch me more, to play the way we used to?"

"Because it's hot and I'm exhausted."

"That's not why."

"I don't know. We get so carried away sometimes that I become scared I'll hurt you, that I'll stab the poor thing inside or . . ." I shrugged. "I don't *know*."

She kissed me, then left. A few seconds later I heard her turn on the shower. I went to the kitchen to get another Coke. I put the shopping bag on the kitchen table and began taking the baby clothes out, setting them down neatly around the table, keeping the stacks even. I put the package from Beau Jack in the center. I was happy to be home. I put away the dishes we'd left in the rack, from lunch, then cleared out the drain in the sink, scooping up the little bits of food with my fingers and dropping them into the garbage pail. I felt drowsy. *Dress British. Think Yiddish.* That was what Mr. Rothenberg said I should remember if I wanted success in this world. I smiled. I liked being alone in the kitchen, taking care of things, letting my mind float while the city slept, while all around me the world seemed motionless. I tried to imagine what Beau Jack had looked like as a boy of ten or eleven, and when I did I saw regiments of sea scouts—black boys eight and ten and twelve years old —marching down Linden Boulevard on Memorial Day. I saw their mid-night-blue uniforms, their white belts, their black boots and white gaiters, heard the crunching sound they made as they shuffled along in close formation, eyes forward.

I dropped our paper napkins into the garbage pail, bent over and picked up a crumpled piece of paper that lay on the linoleum next to the pail. I opened it, to make sure it wasn't anything important.

CALL ABE RIGHT AWAY

The fist closed around my heart. I breathed in, told myself not to panic, not to jump to conclusions. I'd seen Abe in the morning and we'd gone over things he wanted me to take care of—rentals in some of his buildings, breaking in a new man for the Church Avenue collection route, getting Avie's mother into a hospital for tests—and he'd seemed distracted. I stood up straight, leaned on the sink, took in an enormous gulp of air. Damn! I recalled how, in the Classic Comics of *The Corsican Brothers*, whenever one of the brothers was in danger or pain, the other brother would know it and feel it, no matter how far apart they were.

Gail came into the kitchen, her hair wrapped in a blue towel.

"You should take one too, sweetheart. You'll feel so much better."

I shoved the note in front of her. "Talk and talk fast."

"Uh-oh." She backed away. "Methinks the evidence hath been discovered."

"When did it come?"

"I don't know." She turned. "Time for a swift exit, folks. And as our poor heroine leaves her brave and beleaguered husband, our hearts are heavy, for—"

I grabbed her by the arm and whirled her around. "Don't lie to me. When did it come?"

"I'm not lying. That was a true answer. I know when I found the note, you see, but I really don't know when it came. You asked the wrong question, to which I gave the correct answer."

I squeezed her arm as hard as I could. "Don't be so smart. There's no time. When did you find it?"

"You're hurting me. *Jesus!*"

"I'll hurt you more if you don't tell me when you found it. You talk and you talk fast."

"Jesus, David, your eyes are popping worse than mine do. Have you caught that from me too? Now we know that husbands and wives, living as they do in close proximity, are often said to—"

I slapped her. "Now you listen to me. When I get a message like that, you let me know at once, do you hear? And when I ask a question, you give me an answer."

Her mouth was wide open, her hand on her cheek.

"You hit me."

"That's right, and I'll do it again."

"No you won't. Because I'm getting away from you—far, far away."

She twisted from my grip, but I pulled her back, shoved her against the wall. Her head snapped backwards and her eyes closed, the lids clicking down like a doll's.

"Now we'll try it again, all right? When-did-you-find-the-message-and-why-did-you-hide-it-from-me?"

She was crying, softly.

"I would have told you in the morning. Jesus! It was just that it was so late and you'd been through so much already today and my cheek stings like hell, as long as you're so concerned. May I go get some ice so that the welts won't show tomorrow? I mean, let's be practical, after all, darling. Let's think, at least, of the neighbors and the family, of what others will think. Let's think of your mother's response. 'Gail darling— didn't I warn you about that terrific temper he got? So now you know what I mean, yeah?' "

"Don't get too smart."

I pulled her toward me and slammed her against the wall again, the back of her head thudding against the plaster. She blinked, shook her head sideways.

"Well, folks. I guess it must be a matter of life and death if our hero is so upset. Is that so, David? I'll answer you if it is. Is it a matter of life and death?"

"Maybe. Yes."

"Abe's death?" Her head wobbled as if she were drunk, but her eyes were bright with tears. "Then I'm really sorry. If I'd known that it was a question of life or death—especially Abe's death—I would have told you at once. You should know that."

I slapped her again, with the back of my hand. I watched the red marks rise at once. "You just cut it out and stop making me do this," I cried. "You just cut it out, do you *hear*?"

"I hear, but frankly, my dear, I don't give a shit." Her voice was calm. She raised her two little fists and they trembled, as if she'd caught a chill. "Beat me up, lay me out, kick the shit out of me—what do I care anymore? Come on! We might as well get all the brutality over with early in life and avoid the rush later, right?"

She banged on my chest with both fists and, using all her force, shoved me back. Then she opened her robe. Her stomach was round and powdery, glossy with talcum. "Here—why don't you take care of him too while you're at it, big shot? Come on—"

"When did the message come?"

"Tonight." She was heaving in and out, trying to catch her breath. "Okay? It came tonight. The message came tonight. The paper was inside the door when we entered and I put my foot on it while you went by and then I read it and I crumpled it and I threw it in the garbage, or so I thought, and then you must have fished around in there because you don't ever really trust me, David, do you?—or anybody else in this world, for that matter—and then you found it and then you decided I'd betrayed you so that you'd have the right to beat me up, and then you did, and do you know what? I'm *glad*, David. I'm glad you know I hid it and threw it away, because now you won't ever have any doubts about the way I feel about your goddamned uncle."

She looked as if she had knuckles growing under the skin of her cheek. I thought of getting her ice, but I couldn't move. I stared at her mouth, at the words that poured from it.

"Abe said to call. Abe the King, right? Abe the big shot. Big shit, if you ask me. Abe once said that even brave men get scared shitless. Abe once said that happiness is like taking a piss in a long, bad movie. Abe once said that paradise is when you can wipe your feet on your enemies without fear. Abe once said this and Abe once said that and I'm tired of hearing about it. Abe promised this and Abe promised that and Abe is just full of shit. What about *Davey?* What does Davey say and what does he promise and what does he believe? Can you answer me that? Davey says that if Abe told him to jump off a roof, he'd do it. Davey says that if Abe told him to take a long walk on a short pier, he'd do it. Davey says that it's okay to kill people if your uncle says to do it. Davey says that it's okay to hurt people if your uncle says to do it. Davey says it's okay to slap your wife around if she tries to save you from harm and that some-day it'll be okay to bang your kid around too, won't it? And what will I do then? What the hell will I do then? Can you tell me that? What will I do *then?*"

She was pushing me across the room, her eyes clamped shut, her head thrashing wildly the way it did sometimes when we were making love, when she'd lost all control. I tried to grab her arms, to get her to stop.

"So why don't you start punching the kid tonight, here in Abe's place, right? Why don't you beat him up now and finish the job off? You don't want him to live anyway, don't you think I know that? You never wanted him. You did the whole thing out of your crazy nobility and guilt and I thought it might work but it didn't, so fuck everything, all right? Just fuck everything! You don't want him to live anyway and you never did. You don't give a shit about me. You—"

"It's not true," I said quietly.

"It *is!*" she cried. "Don't you lie to *me*, do you hear? You don't want him to live and I know it. I know it! I—"

She raised her fists as if to punch me again, but instead she brought her arms down and began pounding on her own stomach. She was puffing, out of breath. She smiled, tears dripping along her cheeks and across her mouth.

"Are you happy now? Are you? Or should I use a crochet hook this time, for insurance? Up your hole with a Melorol, twice as far with a Hershey bar. Up your twat with a ball of snot. Remember? Up yours with a meat hook . . . it doesn't rhyme, folks, but it sure hurts. Your favorite schoolyard sayings, brought direct to you from Davey Voloshin's House of Horrors. See the anger vein throb in our hero's forehead! See him batter his wife and child! Step right up—"

She bumped her stomach against me.

"Come on, big shot, you take a punch too, okay? If your demure little wife can do it, why not a big hunk like you? Let's get rid of the damned thing right now and then you won't be able to tell me for the rest of my life that I trapped you. Come on, big shot. Punch me, kick me, whatever you want to do—now's the time. Come *on*, I said—"

"I don't want to."

"Scared, huh?"

"No."

"Okay then. How about you go call your uncle while *I* beat up the baby. Division of labor, right? Get it? Division of *labor.* Oh Lord, but you do have a way with words, Kogan. So let's divide the labor from the mother and the mother from the labor and kill two birds with one stone, okay?"

She swung her arm to the side, as if taking a backswing in tennis, and then she banged herself in the stomach with a vicious roundhouse. I gasped, felt my own stomach close on itself. She gagged, doubled over, moaned.

"Oh Jesus." She groaned and looked up at me, her arms locked around her stomach. "I think I went too far. I think I finally did. Oh Jesus, it hurts, David—oh fucking Jesus. Oh Jesus F. Christ—help me lie down. Please? It hurts so bad. . . ."

I helped her to the bedroom. She lay on her back, knees up, her forearm across her eyes. I sat next to her, watched her cry. She stopped for an instant, then let loose with a long high-pitched wail. She clutched her stomach and began sobbing, rolling from one side to the other.

"Should I call your father?"

She shook her head sideways, bit down on her lip.

"Oh Jesus, it hurts so bad, David. I—I—" She groaned, then exhaled. "I'm sorry. I'm sorry, but it just hurts so bad. . . ."

I put my hand on her forehead, then on her stomach. She made rasping noises when she breathed in. She lowered her knees.

"That helps."

"Stretching your legs out?"

"No. You touching me, stupid." She moaned. "Oh God, David. Do me a favor and see if there's any blood leaking out. I'm afraid to look. I think I feel something wet."

I looked. "Just sweat. But what should we do? Tell me—I'll do anything. . . ."

"Just wait. Try not to *imagine* things, all right? Please?" She breathed in, sighed. "I think I'm getting some relief. I think it may just be a big muscle cramp. Can you really knock the wind out of yourself?"

"I don't know."

Her stomach was hard as a rock, like a smooth piece of round marble, a thin layer of skin pulled tight over it. I remembered how we'd argue when we were kids: could you actually kill yourself by running as fast as you could and ramming your head into a wall, or would you always pull back just in time? Was there some built-in reflex that kept you from committing suicide that way? Had guys in jail been able to commit suicide by cracking their heads open when everything else—ropes, belts, spoons, knives, blades—had been taken from them?

"Do you think the baby's starting to come?" I asked. "Are you contracting?"

"I don't know. Subcontracting maybe. Putting the burden on you."

I massaged her stomach, using both hands.

"I'm sorry," I said. "Really."

"Me too."

She let her hand rest on top of mine, took in a long breath, let it out.

"Did you hurt him?" I asked.

"*Him?*"

"Him. Her. Whatever's in there. You know what I mean."

"No. I don't think so. I'd be bleeding or breaking water or something like that if I had, I think. It just hurts like hell. That's all. I never felt anything hurt so much."

"Worse than when I slapped you?"

She lifted her head, propped herself up on her elbows. "I did mean a lot of what I said and I don't want to take any of it back and I won't. I've been wanting to say those things for months, David. Half the time when you're gone with him I roam around the apartment making speeches in my head, trying to come up with the right words so that I can persuade you, so that I can *force* you to change. I know how much your uncle means to you, but I don't really think it's him you love. I figured that out way back. I don't really think you even know who he is anymore. I think it's some *idea* of him you're still in love with, and I guess I keep hoping you'll outgrow it."

"And use your love instead?"

"Exactly." She smiled. "I've got lots. Endless reservoirs. Wells at the bottom of wells. I'll never run out of love for you, David. And everything I want to say comes down to this: that he'll ruin your life, and mine with it."

"You don't know everything. You don't know what his life was like."

"I'm sure. But I don't *need* to know everything either. I know enough. Like you said he says—people always have choices. He may not have asked for the life he has, but he didn't have to keep it either. It seems so crazy, doesn't it?—us talking calmly like this, and then you off with him, getting in deeper and deeper. What I keep thinking is that you're so *young*, David! We are. We have so many years ahead of us—"

"It's mostly legitimate now. The rough stuff ended with the war pretty much. He's always been good to me, to us. Who else ever cared? My father worked for him. He's taken care of my mother. He knew how to be very gentle with me when I was a boy in a way no one else ever was."

"I think I'm all right." She lay back down. "Can you touch me a little bit to be sure. Press here and there and I'll tell you if it hurts. Like playing doctor, all right?"

"Does this hurt?"

"No."

"This?"

"No."

I probed, pushed with my fingers the way I recalled our doctor doing when I had exams. A muscle along the outside of her right thigh was twitching.

"David?"

"Yes?"

"Are you afraid to make love with me now because I'm bigger and fatter?"

"I don't know. It's not what you think. I mean, since we got pregnant, it's what I said before—that I'm just afraid of hurting you."

"Do you still look around a lot? I mean would you rather be doing it with somebody who looked more like Sheila, who had a figure like hers?"

"I'd rather do it with you, but—"

"I feel better. You said 'we' before, did you know that?"

"We?"

"When *we* got pregnant."

"I've been distracted too. I didn't want to tell you yet, because I guess I keep hoping things will blow over peacefully, with my uncle. The stuff with Vincent wasn't only about Sheila."

"I figured."

"And I was thinking too—about your question—that when you were screaming at me I wanted to shout back that this wasn't the first time you'd lied to me."

"*Really?*" She looked hurt. "I didn't mean to, if I did. I don't want us ever to keep things from one another—"

"What you said to me the night we got married, that now we could do anything we wanted, remember?" She nodded. "It's not true." I stroked her stomach, felt it softening. "Even after you're married the way we are—"

"Is there something special you'd like to try, darling?"

"Don't make jokes. I'm serious. I thought a lot about that and what I decided is that it's not true. You *can't* do whatever you want in life, and it's not always because of others, because of the world. It's—"

"David?"

"What?"

"I *meant* what I said before about your uncle. It gets so complicated sometimes and day follows night and night follows day and we just get carried along, trying to cope, and I guess I'd stick by you no matter what, but it does make me so very unhappy. I mean, it's complicated but it's simple too." She looked straight at me and spoke very deliberately then, as if trying to pour the words through my eyes and down into my heart, to fix them there. "Because your uncle and the men he deals with, they kill and they steal and they hurt."

"Not anymore."

"Not unless they *have* to," she corrected. "Despite his great love for you, your uncle won't be able to protect you from that part of his life for five seconds if he gets squeezed badly, and you know it. All I want is to look at you and for you to look at me and to say what I said: that it's bad to kill and to hurt and to steal and that you're a good person, and that you shouldn't ever do it. You're not your uncle, David. Not really. You still have choices—"

"Your father said the same thing."

"Don't hold that against *me*. I'm not my father either—"

"I think about it, though. I can't *not* think about it lately. Only sometimes it's hard to know what to do."

"Yes, but is it—dare I hope?—is it because you're beginning to agree with me, to see a way out for us?" She put her fingers to my lips. "Don't answer. That way I can hope more, yes?" She smiled. "Do you know how I used to think of you up at Smith? I used to get this picture of you in my head, as if you were the hero from one of those medieval plays I studied—a kind of Everyman—and you were walking through a dark and terrible world, along a subterranean corridor of some kind, and

being pulled at from all sides, being stretched one way and then the
other: by Beauty and by Ugliness, by Love and by Hate, by Helplessness
and by Anger, by Darkness and by Light, by Cruelty and by Tenderness."

"You still idealize me."

"Aren't you glad?" She kissed the back of my hand. "I'm okay now, I
think. Nothing hurts, except that I'm a bit bruised. I can feel him moving around the way he always does."

"*Him?*"

"Oh you are so good *inside*, David, don't you know that? You're a
truly good *and* strong person, and there aren't many of your kind left.
It's just so hard for me to watch you walking through the world, pulled
on from so many sides, without my being able to help. I keep wanting
to run out in front of you—the court jester, yes?—so I can steer you
away from Evil and Hate and Anger and Cruelty and all the forces of
Darkness—so I can point you to the true path—to righteousness and to
light and to happiness. To a world that doesn't turn in on itself only. To
contract and grow narrow. That's so much the style these days—to
contract and compress life—and what I want for us is a life that keeps
expanding, that keeps opening and growing larger and larger and richer
and richer. Let me be your guide and companion, please, David? *Please?*
You won't be sorry. Not ever—"

"I know." I felt light, weightless. The words were there, waiting, and
they came easily: "I'll call Abe in the morning."

"May I take the phone off the hook, in case they try to get to you
before then?"

"Yes." I pressed my lips to her stomach, kept them there. "It makes
sense—that play you saw, with me in it. I don't know why, but it makes
sense to me. I like those pictures you get inside your head. Is that okay?"

"At least."

"Beau Jack wanted us to look at his present before we went to sleep."

I went to the kitchen, came back with the package and with a dish full
of ice cubes, for her cheeks. She smiled, said that with her complexion
nobody would notice the marks anyway. I untied the ribbon, opened
the white paper. There was a box inside. Gail opened it, lifted the lid.
Two small gold hearts, about an inch high, rested on cotton.

I lifted one heart, turned it over. There was an inscription on the
back:

David loves Gail.

"This one is yours."

I gave it to her and she turned it over, read the words, pressed the
heart against her own. I looked at my gift.

Gail loves David.

I turned out the light and lay down next to her.

"I'm glad you don't do *every*thing I say," Gail said after a while, and she could hardly get her next sentence out, she began weeping so freely. "I'm glad you didn't whack the baby when I told you to. Because you are strong, and if you had . . ."

"Shh."

10

WAS IT POSSIBLE that so much life could be contained in such a small body, and that merely to hold it close to me could fill me with happiness? Her head was nestled now against my neck, her soft body curled around my shoulder. Her thin legs hung down, kicked every time she let loose with a pained cry. I kept one hand on her bottom, the other on the back of her head, and I talked to her, told her that everything would be all right, that her father was with her. Did she know how much I loved her, what a sweet thing she was? Did she know that she weighed just a little more than a bag of sugar?

Her body contracted, eyes pressed tight so that they were two black dashes, and she let loose with a long, watery explosion of gas that, for such a little thing, seemed miraculous. Then her body sagged and she nuzzled against me as if she were trying to crawl inside my neck head-first. She breathed more easily, regularly. I set her down gently on the changing table, careful to cup the back of her head with my hand, but she whimpered and clung to me. I told her that we had to change her diaper again because if we didn't her rash would get worse. But when I took my hand out from beneath her head, a head no larger than a softball, she started crying hysterically again. I lifted her to my shoulder and she stopped. I walked back and forth with her for a while, until she seemed relaxed and drowsy, then tried to set her down again.

She wailed furiously, tiny legs thrashing. I gave in. I cradled her head against my shoulder, kissed her tiny ears and the top of her downy little head. I sniffed at the indentation there, the fontanelle, where the skull had not yet closed. Such a sweet, vulnerable little thing! Was it possible that everyone in the world had once been this small and weak?

"Are you still *up*?"

Gail stood in the doorway, shielding her eyes from the light. Emilie was asleep in my arms.

"Have you been walking with her like this all night?"

"Come look—"

Gail leaned on me lazily, kissed my breast, then kissed the baby.

"See how beautifully she can sleep? Isn't she amazing?"

"No more amazing than you are, sweetheart. It's almost four in the morning. I gave her her last feeding before eleven. You've been doing this for hours. Come on. Come to bed and let me feed her and then she'll go back to sleep again." She sniffed. "You forgot to change her—"

"Every time I tried to put her down, she squawked."

"But *David*—!" She sighed. "Come on then. My breasts are starting to drip."

"She *knows* me, Gail. She knows who I am. I mean, her body knows my body in some mysterious way, don't you see? And when her body is unhappy—"

"Come on, Dad. You may have manifold and marvelous powers, but the power to produce milk from your breasts is still not one of them."

I brought Emilie into the bedroom and set her next to me. Gail lay down, flicked her nipple against Emilie's lips. Emilie gurgled, whimpered, reached up with her fists. Her mouth closed around Gail's nipple and the last thing I heard before I tumbled into sleep was the liquid sound of Emilie's mouth drawing the sweet, warm milk into her.

Abe sat at a table in the rear of Garfield's, his back to the wall. He smiled at me, but I sensed that something was wrong. His smile was too broad. It reminded me of my mother's smile.

"How's the proud father this morning?"

"Kind of beat. The baby was up most of the night."

Abe stood, offered me his hand, and I felt a piece of cold metal between his palm and mine. Still smiling, he sat and whispered through his teeth that I was to show no reaction. I was to reach for a handkerchief, wipe off some sweat, drop the key into my back pocket.

I did what he said. He talked about having visited my mother the day before, having seen his father for the first time since the war. While he talked he motioned with his eyes, toward the window. I waited a few seconds, took my grilled cheese sandwich and Coke off the tray, turned to set the tray down on an empty table, and saw that two of Fasalino's men were sitting near the entrance. Abe talked about the fur blanket his father was making for Emilie. He twisted his Army ring, red stone to palm, and laughed to himself.

"It was crazy, the way I felt warm toward him suddenly. He was good to me when I was a kid, Davey. Proud of me. *Maladyets*, he'd say, when he took me around with him. '*Maladyets*—my fine American son.' I loved to watch him work. I give him credit there. He had a real talent."

Abe reached across, touched the back of my hand, then looked away quickly, as if embarrassed.

"I found myself thinking of you, of the way you used to draw so well, of what a good ballplayer you were. It's hard to do something well in this crazy world, don't you think?"

"Yes." I hesitated, then asked the question that had been with me all morning: "What was I like when I was a child, Abe? Would you tell me?"

"What do you mean, what were you like?"

"I mean, what was I like when I was a baby like Emilie—what did you feel toward me when I was her age and you held me—when I was the age before I can remember things about myself?"

"You were a swell kid, Davey. The best."

"You're not answering my question."

"Now you listen to me and you listen carefully," he said. His voice was low and hard. "And while you do you nod and you smile and you eat as if we're talking about your kid, or about why the Dodgers keep losing to the Yankees in the World Series. Do you hear me?"

"I hear."

"The key is for a safe-deposit box in a bank upstate. It's in the town where we used to go before the war, to the bungalow colony. You take a bus from the Port Authority Terminal to Ellenville, and from Ellenville you go to Parksville. The Parksville Savings Bank. You get a taxi or you hitch a ride. If anything happens today—I'll get a message to you at suppertime, so you be at your mother's place then—you don't wait, is that clear? You don't go back home and you don't telephone anyone and you don't send any messages. You just get your ass to the bus terminal and you get on the bus."

"But why—"

"There's no time, and even if there were I wouldn't explain things to you. The more you know, the more danger you'll be in. You just listen. The box is in your name, with your signature on file. There won't be any problems. The Parksville Savings Bank. Do you understand?"

"I understand. But what if I don't go?" His brown eyes softened, as if they might melt. My question frightened him, and I realized that this pleased me. "What if I just stay here until you tell me all the things I want to know?"

"They won't touch Emilie and Gail. They won't bother Evie. If we're no longer a danger to them, you and me, they won't ask for trouble they don't need."

"Why should I believe you? How do you know what they'll do?"

"I know because I'm not that different from them."

Silence.

"What about Tony then?" I asked. "What would you *not* do to him? What if I said I won't—"

"There's no *time*, goddamn you, Davey. Don't you understand? There's no time for this. Just trust me."

"You taught me never to trust anybody."

"Don't get too smart. You go. Do you hear me? You do what I say."

"I'll do what I want."

He lunged for my wrist, stopped himself, glanced toward where Fasalino's men were, reached back and, in one fluid motion, smoothed his hair down with the hand that had started for me. He swallowed, and when he spoke again, his voice was soft.

"Do what I say, Davey, please? Things don't always work out exactly the way you think they will. I made myself believe that things could go backwards, that we could wipe out the past. I should never have let you get involved."

"I made my own decisions."

"Maybe. Who knows? Who knows about stuff like that, if we choose or if things choose us? For now just *try* to listen to me and to trust me. And try to get that look off your face if you can. Work on your sandwich. Your jaw is set like a crowbar."

I bit into my sandwich. The melted cheese was cold and dry, like plastic.

"I'll do what I want."

"Now isn't the time to play big shot, all right? Do me that favor. I don't want your family to be hurt. If you're still here—if things don't work out today—they won't hesitate to use them to get at you and I wouldn't like that. I figured that much out, at least. Just believe me that—"

I saw their shadows move across our table an instant before I saw them. They were on either side of Abe.

"You just stay put if you know what's good for you, kid. Don't try to be a hero like your uncle here. And you keep your hands on top of the table, Mr. Litvinov. No trouble, okay? We don't want nobody getting hurt."

Abe picked up his coffee mug. His hand was steady.

"We'd like for you to come with us. Somebody wants a word with you in private."

"Who?"

"Mr. Fasalino."

"Our appointment is for five this afternoon. You're early."

"Mr. Fasalino changed his mind."

"I didn't."

The man to Abe's right put his hand on Abe's arm, and the instant he did the other man was at my side, his hand pressing down on my shoulder to keep me from rising.

"I think you boys are making a mistake," Abe said. "Why don't you go pay for your lunch, then haul your butts out of here. Tell Mr. Fasalino that I have a busy schedule today but that I'll be there when I said I would. I'm making time for him, you see."

"We don't want no trouble. We don't want no business with the boy."

"And if you were thinking of trying to force me to come with you, I'd advise you to look back at your table first, where you were just sitting."

The men looked. Little Benny and Turkish Sammy were there. Turkish Sammy had both hands on the table, palms down. Little Benny touched his jacket pocket, breast high, where it bulged. Behind them, on the other side of the window, Lefty Kolatch and Monk Solloway stood waiting, hands in pockets. Abe smiled. Benny rose slightly from his chair, showed his yellow teeth in a broad grin and, just like a tap dancer at the end of his routine, he tipped his fedora toward Fasalino's men.

"Mr. Goldstein called me last week," I offered, after Fasalino's men were gone. "I wanted you to know. There's a college in Kentucky that's interested in having me play for them. They're willing to give me a full scholarship, to pay for housing, to pay for Gail's tuition too, if she wants to take courses."

"I always felt bad about that, didn't I? About the way they blacklisted you because of me. I'm pleased, Davey. I'm glad we can make that right. I told you things would work out, one way or the other."

"It's just a small liberal arts college and they don't play in any of the big tournaments, but Mr. Goldstein knows the coach—they went to City College together—and there's a large Jewish community nearby in Lexington with lots of rich doctors and lawyers. The college is trying to get some of them involved—for donations, I guess. They're trying to upgrade their athletic program and—"

"—and they're looking for some talented Jewish city kids, right? Some shrewd, hustling, driving school-yard players who'd go through brick walls to score, right?"

"I suppose. I'll be older than the others—the freshmen anyway—but I think I'd like to go to college. Gail and I have talked it over. Her parents have offered to help. Do you mind?"

"Why should I mind?"

"Because I'll have to leave Brooklyn. Because I might never come back. Because we won't be working together."

"So?"

"So won't that bother you?"

"No."

"Not at *all?*"

"Look, Davey," he said, smiling. "I'll miss you, sure, but I think this is what I've been trying to tell you today, don't you see? That it's time to go our separate ways. I think I knew it when we talked that time you didn't call me, when Gail kept the note from you. I was angry with her too, but do you know what? The more I thought about it the more I liked it. Not what she did, but that she did it." He laughed. "It was the kind of thing I figured I might have done if I was trying to protect somebody I cared about. Sure. And we've both noticed the changes, the new way you've been with me ever since she came into your life. There's nothing like the love of a good woman to bring out the best in a man. I always said so, didn't I?"

"Did you ever have that kind of love?"

"Yes."

"Then why—?"

"What kind of life would it have been, married to me? I was ahead of them today, sure—but to make someone you love wait at home day after day, afraid—?" He shrugged. "The story I told you about me and Lillian was true. It's just that it's not the only story. What I figured out, see, is that there's no need for you to repeat my life in order to understand it."

I swallowed hard and began talking quickly, so that he wouldn't see how upset I was. I talked about what Gail said: that it would be good for us to get away from the city for a few years, from her parents and my mother, that it would be good for us both to get college degrees, and even though Abe nodded, I could tell that he had stopped listening to me. He talked about Fasalino. The fact that Fasalino's men had tried to strong-arm him only proved what he'd suspected: that there was little to worry about. If Fasalino had had any real leverage, he wouldn't have needed to try something cheap. Why, then, I asked, had Abe given me the key and told me about the safe-deposit box? Abe smiled easily, said that he had done so just in case—that it was always good to have a contingency plan, to be careful. Now that Fasalino's men had made their move, though, he was less concerned. Was he telling me the truth, I wondered, or, having noticed how upset I was, was he merely using what had happened to reassure me?

He leaned back, eyes misty, and said that he envied me going to Kentucky. He'd always loved the horses—touching them, watching them. He'd never ridden, not even along the Ocean Parkway bridle paths, but he had been to the Derby in 1941, when Arcaro rode Whirla-

way to the roses. He was stationed at Fort Benjamin Harrison, outside
Indianapolis, and he and three other guys from his unit had gone down
there together. Did I know that he used to hitch rides up to Saratoga
from Parksville in the summers, to watch the horses? The horses and
the women.

He liked things that were strong, beautiful, and draped in silk. Why
not? He blinked, as if it confused him to be telling me about what he
remembered. Had I ever tried to draw a picture of a race horse? He
didn't remember getting pictures of race horses when he was overseas. I
said that I'd once copied a picture of the Lone Ranger and Silver from
the back of a Cheerios cereal box, but that was all. I might try again,
though, when I got to college. I was thinking of taking art courses.

"Sure, Davey. Sure. The sooner we all get out of Brooklyn the better,
I guess. Only I want to get out of here in my own way and in my own
good time and on my own terms."

"Fine."

"You don't like it when I talk this way, do you?"

"You can talk any way you want."

"I never *bet* the horses much. Gambling like that, where there's no
real control, never interested me. I liked cards—poker, blackjack, pi-
nochle—but I never played the horses. Mostly I just liked being away
from home on my own, hitching rides and talking with strangers, watching the thoroughbreds run, chasing after the two-legged fillies. I liked to
watch the pretty women, Davey. I was always a sucker for a beautiful
smile. I had a system, see. I'd spot a few good-looking women and I'd go
around and give six or seven of them tips on a race—a different horse
for each woman—and then I'd go back after the race was over and see
what I could collect from the one I'd given the winner to."

Abe leaned back, eyes closed. When he looked at me a few seconds
later, there was something very peaceful in his expression, as if he were
waking from a pleasant dream.

"Just a little more time, Davey, and I think we can close the books on
a lot of stuff neither of us really likes. Be patient with me, all right? All I
want, see—what I'm angling for—are certain assurances about how
things will operate when I'm no longer in charge. Can you understand
that?"

"No."

He nodded, as if he understood even better than I did why it was I'd
answered him this way. He reminded me of what he wanted me to do
for the rest of the day: I was to go around as if it were a normal day—
collect the rents, check up on Benny and Lefty, look in at Mr. Rothenberg's restaurants, make sure the routes were in order, see if any of the
apartment houses needed attention. Then I was to go to my mother's

for supper, and to wait for his call. If the message said to call Ellen, that meant I was to head for Ellenville, without going home, without waiting. If the message said to call Gail, that meant I could go on home, that there were no problems. He pushed himself away from the table and turned toward the window so that, in the sunlight, the pupils of his eyes seemed to fade to a pale transparent silver.

"I promised myself I'd give you an escape clause—just in case—and I've done that, all right? The only thing I'm unhappy about is that I set it up for you before Gail and the baby came along."

"What about yourself?"

"Myself what?"

"What about an escape clause for you?"

"It's all taken care of. What do you think—that I want to die? Nobody wants to die." He stood. "You be careful, though. People always let you down."

"I wouldn't let you down."

"Not even if it meant choosing between me and your family—between me and Gail and Emilie?" He picked up the check. His eyes were cold again, like the sky on a day when you can't be sure if it's going to rain or not. "Everybody lets you down in the end. Everybody disappoints you."

"You wouldn't let me down."

He smiled in the most relaxed and natural way. "Who knows, Davey?"

I stood.

"Don't go, uncle Abe. Please—?"

"Sit down."

I sat. He was behind me, his hands on my shoulders. He spoke gently, ruffling my hair while he did. "Trust me about this." He dug his fingers into my shoulder muscles. "Hey—you're almost relaxed. Nice and loose. You stay like that all the way to Kentucky, do you hear me? What you have to remember, though—why we can't kid ourselves—is that they have no reason to trust anybody either. Why should they? Costello and Luciano helped us win the war when we came up through Sicily— they made deals and who knows if we could have won without them?— but after the war the government double-crossed them too, shipped them back. So why should they trust anyone? You be a good boy, Davey. You take care of yourself."

I couldn't see his face, but the touch of his hand on my neck and on the top of my head spread downward, warmed me. Only for a second, though. I tried to concentrate, to think ahead: What if Fasalino, when he sent his two men, had done so anticipating Abe's reaction? What if Fasalino had known that Abe would have himself covered. . . .

"I am sorry. I'm real sorry about some things, Davey."

I'd never heard Abe use those words before. *Uncle Abe!* I wanted to call out, but I didn't. *Uncle Abe! Wait! Be careful!* I turned and watched him walk off, his stride strong and confident, but I couldn't see his face when he passed the table where Benny and Turkish Sammy had been sitting, or when he paid the check, or when he walked out of the cafeteria.

My mother was dancing with Beau Jack. They circled the living room in one another's arms as if in slow motion. The chairs and coffee table were pushed to the edges of the room, the oriental rug rolled up next to the couch legs, the couch shoved back to the windows. The parquet floor, cross-hatched squares of oak, glistened. It was dark outside. The venetian blinds had not yet been lowered. Across the alleyway I could see lights on in other apartments.

Beau Jack held my mother at arm's length, and I thought of Confederate soldiers in Civil War movies dancing with beautiful girls under crystal chandeliers. Beau Jack's skin glittered as if dusted with a fine golden-brown powder. My mother's head was tilted back, her cheeks flushed, her eyes closed. She seemed very young and happy. She wore a white peasant blouse, a flowered skirt, sandals. My grandfather sat in a wooden chair between my bedroom and my mother's, patches of fur on his lap, a thread looped across his mouth, a silver needle hanging from the thread. How could my mother and Beau Jack dance so gracefully in such a small space? They moved like porcelain dolls I'd once seen on a music box, as if they had made the same circles a thousand times before. Beau Jack wore a yellow-and-brown-striped shirt, blue pants hitched up high and held by black suspenders. Instead of his Dodger cap, he had a red paisley kerchief tied onto his head, piratestyle. I smelled rose-scented hair pomade.

Was I dreaming? The music seemed too loud. Beau Jack and my mother swirled in faster circles. They seemed larger suddenly, impossibly large for the small rectangle they were moving within, and for a moment it was as if they were taller than I was, as if I were a small boy coming out of my bedroom late at night, sleepy-eyed, to find them there.

Had Gail telephoned yet? Would she worry about me because I was already late for supper? I didn't want to phone her until I knew more, until I heard from Abe. I tried to picture her in our bed, cuddling Emilie. Gail's skin was smoother than it had ever been, a change she attributed to the pregnancy. They hadn't heard me knock at the front door, but my mother was coming toward me now, her right hand across her mouth, her eyes wide, and she was laughing in a way that made me know she was pleased that I'd found her there dancing with Beau Jack. She said she was glad that I was home, that they'd been expecting me.

"Expecting me?"

"Abe called and said you'd be stopping by about suppertime."

"When?"

"Didn't you hear me? About suppertime."

"I meant when did he call?"

My mother turned to Beau Jack. "Hello, Davey," he said. "Your uncle called about two hours ago."

"Not since?"

"No."

I touched my back pocket, felt the tiny ridged teeth of the key. My mother's hand was on my arm.

"Hey listen—you won't tell Sam, yeah, about me and Beau Jack? When it comes to other men Sam got a temper like I never seen." She slipped her arm around my waist, kissed my cheek. "Doesn't Beau Jack dance beautifully?"

"I learned to dance at the Hostess Houses. I told Davey about them before. They had us dance with the nurses, and with the women who came overseas to see that we had a normal life sometimes. They gave lessons."

"Oh I love to dance, Davey! Do you and Gail like to dance?"

My mother twirled around so that her skirt rose in a wide arc. I saw Ellen, turning blindly in her garden. I thought of ripples on a lake moving outward. A stone floated down, lost in the center. The lake was dark, muddy. *A fool can throw a stone into the water that ten wise men can't recover.* Abe's favorite saying.

"Beau Jack's been coming up here every Tuesday and Thursday afternoon, giving me lessons. It's nice, ain't it? I mean, who does it hurt? Before your father and me got married I used to go dancing with my friends down to this place called the Chateau Pierre, in Sea Gate. Abe didn't like me there, said I had to be careful of all the mashers." She cupped my ear, whispered: "Abe visited us yesterday. He spoke to Poppa!"

I said that Abe had told me. My grandfather was sucking on a thread, drawing it to a point, pulling it through the eye of a needle. He grinned at me toothlessly. I wanted to get away—to be home. Make a spoon, Gail would say in the morning when we were snuggling, her back to me. Make a spoon.

"You won't tell Sam, then?"

The phone rang. I started for the kitchen, but my mother held my arm, told me that she had discovered that Sam Lipsky was the most wonderful man in the world.

The phone rang again. My grandfather shuffled by, returned a few seconds later, told me the call was for me. I went into the kitchen.

"Davey Voloshin?"

"Yes."

"It's Vincent. Listen, I was wondering if you saw the evening paper yet?"

"Why are you calling me here?"

"It's just that when I saw the news in the paper, it made me think about you. I called your home first, see, but your wife said you weren't back yet, so I figured I might catch you at your mother's place."

"What do you want?"

"To be your friend. So you go take a look at the paper and then maybe if you want to talk about the news, we'll be in touch."

He hung up. I told my mother that I was going downstairs to get the paper. She asked me who had telephoned.

"I'll get the paper," Beau Jack said. "You stay with your mother and grandfather for a while."

"Come here."

My grandfather was beckoning to me with a finger. Beau Jack left the apartment. My grandfather lifted the small blanket so that I could feel the fur, admire the stitching, the black satin lining. He bit off some thread. I turned to my mother, thought of asking her how he could bite off thread if he didn't have his teeth in.

"Do you want your room back?" my grandfather asked.

"Davey got his own place now, Poppa," my mother said. "He got a beautiful wife and daughter, remember? And you lived to see it."

"You're right. I forget things sometimes. I'm an old man. Abe visited me yesterday—did you know that?"

"Yes."

My grandfather nodded once. Then his eyes closed, his chin slumped to his chest. His eyes were black slits. Slit trenches, I thought. That was the name for the holes the German soldiers would hide in to snipe at G.I.s after our men had passed over them. I went to the kitchen with my mother. She told me that when she was with Sam she always thought of the actor from the movie *The Best Years of Our Lives*, but she didn't know why. Did I remember seeing the movie with her and my father, at the R.K.O. Kenmore?

"The guy I mean is the one who had mechanical claws instead of hands. Is that crazy, do you think? Because that was my favorite movie that I ever saw—I never cried so much—and I always thought afterwards that I could love a man like that more than anyone else in the world—a man who could be as gentle as he was strong, who didn't know how to quit on life. Do you remember going with us?"

"Yes. The actor's name was Harold Russell."

Her eyes brightened. She held my hand, her cheeks wet with tears. I recalled trying to imagine what it would be like to live without hands, to have to draw with stainless steel claws. I recalled practicing with a ball and glove, imitating Pete Gray, the one-armed outfielder for the Saint Louis Browns—tossing a ball in the air, tucking the glove under my left armpit, catching the ball in my bare hand, throwing it. . . .

"You don't hate your mother no more. I can see that. You don't hate me too much, do you?"

"Why should I hate you?"

The door opened. Beau Jack came toward us, his face the color of ashes. I reached for the paper, but my mother snatched at it, pulled it from Beau Jack's hand.

"Davey should read it first," Beau Jack said.

She spread the paper on the table, looked down, screamed. I pushed her aside. She kept screaming. She backed up against the refrigerator, one hand to her mouth, palm forward, the other hand in her hair, like a rake, pulling.

I looked at the photograph of Mr. Rothenberg on the front page of *The Daily Mirror.* He was lying on the floor of his kitchen, his feet tucked under him. His wheelchair was halfway into the picture, tipped upwards as if somebody had lifted it like a wheelbarrow to let him spill forward. He wore a dark business suit. There was a patch of blood on his cheek that ran from his left ear to his chin, and the shape, a long irregular triangle that tapered toward a point, made me think of a contour map of Mexico I'd made in the fourth grade. His body seemed to be folded at the waist. I stared at the tiny dots of black ink that flowed evenly through the map of blood on his cheek, and I thought of Mr. Rothenberg's power leaking from his ear, clotting.

UNDERWORLD FIGURE KILLED IN HOME

"Abe! My baby brother Abe! Abe! Abe! Oh Abe . . . !"

My mother backed up to the windowsill, bit down on her right hand until pinpricks of blood appeared. The blood stained her teeth. She had one leg lifted, knee bent, as if she were trying to keep herself from urinating. Beau Jack was talking to her softly, trying to soothe her.

"Stay here," I said. "Don't go out of the house. Don't go anywhere."

"Davey!" I moved to the door. "Oh my little Davey! Don't leave me—"

When I heard the window slide up, I turned. My mother had her head out and was screaming my name down into the street, calling me to come home. I grabbed her, pulled her back, slammed the window down. She screamed louder and I looked down quickly, afraid for a second that I'd shut the window on her fingertips. My grandfather stood in the doorway, smiling. He held a glass in one hand. His false teeth were in the glass, a small white tablet next to them, the water fizzing, the tablet sending a spray of bubbles upwards.

"They should all rot in hell," he said. "The earth should open and swallow him up, but they should cut him down from a tree after one day, do you know why?" His small eyes were clear now, like a young man's, like Abe's. "Because an evil man is a reproach to God. That's what God said about Korach, why they should cut him down after they hanged him."

"Stop!" my mother cried. "Stop talking crazy!"

"I'm an old man."

My mother dug her nails into his wrist. The telephone rang and I grabbed at it before anyone else could.

"Davey—is that you?"

"It's me."

"Listen, hey—this is Vincent again. I wanted to call and give you my condolences, see. I mean, you didn't call me so I figured now that you got the news I'd be big about it and I'd call you. What do you think?"

"I think you're a dead man."

"Nah. Come on—let's not talk like that. I mean, you're all upset and worried, which is why I called. You must be very scared about your uncle. We've been trying to reach him, see—to get the news to him too, but nobody can find him, so we thought maybe you could help us out. Can you help us out, Davey?"

"What do you want?"

"Just that if you see him, you tell him Mr. Fasalino's still waiting."

"Didn't he show up at five—?"

"It's why we're all so concerned. It's why I called you. I figured you might need a good friend now."

The line went dead. My mother started screaming again. Beau Jack asked if I was all right.

"I know what to do."

"You be careful now. You use my place downstairs if you have to. Do you have a gun?"

My mother tried to punch at Beau Jack's chest. He grabbed her wrists.

"No."

"I have one there. It's in a space outside the fuse box, to the left. You got to move a piece of two-by-four."

"You'll take care of her while I'm gone?"

"Yes."

My mother shrieked and her hands were on my shoulders, her nails tearing into me.

"Will you be all right?" I asked.

"A lot you care. You and your big shot uncle. My big shot brother."
She was suddenly calm, and it was her calmness that terrified me. "Listen. I'm sorry if I got so carried away, only I had a real throwback, see,
looking at him in the picture, to when he was alive and how it all started.
Momma never knew what he did for her, how he saved her. Abe made
me swear never to tell Poppa either, see, so . . ."

Beau Jack sat next to my mother, told her that everything was going
to be all right, that I was a smart boy.

My mother patted his hand. "So why should I cry so much, right?
Didn't I cry enough for one lifetime?" She closed her eyes, tipped her
head to one side, spoke in Yiddish, then translated: " 'If you dance at
every wedding, you'll weep for every death.' Poppa taught me that."

"I'll be back," I said.

My mother followed me to the door. "Listen. Mr. Rothenberg was an
old man anyway. I mean, how many years did he have left? The way I
look at it is that if you'd picked up your things right away after you
moved out, I wouldn't have had to throw them out. But who am I, the
Acme Storage Company? I mean, how much notice did you give me
that you and your little girlfriend were already married, that you'd
knocked her up, you should forgive my frankness?" She turned to Beau
Jack. "Would you put another record on? To me she's just like my own
daughter, only when a girl lets herself get into the worst kind of trouble
and the boy marries her, then we know who the sucker is, yeah? So to
show you how I got no hard feelings, I'll phone her now with the news
about Mr. Rothenberg so you'll see I ain't carrying a grudge."

I knocked the phone from her hand. It swung back and forth on its
black cord, tapping against the wall. She smiled at me, as if it made her
happy to see me angry.

Beau Jack put a hand on my forearm. "You'll be all right, Davey? You
won't do anything foolish?"

"I'm all right. Abe told me what to do, in case." I tried to smile at him.
I wanted to ease the hurt I saw in his eyes, to make him believe that
everything would be fine. "Do you know what I just thought? I just
thought that if things get tight, I'll try to imagine what Jackie would do
if he were in my shoes."

"I don't understand."

My mother was showing us the newspaper. "Hey look—they got a
picture here of Mr. Rothenberg from when he was on TV in those
hearings, talking with Senator Kefauver. See how handsome he looked?
He always dressed like a real Beau Brummel and he wasn't even that
much younger. What was it, four years ago? Five? He got old very fast."
She put the paper on top of the refrigerator. "I remember when he came
to the store and how he would never look at the mugs who held the car

door for him. Like they didn't exist. Remember how distinguished he seemed compared to all those other gangsters—like he was one of the senators himself. He had class only, like Sol used to say, everybody got a number, and when your number's up, it's up. This is it and this is it, yeah, Davey?"

"You go on," Beau Jack said. "I'll take care of things. She'll be all right. You call when things are okay."

"I mean, maybe the truth is that his own men did it to him. Who knows? Maybe Abe went and did it himself so he could be in charge now and avoid trouble later. And Davey, my precious, that reminds me that before you come to visit next time I'd appreciate it if you'd call first. Also if you could maybe bring Emilie, only without your wife for a change."

I opened the door and she began pounding on my back, screaming that if I left she knew she would never see me again. Beau Jack tried to pull her backwards and she smashed him in the cheek with her fist, told him to get his filthy black hands off her. She was my best friend, she cried. She had tried to save me, hadn't she?

"Did I try or did I try?"

"You tried," I said.

Her body sagged. She looked towards Beau Jack as if she might apologize to him. "Did I really like Abe?" she asked. "Who can tell? I mean, how can you not like your own brother?"

"Lots do, Evie," Beau Jack said.

"*Really?*"

I kissed my mother goodbye and headed down the stairs. She cried after me that she was my best friend. I was her only son! I was the light of her life. . . .

One flight down, I stopped and waited. Should I telephone Gail? If there were no need, I didn't want to alarm her. Could I dare try to get her and Emilie out of the apartment and to her parents' home? Would Fasalino's men trail me, hoping that I had a rendezvous with Abe? I took a deep breath, moved down from the second to the first floor, looked into our mailbox. No message. I stopped. My head was spinning with questions, with pictures, and I felt that if I could only get one clear picture in my head at a time, and fix it there and stare at it—if I could imagine scenes *before* they happened—then I could be ready for anything.

I stepped down from the landing, into the front lobby, and before I felt my heart tumble, and before I realized how stupid I'd been to go out the front way, I heard the breathing that was not mine, felt the hands grip each of my arms, the gloved palm press my lips back against my teeth so that I couldn't call out. Two men dragged me into a corner. Vincent came toward me. He wore a dark topcoat, and under it, in the dim light that came from the courtyard, I saw him smile, saw his gold medallion swing lightly from one side to the other.

"Hey Davey—you sounded so upset on the phone, I figured I'd get here right away to see if I could help."

There were no lights on in the lobby. Why hadn't I noticed that when I came around the second floor landing or when I squinted into the mailbox? The men frisked me. I told myself not to resist. Vincent apologized for having to use force, said that sometimes you couldn't take chances, even with guys you trusted, even with family. He told the two men to take a powder, that they would all meet later at the party. Later? I kept my eyes on Vincent's eyes. He talked softly, telling me that he was upset too, because he'd had to break up with Sheila. Hadn't I heard the news from Abe? Maybe, in time, they'd be able to get back together. Mr. Fasalino was his uncle the way Abe was mine—did I know that? Mr. Fasalino had been good to him the way Abe was good to me. Mr. Fasalino had helped him out of a lot of jams.

I let him lead me to the front door. I looked through the iron curlicues, the plate glass. I thought of Beau Jack unlatching the large glass panels, letting them swing open so that he could wash them down with ammonia, rub them with rags and newspapers.

Then we were on the street, Vincent's hand on my elbow, guiding me. He talked about his two big problems—gambling and women—and how his uncle had always bailed him out, but that—wasn't it always the same?—he had to perform some small services for his uncle to pay him back. He hoped I'd understand. Didn't everybody owe something to somebody in this world?

We crossed Rogers Avenue. On the next block there were no people walking, no kids playing, no one sitting on the brick stoops. A car cruised by slowly, moved to the curb. Vincent nudged me in the ribs, told me to do myself a favor and get in, that we could all go to the party.

"No thanks."

Something hard whacked me between my ribs and my belt. I looked down, saw the black barrel of his gun. He smiled, told me to come anyway, that he had nothing against me, that he was just doing what he was told to do. He got nervous sometimes, he said, and he didn't want to be forced to do anything we'd be sorry for later.

As soon as I was in the car there were hands on me again, pinning my arms, jerking me backwards by the hair, tieing something around my eyes that cut into my skin.

"Listen," Vincent said, his mouth close to my ear. "I give you my word of honor I'd do things different if it were up to me. I mean, like I said, I think of you as a friend—like a kid brother, see? So just give me your word you'll cooperate, okay? Do it for me—"

I said nothing. A hand was on the inside of my thigh and it squeezed so tightly and suddenly that my back arched, my rear end left the seat. Vincent told the guys to lay off, that I was a personal friend.

"He just became a father too, see, and he got this real cute little baby girl he loves, so we wouldn't want to do nothing we'd be sorry for later." His lips touched my ear. "Be careful. Be real careful, Davey." Then, louder: "Listen—my debt with your uncle that you were so worried about, remember? I want you to know it's all taken care of. Wiped out. I got the news just before I come to talk with you."

I tried to calculate the distance, the turns—to figure out where we were going, but Vincent kept talking in my ear, telling me about his gambling problems, and by the third turn I was lost. I tried to imagine how Ellen calculated distances. I thought of myself with Gail and Emilie and Ellen, in the woods. We had talked about going camping together next summer. I imagined Abe coming with us, helping lead Ellen around the woods and the lake, Ellen telling him the names of trees and flowers. I wondered what he would feel. I counted backwards from a hundred the way I did when I was unable to sleep, when I tried to talk myself into drowsiness. Had we driven for two minutes, or twenty minutes? I'd lost track. The car stopped, somebody shoved me out onto the sidewalk, somebody else grabbed my arm, kept me from falling, pushed me through a doorway. I heard music, smelled beer.

Vincent removed my blindfold. "There you go, Davey. Sorry."

I rubbed my eyes, looked up a steep staircase. There was no banister. The lobby was small and square, the ceiling low. There were no mailboxes, no name plates or buzzers. I could feel the heat our bodies gave off, as if we were packed upright in a wooden box. My eyes drew on the light from the street, sand-colored light seeping in through high, smudged door windows. I looked at the two men who were with us and tried to memorize their faces. Vincent told them to get lost, that he needed to talk to me privately.

They walked upstairs. The door opened. A fat man holding a ruby-colored glass looked down at us, lifted his glass in a mock toast. His shirt was split open at the waist. He scratched his stomach. Vincent came closer, his shoulder touching mine. Upstairs the door closed, but not all the way. The light seemed heavy with yellow, as if there were tiny motes of pigment floating in it. Cigarette smoke hung on the upstairs landing like fog, then drifted toward us, and I thought of droplets of water sliding down our bathroom wall, my mother yelling at me to wipe the wall dry after I showered.

Was Abe upstairs? If he was already on his way to Cuba or Miami or Las Vegas, would he be safe? Had he planned—before I met Gail—to settle in one of those places, to leave the neighborhood to me? Gail suspected it, hated him more when he was away from Brooklyn. Vincent's back was against the front door and he had a gun aimed at my chest. Why? He seemed embarrassed. I was certain he did not intend to use the gun against me. If he'd intended that, he wouldn't have needed so many words, he wouldn't have had to bring me here where people, passing by, might hear the shot.

The truth, I wanted to tell him, imagining the questions about Abe, was that what I knew about Miami and Cuba and Vegas came pretty much from the newspapers and the TV hearings. Abe never talked to me about what he did when he traveled for Mr. Rothenberg. Had he kept things from me because he wanted to protect me, or because—the thought had occurred before—he didn't want me to see that, outside our neighborhood, he was small-time, nothing more than a delivery boy for Mr. Rothenberg? Abe always liked being a big fish in a little pond, my mother said. Couldn't I see that he needed me to worship him? Vincent put the gun back inside his coat, told me how smart I'd been not to fight. He laughed. Nobody wanted me to cry uncle, right?

I didn't smile. Maybe they were bluffing. Maybe what they planned to do was to tell me that Abe had said things about me. Maybe they planned to tell me that Abe was already dead so that I would fall apart and agree to help them, so that I would betray Abe. The oldest trick. I tried to anticipate all the things they might say to me. If they told me that they had taken Gail and Emilie and were holding them somewhere . . .

It seemed crazy to me that a few hours before I'd been kissing my wife and nuzzling my daughter—touching skin that was, in memory, like satin—and that now I was trapped in a dark space waiting to find out if I would live or die. I imagined Gail looking out our living room window, watching the street, waiting for me. Would she be nursing Emilie? The body didn't know how to lie, she said. When she was upset or worried, her milk was different, and Emilie would sputter, would draw her knees up in pain.

Gail would, at this moment, I told myself, be looking out the window, watching the street, hoping to see me, while I was here, watching Vincent's hands and eyes, measuring distances and gestures, calculating my chances. What made sense?

"Listen. This ain't easy for me, Davey. Believe me. Only since I'm the one that knows you best, they chose me to give you the message."

He rubbed his hands together, light flashing at me from his pinky ring.

"If I try to leave?"

He shook his head sideways, like a bulldog shaking off water.

"Ah, you wouldn't be that stupid. You got a good brain, Davey.

Everyone knows that. You can make something of yourself in this life.
You ain't a bum like me. Now Rothenberg, he had a good brain too and
he got to use it for more years than you would of expected, all the dirty
deals he pulled. But in the end the chickens all come home to roost,
right?"

"You're stalling."

"Sure. You would too, if you had to deliver a message like the one
they gave me for you."

"Tell me."

"No rush, kid. No rush. Bad news is never in a hurry. I mean, I
figured you and me would want to be alone here for a few minutes when
you got the news, away from what they got going on upstairs, see, where
we got to go in a minute to get the other things straightened out."

"Tell me."

I thought of myself with Gail, heading west on a train, gazing out at
low hills, at fields of Kentucky blue grass. Emilie had her nose pressed
against the train window. She was pointing to the horses.

"Sure, kid. Only see what a friend I been to you—how I made sure to
get you away from your mother and your kid so they ain't in trouble?
Because, okay, since I don't mean to tease you or nothing, the news is
that your uncle had a bad accident—the worst kind—and that Mr.
Fasalino wants to express his condolences to you personally. He's waiting upstairs so—"

I moved for the door, but he was ready for me, his gun in my stomach.
He talked softly, told me he knew I was upset, but that I should be
careful so that we could both live longer. I felt the blood surge through
me, crash against my chest, and even in my rage I knew enough to
remind myself that he might not be telling the truth, that he might be
trying to set me up, to use me. But for what?

"Accidents happen, right? I mean, kids can fall off sliding-ponds and
break their necks, and pretty young mothers can slip in bathtubs and
crack their skulls, and whole families can go up in flames because a
piece of newspaper happens to float down over a gas range at the wrong
time. Even the insurance companies tell you that most of the worst
accidents happen at home."

His gun was pushing my lips against my teeth, forcing my mouth
open, making me back up against the wall. I tasted cold metal, smelled
burnt gunpowder, listened to him give me advice: I couldn't be too
careful. Did I understand? Accidents could happen, and if he were in
my shoes he would think mostly about looking out for number one. Did
I hear him?

"I hear."

"That's a good boy, Davey. You said the right thing."

His gun was gone. I wanted to spit, to get rid of the bitter taste. What good was anger, he wanted to know. He knew how much I loved my uncle, but what good would anger do for me now? What was gone was gone. I should calm down and let myself feel what lay beneath the anger. I should act on that.

Then, smiling warmly, he whacked me across the midsection with all his might. I was too startled to cry out, and I heard him cry too, as he swung, so that the breath burst from me as if a bag of it had exploded. I gagged, doubled over. I heard his voice tell me that I was to take his word that all they wanted was for things to be peaceful. They didn't hold me responsible for anything Abe or Mr. Rothenberg had done. I gasped for breath, my hands clutching at my stomach. The world went black. I let my head drop lower. Vincent pulled me up by one ear, so that I would look into his face. Now did I understand?

"Nobody wants blood," he said. "Nobody likes accidents, Davey. Mr. Fasalino ain't interested in your wife or your kid or your mother. Mr. Fasalino don't want nothing from you but your good will, see. Like when somebody buys a candy store or a small business, they don't want the guy they buy it from to be going around bad-mouthing them, you know what I mean? They want goodwill in the community so they can keep the customers along with the fixtures."

Somebody called down to us and Vincent yelled back that things were under control, that we would be up in a minute. Men seemed to be floating around in the smoke, drinking and laughing. I thought of Abe and his friends, naked, walking around Al Roon's Health Club, their bodies moving in and out of the clouds of steam like ghosts. Vincent said that Mr. Fasalino had children and grandchildren of his own, that he wanted me to have a good life. Mr. Fasalino was a generous man. I looked at Vincent and I imagined Gail, retching into the toilet. I saw my mother, in the kitchen, raking at her hair. I saw Abe, a gun in his hand, standing in the bathroom doorway, staring at Gail. She screamed. She flung herself at his face, screeching, clawing. Emilie was in the bathtub, and while Abe tried to get hold of Gail's wrists, Emilie slid slowly down the side of the tub until, inch by inch, her head disappeared under soap bubbles.

"You can't have everything in life," Vincent said. "I mean, like with me and Sheila. We all got losses, Davey, and we gotta know when to cut." His eyes were actually watering. He assured me that he'd spoken to Mr. Fasalino on my behalf. He rubbed his hand across his forehead. The handle of his gun was slick with sweat. The light was spilling down on us now, thick with smoke. Somebody yelled at him to haul his ass upstairs, that Mr. Fasalino was getting impatient.

"Sometimes when we get real sad we think we gotta act like we're angry, but ain't that crazy, Davey? My Momma used to say to me, 'Vincent, if you're sad, you gotta let yourself be sad.' I mean, you think I asked for this job? So you just relax, okay? The worst is over." He shook his head. "Jesus. If I had a mirror you could look into, you'd see how crazy you are with anger, what a face you got on."

He gestured to me to start up the stairs with him, and as he did I saw that there were two rings on his left hand, the tiger's eye on his pinky, a second ring on his wedding finger. Had I lived through this scene before? Had I imagined it. He turned to me, eyes moist, a strange sick smile on his lips, and as he gestured to me again to follow him—while he said things about being sincere, about really being sweet on Sheila— I saw the stone from Abe's ring glow red through the smoke, and I wondered if I'd known all along that it would be there. *Abe!* The light seemed to tumble down the staircase now, brighter than ever, the smoke curling and turning in balls, and when Vincent raised his right hand, the gun in it, to shield his eyes from that light, I had him against the staircase wall, my right arm jammed against his windpipe. *Abe!* I slammed Vincent's wrist against the wall and the gun fell. The doorway upstairs was wide open, a high foreshortened rectangle of light and smoke. Vincent squirmed, kicked out at me, tried to call for help. *Abe!* Vincent's eyes blinked furiously with fright, with panic. I bent down, wiped along the step with my palm, found the gun, and even as the noises and voices descended from above, I felt calm and ready, so calm that I could not even hear the sound of my own heart.

The light on the staircase changed from yellow to white—brighter and brighter—and it was as if, inside my head, within that white light, I could suddenly see all the years of my life stretched out to the end of time like a series of empty rooms in a vacant apartment, all the doors open, all the rooms clean and white. *Abe!* And when I heard the shot and felt the gun slam backwards against my palm, and when I heard Vincent moan and slump against me, his hand on my shoulder, it was not at all as if I were dreaming, but more as if I were remembering a dream I'd once had. I was walking out of the apartment slowly, room by room, backwards, across waxed floors. Abe stood in the doorway behind me, gun in hand, looking down at the body. Gail and I sat on the bed, unable to make him see us. Vincent held his stomach, looked at me with pinched, bewildered eyes.

"Oh Jesus, kid, why'd you do a stupid thing like that? How you ever gonna fix a thing like this? Jesus Christ, kid . . ."

But I was already moving down the stairs, leaping the last four steps, flinging the door open, running for my life.

"*Hey*—! Hey you—"

I turned and fired in the direction of the voice. Then I ran again, between cars, across the street, around a corner, and I was astonished at how wonderful it felt simply to be running, to feel my legs stretching and pumping, to be sucking cool air into my lungs. *Abe!* I ran and I ran, the black street racing backwards beneath my feet, my toes skimming the concrete, and it was as if I were running across the grass at the Parade Grounds in full stride, going way out for a pass, knowing I could catch up to any ball that anybody could throw. I felt as if I could run forever.

I saw lights ahead, heard a subway train. I was streaking down deserted streets, past warehouses and small factories and abandoned buildings. I was moving too fast to make out street signs. I headed towards the lights and the noise, at a diagonal, between moving cars. Where had they come from? I heard screeching, horns. I kept running. I saw people in front of me, heard music. I slowed down, stopped, looked back. I smelled sea air. My chest heaved in and out, rasping. How far had I come? Was I in Sheepshead Bay or Canarsie or Red Hook? I remembered fishing with a dropline from a pier at Sheepshead Bay when I was a boy. My mother took me there on the Ocean Avenue trolley. We bought clams and I smashed them on the sidewalk, picked out the white flesh from among pieces of shell, pressed the flesh onto my hook.

Trust nobody. Abe was right. If I'd gone upstairs and made the wrong move, said the wrong thing . . . If I'd lost my temper . . . I backed into a doorway, looked out both ways. Nobody was following me. I lifted the gun barrel to my nose, sniffed in. I saw myself in our apartment house courtyard and I was on my knees, banging down on rolls of caps with a stone, letting the red paper unroll, pounding on the gray dots.

I shivered, imagining myself biting down on the barrel, recalling the awful feeling when I'd bit down through a steak onto the tines of a fork. I walked at a normal pace, staying close to the buildings, watching the street, on the lookout for slow-moving cars, wondering why I didn't feel more about Abe, why I wasn't crying, why my heart wasn't breaking. I was relieved that he was gone, I realized, and the feeling, to my surprise, did not displease me. Why not? I kept the gun ready, pressed to my leg. I heard men speaking in Spanish, arguing and laughing. In front of an apartment building, four men sat around a small bridge table, drinking beer and playing cards. Behind them, two men straddled chairs backwards. I saw dollar bills held down by rocks. A stand-up lamp was next to the table, its cord running through the air, looped into the window of a first-floor apartment. I didn't want any trouble. I veered sideways, toward the curb, so that I wouldn't have to duck under the cord.

I unzipped my jacket, slipped the gun inside, tucked it under my belt, between my pants and my shirt. Two dark-haired girls were leaning backwards against a car. I could smell their perfume, see their chests rise slightly. They giggled, spoke to me in Spanish, asked if I were lost. One of the men looked up at me from his cards. I smiled with closed lips to show him I meant no harm. He gestured to the girls, winked at me, tossed a card onto the table. Coins clinked in a glass ashtray. The girls laughed, asked me what food I ate to have grown so tall. "¡Mira! ¡Mira! Hey, muchacho grande, you real cute, you like to meet my friend Nydia?"

Could they see my wedding ring? The girls called to me, asked my name. I didn't look back. I saw the phone booth on the corner, hesitated for an instant, realized that I had already made my decision: I would not telephone. I was on a wide street where the lights were brighter, but the night sky, blocked by the elevated subway above me, the crisscrossing of girders and tracks, was darker. Where was I? The sign said Liberty Avenue. A man in a stained camel's hair jacket, no shirt below, sat in the alcove of a liquor store, a paper bag in his lap. I looked down at a sewer grating, blocked by wet newspapers and garbage, by a mass of something brown that looked like a clump of human hair.

I thought of Beau Jack's wolf-children, racing beneath the city, chewing at Vincent's face, stripping his cheek from the bone. I looked back. A pair of headlights seemed to float along the street toward me, as if in water. The headlights stopped where the men were playing cards. I moved out of view, crossed over, then ran. I heard a train rumble out of the station, saw the entrance on the next block, felt something wet hit the back of my head, glide down my neck. The gun dug into my waist, scraping, knocking against my hip bone. Liberty Avenue. The Fulton Line. I could take it to downtown Brooklyn, to Atlantic Avenue. I could change there for the uptown Seventh Avenue IRT. If I made good connections I could be at the Port Authority Terminal in Manhattan within forty to fifty minutes.

I took the stairs two at a time, fished in my pocket, found change, pushed through the turnstile. They would look for me first at our apartment, then at the office on Flatbush Avenue. They might return to my mother's building. They might figure I'd want to go home first—to Gail and to Emilie, to pack—or that I would go to Abe's apartment. Abe was probably right, that they would never count on me being ready to head straight for a bus station. I walked to the far end of the platform, leaned against a billboard.

If they found me and brought me back to Fasalino, and even if he didn't get rough with me . . . I clenched my fists, wanted to pound the billboard, to punch through it, through the teeth of the blond model smiling coyly at a man in a tuxedo who was pouring a glass of Scotch. I blinked and experienced one of those moments Gail and I often talked about, of being in a place I'd never been, but of sensing that I'd been there before. Gail had shown me an article that tried to explain *déjà vu* by talking about the images our retinas often took in during the split-second before our minds registered, rationally, what it was we were actually seeing. In that split second, as in a dream, whole stories—entire lives—could pass, and we would think those moments and lives had taken place, not an instant before, but in some other distant time, in some other life.

What I saw in that moment was a dream I once had, or thought I'd had, of being on the subway platform late at night, alone, on my way to a party. I'd forced Gail to stay home—we'd argued, she'd pouted— because I knew, somehow, as surely as I'd ever known anything, that if we went together, leaving Emilie behind, we would all die.

I was very frightened. Gail and I lay in one another's arms, my head on her chest, my cheek against her swollen breast, and it was clear to me that I had told her of my fears—my dream—for she was soothing me, telling me that it wasn't so, that it was only a dream. Why should I continue to believe that I would poison her life with mine? Why should I be so frightened of my feelings—of my desire to be tender and gentle?

I was nineteen years old, almost the age Abe was when he had gone to Mr. Rothenberg the first time. I was nineteen years old and I was living my first life, and in that instant when I wondered if what was happening was happening for the first time or if I were only reliving the remembered moment of a dream I'd once had, what I wanted more than anything in the world was simply to be holding Gail and explaining to her that what seemed so crazy to me was not that men like Abe and Rothenberg and Fasalino and Vincent led the lives they led and did the things they did, but that their lives existed at the same time ours did— parallel to ours somehow—within the same universe. How could it be? How could we be in our bed, the lights out, fondling Emilie, while at the same moment a man like Vincent could be a few miles away firing a small piece of metal into the skull of someone I loved? And where, I wanted to know—this was the part that made my stomach tighten, that was hardest to make sense of—where was the difference?

I heard the girls laughing. I looked up, muscles tense, expecting, I realized, to see that the two Spanish girls had followed me. How long had my mind been drifting? Two couples were coming toward me, their arms around one another's waists. The girls wore silk kerchiefs, tight skirts split at the calves, high-heeled shoes that clacked on the concrete like cleats in a locker room. The guys were about my age and wore black motorcycle jackets, pegged pants. They stopped and kissed, their girl-friends' mouths pumping and sucking. I tried not to stare. I tried to look at them without looking at them.

You won't hurt yourself, will you?

No. I wouldn't hurt myself. Not if I could help it. Gail's words were the same, each time I left home. One of the girls tugged on her boyfriend's sleeve. He was tall, only an inch or so shorter than me, oily black hair slicked back into a D.A. He tossed a penny onto the tracks, then another. His girlfriend told him to stop, that the train was coming. In the distance, at the vanishing point of the tracks, I saw small dots of white and red. The tall guy pushed his girlfriend away. "Geronimo—!" he shouted, then leapt down onto the train tracks, landing squarely. The girls shrieked. People from the other end of the platform hurried toward us. Was the guy crazy? The train was roaring toward us, banging from side to side, the lights growing larger. The guy stood on the tracks, feet spread on the gleaming rails, smiling broadly, head thrown back as if he intended to let the train roll right over him, to catch it in his teeth.

He was playing it awfully close. My heart bumped. What if his shoe got caught, if he tripped? I remembered an old war movie in which a soldier gets his boot stuck in a railroad track while crossing a train yard. When the train roared across the screen, blacking it out, the whistle blasting, I'd covered my eyes and felt sick.

I moved fast, to jump down, but the other guy held my arm.

"Don't be crazy, guy—Frankie, he does this all the time."

Frankie, in the well of the subway, had two hands on the platform, for leverage. He vaulted up easily, as if he were getting out of a swimming pool. He brushed himself off.

If the word were already out, or if they heard about what happened later on, after they got home. If they remembered me . . .

I put my hands in my jacket pocket, felt the gun through the inner lining of my pocket. Frankie's girlfriend was all over him, yelling at him about how scared he made her. She was shrieking and laughing, mascara running in a thin black line from the corner of her right eye. One hand on her ass, Frankie brushed his hair back with his other hand, stared at me across her shoulder, then plunged his tongue into her mouth. The train bore down on us. The other girl had both hands pressed over her ears. The train doors slid open. When they entered the rear door of the front car, I moved sideways, walked through the first door of the second car.

I sat by myself, picked at the cane cushion. There were eight or ten men in the car—no women at this hour—and a few were asleep. When his own father died, my father told me, they placed pennies on his eyes. The train windows were smudged a watery tan. There were always choices. Abe was right. I was choosing not to telephone Gail. I closed my eyes, tried to force my father's face into my head. I wished he could have lived long enough to have known Gail, to have held Emilie. The train swung from side to side, out of the station, high above the street,

rocking around curves. From a distance it would seem tiny, these tons
of steel and glass and wire—a mere necklace of pale-yellow beads moving noiselessly across the horizon.

The train was slowing down. Grant Avenue. We were near the Cypress Hills cemetery. Why was my father still crying? Why did he love
me? Did he agree with me that, for the sake of my wife and daughter, I
was doing the right thing? I wanted to have the chance to be the kind of
father to my own child that I'd always wanted him to be to me. I smiled.
Gail would understand that, wouldn't she? Later I would tell her all
about what had happened and why I'd done what I'd done, though she
would probably turn her back·on me at first, fold her arms across her
chest. The train doors closed. We moved again. I kissed Gail's cheek,
from behind—she was at the window, looking out—and when I saw her
turn on me, her eyes were filled with something beyond rage. A fist
closed around my heart.

Later?

I rose from the seat, one hand pressed over my heart. Didn't I know?
Couldn't I understand? My mother was shaking her head, laughing at
me for my innocence. *Later?* Didn't I know that I would never see Gail
or Emilie again?

The train heaved to one side and I stumbled, grabbed at an overhead
strap. Below me, an old man looked up from his newspaper. His eyes
were kind and he set the paper down beside him, ready to help me if I
fell. He put one hand over his right eye, to keep away the glare from the
ceiling lights. I moved backwards, sat. The man disappeared behind his
paper. I heard my heart tapping steadily against the wall of my chest,
but there was nothing squeezing it anymore.

It had probably never occurred to Abe that a loser like Vincent was
capable of doing Fasalino's dirty work. Did he have a moment at the
end, I wondered, like the one he'd wished for—a second or two to look
back, to take stock?

Things seemed clear enough. With Abe and Rothenberg gone, I was
no real threat to the others. Still, they would probably keep after me for
a while. Little Benny and Lefty and Monk and Turkish Sammy could
be taken care of easily enough. If they survived, they'd work for whoever
paid the rent. As soon as the killing stopped, the police would lose
interest. I looked through the window to the city beyond, out over all
the rooftops and on to the horizon, where the air was such a pale, misty
black that it was hard to see the dividing line between city and sky.

The less Gail knew, the safer she was. I would protect her the way
Abe had protected me. No letters, no calls, no messages. I leaned back,
closed my eyes, saw my mother dancing in slow circles with Beau Jack.
I looked at the station signs, thick black letters on white. Crescent.

Chestnut was next. Then Montauk and Linwood and Van Siclen. We'd
be at Atlantic Avenue in less than ten minutes. I looked behind me, saw
the two guys and their girlfriends out on the platform, moving backwards as the train began to move forward.

I knew, of course, what would be in the safe-deposit box. It was simple
enough to take on a new identity. All you had to do was keep your eye
on the obituary columns until you found somebody your own age who
had died. Then you went down to City Hall, bought a copy of his birth
certificate, took his name for your own. The rest was easy. The lights
raced by, flickering like enormous fireflies. I stared at my reflection,
suspended in the dusty window above the city, superimposed on the city
as in a double exposure.

The train was rocking us gently. I imagined that we were moving out
past the Philadelphia suburbs. Gail's feet were tucked under her, her
head on my chest, and we were heading for Maryland. We kissed, and
at that moment the train swerved, our teeth clicked. We laughed. Gail
touched my mouth with her fingers. Was I sorry about our decision?
Would I regret it later on? Would I hate her and resent her for taking
away my freedom, for stealing from me all the other lives I might have
had? She hated it when we were apart. She wasn't tempted by other
men, but it made her feel crazy and scared—as if she were going to
crack open, as if her parents were right to worry about her—because
without me there she would begin to feel that she couldn't remember
me. She would begin to feel that she couldn't hold onto the feelings she
had toward me when we were together. Would I forgive her for being
weak in that way? When she concentrated, trying to envision me, to
conjure me up, she would lose a piece of me at a time, as if I were being
erased—first my hair, and then my forehead, and then my eyes, and
then my nose, and then my mouth . . .

Distance, like memory, she said, was painful. She had never believed
all the nonsense about absence making the heart grow fonder. The heart
could easily forget what the eyes could not see and the lips could not
touch and the fingers could not feel. Distance, like memory—like anger,
I wanted to add—like rage!—was a veil.

BOOK
TWO

11

GRASS LIKE ICE—mint-green, frosted. Aaron Levin slides the curtains apart, the brass rod cool to his touch. Outside, nothing moves. Tapping. The sound of his own heart? The green world fades to gray, filters through dull glass, through frayed threads of cream-colored curtains. An early morning frost covers the grass like fine netting over crushed velvet. The hill slopes gently away from the window, down toward the dirt road. Gray gravel. Fog. Dust. The brass rod catches light from the window, glistens under his fingertips, and he recalls shiny copper pennies set on trolley tracks, sparks spraying from wheels. He thinks of his son Carl, seven years old, cleaning coins in a solution of water and bicarbonate of soda. Carl dries them under a heat lamp, buffs them, slips them into glassine envelopes, hard plastic with black backing, so that they sparkle. Aaron imagines his children waking, dressing, eating breakfast, walking down the hill to wait for the school bus. The brittle surfaces of puddles crack and shatter, spider webs of dark-gray crystal. Larry, his youngest child—six last May—likes to wake early, to knock at his parents' door, to enter their room, to climb between them and snuggle. Tapping. Aaron touches the curtain. Is he home already?

He rubs the frail cotton with thumb and forefinger, absently, measuring the thinness, feeling, in his mind, his wife's favorite dress—a faded yellow shirtwaist flowered with pale-blue forget-me-nots, flecked with darker greens of stem and leaf. Aaron lets the curtain fall, rubs his eyes, tries to make sense of the fog inside his head, of the strange white light that makes the grass shimmer, that draws his eyes downward, past the road, to the ghostly dull-gray trees beyond. What hides there? He sees, again, the curve of his wife's hip, believes that he can feel her warm body as, in memory, he traces its shape with his palm. Tapping again. Larry at the door? The air in the small room is warm, moist, mildewed. He glances behind, at the bed, as if he expects to see Susan there, lying on her side, her back to him. Is she awake? He shivers, desiring her, longing to be inside her, to feel her moistness grip him. The lawn is silver-green now, brighter. The hem of Susan's skirt billows up slightly as she kneels. She raises it so that she can weed, can avoid grass stain. She brushes back her hair, smiles up at him, digs her fingers into the soft brown earth, licks her teeth. . . .

"Who's there?"

"It's just me—Nicky. Can I come in?"

Aaron opens the door, tucks in his shirt. Nicky closes the door behind her, doesn't move. She is nineteen years old, from a small town in eastern Pennsylvania, a Freedom School teacher like himself.

"Did I wake you?"

"It's okay. I had to get up anyway to go to the door. Somebody was knocking."

"Very funny."

She walks to the window, pulls the edge of the curtain back with a hooked forefinger.

"The moon sure is bright," she says.

The springs squeak when he sits on the edge of the bed. The sheet, where he was sleeping, is damp. His lower back aches. Tomorrow he'll get a board to stick under the mattress. He puts on his shoes, laces them.

"Boy, I was really lost," he says. "No wonder the light's that way. I couldn't figure out where I was for a few minutes. It's evening then?"

"Night. I was scared and I needed to talk to somebody—not to talk, just to be with somebody. You. Do you mind?" She pulls the right side of the curtain to the center and he thinks of Jennifer's puppet theater, of his children giggling and arguing below the stage. Jennifer is thirteen. "Do you ever get scared?"

"Sure. I'm scared now."

"You could have fooled me."

She walks around the room, picks at the wall, which is bare wood, pine slabs. She recites the security rules to him: beware of cars without license plates; never be the last one out of a mass meeting; never go out alone; watch out for cops who wear no badges; listen for accelerating cars; if you wake up at night thinking there's danger, wake everyone.

"So I woke you, but I guess there's no danger. Would you like me to leave?"

"No."

"You sure?"

"Yes. I like having you visit me. You know that."

Her body is lean and wiry, her straw-colored hair pulled back into a ponytail. Her ears stick out. He thinks of a gold loving cup. She is only an inch or so taller than Jennifer. He can smell her hair, cool and lemony, freshly washed. She wears dungarees, a loose-fitting gray T-shirt, a small round black-and-white S.N.C.C. button pinned just above her left breast. She has the gait of an athlete and he imagines her streaking over hurdles, hair flying, legs split wide.

She sits next to him. "What do you do when you get *real* scared, Aaron? I mean, I know how to cover up and protect what they taught us to protect, all that private, vulnerable stuff—but when you feel your stomach start to come apart and turn to water—heading South, right? —and you want to kind of creep off, just go back home and be like everyone else and forget the whole thing—what do you do then? What do you do when you get scared like that?"

"Nothing. I wait it out."

"Me too, I guess." She shrugs. "Okay. Where do you do *your* waiting?"

"In dark rooms."

"Wanna tell me about it?"

He smiles. They talk like this often, tease one another gently, playfully. The kid sister he never had? "Like in dreams," he says. "Don't you ever have dreams like that—that you're in an old house, say, trying to escape from people pursuing you, going from room to room, all of them pitch-black, full of danger, people who'll kill you and torture you, and you're scared to death in each room? So what you do, instead of waking up, is just stand stock-still inside the blackness until the fear penetrates as far as it can."

"Jesus! I'd wake up. Don't you wake up in that kind of dream?"

"No. I just stand there."

"And then what happens?"

"After a while I move. I kind of grope around until I find a wall, a doorknob, the next room."

"Do you get out of the house?"

"Yes. I always get out."

"And then—?"

"Usually I find that I'm holding one of my kids' hands—Carl or Larry —that we're escaping together."

She shakes her head. "I don't have dreams like that." She grabs his arm above the elbow, squeezing hard. "But I'm not a quitter, Aaron. I *will* stick it out—you'll see. We *will* overcome, won't we? We will turn all this hate and death around, won't we? *Won't* we?"

He puts his arm around her. His dream scares him more now, when he remembers it, than when he was in its midst. "I hope so. If we have enough brave teachers like you—"

"Shit on that. I'm just scared. I'm not brave at all."

"You're tough as nails, Nicky."

"Sure. And about as thin. I wish I was as big as you and could talk to people the way you do. That must help, being big. Take me to my leader." She looks up at him. He is a foot taller than she is. "Take me to my ladder, I'll see my leader later, right?" They laugh. "I guess I'd follow you anywhere, Aaron. That was some speech the other night. They've been calling you Aaron Luther King since then. Even the Negroes, did you know that?"

"That surprises me. Would you believe that I used to be very shy and quiet?"

"You still are. When you're alone with people. . . ."

"Yes. But when I see faces out there, the words seem to come of their own. It's as if, with everyone's eyes on me—trusting me—I can take power from your eyes and your trust, as if I want more than anything to send words out there that are so solid you'll be able to climb right onto them, to stand on them and be safe, to ride those words until . . ." He lets his hand caress the shape of her head. He fingers the rubber band that holds her ponytail. He feels sad. "Sometimes when I get depressed —low—I feel that I'd just like to give one long cry, Nicky, and ride that cry to the other side."

"And take me with you?"

He rubs the knobby bump behind her left ear. "Words aren't ever enough, of course, but I keep feeling that if I can reach down into what I feel and know, and if I can use words to give some of that to others, then maybe we'll have a chance, maybe things can still change. . . ." He stops. "Words help me cross over, I guess."

"From where to where?"

"From fear to hope."

"Could you do me a favor?"

"Yes."

"Could you hold me real tight?"

Her teeth are clicking, out of control, and he takes her to him, feels her tremble. Her small heart beats against his own, wildly, as if it might crash through her chest and drive itself into his body. He feels the firm mounds of her breasts. He glances past her to the night table, where a photo of his family—himself, Susan, the four children—is propped against a stack of paperbacks: *The Plague, Borstal Boy, Emerson's Essays, The Fire Next Time.*

The frost, then, he realizes, is moonlight reflecting off evening dew. It is summer, not winter—nighttime, not morning—and he is in a small house at the edge of Greenwood, Mississippi, not in his own home outside Northampton, Massachusetts. Nicky sits up straight, wipes her eyes with the backs of her wrists. Her wrists are thin, freckled.

"Would you come with me to the store?" she asks. "We're not supposed to go out alone. It's the other reason I'm here—my pretext—but I need to go to the shopping center before it closes, to call home. I don't want my folks to worry too much—especially now that they found the bodies. In addition to which, it's that time of month, but I've been too busy to remember to stock things in." She puts her mouth against his bare arm, below the sleeve, and kisses him there. "So you're safe with a girl like me, see?"

The five black children sleep in one bed, pinwheel fashion, heads to the center. Nicky goes around the bed, kisses each of them. The two-year-old, Cephas, sleeps thumb in mouth, sucking away. His navel protrudes like a small brown stone, and Aaron touches it, then pulls the boy's shirt down, circles his ankle with thumb and forefinger, strokes the slender pointed bone.

"Tell Aaron what you just told me," he hears Nicky say. "Softly, though. Don't wake the others. Go on . . ."

Billy grins. He is seven years old. His eyes sparkle. "All I say, Mister Aaron, is that if you all keep teaching in them schools here, they gonna kill you for sure, so I wouldn't do it less they payin' you real good."

Aaron smiles. Billy is delighted, knowing he has pleased them both. "I'm getting the best pay in the world," Aaron says, and he lifts the boy, hugs him.

The mother is on the porch with the three other civil rights workers, her feet in a bucket of ice water. Her name is Rose Morgan and she chops cotton for three dollars a day. She is a few years younger than Aaron—twenty-six or twenty-seven—yet he thinks of her as being ten years older than he is. She rarely speaks and when she does her voice is flat, her eyes dull, filmed over. The workers—George, Dwayne, Holly —are trying to get her to talk with them. They try every night, with no evidence of success, and Aaron admires their persistence, their innocence. This is where the work has to be done, he knows—one-on-one, person-by-person, helping others take control of their own lives. At its best, the Movement knows what a loving parent or friend knows: that you need to love people not for what you want them to be, but for what they are.

Rose's boss has threatened to take away her job because she allows the workers to stay in her house. If he does, Dwayne asks, will she let the S.N.C.C. legal staff take up her case? She fans herself with a paper fan—"Imperial Funeral Home" lettered on it, in black and purple—and shrugs, sullenly. What does she think about all day, all those hours in the sun while she works? Would she be willing to go down with some of them to the town hall, to try to register to vote? Would she like to go to school the way her children do? Does she know where her husband is? What does she think about the three civil rights workers, two of them white and Jewish, who were killed down in Philadelphia, on the other side of the state?

"I'll tell you what," she says. "I'll let you take one of my children back up North with you—you choose any one you want—iffen you get me a TV set in exchange."

Nobody laughs. Aaron puts a hand on her shoulder and looks into her eyes, to see if she is joking. He thinks of Billy's eyes, shining up at him. He has been living in her house for over three weeks, yet he can never tell whether she is serious or whether she is putting them on.

"One child for a regular set, two for color?" he asks.

"That's okay too."

George, a sophomore economics major from Yale, ever serious, asks her what she felt when they were dragging the Mississippi River for the three missing civil rights workers and found, instead, the bodies of two Negroes, one of them cut in half and decapitated. Rose shrugs, shows no surprise. She didn't feel anything because she didn't know them.

What if one of the bodies was one of her own children?

"Then I'd have four left," she says.

Dwayne talks bitterly about the fact that you can find a dead Negro anytime you drag a river in Mississippi—that most of the time the parents don't even report them as missing, for fear of retaliation from the law. He curses and walks off, begins whacking at a tree with a board, the way he does whenever he is upset. Aaron tells them that he and Nicky are going into town, to the shopping center. Does anybody want to come? Nobody does. Rose says to watch out for the night riders, who can come up to you in the dark and steal away your children.

"My children are all up North," Aaron says. "They're all safe in their beds by now."

"That don't matter to them none," Rose says. "They can be meaner than you think round here."

"Do you mind if I hold your hand?"

"No."

They are out of the car, walking across the unlit parking lot.

"How'd you lose your two fingers?"

"Horsing around when I was a kid. We had kitchen duty—grinding up old bread for meat loaf, and one of the old guys shoved my hand in. We'd been fighting a lot—throwing stuff at each other."

"Brr. I like to touch the stubs—you don't find that strange, do you?"

"No. Susan does it too. So do the children. It's been a long time since I was embarrassed." He holds open the door of the Walgreens Pharmacy. They step into bright fluorescent light, aisles of brilliant color—reds and blues and pinks and greens and whites—and he squints. It is as if, he thinks, they are living within a movie that has suddenly switched from black-and-white to Technicolor. He felt the same way, he realized, when Nicky came into his room earlier—as if he'd been living in a world of muted colors, dull grays and browns and greens, until the moment when she first touched him, when she sat beside him on the bed, when his head began to clear.

"I made the best of it—threw a mean curveball, a natural forkball. Like Three-Finger Mordecai Brown."

"Was he at the orphanage too?"

They walk toward the rear of the store, where there are three phone booths.

"Three-Finger Mordecai Brown was a baseball player who lasted thirteen seasons in the majors with four teams, from 1903 to 1916. He also played a stint in the old Federal League, which was a kind of outlaw league some of the players jumped to, like the Mexican League after the Second World War. The Dodgers and the Giants—those were the teams we rooted for—they lost a lot of players to them: Luis Olmo, Mickey Owen, Sal Maglie, Ernie Lombardi, Danny Gardella. . . ." Aaron smiles. "No Yankees went south of the border. Nobody in the orphanage rooted for them. The Yankees were always a rich man's ball club. But Brown—Three-Finger Brown—he wound up winning 239 games, lifetime. I kept a picture of him on the wall next to my bed."

"You know a lot about baseball."

"It kept us alive—dreaming about becoming stars. It was a way for kids like us to believe we could join the rest of America, I guess."

She slips into the phone booth. She smiles. Her left front tooth, chipped, looks like a giant white apostrophe. "Is this America?" she asks, repeating the question civil rights workers have been asking one another—a running joke—ever since their training school at Western College of Women, in Oxford, Ohio.

"This is America. You bet your sweet life it is."

"Babe Ruth was an orphan, wasn't he?"

"No, but people thought he was. We thought he was. Some people thought he was Negro too."

"*Really?*"

"It's possible. I once read a book that tried to prove it. I mean, think of his face—the moon shape, the fat lips, the squat, pushed-in nose, the downward folds of his eyes, the way he loved getting black in the sun all summer long."

"Let me call home. Stay here, though, okay? Don't go away. I like talking with you."

Aaron stays. He watches the shoppers, glances in at Nicky every now and then. She bites her lip, rolls her eyes. He hears her yelling, taps on the glass, cautions her to cool it. He sees three men staring at him from the entrance. One of them wears a sheriff's uniform and hat. Aaron does not smile at them, nor does he look away.

"Oh shit," Nicky says when she comes out of the phone booth. She chews on her lower lip, forces back tears. "They don't understand anything, Aaron. Not *anything!*" She begins to lean against him, her forehead to his chin, but he steps back, keeps her at a distance. "Oh shit and double shit. If they lived down here they'd be worse than the damned peckerheads."

"Peckerwoods," he says softly. "They call them peckerwoods here."

"Peckerheads. That's what I said. Damned peckerheads."

She slips her hand into his and squeezes until his fingers hurt.

"Be careful," Aaron says, nodding toward the door.

"Why? We're both still white, aren't we?" She stops. "Go make your goddamned phone call, okay? I'll get over it. Just shit and double shit is all." She sucks in her lips, screws up her eyes, mimics her mother: " 'Now Nicky, why don't you just let them little pickaninnys alone so that . . .' "

"Shh," he says, and tries again to get her to acknowledge the three men by the door. "Come on now—"

"They think the only reason I'm here is to make them angry. How can people be so small-minded, Aaron? I mean, can you believe my mother going on and on about shopping with me for a fall wardrobe for college while . . ." She stops, looks down. "They're proud of me for going to college, I guess. They grew up poor and dumb and all they want is for me to be happy. I know all about it, only—"

"Hey," he says, wiping a tear from the corner of her eye. "Get hold of yourself. We'll talk later, okay. This isn't the place."

"Do you promise?"

"I promise."

"Well. A parent is still a parent, I guess. No matter how far from home you stray, you keep on searching for the love you never got from them."

"Yes."

"How would you know? You were a goddamned orphan."

"I had parents. I just lost them early."

"Tell me about it."

"I already did."

He leaves the door of the phone booth partly open, for air. He dials, and while his children talk to him, from different extensions, he thinks: sometimes we know things most by *not* having them, by desiring them. Had he ever imagined having children like those he actually has? The children have just returned from two weeks at a sleep-away camp and they want to tell him about it—about the raids and the food and the counselors, about the jokes they learned and the field trips they took and the friends they made. Carl says that he received lots of flying-wedgies, and explains that a flying-wedgie occurs when an older guy picks you up by your underpants and flings you. Larry interrupts to ask Aaron if he knows what "no-slugs" means, if Aaron will be home soon. You say "no-slugs" after you fart, or else the guy who says "slugs" can give you one punch for each second he counts off. Aaron is amazed— that they are so happy and excited merely to talk to him.

"I like your articles," Jennifer says. "At camp they posted them on the bulletin board in the social hall. We had a rap session one night based on what you wrote and my counselor said she wished she was where you are instead of up here."

"I like the drawings a lot," Larry adds. "You sure can draw niggers good, Dad."

"*Negroes!*" Jennifer corrects. "Good God! Did you hear that? How would you like it if somebody called you a kike?"

"They already do."

Susan cuts in and tells the children that she wants to speak with Aaron privately. The children say good night. Aaron tells them that he loves them, that he thinks of them constantly, that he will see them before too long. He hears clicking sounds.

"Susan?"

"I'm here."

"What did you want?"

"To know if you miss me or not. Do you miss me, Aaron?"

"Sure. But—"

"How much?"

"*What?* Now listen. I—"

"Oh Aaron, I'm sorry to be this way, but I've been so worried about you. Would you just tell me, for a minute or two, how much you miss me—would you tell me about when during your days there you think of me, about what pictures come into your mind? I want to be there with you and I'm scared that if I'm not—" She stops. He is surprised by the intensity of her voice. There is a slight raspiness to it, like that of a teenager's voice shifting ranges. "It's just that I've been so worried ever since they found the three bodies. Are you being careful, sweetheart?"

"Sure."

"Have you considered coming home early?"

"No."

"Don't be angry with me for asking. But listen to me for a minute. I was having a drink before—two drinks—and I went down to your studio after the evening news so that I could feel we were together, and I looked at your sketches and I found myself wondering if the truth wasn't that I was so worried about you since the three workers were killed just so I could think about getting you to come home, so I could have a legitimate excuse. What do you think?"

"It's possible."

"It's possible." She laughs. "Oh Aaron, you're wonderful. Do you realize that this is the first time in the eight years of our marriage that we've been apart for more than a long weekend? I mean, isn't it crazy—two independent beings like us? But if we are so independent—if there's truth to the pride we've taken through the years in not being one of those couples that sits on a love-seat-for-two that's really only your run-of-the-mill throne-of-judgment—then why am I feeling so forlorn and lost with you gone?" He thinks of telling her that it's because she loves him as much as he loves her, but he decides not to say nothing. He is annoyed with her for talking this way, for laying even a small guilt trip on him, and he'll be damned if he'll tell her what he knows she wants to hear. Then, too, he senses that if he admits how much he misses her he'll be more vulnerable than he can afford to be—as if merely acknowledging the feeling may somehow bring harm to him. The times he has spoken to Susan about his dreams, about being able to stand inside dark rooms without fear, she has said that she has never doubted his ability to face fears and dangers; what she has wondered about is why he insists on imagining that he must do so *alone*. "Your drawings are splendid—the best you've ever done," she says now, "and the letters are wonderful, especially the parts about the children you work with. But they're addressed to *me*, Aaron, yet there's never anything personal in them, and I—"

"Listen. We agreed before I left that if the newspaper thought they were good enough, I'd let them run the stuff."

"But you could *add* something, couldn't you—on a separate sheet? *Not* for publication? Oh God, I know I'm being childish and selfish and petulant, and you're being noble and heroic and grown-up, but do you miss me at *all*?"

"Sure. It's just—" He decides to tell her about how he felt when he woke from his nap, but before he can begin he glances sideways, sees that Nicky has her face pressed against the glass, her nose and lips squashed flat, her eyes bulging, crossed. He laughs.

"What's so funny?"

"Nothing. One of the young workers is cutting up a little. The tension gets to us and—"

"A female worker?"

"Yes."

"Oh Aaron." She sighs. "Listen. I love you and I guess I'm getting horny." She laughs, awkwardly, and he imagines her brushing her hair from her forehead, smiling easily, relieved and happy to be able to talk to him this way. Had he ever imagined that a woman as beautiful as Susan would be so willing to show him her childishness, her needs? "Let others idealize me, all right?" Susan says. "I can't hide from you, Levin. The truth is that one part of me is proud as hell of you, but there's another part that simply longs to be near you, to be touched by you, to be loved. Is that all right? The newspapers and TV are so full of stuff hinting at all the sex going on—everybody arm in arm and hand in hand, black men and white girls—"

"That's bullshit," he says sharply. "And I don't want to hear it."

"Don't be angry with *me*. I'm only—"

"Didn't you read what I wrote from the orientation school the first week? Damn, Susan! All the fucking media people care about is sex—they're worse than the white trash down here, hoping to catch some young blond in bed with a big black buck. Can't you see through that?"

"Of course I can. It's just that I miss you terribly. Can't you understand *that?* I worry about you too. I'm in pain *for* you, Aaron—for what you're doing. I wish *I* were doing it. And the way I deal with that—same old Susan—is to cover up my pain with anger. We're not so different, after all. And how do I get myself angry with you? By imagining that you're playing around or flirting. Then I have cause to reject you—in my mind you've betrayed me—and I don't have to worry so much, or hurt for you, or hurt because I miss you. Preemptive rejection. Susan's best defense." She stops. "Oh Aaron . . ."

"It's all right," he says, comforted to hear the sadness enter her voice. "It *will* be all right. I love you. I wish you were here too."

"Thanks."

"But try not to let that other stuff get to you. It's just the same old story—sex and violence, violence and sex—only that's *their* story, don't you see? All they've really been waiting for is to have one of us nice middle-class whites killed and chopped up, and if those three poor kids hadn't been murdered, I think CBS might have flown in some actors and corpses and *staged* a damned killing, they wanted one so bad. Well. Now they have it, goddamn them. Now they have it. As if all our work existed so that one of us could become a stiff for five minutes on their fucking TV show. The way people *use* people, Susan! As if—"

"Oh sweetheart—calm down. I'm not *against* you. This all started because I said I missed you, remember? Don't be angry with me."

"I'm not angry."

"Not much." She laughs, but with affection. He imagines her above him, her golden hair falling on his face, dusting his chest. "Same old Aaron—nick him and he bleeds in V's—venom, vengeance, vituperation. . . ."

Her voice shifts, the sarcasm dropping away. She would be there with him if she could, she reminds him, but they agreed that he would be the one to go and she would be the one to stay home with the children. Still, their agreement doesn't stop her from feeling frightened and frustrated, from telling him what she feels. If he weren't so upset and frustrated himself, she says, it might even occur to him to be flattered by her jealousy.

The store lights flash on and off. Nicky taps at the glass. Aaron tells Susan that he'll call her again soon, that she should try not to worry, that he loves her. He'll write to her in the morning, he promises. *Not* for publication.

Aaron and Nicky leave the store, get into Aaron's car and drive out of the parking lot, onto the main road. Nicky leans her head against his shoulder.

"You're nice with your kids. Your voice gets so warm when you talk with them," she says. "If I were one of them I'd just want to rub against it and purr. You like being a father, don't you? I mean, it's very *important* to you, isn't it?"

"Yes."

"You like family life."

"Sure. Doesn't everybody—everybody who has people in their family they love?"

"I wouldn't know. But your wife—Susan—is she good to you?"

"Most of the time." Aaron laughs. "We *like* each other. That helps."

"Do you still love each other too?"

"Yes." Aaron turns off onto a dirt road, checks the rear-view mirror. How can he explain it to Nicky—how lucky he feels to have found Susan, to have the life he has? He sees a pair of headlights turn in behind them. "You'd like Susan. She'd like you."

"No she wouldn't. I saw her picture. She's too beautiful and sophisticated for me. She probably went to one of those fancy girl's schools where they teach you how to serve tea."

"She looks like that kind of woman, but she went to Smith College because it was free. She grew up in Northampton and she was allowed to go there because as a resident—" He glances into the rear-view mirror again. The headlights are larger, closer. He thinks of an owl's eyes. He presses on the accelerator.

"I mean, does she know what a good deal she has, married to a guy like you?"

"I'm no saint. You don't know everything, Nicky. You don't have to live with me day after day."

"It doesn't matter what you say. Nobody's easy to live with who amounts to much." Nicky takes a deep breath. "Oh I may not know a lot, but I know that men like you don't come down the pike every day and that I never had a crush on anyone this bad. Shit. Leave it to me to pick a happily married man who's old enough to be my father."

"Not so. I'm only twenty-nine—I'll be twenty-nine in September."

The speedometer passes fifty. They are still three miles from Rose Morgan's house. Aaron tries to remember the roads, to figure out if there is a way to cut back so that he can head for the S.N.C.C. headquarters in town.

"I'm still a virgin, you know." She moves away from him, her back to the door. "There. I said it and now you know and now you'll feel responsible for me, right?"

"We're being followed and I'm going to try to make some speed. I only wish I knew these roads better. Damn! Hold on—"

Nicky sits up straight.

"Don't fight them, Aaron. Promise me that? If they catch up with us and do nasty things to me, don't fight them. Promise. Promise me now."

"Shut up." Aaron floors the gas pedal. The car lurches over a rise in the road so that their heads bang against the car's roof. The road is dark, without houses.

"I won't shut up. I'll be a broken record. I'm very talented at repeating myself. You have to promise me not to fight them. Promise me that if they catch up with us and try dirty things with me, you won't fight them or try to protect me. You have to remember that I'm just a friend, that I'm not even your daughter. You have to start talking to yourself now, so you'll be ready for them. Remember the games we played in Ohio? We have to start following our better selves, trying to remember that their meanness and hatred come from the absence of love. Their hatred is not a force we have to resist and fight against, for nothing is there. We must descend into that part of ourselves we've been reserving for just such a moment. Blessed are the pure in heart; for they shall see God."

"Shut up."

"Blessed are the peacemakers; for they shall be called the children of God. Blessed—"

"*Just shut your fucking mouth!*" Aaron strikes out sideways, his knuckles catching Nicky on the side of her jaw. The car skids, barely misses a tree, barrels along, two wheels on gravel, two on grass.

"Hit me, but don't hit them," Nicky says. "There you go. You're listening to me. Get it all out, Aaron. Hit *me*—"

They make a sudden right angle turn, the rear wheels spitting stone.

"Don't look now but I'm putting in one of the things we went to the store for." Nicky speaks in a monotone. "I'll tell them I have the rag on. The rest is up to them. Wanna play stinkfinger with me? Goddamn Tommy Huckowicz. I had a mad crush on him our junior year and all he wanted to do was play stinkfinger. Once you get past the smell you've got it licked, right? Shove it already, I'd say. Where? he'd reply. I like to talk tough and dirty so people think I'm experienced, but oh God I'm scared, Aaron. I'm awfully scared."

Aaron sees light ahead, something flat and glittering and wide. A lake, reflecting moonlight. A thin layer of silver on water, like dust on furniture. He sees a spray of orange flames, men huddled around a campfire, squatting, as if the evening is cool. What makes sense? They repeated it to one another every day: when they are in Mississippi, the rest of America seems unreal; when they are in the rest of America, Mississippi seems unreal. He starts to steer left, sees two headlights turn on, from the lakeshore. White light blasts through the rear window, a police spotlight illuminating the inside of the car, the dashboard. Nicky lowers her head. He remembers a dead owl, ravaged by heat, caught in the crawl space of a house he was building two summers ago. The owl's skull, beneath all the feathers, was astonishingly small, the size of a lemon.

"I think we've bought it," he says.

He turns the car around so that they are heading in the direction from which they came.

"You didn't promise me yet. If you don't promise me not to fight them, I'll fall apart and do something crazy right now. I swear. Promise me you won't fight back."

"What I want to do is to ram straight ahead and take a few of the bastards with me. *Damn!*"

"We have to love them too, Aaron."

"No we don't. Not me."

"Hold my hand, please? I put the plug in and my hand stinks bad, but I'm shaking like crazy and trying to remember what we learned to do in a situation like this, but I can't do anything except be scared and want you holding me. I wish I was dead. I wish I could die and come back to life later on, but I doubt if we can arrange that. Oh Jesus Christ, Aaron, somebody inside my head is starting to pray for me and I think it's my mother."

Aaron stops the car, puts it in park, turns off the ignition. He takes

Nicky's hand, which is ice cold. She holds onto his middle finger—the
shorter stump—so tightly that he thinks she may squeeze blood from it.
He imagines the top of the stump opening, a slit like a small eye, red
juice spurting upwards.

"I promise."

Her hand relaxes. A man is at his side, peering into the window,
reeking of beer.

"You're a long way from home, ain't you, boy?" The man wears a
sheriff's hat, but there is no badge there, or on his shirt. His face, lit
from behind, is flat and gray, like the blade of a shovel.

"Yes," Aaron says.

"You lost?"

"Yes. I think I must be, officer."

Aaron hears voices tell the sheriff—his name is Ben—to stop wasting
time, to enforce the law. Ben's eyes seem, to Aaron's surprise, kind.
They are soft and brown, the left one scarred, a vertical yellow crescent,
like a fingernail paring, slicing it. In a different uniform—a white smock
—Aaron imagines Ben behind the counter in a drugstore, filling pre-
scriptions.

"I think you'd best step out of the car, boy. We got to do an inspec-
tion, make sure you ain't hiding any contraband in here. Lots of guns
and stuff been coming down here from up North, you know."

"Me too?"

"You too, ma'am."

They step out and are shoved forward into the crossfire of headlights.
Nicky stands next to him quietly, eyes downcast. She trembles. Aaron
sees men emerge from the shadows, moving up from the campfire, from
the woods that surround them. Some of them carry clubs, some carry
rifles. He sees two large russet-colored dogs—Irish setters? retrievers?—
straining against leashes.

"Hey Dad—you want me to see what they got in their car here? Want
me to open the trunk?"

"Sure, son. You go ahead. Take the key from in front."

"Maybe we can talk things over," Aaron offers. "We mean no harm."

Something stings his mouth before he is aware that anyone has come
close enough to touch him. He tastes blood. His lower lip is split.

"Don't want none of your smart city talk, neither," a man says. A dog
snarls, snaps at Aaron's leg. "What for all you nigger-lovers comin' down
here anyway? Whyn't you stay home in Harlem where you belong, burn
them cities to the ground?"

Aaron sucks blood, touches his lip, and something whips him across
the back, low. He is on the ground at once, head down, knees to stomach, hands covering his back. He glances sideways and sees that Nicky

has done the same, her forehead touching earth. He hears men laugh, feels the lash on his rear end, on his fingers, on the backs of his legs. The pain is extraordinary, lightning-white. He hears a dog close by, panting.

"Get on up, boy, and get them hands off your back. We want to see that yellow streak you got there. You get on up so we can make sure you are who you are. You got identification?"

Aaron hesitates for a second—will he be safer obeying them or covering up?—and in that second something crashes against his ear and cheek, sending him sprawling, a streak of fire searing his brain. Fiery white stars explode, filling his skull with heat. He rolls over, feels warm liquid pour down along his neck. Nicky is bent over him before he can move again, covering his body with hers, sideways, her stomach across his back, her hands cupping his ears, and she is screaming at the men to leave him alone. Doesn't she know what they'll do to her? Is *this* how he'll die, then, far from home, a thin young woman draped across his back? He hears himself moan, wonders if he has been hit with a baseball bat, wonders why he is still conscious. What will Susan think when she gets the news? *Do you miss me, Aaron?* Nicky screams at them to go away, to get a doctor. The dogs howl. Aaron's mouth is clogged with dirt, pebbles, blood. He spits. He lets his tongue roam, searching for open spaces, for missing teeth. *You won't hurt yourself, will you?* Nicky keeps screaming: do they want to kill a man who won't fight back? Can't they see that he is unarmed, that he was telling the truth, that he means no harm. They threaten Nicky, tell her they will ram red-hot pokers up her nigger-loving cunt, feed her to the dogs, bury her alive in horse shit, coil her in barbed wire and sink her in water, cinder blocks on her ankles. They will split her wide open but give her what she really wants first. They will make her beg for it. She recites words they had rehearsed during role-playing sessions in Ohio. Her voice is calm, like that of a schoolteacher addressing fourth-graders.

"We've got nothing against you. We are not your enemies. We're just here to help teach some children for a short while, and we'd like to hear your opinions too and understand how you feel about us. We're human beings just like you are. We have nothing against you. We know some of you have wives and parents and children you love as much as—"

He feels her weight being lifted from him, and he crouches again, covering his neck and ears this time. His left ear and cheek feel pulpy.

"But you got something against him there, girl, don't you? You got your goddamned filthy body right up against him, you little cock-teasing slut. Same cocksucking body you been giving to all them niggers. Don't you spread them legs for every black dick you smell?"

"No!"

"You been suckin' black cock, ain't you, girl? Your teeth ain't fell out yet but you been doing it, ain't you? *Ain't* you?"

"No!"

Aaron lifts his head. Nicky stands with her hands pressed flat against her thighs, her head held high, eyes blazing.

"No! I'm not like that. I'm here to *teach*. I'm a member of the First Baptist Church in my home town and I know you don't really believe that I do things like you say I do. Why should you think so? Let us talk about this reasonably, so that—"

"Iffen you ain't done it yet, you're gone to before the night's over, ain't she, Homer?"

"Like they say, lots of plowin' gets done by moonlight. Lots of plantin' too."

"But I could be your own *daughter!*" Nicky pleads. "I could—"

Before she can finish, the man named Homer whacks her so ferociously across the face with the back of his hand—Aaron hears a cracking sound, like that of a thick branch breaking—that Nicky rises bodily from the earth before she falls.

"You watch your goddamn foul mouth, girl. No daughter of mine ever sucked black cock."

Aaron realizes that he is standing. Nicky screams, her body heaving up and down, but Aaron knows he helps her most by not going to her, by not touching her.

"I brought the girl here," he says, his tongue thick. "It's my responsibility that she's here. Why don't you let her go and just deal with me?"

"We'll do that too, boy. Don't you worry none."

"You could let us both go. Haven't you hurt us enough? I'd like to take her to a doctor."

Nicky is on her knees and Aaron hears a man talk about dog-fucking her. Nicky rises, eyes glazed. She steps one way and then the other, her hand outstretched as if she is blind. Aaron estimates that there are twelve to fifteen men around them. He tries to find a picture inside his head that he can fix on, a picture that will enable him to restrain himself, to keep from erupting, from trying to kill the bastards.

"I can't find any of your goddamned dark rooms," Nicky whispers. She stands beside him. "I'm losing everything, Aaron. Oh good Christ Almighty but I'm scared—"

He sees her hand reach toward him.

"Don't," he commands.

"Bring 'em down to the water," Ben says. "Let's go now."

"Oh good Jesus Christ, Aaron—we're all gonna gather by the water, like in the hymn, only—"

"You wanna pray, girl, you get down on your knees the way you know how, like you do for all them coons."

Aaron eyes the gun barrels, thinks of how beautiful the blue metal is in moonlight. His left eye throbs, but behind the pain there is a picture now, and the picture is very clear. He, Nicky, Holly and Dwayne are driving across the state to attend James Chaney's funeral. Chaney is the black civil rights worker whose body was found, along with Andrew Goodman's and Michael Schwerner's, in Philadelphia, Mississippi. The funeral is in Meridien. Chaney, who was twenty-one, has a twelve-year-old brother, and at the Freedom School in Meridien, the brother plays in a jazz band: piano, washtub bass, cardboard boxes, bongos. Is he pleased, in the midst of grief, to have so much attention paid to him because his older brother has died? There are about 150 marchers, and Aaron walks with them, from the church to the school, in silence. A phalanx of TV personnel and vans move along with them, drawing closer each time they find a pair of eyes in which there are tears.

Walking down to the lake, beside Nicky, he tries to recall what he felt during that other walk, that hour of silence. He sees James Chaney's face, as if in a sketch: brown pencil on beige paper, tints of rose-red. He hears Dave Dennis's voice—Dennis, the Assistant Director of the Mississippi Summer Project—and Dennis is calling out the roll of death: Mack Parker, Medgar Evers, Herbert Lee, Lewis Allen, Emmett Till, four little girls in Birmingham, two boys in the Mississippi River. Dennis says that he is sick and tired of attending funerals. If you cannot go ten blocks to the courthouse, he asks, how will you ever go nine million miles up to heaven? Dennis damns the souls of everyone in the church where James Chaney lies dead. He is angry—sweet Lord, he is angry!—and it is high time others became angry too, angry enough to go to the courthouse and register, angry enough to teach children to read and to write, angry enough to do whatever they have to do to stop the murder and the hate. . . .

Aaron feels a gun barrel jab the small of his back. Nicky's face is twisted, swollen.

"I won't hurt myself," he says.

"Them neither. You promised."

"Hey, wait a minute, Dad. Look here what they got hidden away—"

Aaron turns. To his surprise, he and Nicky have walked only a few feet. Aaron remembers James Chaney's mother, in the front pew, weeping. Will what he felt then give him strength now? He recalls believing that Susan was there with him, and he wonders why he never told her so.

Ben's son drags a young, shivering black boy—Aaron does not recognize him—into the circle of light.

"You hold on to him, son."

The sheriff takes Aaron's wallet, looks through the cards and photos, counts the money.

"What's a nice clean-cut young guy like you want down here with us?" he asks. "I see you got a family. What for you want to go messin' around in other people's yards for?" The softness in his eyes fades. "Now what you got to see, Mr. Levin, is that we heard all about how you roused up them people last week like you was savin' them for Jesus, and what you got to see too is that we know it was some lying son-of-a-bitch Jew like you that cut up them other three so's you could bring the feds in, ain't that right?"

"No. I don't know why you—"

A blow to his right kidney sends Aaron staggering forward. The sheriff sidesteps, lets Aaron fall, kicks him in the stomach.

"A big boy like you, got a shave and a haircut and a wife and kids, you could be up home doing good works for that family instead of messin' around where you don't belong, makin' trouble for honest folks. I got a mind to cite you for loitering and insurrection and intent to cause a riot and speeding and operating under the influence—" Aaron feels beer splash in his face, drip down. "I got a mind to cite you for all kinds of things. There ain't much I couldn't cite you for. You know that, don't you? I could find things to cite you for would keep you locked up down here till your own kids wouldn't recognize you no more."

"He'd make a good tight end, Ben, if he don't get all his muscles broke first."

"Where'd you find the little boy, Horace? You tell your father the truth."

"He was locked in their trunk, Dad. I think they was fixin' to kidnap him up North, sell him to somebody."

"Jesus," Nicky whispers. "Oh sweet Jesus, Aaron—"

Aaron and Nicky are pushed forward. They stumble down toward the lake, hear the men jeer, hear the men ask if they want to go wash the nigger smell off. Will putting them in the lake kill all the fish? The men laugh. Aaron thinks of escape. There are no lights—no houses—on the lake that he can see. No boats. He imagines himself and Nicky holding hands underwater, swimming along the bottom, bullets spraying the lake's surface like pellets of hail. He sees blood burst from their ears, dark streams of it rise through the water like smoke. He thinks of old Jon Hall movies, South Sea natives diving for pearls, staying underwater too long, legs caught by giant clams. When he and Nicky are near the campfire, about fifteen feet from the water, they stop. Aaron sniffs in through swollen sinuses and he can tell that the black boy has lost control of his bowels.

One of the men presses the barrel of a revolver between the boy's eyes.

"You wanna fuck this white girl?" he asks. "Iffen you do, now's your chance."

The boy gapes. The man cracks the boy across the cheek with the butt of his pistol and Aaron sees the skin peel back at once, as if chiseled. The boy does not lift a hand to protect himself. He does not seem to know that he has been hit.

"They all want it," the sheriff says, "only when it's been given to 'em free, they're too scared to take it."

"How 'bout a kiss for the boy to get him started?" Horace says. "He's so shy, ma'am, you gonna need to help. You come on now and do what I say, hear?"

"Don't," Aaron whispers. "Don't do it."

"You keep your lip buttoned." The sheriff has his service revolver in Aaron's midsection. "You let the girl do what she wants. Freedom now, boy, right? Maybe she's got a thing for little fellas, likes to play games with them."

A man approaches from behind the campfire's flames, a barber's razor across his raised palm.

"Take the little fucker's pants down, Horace, and we'll take care of his problem right here and now. Then he won't have to worry 'bout temptation all the rest of his life."

Aaron sees Nicky sway, as if she may faint. He sees them lift the boy, jerk his pants down. The boy falls face forward toward the campfire, lurches along the ground as if having a seizure. The surface of the lake is absolutely still, a disc of dusty tin. The sheriff's son grabs the razor from the other man and straddles the boy, turns to Aaron.

"You love this nigger so much, mister, whyn't you come fight for his little pecker now? I givin' you a chance to come try and take this razor from me so you can save the boy you love." He laughs, turns to the other men. "Think the fish gonna bite for it if we put it on a hook after? Looks just like a nice fresh brown earthworm, don't you think? Don't it, Dad?"

"Too small, Horace. Fish is smarter than niggers."

Aaron's throat is dry. "Please don't," he says. He tries to recall the words they were taught. "You'll only be sorry later. Can't we talk this over? We won't tell anybody about what you've done, but I think—"

"Who's he gonna tell, Ben? You're the law. Maybe he's gonna tell you."

"I got to warn you it's against the law in the state of Mississippi for two people to fornicate in public places," Ben says. "This here is public land, boy."

"The nigger's out cold, Ben. How about letting her do it with the big white fucker, give us a show—teach us all them tricks they been learnin' the niggers in their schools?"

The men mumble, shuffle. Have they lost interest already? Aaron wonders: when their imaginations run dry—when words and taunts fade —will the need for violence still be there?

"You heard them," Ben says. "You be a gentleman and you give the pretty girl here a kiss, then maybe we'll let you go." He grabs Aaron's jaw and squeezes with such terrible pressure that Aaron believes the top of his head may pop off. Ben whispers, his eyes pitiless, his voice low: "You want to get out of here alive, you do what we ask, you hear? I'll handle the rest."

"She ain't so pretty with all the blood swole up on her mouth, Dad."

Ben's voice is harsh: "You *move*, girl—"

Nicky is in front of him, her hands light on his shoulders, her lips against his. She is on tiptoes, and all the pressure of her wiry body is set against his mouth, a strip of air between them. He does not close his eyes. He hears the men holler, making jokes, urging him to cornpole her. He feels a lash on his cheek and knows it has drawn blood from Nicky too. Still, she does not pull away and the desperation of her passion startles him. Her tongue searches inside his mouth hungrily. Her lips are surprisingly warm, her tongue sweet with the salty taste of blood. Her blood? His own?

Aaron is pulled backwards violently. Somebody says that he is enjoying it too much. Nicky licks her chipped tooth. The sheriff's son passes the razor in front of Nicky's eyes and Aaron does not move.

"You stay where you are, boy," the sheriff says, a hand on Aaron's arm. He turns. "What you aim to do with that carrot peeler, Horace?"

"Cut me some bait," Horace says. He jabs at Nicky's waist. "Smells like rotten shrimp down there. Fish gonna like that, I bet."

"No," the sheriff says. "You got to be smart, Horace, like I always say. You know how many feds they got in Philadelphia and Meridien now, more coming? You kill a white girl, they gonna be down our necks before the sun comes up. Now, you got business with the poor colored boy, you finish that, none of us around to see. They don't care so much about that." He turns halfway toward Aaron. "Didn't Jesus himself say, 'I come not to bring peace but a sword'? Didn't he now? So you tell me, if you're a smart man: who brought the sword down here, who's doing His work best—?"

Horace bends over the boy, razor high, and Aaron is aware of the hush, the sudden silence. He is afraid that he is going to retch, and he doesn't want to give them the satisfaction. He sees a few men turn away, hears the sound of a car engine start up, measures his chances, tries to

take into account what they might do afterwards to Nicky, to the boy.
Horace hunches over, razor held sideways, as if he will slice back-
handed. But he hesitates for a second—his other hand, directly above
the boy's groin, twitching a bit, as if afraid to touch the boy's penis—
and in that second, the sheriff reaches for the razor and Nicky begins to
sing: " 'Amazing grace . . . how sweet the sound . . ./That saved a
wretch like me—/I once was lost, but now I'm found . . ./Was blind,
but now I see. . . .' "

Aaron feels his heart stop, then pound harder. A pulse beats in his
neck. Nicky's voice is not beautiful, yet it is surprisingly full and lusty,
rasping a bit on the low notes, breaking slightly in the falling cadences.
He imagines her in a long white robe, walking out into the water, being
held by the minister, being dunked backwards. He sees her rise, hair
dripping. They sang the song in Ohio, holding hands, and in the church
in Meridien. The sheriff has stopped, his hand poised above his son's
hand. Does Nicky see him? A dog begins to howl, then another, and
Nicky keeps singing, eyes closed. Aaron sees a man, to his right, squat
down the way the Polish farmers do where Aaron lives, forearms on
thighs for balance. The man removes his orange hunter's cap. Horace's
eyes bulge even while his hands relax.

Aaron watches a man ruffle the fur on his dog's neck. Doubtless what
they were taught, again and again, in training sessions, is true: the same
man who will horsewhip a Negro will be kind to wife and child and dog,
and will perceive nothing contradictory in his behavior. Aaron watches
Ben take the razor from Horace's hand.

"Well," Ben says. "All we said we was gonna do, remember, was to
put the fear of God into these troublemakers, and I guess we done that.
No need to bring trouble down on our necks too."

Aaron watches his car slide by, pushed by three men. It rolls forward,
glides into the lake, stops when the water is just below the level of the
front windows.

A minute later they are alone, though Nicky does not seem to realize
it.

"We're okay," Aaron says.

She reaches for his hand, then collapses against his chest, clutching
at his back, beginning to sob. He smooths her hair, feels pinpoints of
pain explode within his head and chest.

"We need to get the boy to a doctor. Us too."

"I don't think my jaw is broken—not really."

Aaron listens to the boy's heart race, feels the cold, damp skin. He
takes his own shoes and socks off, rolls up his pants and walks into the
lake. He reaches into the back seat, takes out a blanket, holds it above
his head, wades back to land. He washes the boy's forehead and face,

dries him, then wraps him in the blanket and lifts him in his arms. The
moon is gone. In darkness they begin to walk toward the road.

"It worked," Nicky says. "Jesus Christ Almighty but it worked, Aaron.
We're still *here*. I was so scared, but . . ."

"It's all right."

"I imagined it happening like this a long time ago—what I'd do in a
jam like this, when I was down to my final out—and I figured when
you'd used up everything else, music would be the only answer, for . . .
for it alone has charms to soothe the savage beast, right?"

Briefly, as they stumble together through the woods, she leans against
him. He tells her again that everything is all right. He does not tell her
that the sheriff had moved toward his son and taken the razor before
she began to sing.

Much later, when they are back at Rose Morgan's, their wounds
stitched and treated by a young doctor called to the S.N.C.C. office, the
boy taken to a county hospital, the incident reported by telephone to
state police and federal agents, and after they have told the story to the
others, Nicky goes with him to his room. He sits on the edge of his bed.
She looks out the window.

"The one rule I forgot to mention," she begins, "was that you
shouldn't ever go out after dark, only I just . . ."

"It's okay. You did fine. We knew this might happen. It happens every
day to somebody, so why not us? We'll heal." He is puzzled. "But it's
like a summer job for us, isn't it? I mean, we go back to other lives when
this is over—"

"You sure kiss good," she says. "At least I can have the memory of
that to warm me some long winter night."

He sees that, despite her smile, she is trembling. He puts his arm
around her.

"Would you like to sleep here tonight?"

She starts to speak, but her lips quiver. She bites down, winces, then
nods.

"Come on," he says. "It's all right. This is the life we have, right? And
not another—"

They lie down. He expects that he will not sleep until the sun rises.
He turns onto his side, his eyes on the window, and she presses her body
against his. Her arms are around his waist, her cheek against his back,
her knees pressed against the hollows behind his knees, her feet cold
against his ankles. She tells him that he should not be frightened, that
she will try not to take advantage. He puts his hands on top of hers.

If things were different, Nicky asks—if they had different lives—she knows they don't, but if things were different and they had met the way they have, but in some *other* time and place, does he think he might have fallen in love with her? Could he love a girl like her?

Yes.

That's all she needs to know, she says. She burrows close to him, as close as she can get, rubs her damp nose back and forth against his shoulder. She talks softly, tells him that she likes to hold him this way so that he can't see her face, so that he has to imagine it. He thinks of Ellen's fingers, touching his face, reading it. He sees Ellen in her garden, bending down, reaching for flowers, and he suddenly sees his children —Carl and Larry—in that garden, sitting on the grass, waiting for Ellen to find them. He loved Gail and yet, in his memory, it is Ellen he sees most often. Why? Is it merely because, like her, he too is now cut off forever from seeing the world he once loved so dearly? Is it because, like her, when he wants to see this world, he must now imagine it into being? Perhaps. But he senses that even when he was living in his first life, his affinity with Ellen was as strange and deep as it was mysterious. The world was there for both of them, yet neither of them could live within it in the ordinary way he yearned to live in the world. His desire to imagine a life other than the one he had been given—a desire that he refused, back then, to acknowledge—must have been at least as strong as her need to imagine a world she could never see.

Nicky clings to him, talks about how frightened she was, and while she talks he thinks of Emilie, who would be almost ten years old by now, if she is alive, and he tries to imagine *her* smile. He sees himself squatting, letting her climb onto his back, grasp him around the neck, press her cheek against the nape of his neck. He sees Gail in the doorway and she leans back, hands on her stomach. She is pregnant again. Has she remarried? How often does she think of him? The last time he saw her she was the age Nicky is now. He imagines Gail passing in front of the window, her back arched. The window is a dark-blue mirror. He wants to press his palm against the small of Gail's back, to hear her sigh with pleasure at the relief he can give to her in this way, and for a few minutes, before the world spins into blackness, he is comforted by imagining that Ellen sometimes wonders what became of him, and that Gail can see him here, with Nicky.

12

THEY DRIVE HOME, through the hills of Ashfield and Conway, and down across the flatter landscape of Hatfield, Lucius delighting in the light snowfall. It is the first snow he has ever seen, and he keeps his bare hand stuck out the side window so that he can catch the flakes, lick them from his palm. The road is slick and black, the wet flakes dissolving the instant they hit pavement. Aaron watches a lone car, a dozen yards ahead, skid sideways, fishtail, recover. He downshifts from third to second, keeps the van in second gear, listens to Lucius talk about what people back home would think, could they see him now.

"Instead of flowers," he says, "I gonna bring some gal a snowball when I come courtin' next time, don't you think? She can keep it in her icebox."

Aaron smiles, but his smile falters. He is never comfortable when Lucius talks this way—back-home talk—and he feels that Lucius uses talk like this to put distance between them.

"Can you close the window? We'll both catch a chill. The sweat's not dry on me yet."

Lucius rolls the window up, puts his hands between his thighs to warm them, laughs easily, then pats Aaron on the shoulder in a way that lets Aaron know that Lucius senses what Aaron feels. Lucius talks naturally—his voice guttural, his inflection almost without southern accent—asking questions about snow: what makes it stick? what makes it melt? how deep can it get in how much time? what's the worst snow Aaron has ever seen? what happens if the snow comes down mixed with rain. . . .

The world is dim, all whites and grays except, in the patch of light illuminated by their headlights, the snow falling at a slant, a lemony-yellow. The fields stretch away to either side, cabbages and cornstalks visible here and there where they have not yet been plowed under. Thanksgiving is still ten days off. Aaron cannot remember snow having come this early, and he says so to Lucius. Lucius says that the cabbages, like soft babies' bottoms, look as if they've been sprinkled with talcum. To their left, where the Connecticut River flows less than a hundred yards away, they see nothing but white—and the whiteness does not please Aaron. He cannot see the river, or the line of trees that borders it. He senses a wall of black behind the whiteness, pressing against it: a thin, hard veneer. Aaron loves the land when he can see across it, when there are wide horizons, endless vistas. His favorite time of year—between autumn and first snow, when the leaves fall from the trees little by little, slowly revealing the landscape beyond; when he can see the hills and green fields that have been hidden for half a year, even as the green itself begins to fade to browns and lavenders and yellows and golds —this is gone now. He feels as if he is driving under an enormous dome of snow, the dome moving along with him, the side walls remaining equidistant from his van. There are pinpoints of color here and there— a splash of orange on a billboard, a yellow porch light, a green highway sign, black shutters on an old farmhouse, silver mailboxes on dark posts. Is life like that—an endless haze of gray and white, without beginning or end, with here and there a flash of color, a spot of something that suggests the *possibility* of beauty? Can one enter these points of color— of light—and pass through to the other side, to some other world?

Aaron chides himself for such musings, yet finds that he is less irritable, less tense, for letting thoughts come this way. Until recently—he has been talking with Susan about this—he had never thought of himself as a man with imagination. He could draw well, of course. He could design houses and, his great pleasure, make beautiful architectural renderings of them—design sections or construction drawings, architectural elevations—but in doing so he felt for the most part that he was only setting down what was already there, or would be there, in the physical world. He was collaborating with clients, working to order, rendering the actual: what could, in fact, in the physical world, be constructed out of wood and metal and glass and cement. But to have thoughts beyond things physical—to consider the presence of things not visible in the world—this was something he couldn't remember having done often. In the portraits he drew when he was a boy? In his drawings of apartment buildings and storefronts? Perhaps. For much as he wanted to render things as accurately as he could, he was aware that he was also trying to get at something else, that he was trying, somehow, to draw through the details to something more real, to some quality of the person or of the place that could *not* be expressed by things merely physical.

His mind drifts, whiteness swirling softly inside his brain like plaster dust caught in an updraft. A cluster of houses set back from the road, to the west—a dairy farm, a four-walled fortresslike layout of buildings, with a red and silver silo jutting upwards like a bullet—makes him think of the dark, close barn, the warm bodies of cows, the sweet, musky smell of silage. He imagines a cardinal passing in front of the car, from west to east—a streak of crimson that bleeds across the white landscape, coming from nowhere, disappearing forever. He looks sideways at Lucius, and he recalls the easy way his father would sit in the bedroom with him while he drew, and of how, when he would look up from his paper, he would never know how many minutes or hours had passed. Were those happy times? Was he *ever*, in the four small rooms of that apartment, happy—at ease in *this* world?

Lucius asks him what they will do for work—for money—when they are finished with the house they are building. They are down to minor items now—cabinets and countertops in the kitchen and bathroom, paneling in the study, moldings—and Aaron says he has a few small jobs —bookcases, kitchen renovations, taking out walls, putting in walls, finishing a family room—that should keep them busy through the end of January. Other things may come along. He has a contract for a new house in North Amherst, and they can start on that in mid-April, when the frost will be out of the ground.

"Maybe something sooner. When I called Susan at noon she said that somebody's coming by tonight to talk about renovating a big old farmhouse, in Hadley. Says he admires my work." Aaron feels the sweat evaporate, warming the air trapped between skin and clothing. A vapor barrier. "You'd like that, Lucius—restoring an old house. When you cut into the walls and floors, get past the lathing, tear away a chimney and see the innards—building the house backwards in your mind is the way I think about it, from the inside out—that does make the blood flow."

"Well. We want to keep the blood flowing, don't we? Like the man says, gonna be one long ball-breaking winter—snow balls and blue balls —and me without a woman."

"You can sleep a lot. Have good dreams."

"Oh yeah. You bet I'll dream, Aaron. Dream lots. Dreams are what keep us alive, right? I had a dream. Sure. I had a dream that someday the sons of black sharecroppers would lie down with the daughters of white millionaires. Oh yes, Lord. I had a dream. . . ."

Lucius laughs. Aaron looks out through mists of white, imagines a fawn and its mother staring back at him, bending over to pick at grass, at tufts that rise through the snow like green hair.

"There's a bone in the middle of a deer's heart. Did you know that?"

"Coon got one in his dingus, makes a good toothpick. You know *that?*"

"The truth, Lucius," Aaron says, laughing easily, "is that the winters *are* long and dark and cold here. You should think about that part of your life too."

"Don't do much some evenings *but* think on it. Trouble is, my boss works me so hard, all I want to do at the end of day is to lay down my weary bones and sleep."

Aaron makes suggestions he's made before, ever since he brought Lucius back with him at the end of August: that Lucius consider enrolling in courses at the university; that Lucius go to S.N.C.C. meetings or C.O.R.E. meetings; that Lucius do *something* so that his entire life does not filter through Aaron's life, so that he can begin to meet and know other people and families, so that he can meet women.

"Blow it out your ass with that line," Lucius snaps. "You white guys been in the Movement get me, plugging all the white and black ass you can all summer long, then reaching out your hand to help us poor niggers, except we gotta do our plowin' in black soil only. Damn! You don't know shit sometimes, Levin, you're so fucking pure."

"Pure?"

"Yeah. Pure. You probably the only guy down there, all them babes creamin' over you, who *didn't* get anything."

"I'm a free man, too," Aaron says. "And a happily married one."

"I know *that.* Everybody round here knows about your famous happy marriage. Only you got to be human too. Otherwise you put strains on things natural, don't you see? I mean, when I was married, what I said was, 'Oh, yeah, I'm married, only I ain't a fanatic about it.' "

They ride in silence, south along Route 5, Aaron concentrating on the driving, on the dots of color in the landscape: crimson, pea-green, gray, orange. The houses are closer to the road now, closer to one another. Aaron thinks of replying, of saying that he's human enough, that being married to one woman—one *interesting* woman—for eight years is no easy thing, but his mind veers to something else.

"Do you want to go back?" Aaron asks.

"Sometimes."

"You miss Carrie?"

"Not much."

"The child?"

"Some."

"Well." Lucius is Rose Morgan's cousin and Aaron knows Lucius can trust Rose to keep an eye on Carrie and the boy. "You're a free man too now. If—"

"Oh shit on that, Aaron. A free man. Come *on!*"

"If you want to go back home, I'll take care of it. The money, I mean."

"Is that a promise or a threat?"

"Neither."

"You still gettin' them calls about me?"

"What calls?"

"You know what calls. Susan told me—nasty calls about all I been doing to your wife and daughter, what you been doing to me, what I been doing to your boys—"

"I didn't know Susan had told you."

Lucius shrugs. "*I* didn't know she kept anything from you. Thought you two shared everything—no secrets—the famous happy marriage you got."

"There's lots about me that Susan doesn't know, or have to know."

"Well, I'm glad to hear *that*," Lucius says. "Relieved too, you want the truth. Only there's something else I been wanting to tell you."

"Yes?"

"I was never married. Not legal anyway. Rose must have told you."

"No. But I figured."

"You did?"

"Do you think a man as pure as Aaron Levin would have taken someone North who was abandoning wife and child?"

"I been sending money back home for the boy—to Rose—only the main thing is that I wouldn't put a bet on him being mine."

"So? What difference would that make?"

"The difference is some men ain't so bighearted like you. They get a son, they want that son to be son of their blood, see? The difference is all men don't feel about kids not their own the way you do about Susan's." Lucius pauses. "Anyway, jealousy's never been one of my depths. I look at that boy and I think of all the men been in Carrie's body."

"Why did you marry her then—stay with her?"

"Never *married* her, didn't you hear me? Don't you *listen*, man?"

"I listen."

Aaron turns off Route 5, heading west. He is pleased to be able to get a rise out of Lucius. He loves the easy way they have of bantering, teasing, and of how their conversations will suddenly, unexpectedly, become serious. When they work, eight and ten hours a day, they rarely talk, except about the business at hand. Aaron waits, knowing that if he does, Lucius will speak. Aaron feels warm and drowsy, safe within the van, the van safe within its dome of snow. The snow is less wet now, the flakes larger, falling more densely. If the snow sticks, the children will be able to go sledding in the morning. Aaron imagines Lucius on the toboggan with his children, all six feet three inches and 220 pounds of him bundled in wool and down, his coal-black face swathed in bright Scandinavian colors. He thinks of Tony and Regina, in the subway, heading for Coney Island, Regina bundling close to Tony for warmth, and he realizes that Tony will never be able to see Aaron's drawings— how good he's become—and that he will never be able to tell his friend Lucius about his friend Tony.

Lucius sighs. "All right. Story time, then?"

"Sure," Aaron says. "I'd like that."

Lucius shrugs, as if to shake off the last of his anger. "Why I stayed with her, crazy as she was? Took the easy way out maybe. My old man used to say, why go hunt up some new woman and get her broke in right when you already got one in your bed? After all the shit I lived through in prison, it was good to be with somebody wasn't wanting something from me every minute of my life. It was good not to be scared. She was good to me, Aaron. Real good. *Kind.* You seen that."

"Yes."

"What you didn't see was why everybody was so surprised, why they thought she was crazy. What everybody knew about her—why they couldn't figure me and her together—was how, from the time she started dropping her drawers for whatever came along, she used to have this thing, see, where if a guy came too soon or wasn't doing it the way she liked, she'd pull out this little penknife, stick it in the guy's ribs, make him stay there till she got what she was after."

"Freedom *now.*"

"You got it." Lucius laughs. "Only problem was, it ain't easy for a guy to keep it up when he got a knife in his ribs. By and by, when they found out she was doing the same thing to them all, the guys got wise to her, they just started in beating up on her and I guess I wound up feeling sorry for her, dumb me. See? I ain't so much *un*like you as I make out when it comes to wanting to help the colored people. Oh yeah. So when I come on three guys knocking the shit out of her back of the high school one night, her screaming like a cat with its ear ripped off, I let loose, picked up two of them at once, banged their heads together, then took the other guy and heaved him at the wall, broke bones.

"Well. Our size count for something once in a while, Aaron. And Carrie, by the time I got her fixed up she started being so sweet and good to me—thanking me, loving me up, telling me how she gonna change, how if anybody pulled something on me she gonna kick *their* ass—I just found myself staying on with her. Seemed easy. The real crazy thing was how I got to like her more than anyone I knew, how we could talk with each other, say all we wanted to without being scared. First time I ever had that with somebody—what I guess I got with you, brother—so when the kid started showing, and her telling me every day

I better move my ass out or people gonna think it was mine, I just said 'Fuck what people think,' and stayed on."

"But you don't want to go back to her? You don't ever *think* about going back?"

"No."

"You're sure?"

"I'm sure."

"Not to your own family either?"

"My old man, I see him again, I might kill him, make the buckle on his belt mighty sharp first." Lucius smiles slowly. "Know that belt well. Too well. Only I figure I gonna do something like that, I save it for somebody *worth* killing."

The porch light is on, and in the amber haze Aaron stamps his feet on the black rubber mat, pushes the door open, enters. They are assaulted at once, Carl on Aaron's back, Larry all over Lucius, both boys shouting that there is a surprise waiting in the living room—someone—and Aaron has to guess who it is. Susan touches Aaron's ear with her knuckles, lovingly, kisses him, remarks on the crazy weather, on how bitter cold it is. Didn't Aaron wear a hat? Was their space heater working? Aaron jokes with Lucius about Jewish wives being Jewish mothers to their husbands, and Lucius smiles, accepts a kiss from Susan, blows into his hands, the palms bright pink like the insides of conch shells.

Aaron is pleased to be home. His nostrils quiver, take in the fragrances of things baking: potatoes, he guesses, and a pork roast. Buttermilk biscuits. His eyes take in color: forest-green carpeting, blue and purple Venetian glass in the bay window, ivory-white drapes, a brass menorah and silver spice box on a cherry wood table, a rose-colored smoked-glass fixture suspended from the ceiling, brightly colored hand-woven pillows on the window seat. Susan is happiest, Aaron knows—despite all her worldly talents—when she is in their upstairs bedroom alone, looking out at the backyard, working at her sewing machine, making things for the children or the house. He listens to her tell him about her day, about how peaceful it was until the children arrived home, about how they were excited by the sudden snowfall, and as she talks, leaning against the doorjamb, her head tilted, her cheek on the back of her hand, he is struck again, as if for the first time, by how extraordinarily beautiful she is.

Whenever he is away from her for more than a few hours—whenever he leaves home and returns, if only on an errand—it always seems a small miracle to him that this woman, who is more beautiful than most movie stars—a talented actress who, before she had children, probably

could have *been* a famous movie star—is there waiting for him, that she
is happy to see him, that she loves him, that she is his wife. How can it
be? Sometimes when he tells her how lucky he feels—to have her, to
have the family they have—she becomes annoyed, tells him that she is
only a woman who happened to be born with the features she was born
with. Were she not so physically beautiful, she will ask, would he love
her as much?

Still, when he is with her, he often feels somewhat adrift, as if he is a
small boy who needs to ask her permission for things. Why? She talks
with Lucius now, laughs with him about snow, then bends down and
explains to Larry that Lucius has never seen snow before. As good a
wife and mother as she is, Aaron often feels that there is a curious
distance between them—air—that they remain, in part, strangers, that
they are never as easy with one another as she is with the children, and
it occurs to him that this is so not only because they have chosen, he
more than she, to hold back their full histories from one another—who
they were and what they did before they met and fell in love and married
—but because when he is with her, her beauty allows him to forget what
he often feels when they are apart: that there is something missing. It is
as if, he will imagine, she is not solid all the way through—as if several
layers down there are air chambers instead of organs, tubes instead of
bones—and he has to ask himself if he is only, when he feels this way,
to use one of Susan's favorite words, projecting. The truth, he knows, is
that he cannot imagine, no matter how good his new life seems, ever
being able *not* to feel that he is the one who is hollow, that some part of
him is missing.

Susan moves to the alcove, between the foyer and the kitchen, inviting him there, he knows, and he goes to her, tells her that he and Lucius
will have drinks—bourbon on ice, with a splash of water—and as she
turns to him, smiling, he seizes her wrist, presses her against the closet
door, lifts her honey-colored hair with the side of his hand, nuzzles at
her neck. She hums, embraces him, takes his chin with her hand, kisses
him hard. She pulls back, shows him her forearm, where the goose flesh
has risen. She tells him that she misses him, and he laughs, tells her he
is there. Her eyes are a strange winter shade of blue—almost transparent, like thin ice at dusk. She has never seemed more lovely, and when
he thinks this he realizes that in another part of his mind he has been
imagining that it is Tony and not Lucius who has come home with him,
who is watching him and smiling. Poor Tony.

The children jump on them, try to pry them apart, tell him to hurry
and come with them, to see who is waiting in the living room. Can he
guess?

"You go—I'll be right there with the drinks," Susan says. Her eyes show puzzlement. Is she warning him of some danger? Have there been more calls?

He enters the living room and Paul Steiner smiles, rises from the couch, hand extended. Aaron hesitates, startled momentarily by how handsome and healthy Paul looks—as if time has gone in reverse—then moves forward, shakes Paul's hand.

"Good to see you, Aaron. Good to be here."

"How are you, Paul?"

"Better. Much better."

Aaron nods. He does not, he realizes, want Lucius to sense his tightness. "I see that. I'm pleased for you."

Jennifer and Benjamin, waiting politely, come forward now, kiss Aaron, but he knows that they can sense his unease in Paul's presence. Benjamin sulks. Aaron turns, introduces Lucius to Paul, says that Lucius works with him. Paul tells Lucius that the children have been singing his praises.

"Will you show uncle Paul your scars?" Larry asks Lucius.

"Not now," Paul says, touching Larry's head, with affection. "Not now."

"I told him about the scars you have on your back from being whipped in jail. But I bet in a fair fight you would of busted those guys good, right? You're as strong as Daddy—"

"Lucius comes from Mississippi and he was in jail because he stood up for his rights," Carl begins, as if reciting a speech for school assembly. "When he entered prison he weighed two hundred and fifteen pounds and when he was finally freed he only weighed one hundred and twenty pounds."

"Hey now," Lucius says. "No need. No need."

"Paul is Benjamin and Jennifer's father," Aaron explains. "Susan's first husband. We haven't seen one another for a long time."

"I've been away." He glances at his children, as if for encouragement, and then continues, speaking deliberately. "I wasn't well, you see. I had some problems and tried to take care of them." He smiles. "They tell me I did—that I took care of them."

"Daddy was in a private psychiatric clinic," Jennifer says to Lucius. "Many people believe that it's a sign of weakness to ask for help, but it's really a sign of strength is what I believe. It took a lot of courage for my father to say 'I-have-a-problem-that-I-cannot-solve-alone-and-I-need-help-with-it.'"

Well, Aaron thinks: she is her mother's daughter.

"Jesus!" Benjamin says, turning away. "Why'd you have to tell Lucius? You suck, Jennifer, did you know that? You really do. You're a real priss-ass."

"And you are a narrow-minded immature twit."

"But why did Lucius have to *know*? Jesus—"

Paul takes Benjamin by the shoulders, bends down so that they are at eye level. "There's nothing to be ashamed of," he says. "Mental problems are problems too—the brain and the heart are organs just as the kidneys and the lungs are—and if you have problems with your mind and your feelings, you go to the doctors and the places that fix them up."

"Just leave me *alone*," Benjamin says, pulling away from Paul, striding across the room. "Just leave me alone already."

Carl and Larry stare at Benjamin, and in their eyes, Aaron can tell, is the hope that things will escalate—that Benjamin will lose his temper, that he and Jennifer will go at each other, that people will start arguing and screaming, that they will get the chance to gang up on their older brother. Paul is, clearly, upset by Benjamin's surliness, by being its cause. What Paul lacks in character, Susan has always said, he makes up for in charm. Now that he is less charming—a bit humbled—will he gain in character?

Paul wears a brown tweed jacket, a button-down shirt, a soft, gray silk tie patterned with wine-red wagon wheels. He looks, Aaron thinks, exactly like the headmaster of one of the local private secondary schools —the Williston School, Deerfield Academy, Mount Hermon, Northfield. All he lacks is the pipe in hand, the Irish setter at his knee, the crest on his jacket pocket. In photographs taken during their years together, he and Susan look like the ideal Wasp couple—blond and blue-eyed, patrician, cool—and he knows that this was part of the attraction for Susan: that a man who looked like the head of a Christian fraternity had been born of a mother whose flesh floated up through a chimney in Auschwitz, whose ashes served as compost for hard winter fields. Aaron thinks of the cabbages in the snow, of a man on a tractor, bundled behind a plastic wind screen against the gusting wind. He sees the tractor's blades grind up the cold earth.

"I hope you don't mind, my just stopping by," Paul says. "I thought it might be easier that way. Susan told you I'd be here, didn't she—that I have a project I hope you'll be interested in?"

"Yes."

"I wanted to talk to you about other things also, and I will: I wanted to say thank you for all you've done for my children these past years, while I was away."

"Save it," Aaron says, and he feels heat rise around his collar. He does not look toward Lucius or the children. He feels angry, uncomfortable, used. He imagines Paul rising from a sewer, pushing the grating aside, hoisting himself up. He sees Paul following him through the city. Why?

Is he only feeling what Lucius felt looking at Carrie's child—an adolescent jealousy towards a man who had once known his wife? Perhaps. He looks at Paul and remembers what Paul looked like the last time they saw him, when they took Benjamin and Jennifer to Stockbridge, an hour west, to the Austin Riggs Psychiatric Center. Paul's eyes were half-closed, his face puffy, his neck rigid. Now Paul's face is lean, well tanned, as if he has been skiing. Aaron wonders if Jennifer is recalling that last visit, if that is why she is pleased, and he wonders too if that is why Benjamin, for the same reason, is so surly. How can his father be two such different men?

Susan enters, tells the children to leave, serves drinks. Her eyes meet Aaron's but he cannot read them. Is she worried that he will be angry afterwards because she didn't tell him Paul was there? Paul says something to Aaron about how good the children look, how Jennifer looks more and more like Susan. Susan's color rises. Aaron sees her as Nina in *The Sea Gull*, at the Williamstown Playhouse, the summer they met. He recalls something Paul said to him after his divorce from Susan was final and before Aaron and Susan were married: that by marrying a woman who looked like Susan yet was Jewish, they had it both ways— they remained within the fold while at the same time fulfilling all their fantasies about blond, blue-eyed goddesses. Aaron didn't bother to deny it, to tell Paul that as a boy he had trained himself most of the time *not* to imagine the future, the life unlived. But Aaron is disturbed by Susan's presence, by her silence, by the high color in her cheeks. Does she like the idea that her two husbands, present and past, are there with her at the same time? Does this turn her on, as if they are, somehow, sharing her? Or is he imagining this—his version of preemptive rejection—in order to deny his feelings of jealousy, in order to blame the feelings on Susan?

Paul talks about the house he has found, the restorations he wants. Aaron does not doubt Paul's desire to insinuate himself into his and Susan's life, and he figures he can handle that at least as well now as he did before. What bothers him is his need to imagine that Susan likes the idea, that she would want to insinuate her past into Aaron's present, that she would want to hurt him. Why does he think this? Paul is telling Lucius that in the house, once owned by the Congregational Church, they have found secret chambers that they believe were used in the nineteenth century to hide runaway slaves on their way north to Canada. Paul says that this fact was crucial in his decision to buy the house. He says that underground railroads interest him and that, in time, Aaron will discover why. Aaron waits, shows no curiosity. He looks at the straight line of Susan's nose, the almond shapes of her wide-set eyes. She is broadly built, robust. He imagines her on a field in Russia, a black babushka on her head, a scythe in one hand, a bundle of wheat in the other. She smiles at him without coyness, and they move off together across the field until they come to a shaded copse, by a stream. Lucius sets his drink down, half-finished, says that he is going. Aaron senses Lucius's rage, is pleased that it is there. Lucius touches Aaron's shoulder, leaves the room without saying goodbye to Paul or Susan.

"Sure," Paul says. "First love is the one love worth having, I guess—the one we dream about, the one that stays with us forever—but the best *marriage* is often a second marriage. I hope it will be for me. From the look of things, it surely is for Susan."

Paul looks at Aaron for confirmation, but Aaron shows nothing. They are alone in the kitchen. The children are upstairs doing their homework. Susan is driving Lucius home. What, Aaron wonders, is Paul's game this time?

"You'll like Debbie," Paul says, the second time he has done so. "I want you and Susan to meet her soon. I guess I'm even hoping that the four of us might become friends. Could you live with that?"

"I thought you were here for business. Haven't I heard Susan say that you always believed that business and friendship never mixed?"

"You're a hard man, Aaron Levin."

"In business or friendship?"

Paul laughs. "In both, I suspect."

"Maybe. What's on your mind? I have things to do."

Paul opens a cabinet above the sink as if he has done so the day before—as if to remind Aaron of how close, in a daily way, Paul and Susan once were. Paul sets glasses on the shelf. "Look," he says. "I guess my need to make you see how I've changed is a bit larger than your need to see the changes, but I *am* serious about the house. I'd love to have you come out and take a look at it, tell me what you think and take on the job. You're not holding back because of Susan, are you?"

"No."

Aaron knows that he has answered too quickly. "Think about it, though, all right?" Paul says, smiling. "If things work out, you see, the house I'm buying will be one that Benjamin and Jennifer can spend time in, where we can get to know one another again. Susan and I talked it over, before you came home. She told me she thought it would be good for the children to spend some time with me. I think she and I can be friends now in a way that—"

"I said I'll think about it."

"Do you have to consult with Lucius?"

"Why should I have to do that?"

"You two are in business together, aren't you?"

"Lucius and I aren't in business together. Lucius works for me."

"Ah," Paul says. "And if you take on this job, you'll be working for me. Is that the problem—the reason you hesitate?"

"No. There are things I need to think about."

"Such as?"

"The differences between a man like you and a man like Lucius."

"Well," Paul says, smiling. "He wasn't married to Susan, I'll grant that. Still—"

"Be careful," Aaron says. "Your illness doesn't give you license here."

Paul laughs, says he sees that Aaron is still a very literal man. A literalist of the imagination perhaps? Aaron considers asking Paul why he is telling him all this but decides that he has already said too much. He imagines himself outside, in early spring, playing basketball with Lucius and Tony. In three-man ball, could anybody beat the three of them? He recalls walking along Flatbush Avenue with Tony, meeting Avie and Little Benny, Tony telling Benny that he was Jackie Robinson's brother. *Yeah. I just look pale today 'cause of how much you guys scare me.*

He wonders: after he left, did Tony ever visit Gail and Emilie? What would Gail have felt, opening the door and seeing Tony there? What would Tony have felt, embracing her, picking up the baby? Paul is talking about his upcoming marriage to Debbie, about his years with Susan, about how young Susan was when they married, about how neither of them had really tried the world very much. After their early happiness, he says, the banked fires of passion and independence exploded, and neither of them ever knew why. They still believed, all through their last miserable years together, that they loved one another, when all they really wanted was to destroy the other. They nearly succeeded, Paul says.

Does the fact that Aaron now has what Paul once had and still desires —Susan—satisfy Aaron in some way he would rather not acknowledge? Is this why he has enjoyed the bit of competitive edge to their conversation—his willingness to parry Paul's small barbs?

When Paul talks the way he is talking now—holds forth, really—he seems very professorial. Aaron imagines him parading in front of nineteen-year-old girls at Smith College, their eyes full of desire and adulation. Aaron reminds himself that that was, after all, the way Susan met Paul. Paul had been a young instructor in Smith College's Theater Department—Susan's teacher, her director when she had the lead in a production of *Our Town*.

Aaron is relieved to hear the sound of Susan's Ford approaching the house, the wheels squealing against snow and gravel. He will go out

later, shovel the steps, plow the driveway. In the morning he will be
back in Ashfield with Lucius, finishing up the trim, cutting moldings to
length. They will talk about Paul.

Susan enters the kitchen, her forehead slick with melted snow. She
shivers, talks about the snow turning to ice.

"Did Susan tell you how Debbie and I met—the circumstances?"

"We haven't been alone since you got here—how could she tell me?"

"We met at my father's funeral, actually. Debbie was the daughter of
a distant cousin, the part of the family that got out of Germany before
the war. My father—"

"I'm not really interested," Aaron says. "In fact, I think our conversation is over."

"The house is a beauty." Paul talks as if he has not heard Aaron. "A
nice old colonial, Federal style, built in 1835, with an attached barn in
an ell. You can go straight from the barn to the kitchen, which is terrific
for bringing in wood, or getting to the car in winter. From what little I
can tell, the timbers are solid. Post-and-beam construction, chestnut for
the most part, oak in the parts added on to the house in the late nine-
teenth century. Nobody's lived in the house for two winters—the family
was feuding over inheritance—but the roof is in reasonably good shape
and—"

"I said I'll think about it. Don't push."

"Me push?" Paul grins. "I wouldn't think of it."

"Good."

"But how about tomorrow sometime? I can come by late afternoon."

"I said not to push. I work tomorrow."

"The weekend then?"

"Lucius and I promised the Lesters they could be in their house by
December fifteenth, so we may work over the weekend."

"Lucius," Paul says. "Lucius. An interesting man." He smiles at
Susan. "You get the slave home all right?"

Susan's mouth goes rigid, her eyes widen. She looks toward Aaron,
terrified.

"Get out," Aaron says. "Get out fast."

Paul does not move. His eyes show no fear.

"Just testing, old man. Just wanted to make sure the ancient fires of
justice are still burning within you, that the passion for the underdog
and the dispossessed has not—"

"I said to get out. Now you *move*."

Paul turns to Susan, "Have you told him how much I admire what he
did last summer, that I read his articles?"

Susan's fingers, on the back of Aaron's neck, are like ice. He pulls
away, numb with rage. Susan tells him to take it easy, that it's Paul's old

way of trying to get a rise out of others, that he doesn't mean anything by it, that he just can't help being the way he is.

"Call it habit," Paul says. He leaves the kitchen. "Or envy. That would be more precise. N-V—the biggest two-letter word in the English language. Envy can be a habit also, and a bad one. The worst. Imagine being me and seeing you here, Aaron. Can you? Can you imagine that? Imagine being me and seeing the way my children adore you and hang on you. Can you imagine that?" He smiles. "Imagine being me and what I might do next."

"Oh, cut it, Paul," Susan says. "Stop acting out. Just turn the battery to your tongue off before you get into trouble."

"Well," Paul says. "I *am* trying, believe it or not. Will you believe me? I'll tell you what—I'll begin to let you in on some secrets, all right? We all have secrets, and not the kind you give to doctors when you're lying on a couch. We have other secrets, Aaron, men like you and me. How not? What you did this past summer—it's the kind of thing I'd like to do, the kind of risk I'd like to take. And in my own way, I'm going to. Can you imagine that? Can you imagine me bringing somebody out of . . ."

Susan gives Paul his coat. Aaron cannot move. He thinks of the low rolling hills that surrounded them on all sides when they were driving down from Conway—the Holyoke Range to the south, the Pelham hills to the east, the Leverett hills to the north, the Berkshires to the west— all of them invisible behind the dome of snow. He thinks of Emilie, asleep in her crib, Carl and Larry looking in at her. He looks at the hanging plants, the copper pots and Delft tiles on the walls, the children's drawings taped to the refrigerator. He hears the front door open and close.

"It's true," Susan says, moving toward him. She leans against him easily, and in the way she touches his cheek he senses an apology. But for what? "When the children were telling Paul about Lucius before you two came home—when they were bragging about how Lucius weighed so little when he got out of jail, Paul talked to them about his father— their grandfather, after all—and of how he weighed less than ninety pounds when the American soldiers liberated his camp, about how he came to America and made his fortune. He told them how his father was still making deals by phone from his deathbed, and—"

"Any calls today?"

"One."

"What did he say this time?"

"I don't know. Jennifer answered."

Aaron blinks. He is thinking of another call, one he made eight years ago—the only time he tried to go back, the only time he risked touching the other life. He wanted to know if Gail and Emilie were all right, but he didn't want them to know he was asking. There was only one person he could trust, and he recalls, as he dialed from a phone booth in Albany, and then began dropping quarters and dimes in, how, for a second, he began to hope that maybe Tony would be so happy to hear from him that the two of them would start talking about where they could meet, about how they would roam around the country together, how they would get enough money to buy a trailer they could live in. . . .

"I'm sorry. I shouldn't have lost my temper."

"It's all right. Paul still knows how to work you, to prey on your jealousy. Don't worry about it."

"I'm not worried. I'm angry."

"And confused."

"No, not really. Mostly I'm angry that he saw he could get to me."

Is Tony there?

His heart lurches. He puts his arm around Susan, kisses her hair.

Tony who?

Tony Cremona. I know he may not live there anymore, but I wanted to get in touch with him. If—

Susan's hand moves inside his shirt, along the small of his back. He never wished for his first life to end, he tells himself. But he wonders: had he known he would have a second life like the one he has, would he have been willing to see the first life die? And if, in some way that makes him sadder than he ever dreamt he could be, he does believe that living with Susan and their four children is like a dream come true—his deepest wish fulfilled—does that mean, even in part, that he somehow *willed* his new life into being?

Tony's dead, fella.

Dead?

Where you been? He died over in Korea two years ago. Hey—who is this anyway?

"Don't be." Susan sighs, caresses the back of his neck, moves away and starts to put leftover food into containers, to clear the sideboard. She does not seem to notice the sadness that he believes is melting from his eyes. She does not seem to notice that anything is going on inside him besides the feelings he chooses to show her. Poor, sweet Tony. *Go fly a kike, okay?* Sure. Aaron blinks, feels that his eyelids are passing over dry, cold marble. Killers. "Paul," Susan says, "Paul just likes to stage things, don't you know that yet? He likes to set things up so that he can see how people will, under his control, react. He likes to move people around, to play god to a small, enclosed world. Same old guy. He never fools anybody for long."

"He fooled you."

"That's what I said."

13

EARLY MORNING. Aaron sits on his stool, the creamy-white vellum sheet on the drafting table, his hand poised above it. Pull the pencil, he tells himself. Don't push it. Everything is in the line: its weight, its grace, its length. He rotates the edge of the pencil steadily, pressure constant, to keep the width and tone of the line even. Each line must be drawn in a single stroke, for the essence of a line lies in its continuity. On the paper, a two-point perspective of the home's interior —a design section of the entranceway, two stories high, the front hall-way leading to the living room—is half-drawn. Five steps below the second landing, the staircase vanishes. Aaron smiles. It never ceases to amaze, to please: how the drawing of a house seems so much more real to him than the house itself.

Even when, as now, he actually makes his drawings of the house *after* he and Lucius have done most of the work, he still takes great joy from imagining the house into being. He loves seeing the lines appear, en-closing whiteness, the invisible becoming visible so that, where there was nothing, there is now something. Will that magic ever *not* thrill him? He loves the illusion of reality more than reality itself, he supposes. Susan has teased him about this, wondering why, when the actual work is done, he will still finish the drawings that would normally have pre-ceded the work. But no matter how often it happens, he still wonders at the fact that mere pencil line drawn on paper can, within two dimen-sions, seem to have depth—to project solidly in space.

His erasing shield, cool, clear plastic, moves evenly under the edge of his hand. His coffee mug is to his right, next to the pens and pencils, the triangles and french curves and templates, the tin cans and cigar boxes and shoe boxes decorated by the children with wall paper and construction paper. He lifts the mug carefully, using thumb and forefinger, the stubs of his third and fourth fingers against the mug's side for leverage. His hand is perfectly steady. He sips, looks across the drawing and through the sliding glass doors to the lawn beyond, where young grass glistens bright green—unnaturally so—among patches of snow.

He built his studio onto the back of the house four years before, opening up and extending what had been a small unheated work area at the house's west end—an attached, barnlike room used for storing wood —for a workshop in winter. The skylight above his head lets in an abundance of pale morning light, so that Aaron does not have to use the desk lamp that runs the length of his table. He prefers natural light, always, and in the morning, as now, before anyone else in the house is awake, and especially if the sky is clear and cold, backed, as it were, by an infinite curve of silver, he amuses himself with the thought that the light itself is so brilliantly clear because, given the early hour, it has not yet been much *used*. It seems pure, fresh, crystalline—endless particles of no color—in a way that corresponds to the sense he has of his own mind at this time of day, before it has had to expend itself on things worldly.

He loves the stillness, the peace, the thought that in the house that does actually exist behind him—*his* house—his wife and children lie asleep in their beds, dreaming dreams he will never know. He imagines each of them: Susan on her side, golden hair across her cheek in an S-curve, a strand tucked into the corner of her mouth; Jennifer on her back, headgear strapped behind her neck, silver orthodontic band curving from ear to ear; Benjamin on top of the covers, prone, hugging his pillow, arms rigid; Larry in the middle of the bed, on his side, in the same relaxed position he was in when Aaron kissed him good night; Carl jumbled in his blankets, his small fist against his mouth, the knuckle of his thumb pushing his upper lip, pressing against the gum.

Aaron prefers cutaway drawings in perspective to floor plans or architectural renderings or paraline drawings; he likes seeing the series of doors and windows that open, one on the other, within a drawing that he has already sliced, ceiling to floor, and entered. He likes seeing Paul and Debbie's hallway through the severed front door, and the living room through the door that backs the front hallway, and then the smaller door at the far end of the living room that leads to the kitchen and the dining area beyond. The doors and windows, like the staircase, are still partly unrealized—no panes within the windows, no frames around the doors—yet they are whole within his mind, the lines straight and true. At the bottom left he has almost completed a detailed rendering of the front door, six feet high, inch-and-a-half-thick paneled chestnut, vertical sidelights to right and left, a wooden fanlight above. He sands the lead in his compass-pencil to a fine chisel point, draws the outer curve of the fanlight—a semicircle—the curve first, then the straight bottom edge, so that the tangents will match.

He thinks of Jackie Robinson. Jackie is wearing a double-breasted gray suit and is sitting behind his desk at Chock Full O'Nuts, where he is a vice president. Aaron wishes he could reach out across time and space, run his palm over Jackie's frizzy white hair. He wishes he could run the edge of his hand across the planes of Jackie's strong, good face. He is taller than Jackie, and he realizes, to his surprise, that he was taller than him even in high school, during the years Jackie played for the Dodgers. He sees them standing together, his hand on Jackie's shoulder, the two of them posing for photographs. What are they celebrating? Why is he taller than the man who was his hero?

Despite all the lead holders and fancy mechanical pencils he owns, he ends up, most of the time, using a common 2H wood pencil, medium-hard, that does not erase easily. Is it the blackness of line that causes him to feel the edge of Jackie's face? In the newspaper, two days before, he read the item about Jackie's son volunteering for the Army. Why? Why *now*? Jack Junior is seventeen years old, and Aaron senses that the troubles the sportswriters allude to—the special school Jack Junior has had to attend—are deeper than they feel free to say. How can it be? After such a long journey and so many hopes, can one lose all if one's own son . . .

Aaron shifts the straight edge of an adjustable triangle from right to left, the tapered pencil-point moving down from top to bottom, creating each individual strut in the window fan. If Jack Junior is shipped to Vietnam, as seems certain, and if he dies there, and if Jackie waits at the airport, hunched in a black overcoat, hands in pockets, reporters around him, to see the casket come off the plane, to identify the body . . . A line goes over the bottom edge of the window fan. Damn! Aaron feels Jackie's rage surging through his own body, oceans boiling to steam. Aaron slides the shield down, finds a small square, erases through it, moves the shield, dusts away the pale orange dots of eraser with his drafting brush.

The front door to Paul's home is more than 150 years old, yet it is as straight and true today as it was on the day it was first hung. Aaron sketches the details surely, working from top to bottom, using different-size triangles—top rail to frieze panels to frieze rail to middle panels to lock rail to bottom panels to bottom rail. For the house Susan wants, he decides, he will build a door like this, though he will have a hard time getting chestnut. Perhaps he can find enough from an old barn being torn down in the area. The Polish farmers in Hadley and Hatfield do that, to save on taxes, to sell the wood. Aaron likes to knock out the old

beams and walls, store them—air-layered—down near the stone wall.
Later in the day he and Susan will drive out with the children to look at
the piece of property she has found and has fallen in love with—fourteen acres in North Leverett, near the sawmill—and he realizes that he
is already, however wary, and only a month after she first mentioned it
and they first fought over it, getting used to the idea of buying land, of
building on it.

He stands and stretches. Outside, twenty feet from the window, a
chickadee, upside down, moves along the trunk of the silver maple. He
slides the glass door sideways, steps out into the cold morning.

He crosses his arms, rubs them to stimulate warmth, begins to shave
the pencil point, to watch the curls of wood slip off, float. There are, he
recalls with some surprise, only two children in the house. Benjamin
and Jennifer are spending the weekend with Paul and Debbie. They
took their sleeping bags and pillows with them. Aaron imagines them
snuggled inside the sacks, wood shavings around their heads. He and
Lucius sanded the old floors a week before but have not yet stained or
waxed them.

He sees a shadow in the woods, beyond the stone wall. Is it moving?
He shields his eyes to cut the glare of morning light on snow, looks back
at the house briefly—his drafting table and filing cabinets framed in the
door's window—then looks to the woods again. The woods are mostly
gray, tree trunks and branches specked with wine-red dots of maple
buds, with glossy patches of mountain laurel.

Suddenly the questions swarm: Where will they get the money to buy
the land Susan wants? Where, for that matter, will they get enough
money to live on if no new houses come along before the fall? And if he
gets no new work, what about Lucius? What if Lucius returns to Mississippi? Can he hold Lucius back?

What of Paul and Debbie? Aaron's jaw tightens. He regrets having
agreed to do the house but knows that nobody talked him into it. His
own choice. He hates dealing with Paul, receiving his praise, watching
Debbie float by, stoned to the skies. Benjamin and Jennifer come home
from visits with Paul and Debbie in moods that foul the air in Aaron's
home. But what else could he have done? Given Susan's resolve—that
the children should have, her phrase, free access to their true father—
he thought it might help if he showed that he wanted to cooperate, that
he bore Paul no ill will. Still, Aaron will be happy when the restorations
are done and he does not have to see Paul. He senses something strange,
even sick, going on with Paul and Debbie, but he cannot name it or
prove it, and Susan continues to stand firm: Paul is the children's father,
they are Paul's children. It is right and natural for them to spend time

together. How can he argue with her? Would he want never to see Carl or Larry again?

He tightens his grip on his knife, scrapes the lead to a long tapered point, tests the point against his left index finger. Is it that he somehow connects Paul's reentry into their life with Susan's decision to return to work in the fall, to take courses at the university? Susan has been tutoring Lucius on a regular basis, has decided she misses teaching, misses the theater, misses being involved with other people. She has been after Aaron to join her—to take courses, to get a degree. She already has a degree in theater, and now wants to get one in counseling. Does Aaron, she asks, want to spend the rest of his life drawing houses and pounding nails?

He imagines Susan waking, brushing her hair. Sometimes, when he watches her in front of the bedroom mirror, it is Tony he sees, Tony brushing his hair from his forehead, getting ready to ask a question. But what question would Tony ask?

Something *is* moving in the woods. A deer passing through? Aaron tenses. He squints, and before his eyes can register whether what he sees is shadow or form the blade has cut into his left index finger and he watches bright red blood flower from the cut, sees a drop fall and stain the snow, fade to pink. Has he felt pain? All is still. The sun is higher. He recalls, if dimly, waking at night, seeing a shadow on the bedroom door, rocking gently back and forth—Emilie in Gail's arms, her small head against her mother's breast. The truth, Aaron admits, is that even if Paul were deserving of his children's love, Aaron would probably resent him. He turns, goes inside.

He sucks on his finger, presses down, takes his thumb away and sees that the cut is not deep—a slight crescent, like the hinge of a cuticle, along the right edge of the forefinger. Damn! He puts a Band-Aid over the cut, pours himself more coffee, sits. The cut stings and he knows he should put antiseptic on it, but he does not want to leave his studio; if he stays at his desk and works, he thinks he may, in the silence, be able to retrieve the peace that has been temporarily shattered.

He closes his eyes, sees Lucius smiling at him. Lucius will be waking now, getting ready to go to church. Aaron imagines Lucius throwing off a blanket, stretching his long brown body. Lucius's skin seems somewhat pale to Aaron, as if the gray of morning light has dusted it. There is a small community of blacks in Amherst, descendants, for the most part, of slaves who made their way North in mid-nineteenth century, settled in the area as servants, blacksmiths, carpenters. Some of them were free blacks. Lucius enjoys being in their presence. Lucius believes in God. He believes, quite literally, in the Lord Jesus Christ as Saviour and

Redeemer, and his belief has allowed him to take up Aaron's suggestion:
to move out into the world beyond Aaron's family. He has even written
to Rose and Carrie about his spiritual rebirth, has asked them to forgive
him, to think of coming North when he can afford to send for them.
But how strange, Aaron thinks, given Lucius's life, given the brutality
inflicted upon him by God's world, by whites who profess, too, to believe
in Jesus. God's existence or nonexistence does not much interest Aaron
—it never has—though he does wonder at the ability of someone with a
mind as clear and piercing as Lucius's—a mind at least equal to his own
—to believe and care.

Aaron opens the sliding door, closes it, walks down to the woods. He
turns, sees that the doors to his studio look like silver mirrors. Nothing
moves, yet he is frightened. Why? Given what he has already lost, the
threats he has had to endure, what could happen now that can have the
power to terrify? Still, the question is there: if the dangers from the world
are truly gone, will dangers from within now emerge? Will such dangers
be worse? Are there dangers there—fears—that he has been able
throughout his life to deny, to hide from? He smiles, thinks of how
Susan would enjoy knowing that he thinks this way sometimes. When
she talks with him about the novels she reads and the psychology books
she studies, she argues that of the two sets of dangers human beings are
subject to—those from without and those from within—those from
within are infinitely more terrifying. Precisely because, she says, they
are as infinite and unpredictable as they are mysterious and intangible.
Is it so? The danger now, he supposes, is not to his life or to the lives of
those he loves but to what he has *made* of his life. If one of their children
should die? If their house should burn down? If he or Susan should
become seriously ill?

Such possibilities, when he imagines them, do not scare him. But in
that vague distance he often senses between himself and Susan—that
air with no color, that air that also lies, he knows, in an empty room
near his heart—there is, still, something that disturbs. But what?

"Don't move, mister."

He freezes, his hands moving upward instinctively in a gesture of
surrender. The voice is husky, assured. Why didn't he hear any sounds?
He walked down to the woods because he saw something move. Why,
then, wasn't he more alert?

Warm hands cover his eyes, thumbs against his temples.

"Scared?"

"Yes."

"I'm sorry."

Susan's hands grasp him about the chest, so that he can feel the
length of her body against his own. He turns.

"What are you doing here? I thought you were sleeping."

"Benjamin called. He wanted to come home early."

"Why didn't you tell me?"

"You were working and I didn't want to interrupt. And—"

"And what?"

"And I was afraid that if you went, there might be trouble."

"Tell me."

"That's all." She rests her head against his chest, pushes at his chin with her forehead. "God, your heart is beating so wildly, Aaron!"

"*Tell* me."

"I think I'm scared now too, just listening to your heartbeat. I *am* sorry. I only meant to surprise you. Really."

He kisses her forehead, her eyes, tells her that it's all right. He holds her tightly, realizes that what he sees in the empty chamber near his heart is a vial of poison. He imagines a cutaway drawing of the heart, the vial perched now in the upper left-hand chamber. He imagines Nicky reaching inside, taking the vial down, as if from a shelf. He imagines Nicky giving the vial to Gail. He imagines himself watching Gail as she tilts her head backwards, drinks.

In his dream he is, as ever, able to stand inside dark rooms without fear. But what if, instead of being inside the dark room, the room is somewhere within *him*? He shivers.

"Yes?"

"Sometimes I do get scared," he says. Can he ask her about the room? If there is a dark room inside him somewhere, what could possibly be hiding in it, he wonders, that could cause him more pain than memory can? "I know it's irrational, but sometimes I just get scared that everything is going to be taken away from me. You. The children. Lucius. The house. My work."

"Oh sweetheart!" She reaches up and kisses his chin, touches his eyes with her fingers. "I *am* sorry about—"

"It's as if there's this room down here—" he touches his chest "—and as if some little boy who looks like me enters it with a smile on his face and—"

"Yes?"

"I don't know. Awful things happen, I suppose. But I can't *see* them. All I see is blackness, the boy sliding down a dark tunnel. All I feel is the boy's terror, his heart pounding, bursting—"

Susan smiles. "Men do fear death as children fear to go into the dark, don't they? Even if they're as brave as you are. Your fear's not uncommon." She presses her ear against his chest. He thinks of Ellen, when Gail was pregnant, listening to Emilie's rapid heartbeat. He thinks of Ellen's fingers, moving gently along the planes of his face. He imagines himself leading her through a house—he and Lucius have framed it, put on the roof—and explaining to her why he does the things he does. He sees her feeling the nails and hammers and saws, touching the beams, searching the air where the walls will eventually go. He sees her beside him, in his studio, and he is describing a drawing to her so that she can, inside the dark room of her mind, draw the house that he has imagined. He sees his father, in his bedroom, sitting patiently while he copies a picture of Pee Wee Reese from *Sport* magazine. When he shows the picture to his father, his father smiles in an easy and natural way that is surprising. His father's face seems almost handsome in the half-light that slips in across the fire escape. Half-light, half-life, Aaron thinks. Ellen's desire, without eyes, to see a world she would never see —to know exactly what it was like—was this anything like his desire to imagine a life other than the one he had? He must, as a child, despite Abe, have wanted a different life. It was simply that he didn't believe he would ever know how to get one.

"Do you remember the first time we spent the night together and you grabbed me—the sun was just coming up—and started trembling because, you said, you were frightened of losing me?" Susan asks.

"Yes."

"I think I knew I loved you then—might love you forever—even though I hardly knew you, hardly knew anything about you. You were so amazing as a lover—it just went on and on and on—and then you were suddenly such a vulnerable little boy."

"I suppose."

Susan's body, against his own, is warm. He strokes her hair. He remembers sitting with Tony on the cold hard step in front of his building on Martense Street. He wonders: would Tony believe that Aaron is now living within the life the two of them dreamt of that night so many years ago?

"Can we go inside?" Susan asks. "I'm starting to get cold."

"Would you tell me about Paul and Benjamin?"

They walk toward the house, holding hands.

"There's not much to tell. I went and took care of things and then I came back here. I was upset, I guess, but I didn't want to worry you. I wanted to think things through by myself first. So instead of going to you I came down here to walk it off, to be alone for a while."

"Is Benjamin upstairs?"

"No. By the time I got there, in fact, I think Ben was sorry he'd called. He didn't want to admit he'd needed to do so. You know Ben—he hates to admit he ever needs anything or anybody. But it did scare me some."

"What scared you?" Aaron stops. "Paul?"

"No. Paul is Paul. Harmless. Childish. I was scared of *Benjamin*. Of what to do about his anger." She shakes her head, as if to clear it. "Okay." She exhales. "Paul claims that Benjamin tried to kill him—to strangle him."

"Maybe he had cause," Aaron says, and as he does—the words surprise him—something eases in his chest. He puts his arm around Susan.

"*What?*"

"I don't buy the business about Paul being harmless and childish. The man is disturbed. The man likes to prey on—"

"Maybe he had cause," Susan repeats. She begins to pull away, then relaxes. "Good Lord," she says, her hand to her mouth as if to keep herself from giggling. "You may be right, Levin. Do you know that?"

"The boy has good instincts. I've always said so."

"I don't disagree."

"Do you agree with what Lucius claims, though—that Paul is *evil?* That the children shouldn't be there at all?"

"No." She clicks her tongue. "Lucius. Lucius is very much into evil these days. It's become his favorite word. If I believed Lucius, then I—"

"Okay. Tell me the rest."

"Paul took me aside and said that Benjamin had set his alarm clock— it was what woke Paul—and had tiptoed into his bedroom. When Paul opened his eyes Benjamin had his hands on Paul's throat."

"You believe him?"

"Partly. I mean, Ben does have an amazing temper."

"When provoked." Aaron shakes his head. "If he wanted to kill Paul he could have gone into the kitchen and borrowed a knife. Listen. Ben's a smart boy. He knows Paul is too strong for him."

Aaron opens the sliding door. They enter his studio. Susan shakes off her jacket, sets it on top of a filing cabinet.

"Did Ben tell you what he was so angry about?"

"On the phone he said something about Paul wanting him to dance with him and Jen and Debbie, Paul threatening to send Benjamin home if he wouldn't." Susan sits on Aaron's stool, studies his drawing for a few seconds, then looks up. Aaron sees that her eyes are moist. "Do you know what he said, Aaron? He said that Paul threatened to give him up if Ben wouldn't do the things Paul wanted him to. Same old Paul—he threatened to send Ben back to our house, to force him to live with me full-time. 'But he can't *make* me,' Ben said."

"Can't make him *dance* with them?"

"Can't make him leave." Susan bites on her lower lip, gestures to Aaron to come to her. She takes his hands in hers, kisses the knuckles on Aaron's right hand, bites lightly on the stubs of his missing fingers. "Why does that move me so, his saying that?"

"Because Benjamin is Paul's son, but he's stronger than Paul. Because Ben would never reject Paul the way Paul rejects him."

"He'll only try to kill him, is that it?"

"Maybe."

"Oh Aaron, you *are* a smart man." She wipes tears from her eyes. "Only it's just so hard to know what to do sometimes, with Ben. I try to leave him alone, to let him find his own way, but there's something about him—do you mind my saying it—that reminds me of Paul, and—" She stops, rests her head against Aaron's chest again. "I get confused, sweetheart. Sometimes I get confused. About Jen too. Will you tell me why I was so lucky, after Paul, to have found a man like you—a good man, with a good heart—who's so patient with me, with *all* my children? Who understands them so well? What can I do, though? If I forbid them to go there, that may only make the idea more attractive and—"

"And what?"

"And Paul will always find ways to get to them. When he's determined to have his way, he's just like—"

"Me?"

"No. Like Benjamin is what I was going to say."

She walks to the window. Aaron imagines tender shoots of grass being pressed down beneath their shoes, beneath the thin layer of snow. He imagines the snow melting, the grass bending upwards.

"Like you too, I suppose." She talks without looking at him. "I know what the right answer is. The right answer is that I have to trust the children to figure these things out for themselves. Still, I don't think it would hurt to talk with them later, to let them know I'm worried, to let them know it's all right with me if they choose not to see their father." She turns, faces him. Her voice is warm. "You're very happy when you're here by yourself, aren't you?"

"Yes." He smiles. "Happier than I ever expected to be, in this life."

"In this life." She walks around his drafting table, touches the back of his neck, ruffles his hair. He wonders how it was that, in the cold morning air, her fingers were warm. He imagines her sitting at the base of a tree, thinking about Benjamin and Jennifer. He sees her with her hands tucked between her legs. He thinks of Nicky, in Ohio, sitting on the lawn in front of the tents, singing. *You like being a father, don't you?*

"I like talking with you about the children," Susan says. "In addition to being smart, you have good sense, Levin. Did anyone ever tell you that?"

"Yes."

"Sometimes I forget that you're not their real father. Does that bother you still—that they're Paul's?"

"No," he says quickly. *Too* quickly? He shrugs. "What bothers me is Paul."

"And sometimes I forget about your childhood—that would explain it, wouldn't it?—that you weren't raised by a mother and father."

"I suppose."

She asks if he will show her what he was doing when he interrupted his work to go down to the woods. She says that it makes her feel peaceful—it did this morning—to know that he is here, doing the work he loves. Aaron lays a perspective grid over his drawing, to check proportions, and explains to Susan that in the books they teach you to make your grids on the thicker paper and to lay the drawing on top, on tracing paper or transparent vellum, enabling you to see through *to* the grid, to transfer the drawing to thicker paper later on if necessary, but that he can't work this way. There are so many different ways of seeing any house, any one room, so many different ways of drawing them, he says —floor plans, orthographic projections, paraline drawings, exterior elevations, section drawings, perspective drawings, shaded drawings—so many ways of making one's way into any house, into any room, that he often, as earlier, becomes lost in possibility. The children like the shaded drawings best—they seem more *real* to them—but Aaron prefers the simpler line drawings.

Drawings, he believes, should not reproduce the world but should, instead, imagine it into being. He wonders: are there more ways of seeing a house—of imagining one—than of living in one? Does Susan sense that this has been behind his reluctance to build his own home? Susan's hands are on his shoulders. She kisses the back of his neck. He imagines that Ellen is standing where Susan is, that he is taking Ellen's hand, guiding it so that she can touch the paper and trace, with a finger, the lines Aaron has drawn.

"I was thinking," she offers. "If you don't want to look at the land later, it's all right with me. Lucius will be here in about an hour, for his session with me—before church—but if—"

"We can look at the land." Aaron pauses, laughs lightly. "We may not buy—not ever—but we can look."

"Oh Aaron—do you know how much you please me still, and that I really don't, as with buying the land, want to take anything *away* from you?"

"I didn't say you did. I said that I'm just scared things will *be* taken away—"

"Shh. Don't get upset."

Her right hand slips down, inside his shirt. She unbuttons the top three buttons of his shirt, rubs his chest and shoulders slowly.

"I love you," she says. "Can we play here, do you think? You won't be angry? Or I could just stand at the door and watch you work. I could stare at your shoulders, drink in your peacefulness, your strange intensity." She touches his belt buckle. "Or . . ."

He does not want to turn and face her. Although he loves being touched, he wonders how it is that she can be so gentle with him—so in love with him when he has withheld so much from her? He looks down at his drawing, at the white space between the second floor landing and the missing stairs. He tries to stare through the whiteness into the vastness beyond, into all that time and space which is his own life, into a past to which the only bridge, he knows, is memory and pain.

Sometimes, as now, he feels that his second life—all the years that have passed since he left Brooklyn, along with all the years to come—will only prove to be a rumination on his first life. Will he ever be able to talk with Susan about such feelings without destroying the life they actually have? Why is it so, he wonders—that truth sometimes has the potential to destroy, while lies can save?

She untucks his shirt. He asks if they have time and she says that she is a practical woman: the boys will watch cartoons when they wake, she has locked the door, Lucius will not arrive for an hour. He touches her hair, kisses her mouth. She licks his lips slowly, as if drawing them with her tongue. She undoes his belt buckle. He is astonished at how much he desires her, at how wonderful it is to feel her hands move across his body, to have her undress him. He lets her guide him. He lies on the floor, face down, rests his cheek against the beige carpeting, and a second later she is lying on top of him, rubbing her breasts across his back. She rises and falls, rolls from one side to the other, and he floats, finds himself entering a region of his memory which, now that he can dwell in it again, surprises him by the fact of its existence. Are the woods still? He thinks of a dead limb, high on a silver maple, imagines it cracking, falling. Silver maples are very brittle. He wonders why it is that it matters to him so much—that it still thrills him after all their years together—that she is such a beautiful woman.

He smiles, hears his father's voice. *Do you know how come I know I'm the smartest man in the world?*

Susan is breathing hard, caressing him without stop, licking him along the neck, along his backbone, along his buttocks, down along the insides of his thighs. She asks him if he likes playing in his workroom. He says nothing. He knows that she frightens him a bit when she gets like this because he cannot make sense of the strange mixture in her of woman and child. But wasn't that mixture—of man and boy—what she said she loves so about him? She nibbles at his toes, sucks, bites at his ankles, then begins to move upwards again, hands and mouth at him constantly, lightly. He thinks of her as she was the first time he saw her: at

the Three County Fairgrounds, buying cotton candy for Benjamin and
Jennifer. She reaches below, and when she moans he hears, a second
later, a strange involuntary sound, somewhat higher-pitched, come
from his own throat. It was a brutally hot day and it was, he thinks now,
something about her very exhaustion that drew him to her, made him
bold enough to start a conversation.

Both yours?

They're not yours, mister.

Her voice was abrupt and hard—like a man's voice, he thinks; like the
voice in the woods—as if because of her beauty she was used to replying
this way to men who started conversations with her. The strange thing,
though, is that in his memory now her voice sounds like Nicky's, when
Nicky would try to act tough.

She runs her tongue along his waist in a slight upwards curve, from
left to right. She asks him what he likes best, what she can do for him.

"Are you sure we're married?" she asks.

She mounts him, slides down slowly, golden hair falling onto his face.
He grabs at her hair, circles a strand with each hand, as if coiling rope,
tugs until he knows, from her sweet whimpering, that he is hurting her
just enough to please her.

He is crying. Why?

"Are you all right?" she asks.

She has been asleep, her head on his shoulder. He has been floating
through space—feet forward, body horizontal, as if in a state of levita-
tion. He has been gliding through white rooms whose walls seem to
move sideways, the rooms expanding as he enters them, as if perspective
has been reversed and the vanishing point is behind his head.

"I don't know."

She rises onto an elbow, kisses his eyes, his mouth, his chin. "Happy
families are not all alike, or all dull," she says. "Not this one. We're
entitled, Aaron. We've paid our price."

"I suppose."

"Talk to me, Aaron. Please? Tell me why you get the way you do—
not the tears and not what you say, but that other look—the distant
one, the blank one. Sometimes I feel there's just so much of you I can
never get close to, that I'll never know about. Tell me why you were
frightened earlier. What scares you so, sweetheart?"

He swallows, touches her cheek, remembers the feel of Emilie's skin.
He sees Abe's smile, hears Abe telling him that if you were born, like it
or not, there was an admission price. Susan licks his cheeks, his eyes,
the creases around his mouth.

"You're like a woman sometimes, aren't you—the way you're affected by our love-making." She kisses the hair on his chest. "When Paul came back into our lives I was frightened for a while that it might sour things. I was frightened that his presence might make you reject me. I kept feeling you wanted to know all the details of my life with him so that you'd have *reason* to reject me. When I first met you—I can tell you now—I was scared that no man would *ever* love me again after all I'd done with Paul, all the crazy things he got me to do."

Aaron imagines himself leaning on the railing at the five-eighths pole. Abe is beside him, dressed in white—white shoes, white slacks, white shirt, white hat—smiling. God but he loved the man! He sees Abe move off, start a conversation with a young woman. The woman tilts her head, enjoys being charmed.

Why had he loved Abe so? Aaron wants to smile, hearing the question again, but does not. Why, when he was a boy, had he loved Abe more than anyone in the world? In the past, when the question has come, he has usually found himself imagining his father's face, his father's bad eye, and himself, as a boy, wishing that his father could be more like Abe, more of a man. But what he senses now is that when he was a boy what he really felt when he looked at Abe—when he tried to do something that would please Abe—was a desire to change him. If only he could have loved Abe enough, he must have felt, he could have made him less hard, less severe! If only he could have loved Abe enough, the tenderness he sometimes saw in Abe's eyes might not have disappeared! If only he had loved Abe enough, the good and sweet man he knew was there might have shown himself more, might have lived, might have believed it was possible to have lives other than the one he had!

What he wanted, he realizes, was to be able, with his love, to cause the sweetness that was there for him occasionally—in the way Abe would smile, or ruffle his hair, or ask to see his drawings, or tell him a story—to linger and spread. Was it because he believed, as a boy, that his love was inadequate—that it could never change Abe or Abe's life— that he was afraid, except indirectly, to show his love, that he never allowed himself to know just how much he had cared?

"You had choices," Aaron says to Susan. "You could have refused."

"Oh Aaron, I was so *young*—and I did love him. He was a wonderful man in many ways and—" She sits up. "Then you *are* still jealous. You do still disapprove, don't you?"

"I don't know." He blinks. Abe is gone. "No. Not when I think about it. If you hadn't known Paul you wouldn't be the person you are. You wouldn't be the woman I fell in love with. I've thought about that: if I love you, then I love the history you bring with you."

"Too easy." She lies down again. "I'll accept the answer for now, though. I'll try to believe that you *want* to believe what you say and that maybe if you want to enough, you'll come to feel—"

"Stop."

"Are you afraid that I'm still the same woman who once loved him?"

"Maybe."

"Sure you are. And if I am, then what about you, Aaron? If you're afraid of that in me, what are you afraid of that's analogous in yourself? You chose me, after all, knowing about Paul. I mean, if I chose a man like that once upon a time, what was *wrong* with me? What *might* be wrong with Benjamin and Jennifer? What might still *be* wrong—?"

He looks toward the glass door, toward the grass and the snow and the woods. He is certain now that Paul, voice muffled by handkerchief, has made some of the threatening phone calls. But why? Merely to frighten Aaron? If he were in Brooklyn, he thinks, he could have one of the guys —Lefty or Monk—tap into the lines easily enough, trace the calls.

"How much time until Lucius comes?"

"We're all right," Susan says. "We'll hear the children. They'll knock first. The door is locked. Lucius will entertain them. You have your clothes. I have mine. Don't move yet, all right? Listen to what I really think, Aaron. Sometimes, sweetheart—sometimes I feel you're angry with me not for anything I've said or done but for being who I was when neither of us knew the other even existed. Sometimes I feel what you really want is for me to *justify* all those years, and it occurs to me, happy as I am, that I'll be damned if—"

"Shh." He kisses her forehead. It's just that I never expected to be this happy, he wants to say. To have a home, children, a wife. If we're distrustful of others, he imagines her saying next, as she has before, it's usually because we don't trust ourselves. It hurts to realize that they will have no choice but to leave one another in a few minutes. He wishes he could hold to her forever. "Do you ever miss things before they're gone?" he asks.

"Before they're gone? I don't understand."

"Sometimes when I look at Carl or Larry my stomach sinks, feeling their future absence, imagining them at eighteen or twenty or twenty-five—"

"Early loss," she says. She touches his mouth with two fingers. "I was reading a book about orphans last week—I almost drove out to the house where you and Lucius were, just to tell you—and one of the orphans—they're all grown men, older than you, and they have re-unions, play touch football together—one of them says that the home they grew up in ruined them all somehow for adult life. 'We gave one another things families don't give to each other anymore,' he says." She sits up, begins to dress. "Is it so, Aaron? When your eyes cloud over and begin to move backwards inside you, do you feel the same way? Are you remembering some life you used to wish you had? Or resenting the life I had when I didn't know you existed? Talk to me about what it was like for you, Aaron. Was it like that—like what the man in the book says?"

"I suppose. I don't know. It's hard to think that far back."

"You don't talk much about the home anymore, the way you did when we first met. The children say you still tell them stories from time to time, but they wonder why you don't have any friends from back then, why—"

"I'm worried about Lucius," Aaron says. "He seems different lately. Have you noticed?"

"No. What I notice is that you've just changed the subject."

"I was thinking about friends—about Lucius, about friends I lost." He shrugs, begins to dress. He says that the only thing he can figure is that something in Lucius seemed to shift a month or so ago, at about the time Malcolm X was killed. Does that sound crazy? Lucius was never a fan of Malcolm or the Muslims, yet he seemed very upset about it— about the idea of yet another killing, this time up North, this time with blacks killing blacks.

Susan asks if he has tried asking Lucius what's bothering him. She says that Lucius loves and admires Aaron very much. She suggests that Lucius may be withdrawn precisely because he wants Aaron to ask him the questions Aaron is asking Susan.

She kisses him, goes to the door. She nods to herself. She should do the same, she says. About Jennifer. She had been about to ask Aaron's advice but realizes that what she will do is ask Jennifer the questions she was going to ask Aaron. She has been finding notes on Jennifer's desk that are addressed to boys. They are wildly pornographic and Susan cannot tell if Jennifer is actually doing the things she writes about, or fantasizing about them. She wonders if Debbie has been filling Jennifer's ears with stories of her wild life in New York when she was Jen's age, of all the dope and sex she and her friends were into at their fancy private schools. Is Jennifer leaving the notes so that Susan will find them, will ask about them? Is Paul getting Debbie to talk to Jennifer . . . ?

When Aaron turns, to answer her, to suggest that she talk to Jennifer —draw her out the way Susan suggested he draw Lucius out—she is gone.

He closes his eyes, thinks of going to the window with Susan and the children. Aaron never agreed with Malcolm's politics, but he liked the man—he liked to watch the fire in Malcolm's eyes, the quick light that showed forth the mind within. Now that mind is gone. Aaron opens his eyes. He will talk with Lucius about Malcolm the next time he sees him. He thinks of their last talk, five days before, at Paul's house.

When they arrived there was only an hour of daylight left. They carried two forty-foot ladders from the van, extended them, raised them to roof level, steadied them. They took the old wood rain gutter Aaron bought the week before, from the owner of a house being torn down in South Hadley, and attached metal hangers while the gutter was on the ground. The gutter was beautifully channeled, still thick enough in the channel to serve for many years. They called instructions to each other across the length of the house. When Aaron laid a dab of roofing cement onto the tin roof, then banged nails through the hanger and covered the nails with another dab of cement, Lucius did the same at his end. The gutter sagged in the middle, swayed. Aaron moved a step down, tested the gutter, looked up at the cornice—the eaves, fascia, soffit— called across and asked Lucius if, given their mutual dislike of Paul, they might call the work they were doing for him sheer soffitsry. Lucius groaned. They descended, moved each ladder in ten feet, mounted again, nailed in the next set of hangers.

There was no car in the driveway. Paul and Debbie were supposedly in London, but according to Benjamin they had gone there so that Paul could get a flight to Havana. Paul had confided in Benjamin, but Aaron figured that he did so knowing that Benjamin would not keep his secret. It was all the same to Aaron. Mostly he was pleased that the renovations were near an end, that the house was deserted. The less he had to do with the man, the better. The day was mild, the roofing cement soft. Aaron made sure the gutter sloped slightly toward Lucius's end. Perhaps, he thought, what Paul claimed—that he wanted a new and good family life like the kind Aaron and Susan had—was true. Who could tell? Aaron had stopped trying to figure the man out. He only hoped Paul would become as tired of his new life—in which he seemed to be half-revolutionary, half gentleman-farmer—as he had of those lives that preceded it.

The second set of hangers nailed in, Aaron moved down two rungs, glanced into the upstairs window. Paul was there, grinning, pointing a rifle at him. Aaron lurched backwards, grabbed onto the rails, felt his heart thump wildly against his chest. Paul lowered the rifle, gave a half-wave, left the room. Lucius called across, asked him what was up, cursed when Aaron caught his breath, told him. They descended, moved the ladders again, mounted, nailed in the last set of hangers, and then, at the north end, installed an aluminum elbow, a downspout, metal straps to hold the downspout to the building. Lucius tried to get Aaron to talk about Paul—about what they should do—but Aaron said that the only thing he wanted to do was finish the job and leave.

"Hey," Lucius said as they jerked on the ropes that let the ladders collapse to half their lengths. "You'd best calm down or you gonna make that man too happy."

"Happy?"

"To see how he can get to you, slide under your skin—"

Lucius set his hand on Aaron's shoulder, firmly, and when he did, Aaron felt his heart ease.

"Let's move," Aaron said.

Daylight was almost gone, the sky a lovely blend of pink and blue and lavender, the Berkshires themselves a soft, deep purple, the breeze transforming clouds into crisscrossing streaks, like jet streams. Aaron and Lucius carried the ladders to the van. Paul was waiting there for them, and he began talking at once about Malcolm's death, telling Lucius that if he were black he would have agreed with Malcolm.

"I wouldn't want coffee at any white man's lunch counter," Paul said, then corrected himself. "Well. I might want the coffee, but if I drank it, I'd want the pot and the counter and the chairs and the whole god-damned store too. How about you?"

"I want to get home," Lucius said. "Want to get somewhere where the air smells right."

"Ah Lucius," Paul said. "I wish you could learn to trust me more. I want to be your friend, don't you see?"

"Got enough friends," Lucius said.

"What a friend you have in Jesus, is that it?"

"Lay off," Aaron said, and he moved toward Paul. "I'm warning you."

"You and what army?" Paul asked, and the rifle was suddenly in his hands, aimed for Aaron's chest.

"Take it easy," Lucius said to Aaron. He turned to Paul. "You leave off, you hear? You don't start what you can't finish."

"Why are you here?" Aaron asked. "Why did you come back?"

"Do I have to report"—he gestured to Lucius—"the way he does?"

"You talking bullshit," Lucius said. "You making the flowers grow."

"Sure," Paul said. "Planting them row by row, Lucius. But if I were Malcolm—may I tell you this?—I'd be watering them with lots of white man's blood, in *my* dreams. Did I ever tell you the story my father told me, about how in this one camp during the war the Germans went crazy because blood started seeping upwards from the soil, bursting through like swamp water? They were forced to dig up the land all over again. My father told me the story when I was seven or eight and I've always thought that would have been marvelous—to see the land bleed, to have to plant death deeper." He let the rifle drop so that the barrel grazed the ground. "You *are* aware of the camps they've set up for you—?"

"I don't know nothing," Lucius said, "except that your fool tongue don't know when to stop moving."

Aaron and Lucius secured the ladders to the van's roof.

"Where's Debbie?" Aaron asked.

"In London. I had to return early, on business. She's four months pregnant, you know." He lifted the rifle, patted the butt end, then smiled. "I'm sorry if I scared you before, but given the dark road and how isolated the house is—given the strangers passing through, the family I'm responsible for—Jen and Ben, the new child to come—I can't afford to take chances. I need to be ready at all times. I—"

"Who's paying you?" Lucius asked. "Come on, man. Tell the truth— who's *paying* you?"

Paul raised the rifle, the barrel pointed to the sky. A door opened behind them. The three men turned, watched a stocky black man walk from the house to the barn, a rifle in each hand. Aaron tensed—afraid the man might change direction, come toward them—and he realized that in Paul's presence he was, as always, tight, wary, frightened. It was not only, he sensed, because he was reminded that somebody somewhere might connect him to his former life—might unexpectedly emerge *from* it—but because, quite simply, more and more with the years, he preferred life when it was predictable. As much as he was rarely able, as a boy, to imagine scenes before they took place, so now, as an adult, he disliked finding himself inside situations which he had not previously imagined.

"The difference between you and me," Paul offered, "is that I don't fool myself about why I do what I do. Self-interest can be a very firm basis for trust, don't you think?"

"What I think is that it's time to go."

"Yet you and me, we're more alike than you think—than you *like* to think," Paul continued. "Certainly more like one another than you and your black brother here. Why should a black man ever trust a white man in this country? If you were black, would you?" Paul grinned, the way he had earlier, through the upstairs window. "Then too, think of all we have in common, Aaron. Think of Ben and Jen. Think of the times you visited me when I was ill. Think of what we've survived. Think of our houses. Think of Susan—"

Aaron did not react. He opened the door to the van, got into the driver's seat. Paul talked to Lucius about the detention camps the government had set up for blacks in Arizona and Nevada—like those they had used for the Japanese during World War II. Had Lucius seen photos? Paul laughed, suggested that Lucius ask Susan to teach him about the camps during their tutorial sessions. For his part, he said, pointing to the house, he would continue to run his own Upward Bound program. Only his sessions, he imagined, were more practical, less personal. Lucius got in the van, slammed the door. He said that he used to think that Paul was crazy but that he had changed his mind. Paul wasn't crazy. He was just plain stupid.

Paul leaned in on Lucius's open window, said that he hoped he hadn't offended, but given what his daily life was like—the company he kept—he probably enjoyed talking with them more than he liked to acknowledge. Who else could he talk to in this way? He told them not to be strangers, to visit him again soon. He told Lucius that he was serious about Malcolm, about how, if he were black, he wouldn't want ever to beg for what should rightfully be his. Malcolm was right. Why the hell should any black man want to be integrated into a burning house?

What bothers Aaron most, he now realizes, is that in some crazy way, all the while they'd been standing there, outside his barn, Paul had been reminding him of Abe. Paul was about Abe's height, had Abe's build. He was about the same age Abe was when Abe had died.

Your Uncle Abe is coming home, darling. He's coming home now. Everything will be all right.

Aaron imagines Lucius on Paul's roof, looking at the chimney. He imagines one of the bricks falling away, an eye looking out from inside —a woman's eye—and Lucius terrified, tumbling backwards into air. He wonders how many others there are in Paul's house, and if they come out at night from their secret places—from the cellar, from the same narrow rooms beside the chimney where slaves hid a hundred years before. Could he talk with Susan about his feelings, about how Paul always seems able to get to him, to surprise him? The truth, he knows, is that he has sometimes found himself wishing he could be a bit more like Paul—a bit less absolute, a bit less moral—for as much as he despises the man, he can understand why, if he were a woman, he might be attracted to him. He can sense why it might seem exciting, in prospect, to think of being loved and protected by a man who believed that there was no such thing as morality—that you were allowed to do anything you wanted to, that you actually took on power by rejecting society's rules and substituting your own.

In the early years of his marriage to Susan, he recalls, he was afraid to admit to her that he was confused by the fact that he himself found Paul attractive—that he liked being near the man, liked hearing him dispense his theories—and that he often felt that women would find Paul more attractive than they would ever find him.

He smiles. He sees himself standing by Abe's front door, hoping that Abe will notice him—hoping that Abe will bend down, will take him in his arms, will hold him and comfort him and talk to him.

Are you still my boy? Are you still my favorite little guy?

He can recall, that first winter after the war, walking with Abe on Flatbush Avenue and meeting some of his friends, feeling their envy. He can recall how wonderful he felt whenever Abe tossed him in the air or ruffled his hair or played ball with him or admired his drawings. He can recall, when Abe touched him, believing that Abe's strength could somehow pass out of Abe's body and into his own.

Aaron stares at the woods and feels that he is a blind man about to be led through a garden. He knows that he would like to believe that Paul is merely a sick and weak-willed version of Abe. But what if he is not? What if he is as shrewd and canny as he seems while also being sincere in his efforts to aid the Movement, to hide fugitives? What if Lucius is right about what he said to Aaron afterwards—about the need, still, for Aaron to loosen up, to be less pure? Lucius may have hated Paul as much as Aaron did—still, on the ride home he seemed surly, distant, disturbed by Paul's words, by Paul's reminding him of what Malcolm had taught, of what it meant to be black in America.

Aaron recalls sitting in the garden with Ellen, on the stone bench. He can see Gail and her father coming from the house, moving toward him. He wonders what Benjamin and Jennifer will feel when Debbie's child comes: happy? rejected? angry? confused? He thinks of riding in the car, the children asleep, Susan beside him, her head on his shoulder. He thinks of them with their four children, and then he thinks of them with three, with two, with one, with none. Susan loves the time they spend together as a family, but she misses having long stretches of time alone—she misses having time for just the two of them. They have never had that luxury. She often thinks of herself as having three distinct lives, she says: life before children, life with children, life after children. She thinks it will be interesting to see what they will be like, just the two of them, without the constant presence of others, without the intense family life they have shared for all their years together.

Aaron finds himself wishing that he could tell Lucius what his childhood was like—that he could take Lucius back with him, into his apartment on Martense Street and along Flatbush Avenue and into the Erasmus gym. If he had fewer secrets to keep from Lucius, would Lucius be less likely to listen to Paul? Aaron lifts a pencil, rubs the point against his index finger, gently. Why is it, he wonders, that his first life often seems to him a continuous line while his life in the years since seems to be made of fragments? Do most other people see their childhoods in this way—as consecutive, continuous, whole? He floats, as if in warm haze, as if it is summer. He thinks of long days spent in the Holy Cross schoolyard, his ass on concrete, his back against the chain-link fence, Tony or Morty or Julie beside him. He sees himself sipping a Coke, slipping the bottle through the fence to a kid even younger than himself—the kid running off to get the deposit money—waiting for his nexts, talking about the Dodgers or the Knicks, watching the older guys play—Al Roth, Johnny "Red" Lee, Heshy Weiss—wondering if he will ever be as good as them. He recalls his mother asking if she ever wanted more than that they should be a real family together, the three of them, with no secrets.

He can hear Paul laughing at him, asking him why he thinks nonviolence and love will change the world, and when he does he finds that he is clenching his fists, that this time he is seeing his mother's smile—not Abe's. He is seeing her laughing at his father, mocking him.

I mean, is he helpless or is he helpless?

Is Lucius right? Lucius believes that the F.B.I. has something on Paul, knows about his operations, may even be paying him to hide fugitives so that they can keep tabs on them, pick and choose when they want to hang somebody in the wind. Lucius knew enough men like Paul in prison—men who would do anything to save their own skins, who would simply work for whoever bought the bread. Aaron remembers Paul saying that his father used to say something in Yiddish about love being sweet but tasting best with bread—does Aaron know the expression?—but that for the places where Paul has to travel he has invented a variation: revolution is sweet but tastes best with tacos.

Aaron imagines that it is night and that Lucius is waiting inside Paul's house, guns and ammunition at his side. Paul is on the highway, heading for safety. Full moons of yellow light float waist-high across Paul's lawn, police cars closing in. The problem, Aaron decides, is that once you set your imagination free—once you begin to let it imagine *possible* futures—there seems no way to stop your imagination from *being* free.

He remembers Susan's hands, on his eyes, in the woods. He thinks of how cold the plate glass of his sliding doors would be against his back. He looks at the lawn, the patches of snow, and he imagines Martin Luther King and Malcolm X leading one another through the rubble of a bombed-out city—one of them is blind and one of them is deaf and they walk one behind the other, the blind man's hand on the deaf man's shoulder. They are dressed, as always, in dark business suits. He recalls watching boys play baseball in the field behind the Elkton Fancy Diner. He hears a car, imagines Susan opening the door, stepping outside, greeting Lucius. The trouble with blacks like Lucius, Paul claims, is that they are too religious when they need to be more political. The trouble with their Movement is that it is essentially *spiritual* at its core. They dream of salvation in *this* world when their history and religion should teach them to act and believe and hope otherwise. Aaron sees Malcolm and Martin move from the edge of the city, out into the desert. Then the image fades, bit by bit. Which one is blind? Which deaf? Aaron turns, goes to his desk.

14

PURPLE CROCUS tipped with snow. The first week in May, and in the hills of Leverett there has been a light snowfall during the night. The previous week the weather was unseasonably warm and muggy, as if, Aaron thinks, August were lost, wandering through winter. He crouches down but does not touch the flower; under the snow its veined petals curl inward at the top. In the early morning light—in his memory —the flower seems to be made of thick glass stained a wonderful deep purple that is more blue than red, the little cap of snow perched upon it like a drop of liquid porcelain that has spread, thinned, begun to harden. When the sun rises, though, above the line of birch and maple and pine to the east, the white will dissolve and disappear, the flower will open, will reveal the deeper violet within, the soft vertical yellow streaks, the little upright threads that tell its sex. The glass will—in his mind, to his touch—thin to satin. With both hands he grasps the smooth plank on which he sits, feels its grain. He closes his eyes, listens to the pleasant sound of feet pounding on hardwood. He is, he realizes, happy, and it surprises him—pleases—that at his age this can be so. In less than half a year he will be thirty-four years old.

Susan's house. Why, though he designed it and built it and owns it, does he continue to think of it as Susan's house? Is it because he likes adding to it little by little, year by year—because he likes having her think of it, still, as his gift to her? Is it because he is reluctant to admit that he loves it as much as she does—loves especially, he knows, the idea of its being, after three years, unfinished—so that, as with their life together, he can continue to make it, to change it?

Or is the reason simpler: does he continue to think of it as Susan's house because he does not like to admit what she admits—that time is passing, that they are getting older. In three months Susan will be thirty-seven years old. A hand moves through his mind, palming the meadow as if it is velvet, transforming its green from lime to emerald. He thinks of the meadow in winter—as it was this morning: a white field fringed by forest, with here and there a spot of color—evergreens and birch and mountain laurel; tan cedar shakes on the house's roof; Delft-blue curtains in the kitchen window; copper lantern beside the door; a flash of color—brown, red, yellow—as a bird careens across the meadow.

He watches Lucius, who fakes to the left, slips under the backboard, takes a pass, gives it right back and pivots, in place for the rebound. He thinks of Lucius in the van, beside him, and of the snow that surrounded them as they drove home four years before, down from the hills of Conway and Ashfield, across the flat plain of Hatfield, on the day Paul came back into Susan's life, into Benjamin and Jennifer's life. He sees the dome of snow, hazy and infinite. Are the years like that too—his years—lost in white? The meadow in front of Susan's house stretches away, but not forever. The trees form a dark border to it, on three sides. The sky above is pale, washed out, ice-blue. Cerulean. He recalls seeing the word on a tube of paint once, in the art store on Church Avenue. How magical the words were! Cerulean blue. Vermilion red. Burnt sienna. Yellow ochre. Cadmium orange.

He does think of the years as being like that, doesn't he—like spots of color in an endless white landscape. Yet when he thinks of his child-hood, as he does with greater and greater ease lately, he never thinks of white unless he is thinking of blank paper, of his old bedroom, his drawings. He sees, instead, paint squeezed from tubes, bright-colored oil flowing in glossy streams, converging to thick masses of dull brown and gray-black and muddy green. Olive drab. He sees the soiled Army jacket Abe liked to wear on weekends when the two of them would go to the Parade Grounds together to play ball. The jacket fades, threads floating in wind, fraying to air. Curious. If he thinks of these years—before he reached high school—he finds that he has to search for white-ness, for those times when, if ever, emptiness and space existed, for the times when there were expanses of no color: of calm, of peace. To mark the passing of time during those years—to date things—he has to con-centrate, and even when he does he finds that it is not always easy to reconstruct sequences, to determine how old he was when particular events occurred.

The easy way to fix things in time is to link events in his life to events in sports. The dates of particular baseball games, the years the Knicks or the Dodgers won championships, the times favorite players per-

formed spectacular feats—these allow him, with some certainty, to figure out when things happened. He was ten when George "Snuffy"
Stirnweiss of the Yankees won the American League batting championship with the lowest average ever: .309. He was eleven when Jackie
Robinson signed to play with the Montreal Royals and twelve when
Jackie came to the Dodgers. He was a month past his thirteenth birthday
when Cookie Lavagetto ruined Bill Bevens's no-hitter in the bottom
of the ninth with a line drive off the right-center-field wall at Ebbets
Field. . . .

Now he finds that he often marks the passing of time—measures his
life—by each change in Susan's house. He was at the house this morning, awake before sunrise, before Susan and the children began their
day, to haul beams there for the greenhouse he plans to build. He wants
to go back later today, while there is still light and the ground has
thawed, to begin staking out the plot, clearing some trees and shrubs,
figuring exactly where, on the southeast side of the kitchen, he will cut
into the wall. He loves being out in the woods by himself, cutting trees
with his chain saw, letting his mind drift. It drifts, he realizes, the way it
would when, as a boy, he would be riding the subways, nodding off to
sleep, his head bobbing to the irregular lurchings, the rumblings. Susan
worries about him when he is in the woods alone. He doesn't, she warns,
have many fingers to spare.

If possible, he wants to have the greenhouse finished in time for
Jennifer's graduation from high school. That gives him seven weeks. He
would like her party to be at Susan's house. He imagines the greenhouse
filled with flowers, bursting with color. He sees himself at the breakfast
table with Susan—the children are all gone—and they are happy because while they eat and gaze out through the greenhouse at the white
meadow beyond, they are gazing through layers of color: through glossy
green leaves, frilly hanging ferns, baskets of fuchsia, flats and containers
of violets and spices, tea roses and lilies and chrysanthemums. Seven
weeks. In seven weeks Jennifer will graduate from high school, Benjamin will complete his junior year. In seven weeks Carl and Larry will be
preparing to go off to a sleep-away camp in Vermont.

To have the textures and colors of flowers there, between him and the
world, pleases Aaron, mutes the passing of time somehow. But why? To
be able to go from his kitchen directly to the greenhouse, to feel the
sun's distant heat in midwinter, to put his hands into warm earth when
the earth beyond home and glass is frozen, when the world behind him
—his life with Susan—is whole: this comforts him. She was right, he
thinks, to insist on building the house so that they could have a place to
go to whenever one of them wanted to be alone. In the meantime, she
argued, they could rent the house, he could use it to show prospective

clients the quality of his work, they could camp there with the children in the summer, they could use it as a guest house. . . .

Jennifer has a summer job in West Yarmouth, on the Cape, as a waitress. Benjamin has a job at a camp near Pittsfield as a counselor. For the first time in their eleven years of married life, Aaron and Susan will be together without children for four entire weeks—until Carl and Larry return—and she has been teasing him: is he frightened of being alone with her? And just before the first of those four weeks, Aaron thinks, Lucius and Louise will be married.

He nudges Louise, lifts her hand. "Some rock," he says.

"Sometimes Lucius knows how to do the appropriate thing," Louise says. She speaks, as always, with excessive clarity, articulating each word. Aaron touches the engagement ring, turns it, diamond to palm, so that it looks like a silver band. Louise turns it back so that the diamond catches the light, sparkles. Aaron imagines what it looks like within, through a jeweler's glass: the endless refracting boxes and triangles. They are sitting on wooden benches, eight rows up, inside the Curry Hicks gymnasium. On the court Lucius works out with the other players from the All-Star team that will tour for two weeks against a visiting Yugoslavian team. Aaron's fingers itch. He wants the ball in his own hands. He wants to sky high over Lucius, to jam the ball home, to see the surprise in Lucius's eyes. Louise talks about the wedding, about the honeymoon she and Lucius will take—they've rented a cabin on Penobscot Bay, in Maine—about their plans, their future. For all her airs—if she weren't so goddamned proud she's black, you'd think she thought she was white, Lucius always says—Aaron likes her, admires her.

Lucius has one more year of college—he is on full scholarship, for basketball—and while he is finishing his bachelor's degree, Louise will get a master's degree in counseling. She wants Lucius to apply for fellowships abroad, she says, but he is resisting. He is afraid, she reasons, not of failing, but of succeeding. Good old survival guilt. Louise believes in Lucius in the same way, Aaron realizes, that Susan believes in him. Why shouldn't Lucius be able to be a Rhodes Scholar or a Marshall Fellow? His grades are excellent, he is a superb athlete, he has risen from adversity. Did Aaron see the article she clipped and gave to Lucius about Bill Bradley, the All-American from Princeton, in Oxford for two years on a Rhodes Fellowship while playing, in his spare time, for one of the professional Italian teams? Lucius could do the same and that way they would have extra income, he would stay in shape, have some friends—most of the players on the European teams are American blacks not quite good enough for the N.B.A.—and the two of them could travel and see the world.

Aaron suggests that Louise go easy on Lucius. He reminds her that Lucius has come a long way in a short time, that less than four years before the very idea of going to *any* college seemed absurd to him. Until Susan began working with him, encouraging him to enroll for courses, Aaron admits that it had not even occurred to *him* to suggest that Lucius go to the university.

The players move silently—Aaron chooses not to hear the pounding of the ball, of feet—and in his mind's eye he is lying in the meadow in front of Susan's house. A local farmer, who hayed it before they bought the land, continues to hay it each year, and Aaron stares ahead at the expanse of white, through which, as if through the softest cotton sheet, he can discern the pale green below. Can he blow the snow away? The snow rests lightly on the new spring shoots of winter rye as if protecting them. He thinks of being inside the house, looking out at snow. He is sawing through sheet rock, the fine spray of plaster dust coating his neck and arms. He thinks of the sun, rising now above the trees, a squat ball of yellow suffused with clouds of white, like dry ice, that make the yellow unbearably harsh. The sun warms the meadow, turns the snow to vapor, lets the blades of bent grass straighten, rise. If you stared long enough, would you see them move and grow—could you see the color change?

He tells Louise about the greenhouse, about his plans, about how it will be a surprise for Susan. He talks about the new kind of thermal glass he has ordered, which will concentrate and hold the sun's rays, spreading warmth to the kitchen in winter. He imagines the greenhouse filled with daisies. He tells Louise that he will coax Lucius into coming out with him one weekend so they can work together. Louise gives him Lucius's schedule—when he leaves with the team, where he will be playing, when he will return. She has been preparing work sheets for him, charting the homework he will have to do each day. She has spoken with the coach, with each of his professors.

"Lucius going to let your dad work on his mouth?"

"Or I don't marry him." Louise smiles. "Who'd want to marry a man with teeth like his?" She touches her ring. "Oh, I'll marry him. I'd do anything for him, I love him so. But he is one stubborn man sometimes. We had a big fight this morning before he left for classes. Did he tell you?"

"I haven't seen him. It's why I'm here. I mean, I was on campus anyway, to see Susan in rehearsal—her play opens Friday night—so I thought I'd stop by. Lucius and I don't get to see each other much anymore."

"He says that he won't attend graduation—*my* graduation. He says that he intends to boycott it."

"I figured."

"I've told him that I'm not against him or the others, but for the life of me I can't see what having a separate graduation ceremony for blacks is going to *prove* to anybody. Damn it, Aaron—I worked hard for four years to earn my degree, earn it without favors, and without majoring in black studies either—and I'm proud of what I did. I thought what we wanted was to be equal and *not* separate."

"What did Lucius say?"

"That they're his brothers and sisters by skin and history, and that he won't go against them."

"And what did you say?"

"What did *I* say? I asked him why he was choosing them over me— that's what I said. I asked him if this was what the rest of our life was going to be like—him choosing race over reason, him choosing to hurt me just so he won't be called an Uncle Tom." She openes and closes her fists. "Why *should* he choose to be with them instead of me? *Why,* Aaron?"

Aaron says that he can't answer for Lucius, that Louise knows his life better than he does. Louise sighs, says that Lucius is afraid that, if he appeared at her ceremony, he would be betraying the others, and that she argued with him and said that he would be betraying himself if he let himself be manipulated, if he let the others lay a guilt trip on him.

How strange, it occurs to Aaron, that somebody who has lived through all that Lucius has lived through—lynchings and beatings and chains, sadism and Carrie and jail—can still seem such a child, can still need to be taken care of by a woman like Louise, who has tasted little of the world's cruelty. Carrie. Carrie and the boy moved from Greenwood over three years before, not telling Rose they were leaving. Rose does not know their whereabouts, has never heard from them again. Lucius is free then. And if Carrie had not left, Aaron wonders, would Lucius have felt free to fall in love with Louise, to marry her? Has he told Louise about Carrie and the boy? Louise talks more evenly, tells Aaron that she has given in and agreed to be married in the First Baptist Church of Amherst—a concession to Lucius. Louise does not believe in God, but she believes in Lucius's belief in God. Does that make sense to Aaron? Will she regret it later if she defers to him now?

Lucius does have his faith in God, Aaron knows—his belief that Christ reached inside him in an almost physical way, and redeemed him. Lucius claims that whatever he does—whether it be to play ball, or study, or cook, or marry, or make somebody laugh—is part of God, or rather is his way of returning, in part, the gift of life that God has given to him. Aaron has seen Lucius in church, praying and singing. He has seen the peacefulness in Lucius's eyes—the faith. Aaron wonders what *he* has—besides his love for Susan and his family—that is comparable.

What does he believe in that goes beyond his own history, beyond things tangible? Had he believed in God—had he known anything about the history of the Jewish people—would he have felt differently at his father's funeral? Would he have been able to weep?

Louise asks Aaron if he will do her a favor and urge Lucius to take a course next year in the speech department. If the suggestion comes from Aaron, perhaps Lucius will be less threatened than if it came from her. How will they understand Lucius in England if he slurs his words so, if he talks as if he is on a porch in Mississippi? Louise is speaking softly, whispering, yet she articulates her words with such precision that Aaron asks her how Lucius ever stands a chance against her in arguments.

"He glowers," she says. "Lucius is very good at glowering."

"Hey, sweet one—you all angry again?"

Lucius is standing over them, dripping sweat.

"Get away, black man."

"You don't love me in my natural state?"

One of the players calls up to Lucius, razzes him about his love life, tells him to get on down and play. Lucius sits next to Aaron.

"You ready?" he asks.

"For what?"

Lucius taps at Aaron's right sneaker. "I see you got your running shoes on, figure you be ready to step down there with the big boys."

"Come on—"

"That ain't why you here? You ain't here to show me up?"

"I promised Susan I'd stop by," Aaron says, glancing at his watch. "Her rehearsal will be over soon and —"

"Your boys been telling me how good you are, shooting baskets all the time lately. Ben tells me you're better than me—or would be, if you were still a young man." The players call to Lucius from the court. Lucius waves them off, tells them he is recruiting. "Come on, hey—you against me, man—let's us old men show these boys how it's done, okay? Let's show these boys some quality."

Aaron drives home alone in the van, along Route 9. Susan has her car. She asked him to stay, to go into town to have drinks with her and the other members of the cast, but he pleaded work, told her he had to have some preliminary sketches ready for a client within two days. He lied, and he is pleased that he did—that he is less absolute with himself than he used to be. Dump trucks carrying fill pass him going in the opposite direction, toward the university. Cows graze in the lush meadows to the north, and past them, across low fields of rye that are tufted in a miraculous haze of lavender and copper, he sees the new high-rise dormitories jutting twenty stories into the air, red brick laced with wide vertical ribbons of white concrete. So much open space, he thinks, such a lovely valley, and they build these oblong cartons of stone. He recalls photographs he has seen, in *National Geographic*, of buildings rising from the plains of Brasília.

When he and Susan married there were fewer than six thousand students at the University. Now there are almost twenty thousand and new poured-concrete structures rise everywhere on campus. Everywhere there are girders and cement mixers, earth movers and construction trailers. In the center of the campus, overlooking the small pond where he and Susan and the children ice skate in winter and feed the swans in spring, workers are building a twenty-six-story structure that will soon be the world's tallest library, the design by Edward Durell Stone.

With the vast numbers of new faculty and staff and students, and the young lawyers and doctors and teachers and social workers who follow after, it will be a long time, Aaron knows, before he will have to worry about not having enough work. In the past six months he has had to refer over a dozen potential clients to other builders. He likes being able to pick and choose among clients—to do only those houses that please him, to work only with those people he senses will give him the least trouble, will appreciate him most. Susan has urged him, now and then, to expand, to hire more men—aren't you an American? she teases; aren't you ambitious?—but he prefers to keep things the same, to scale: to work with one or two helpers and to let Lucius work whenever he has free time—which has been, the past year, almost never.

He drives through Hadley, past the Farm Museum, the town's center. The steeple of the Congregational Church—an imitation of one by Christopher Wren—rises at a slant from behind the Town Hall. More fields. Long, low tobacco barns. Boulders. Black earth, recently plowed —old river bottom, the richest land in New England. A field dusted with lime. He approaches Coolidge Bridge. His body feels wonderful, as relaxed as it has been for months, and he thinks of the shower he took with Lucius and the other players afterwards, recalls their glances, their questions about what college he had played for. He hears Lucius bragging on him: *This man never went to college. Too smart for that . . .*

He will ache tomorrow, he knows, but right now his body sings to him, the muscles stretched, the blood coursing through them, through veins that he thinks of as being wide open, like tunnels, as having been vacuumed clean. He feels light-headed, ready for anything. He shoots baskets with Benjamin and the younger boys sometimes, plays full court in pick-up games now and then, but it has been a long time since he moved with such fury. Lucius guarded him, talked to him, teased. He felt at first as if he were, despite the bodies and sounds around him, lost, wandering, abandoned. But as soon as the ball came to him, he was all right. He faked, went straight up, watched the ball curl off his fingers, saw it rise and fall, spin straight through—swish!—heard Lucius groan, felt somebody slap his ass as he began to backpedal toward the other end.

In some strange way he had never, despite playing with guys a dozen years younger than he is, felt more on top of his form. When he swiped the ball from Lucius—slapped it ahead, broke, headed downcourt—it was as if the others were moving in slow motion. He would not have been surprised had he, from the foul circle, been able to rise up, as in dreams when a boy, and float through the air, legs pumping as if on a bicycle going uphill so that he would be cruising through the air for twenty feet, then descending slowly, dropping the ball through the orange hoop, his body dropping past the ball as it slipped through the netting.

Oh man, take this little boy to heaven now, Lord. Take him right now! Lucius said when Aaron had put yet another move on him, faking right, gliding left, changing the ball back from right to left hand in midair, slamming it home backwards over Lucius's outstretched arm and body. *Oh yeah. Take this boy to heaven now.*

Aaron smiles. Mercifully, the scrimmage lasted for only seven or eight minutes. Then the players relaxed, shot their fouls. He wonders what would have happened to him had they played for ten or fifteen minutes. He sees Susan smiling into her dressing room mirror, jars of cold cream and makeup in front of her on the table, while Lucius describes the game. Well, well, she says, and her eyes glow, happy for him. Well. Susan is playing Beatrice in Arthur Miller's *A View from the Bridge*— when she was an undergraduate at Smith she had played Beatrice's daughter, Catherine—and Aaron watches her remove the black wig, shake her golden hair free, brush it. She moves her mouth in slow circles, stretching the skin so that she can cream the blacked-in wrinkle lines from around her lips and eyes, from her forehead. He and Lucius arrived in time for the final scene of the dress rehearsal—Eddie being killed by Marco, but by his own knife, his hand held by Marco's turned against himself, Beatrice crying *Yes, yes!* and covering his body with her own; Alfieri the lawyer coming forward, the bodies behind him frozen in a tableau. Susan does not know it, but Aaron knows Alfieri's words by heart. *Most of the time now we settle for half and I like it better. . . .*

Has Aaron settled for half? He is on the other side of the Coolidge Bridge, in Northampton. LaFleur Airport and the Three County Fairgrounds are to his left, the river behind him. He turns right onto Damon Road to avoid the town's center. *Most of the time now we settle for half.* Not me, Aaron thinks. Not yet. Not by a long shot. Aaron has told neither Louise nor Lucius nor Susan his real reason for being on campus. He was there in order to pick up registration forms so that, during the summer, he can attend the university. He has decided to go there, to major in art.

There was a moment, standing at the rear of the small theater, looking through darkness at the brightly lit stage, when he had the impulse to tell Lucius everything. *Everything!* He felt, too, as if Susan's body were lying across his own. They were, perhaps, ninety feet apart, yet he believed that he could actually feel the warmth of his wife's body as it lay across Eddie's, could feel it press against his own. Will he tell her later? What Alfieri says about Eddie—would Susan say this about him —*for he allowed himself to be wholly known and for that I think I will love him more than all my sensible clients.*

For he allowed himself to be wholly known. Is it possible—the question has never been inside his head before in words, and as soon as it is, his heart cramps, lurches—but is it possible, he wonders, that he may someday be able to tell Susan about David Voloshin?

To his surprise he does not have to pull to the side of the road, or to stop driving. To the right, down a steep embankment, a single yellow-and-blue tent is perched on a narrow sandbar. Two boys sit on the old railroad bridge, their feet dangling twenty feet or so above the Connecticut River. He thinks of David as if thinking of one of his own children. *David! Sweet David!* The pressure in his chest eases as quickly as it came: the fist that gripped his heart opens, the sharp pain dissipates, sends heat along the length of his arms, his legs. Is it possible that he may someday be able to tell his children the story of David Voloshin's life?

He looks at his fingers, swallows. New fingers cannot grow from the old. He recalls Carl asking him about that, having read about certain crabs and sea animals that regenerate severed tentacles. His half-fingers live on, can do work he never expected them to do. It has not occurred to him for a long time that he has no trouble shooting baskets with three fingers, no trouble drawing. But how, he wonders—this question is new —can the second half of his life ever be whole, ever have *its* story, if cut off from the first life, from its true beginnings?

Going to the University and getting the forms is a start, he tells himself. Doubtless, if he wanted to, he could figure out ways to fake things —to fill out the forms so that he could fool whoever had to be fooled. He can take one or two courses a semester as a special student forever,

but to apply for regular admission so that he might someday obtain a
degree, for that he will need to produce transcripts and a high school
diploma.

Did the first Aaron Levin graduate from high school, and if so, from
which one? He could find out, he supposes, by going back and spending
a few days in the city, but the easier way is to drive to Boston, to ask
around, to purchase whatever papers he needs. For a price, you can
buy anything. He could, he considers, make up a story about the orphanage closing, the records being burned—he has the name and address of the one he knew: the Maimonides Home for Jewish Boys, whose
history he has given Susan and the children. He could inquire about
taking high school equivalency exams. Better, though, to pay for what
he needs.

Who, he wonders, would care now that he was Abe Litvinov's
nephew, or that once, in self-defense, he killed a small-time thug named
Vincent D'Agostino? Aaron has read stories in the papers of people
confessing to crimes decades after they were committed, of murderers
being let off with light or suspended sentences. But if he reveals himself
—his true life—what of Gail and Emilie? What if his mother is still alive?
What of Susan and Carl and Larry . . .

When he arrives home and finds that the children are gone and the
house empty, he is happy. He walks from room to room, touching
objects in each room—the boy's model cars and planes, Jennifer's collection of shells and dolls, Susan's hairbrush, Benjamin's geodes—and
all the while he is imagining himself in studio classes at the university,
an easel in front of him or a sketch pad on his lap, and he is learning
from teachers, some younger than himself, how, through specific tech-
niques and exercises, to draw and to paint. What he realizes is that his
willingness—his desire—to tell Susan about David Voloshin could be
born not merely because he wants to open the doors to his past so that
he can be free of it, but because he has decided to free himself for the
years to come. This seems so obvious and simple—wasn't it always
there, waiting?—that he is astonished it has dawned upon him so slowly.

He makes himself a cup of coffee, then goes to his studio, locks the
door behind him. He likes the fact that he does not know where his
children are, that they have lives and worlds of their own that exist apart
from him, from anything he has given them, from any knowledge he
has of them. He plans ahead: should Susan or one of the children return
before he is ready to leave for her house, he will slip through the sliding
doors, walk around to the front, get away without speaking to anyone.
He wants to be at her place while there is still light. The sun will not set

until after seven. He wants to sit for a while in his studio, to let his feelings float, to let the world seep into them.

In the upper right-hand corner of his drafting table, under clear plastic tape, is the painting he loves: Vermeer's portrait of a woman pouring milk. The print, eight-by-ten-inches, is in black and white. Two floors above, on their bedroom wall, beside the window that overlooks the back lawn, is a framed print of the same painting, but in color. It was on the wall when he married Susan, and he has never grown tired of it. Susan bought it almost twenty years ago, during her junior year abroad, at the Rijksmuseum in Amsterdam.

When his mind wanders during work, when he rests from his drawing, he likes to stare at the black-and-white print and to imagine colors, as if from below, bleeding through, suffusing the blacks and whites and grays with life. He loves the pale yellow light that comes from the window, from its small square panes, the light that touches, with tenderness, the woman's head and bosom and arms and hands. The woman is neither beautiful nor young, and he cannot tell if she is a mother.

The contrasting textures never cease to fascinate: the wicker basket and the metal one; the bread and the milk; the whole loaf and the broken loaf; the full basket and the empty one; the blue overskirt that is drawn up and the blue tablecloth that hangs down; the earthenware pitcher in hand and the glazed jug on the table. . . . All things seem to be partially hidden: what do the baskets on the wall contain? What is inside the wooden box on the floor? Why is the skirt slightly lifted, the extra blue cloth gathered and laid across the tablecloth? And how can there be so many different textures, so many contrasting shapes—ovals and circles and squares and rectangles and triangles—within such calm?

So little movement, yet so much life! The rough wood of the window casing and the smooth cloth of the woman's head-kerchief; the fresh white milk pouring down near the grainy pieces of the half-cut loaf of bread; the soft curves of pitcher, bowl and bosom, and the hard angles of table, of box, of copper basket. So much light, yet so much darkness; so much that is hidden, so much that is only partially revealed; and beyond the window—into that world from which the woman has come and to which he senses she will soon return—what life out there?

The picture begins to shimmer, to take on color and depth, to glow with golds and blues and browns, and the intensity of the color—its clarity—serves, miraculously, only to soften the effect, to make the moment seem yet more peaceful, more calm. How can it be? Aaron touches the print, runs his index finger along the rim of the pitcher, then traces the oval of the ceramic bowl into which the thin line of milk descends. How easily the woman holds the bowl of the pitcher. Aaron touches the strong muscles in the woman's bare left forearm. He feels

as if his entire being is suffused with the same pale yellow light that
suffused this woman's world. Did she exist? What is the difference between who she actually was and the woman Vermeer painted? The wall
behind her—the great expanse of wall that has nothing on it but a few
nails—seems to surround the woman with radiant light, and staring into
it Aaron feels sleepy, dreamy, happy. Oh how wonderful it would be to
be able to have the knowledge—in craft, in experience—to be able to
paint like this! Can he do it? Is it too late? His drafting technique, he
knows from the admiration of other architects, is excellent. The
sketches he does from time to time are fine. But is there still the time—
and will—for him to learn how to paint like *this?* As far as art historians
know, Vermeer painted only thirty-seven paintings. If there were a
thirty-eighth, Aaron wonders, what would it be like?

His left hand strokes the seat of his stool, idly. He is glad he stopped
in at the gym, spoke with Lucius. He realizes now that the dim memory
he had, sitting there, was of sitting in the balcony of the Erasmus gym
when he was a thirteen-year-old freshman watching the varsity practice.
Afterwards Mr. Goldstein came upstairs, put a hand on his shoulder. *So
you're the Voloshin kid. Davey, right? Well. I hear you're pretty good.*
. . . He sees the photos of former Erasmus stars hanging from the walls
of Mr. Goldstein's office. He sees Leo Durocher, the Dodger manager,
talking to men in business suits. The men are reputed to be gangsters.
Durocher has been banned from baseball for a year, for consorting with
underworld figures. Durocher is in his uniform, the men are in the
grandstands, just above the dugout. The photograph is in the *New York
Post*. Abe laughs. Abe quotes Mr. Rothenberg: the self-righteousness of
weak and envious men is without end.

The woman's face is suddenly less round. The print begins to lose
color, and as it does, the darker hues—the inside of the bowl, the edge
of the tablecloth, the folds of the skirt, the shadows of basket and bread,
the lines of the woman's eyes and mouth—become black, a color that
does not exist in the painting itself. The wall becomes almost as white as
her kerchief. The absence of color does not displease Aaron. Someday
too, he promises himself, he will draw the picture of Beau Jack that he
was once too frightened to draw.

Aaron is for the moment content, he realizes, and in this contentment
he is aware that he feels as if he is somehow living within the epilogue
to one of those nineteenth-century novels that Susan loves so much,
wherein all the couples marry, all evil is dispersed, all good people are
reunited, all the children and grandchildren are seated happily about
the family hearth. How strange to feel that he is living within the *ending*
to such a story when he is barely beginning the middle of his own life.

He looks at the woman again and her color has returned, as if he is looking at the print on the bedroom wall, and he feels that he is somehow alive within the yellow-white light that surrounds her. It is as if he can thin to air and rise like the light itself—the almost invisible motes of pale yellow and white dust—and float back and forth, passing in and out through the panes of the window in the woman's kitchen. Has her life been hard? Has she suffered loss? Is she a mother, daughter, or servant? Is she happy?

Aaron looks out at the lawn, the trees, the blossoms. He is, he knows, living a life he never expected to live, and he can catalogue its riches: he is married to a good and beautiful woman who loves him as much as he loves her; they live in a lovely home in a gorgeous part of the world; they have four bright, healthy children; they do not want for money or for time to enjoy their life; he has work he loves, and can grow in; his wife, having raised the children, now has a life of her own too—with friends, with the theater—that rewards her; he has good friends, and the lives of these friends go well. Nicky is living in a small town in Pennsylvania, married to a man who was her history professor at Dickinson College— they are expecting their first child in the fall. And in his friendship with Lucius, Aaron has something he never expected to have: a close adult male friend with whom, on a regular basis, he shares his work, his life, his family, his feelings. He has a rich family life, work he loves, close friends to share his life with. What more does a man need?

Somewhere behind him, a door opens. Aaron stands, goes to the window. He imagines Martin Luther King going to the balcony of his motel. Now Martin Luther King is dead too, slain in Memphis, where he had come to help striking garbage collectors. The world beyond Aaron's home—beyond his thoughts—rolls on. Outside his house, beyond his safe New England world, wars and famine blaze across the swamps and deserts and jungles of the world. Young Americans and Asians die by the thousands in the heat and mud of Vietnam. Jackie Robinson Junior, home from Southeast Asia, has been arrested for possession of drugs, for carrying a concealed weapon; he is an addict and has said so publicly; he is now living in a rehabilitation center called Daytop House. Jackie himself, silver-haired and paunchy, has been inducted into baseball's Hall of Fame—the first black there—but what pleasure in this public victory when the private grief must be so great?

Aaron opens the sliding doors. Just outside his studio crocuses and daffodils are in bloom, as is the forsythia that grows wild down by the stone wall. He studies the crocus, sees that it is not veined inside, as he imagined. Siberian iris, around the base of the Russian olive, have risen, formed their small slender buds. Soon the redbud and weeping crab apple and flowering dogwood will release wild reds and purples and whites. He thinks he hears Jennifer's voice, mildly raspy, so similar to

Susan's that he cannot be sure. Or perhaps the boys have turned on the television set. Jennifer. Not yet eighteen and leaving home. God knows how many boys and men have had their pleasures with her already, yet this does not bother Aaron the way it used to. Maybe Susan is right: when Jennifer has to make the choices that will mark the rest of her life she will not, at least, be confused by sex itself the way so many are. The way Susan was with Paul.

Paul. That should be in the epilogue, too, shouldn't it—that Paul and Debbie and their child have gone away, have left them in peace. Paul is somewhere in New York City, making money and bombs, Aaron supposes. Out of sight, out of mind. Would he, he wonders, feel differently about Jennifer were she his own daughter? He thinks not. Amazing. All he really cares about is that she be happy. The past is the past and we need to understand it, not to dwell in it. Perhaps if Paul and Debbie had not come along, Jennifer would have been led down the same path— full of drugs and sex and rebellion—that many of her friends have traveled. Who can tell?

Aaron walks along the north side of the building. Jennifer has made the honor roll her last three semesters of high school, has scored within the top 2 percent of the nation in her college board exams, is headed for Tufts in the fall. And Benjamin, to everybody's surprise, has become an excellent student. Susan had good instincts there: his surliness, especially during the months he was going back and forth from Susan to Paul, became almost pathological. Susan insisted that Benjamin go into psychotherapy, where he stayed twice a week for three years. He continues now once a week, and that, along with the passing of time, seems to have helped to straighten him out. The intense irritability that could have turned inwards now deploys itself in a determined will to succeed —in his studies, in sports, with his friends, with girls.

Sports. That has been a bonus for Aaron—that Benjamin has turned into a gifted athlete, star pitcher on the Northampton High baseball team, high-scoring forward on their basketball team. They work out together, and it hardly ever occurs to Aaron that the boy is not his own son.

Aaron feels himself float through the window and into the air of Delft. Flat land with low horizons, endless vistas. Windmills. Canals like blue veins. The wide curving sea. Boats at rest in the harbor, masts bare of sails. He descends slowly, riding warm currents of air, and finds that he is drifting into the courtyard of their apartment building on Martense Street, where he is hurling a pink Spaldeen against the wall again and again, bouncing it off ridges, making spectacular one-hand grabs, imagining himself as different players: Pee Wee Reese, Eddie Stanky, Spider

Jorgensen, Goody Rosen, Augie Galan. His father appears and they throw the ball back and forth. Aaron is frightened—afraid to throw the ball too fast, afraid he will hurt his father. He is surprised that his father can gauge distances, can catch and throw as if he has two normal eyes. For days afterwards he brags to his friends about what a great player his father would have been had he had normal vision. Has there ever been a one-eyed major league baseball player? One-armed Pete Gray, one-legged Monty Stratton, Three-Finger Mordecai Brown. But no blind men.

Aaron is walking across a green lawn with his father at the Brooklyn Botanic Garden. They have just come from Ebbets Field, two blocks away, where the Dodgers lost to the Cubs in both ends of a Sunday double-header. The Cubs will go on to win the pennant. It is 1945, then, and Aaron is nine-and-a-half years old. The war will soon be over, first in Europe, then in Asia. Phil Cavaretta, the Cubs' first baseman, who gets five hits that day, will go on to lead the National League in batting with a .355 average. The Dodgers' Dixie Walker—the bastard who will later lead the rebellion against Jackie's being on the team—led the league the year before, with a .357 average, and Walker is Aaron's hero. Claude Passeau and Hank Borowy, the Cubs' ace pitching duo will, in the World Series against the Detroit Tigers, be no match for Hal New-houser and Virgil Trucks. Newhouser's face, in a full-page portrait in *Sport* magazine, by Jack Sher, which Aaron copies on a long Sunday afternoon, transferring Sher's colors to blacks and whites and grays, is lean and scarred. A gangster's face, were not the eyes so gentle and unhappy, as if in mourning.

Along the mall near the Brooklyn Museum the cherry trees are in bloom, two long alleys of pink and white, the color of strawberries and cream. Double-flowering kwanzans. Aaron has planted three kwanzans in front of the house in Northampton, has given the children stories about the trees in the Brooklyn Botanic Garden, about outings he made there from the orphanage. Aaron hears his father declare unequivocally that the trees they are looking at in Brooklyn are more magnificent than the more famous cherry trees of Washington, D.C., and Aaron repeats this information for his fourth grade class, insists upon it. His father, of course, has never been to Washington.

His poor father, so ineffectual, yet so sweet and gentle! His father, he realizes, would be happy for him in the life he now has. But would Abe? He is not sure. He is not sure that Abe would want to believe it possible that he could have a second chance. He is not sure that Abe would be as interested in his architectural renderings as he was in his portraits of athletes. If he brought Abe with him, to Susan's house, he thinks, Abe would be restless, distracted. He would not wander through the rooms as Ellen might—happy, intense, curious. Abe would have a hard time accepting anything he had not imagined.

Aaron has sometimes said to Susan that he values his privacy and that of his children so dearly because in the orphanage he had so little of it. But surely it was in the four small rooms of that Brooklyn apartment that he had so little privacy, as little as any orphan in any dormitory ever had.

Lately he has been able to think back to those rooms more, to dwell within them, without either annoyance or fear. They seem more ordinary, less terrible: cluttered, low-ceilinged, dimly lit, drab, but not totally without light. He can live in them if he wants to. He can recall any moment of any day, summon up any conversation, any argument, any sensation. Still, he knows that he would never *choose* to live in those rooms again. Not while his parents were there with him. Not for a single minute. Why, then, does he cherish, more than ever, each physical detail of those rooms? If he could be there by himself—without people, without sound, without being seen—he would.

What, he finds himself wondering, is the story of his life? He drives north along Route 5, through Hatfield, turns east onto Route 116, crosses the Connecticut River over the Sunderland Bridge, then heads north again on Route 47. He has left a note in the kitchen—the boys were downstairs, in the workshop—telling Susan that he has gone to the property in Leverett and will be home shortly after sundown. If they are hungry, they should eat supper without him.

What is the story of *anyone's* life? Do lives, as such, have stories? Apart from birth and death, do they have true beginnings and ends? Like pictures, he thinks, stories are illusions, and that is why he loves them so: they are single moments in which time seems to stop, narratives in which events only appear—momentarily, magically—to be connected, one to the other. If he thinks of others—Beau Jack or Lucius or Abe or Jackie Robinson or his father or Susan or Nicky—he can find beginnings, middles, ends. But if, in fact, you trace a person's life from start to finish, there is no real *story*, he decides—no single picture, or series of pictures, that will be equal to the life, or to its essence.

When he recalls how moved he was by the story of Jackie's life—*My Own Story*, by Jackie Robinson, as told to Wendell Smith—he realizes that this book that so utterly enchanted him was made up, even if there were any of Jackie's own words or thoughts in it, of a series of moments, incidents, facts, and that these items, along with all those that have come since, do not really lead one to the other in any *necessary* way.

Jackie's birth, the death of Jackie's brother, the displacement from Georgia to California, Jackie meeting Rachel, Jackie in the Army, Jackie joining the Dodgers, Jackie stealing bases, Jackie having children, Jackie running Chock Full O'Nuts, Jackie worrying about Jack Junior's drug problem—what was inevitable about such things? Where in such a brief catalogue is there cause-and-effect? Lives do not have plots the way stories do, though in following lives, he likes to *impose* story, doesn't he? The events of Jackie's life are random, joined only by the fact of the man who has lived through them. Is this why, when Aaron thinks of his own life, he can never find its center, its story—but why, he senses, looking at him from the outside, as he has looked at Jackie through the years, other people can?

Character is fate, Susan often says, repeating Aristotle's words, words she heard first from Paul when he was directing her in Euripides' *Alcestis*. But the word "fate," for Aaron, always signifies the place *toward which* one is inevitably heading; it does not account for the life led, for all the years, for the texture of individual days, for things pervasive. And even if one's character is one's fate, how does this, from within, become *story*? Will he ever see his own life so that it takes on contours the way Jackie's, or even Susan's life does?

He pulls off the main road, eases the van into second gear. The road to Susan's house is bumpy, the gravel washed out in low spots by spring rains. He drives past the thick woods that shield the property from the road, sees the setting sun, only inches above the far line of trees. The meadow, shaded by trees, the sun at low-angle, is a deep forest-green. He will have good light for at least an hour.

Two cars are parked outside Susan's house: her green 1966 Chevrolet and Lucius's old 1958 Mercury. Aaron pulls up beside the cars, hears loud music. The Beatles. He gets out of his van, enters the kitchen. He is disappointed. She will have seen the timbers, will ask questions.

Lucius and Susan sit at the round oak table, Susan's back to the door; when she catches the look in Lucius's eye, she turns, breaks into a broad grin, rises, shakes out her hair—which is wild and uncombed—comes to him, kisses him on the neck, begins to stroke the small of his back with her thumb and first two fingers. She leans back, body limp, pecks him on the nose, the mouth, each cheek. She is stoned, the pupils of her eyes dilated, the irises a pale, watery blue.

On the table is a gallon jug of cheap Burgundy. Lucius, without rising from his chair, offers Aaron a glass, but as he begins to pour, the wine misses, splashes on the table. Lucius laughs.

"You're drunk," Aaron says, then realizes that lost in the noise of the record, in clanging guitars and shimmering voices, Lucius cannot hear him. Susan is wearing a low-cut cream-colored summer dress, not the one she had on after rehearsal. He watches her bosom rise, sees that Lucius watches it too, bleary-eyed. Her cheeks are flushed and she looks especially young, the way she might have looked, Aaron imagines, when she played Beatrice's daughter Catherine. He thinks of the beautiful young woman in the Elkton diner, the one Gail was jealous of. He goes to the sideboard, turns off the stereo.

"Party pooper," Susan says. "We were playing *our* song—"

"My song," Lucius says.

"Lucius in the Sky with Diamonds," Susan says. She lifts a half-smoked cigarette from an ashtray, inhales, offers it to Aaron. "Want some?"

"No."

"Drags don't take drugs, I guess," she states, then quickly puts a finger to her lips. "Shh. Be careful, Lucius. Aaron's getting angry."

"Hey man, put the music back on!" Lucius commands.

"I think you'd better get going," Aaron says. He hears a high-pitched sound in his ear, the sound spiraling to a single note, higher and higher, as if going backwards through a cone of vision.

Lucius pushes his knuckles against the table, braces himself and stands, goes to Aaron's side, touches Aaron's shoulder. "Hey—we just having some fun is all. Got to have me some fun before I'm a married man, don't we?"

"The longest journey," Susan says. "Forsaking all others. Love, honor and obey. Obey. Oh boy."

"You can have fun after you're married," Aaron says.

Susan bursts into laughter, slaps a hand over her mouth.

"What's so funny?" Aaron asks.

"You," Susan says. "Your eyes are in the sky, like diamonds. You have wonderful eyes. Still. Sometimes I'd like to swim into them, go all the way to the bottom."

"That's Lucy," Lucius says. "Lucy in the Sky with Diamonds."

"Lucius," Susan states.

Lucius takes Aaron's hand, touches the stubs. "You sure shoot good for a three-fingered man. But look now. Been wanting to ask you since we met, a long time gone. Look now. How you lose these things *really?*"

"I told you once. At the orphanage, they—"

"Oh come *on*, man—come off it already—what kind of dumb nigger you think I be? You think I believe all that bullshit about you being a poor orphan boy? Hey! Paul, he straighten me out on that a long time back."

"Oh God," Susan says. "I am really stoned. I think I am fucking stoned out of my mind." She blows lightly in his left ear. "C'mon Aaron

—don't be so damned high and mighty and pure. Try some, please? Don't you want to have fun with me anymore? Don't you want to play games with pretty Susan?"

Aaron pushes her away, feels the blood surge in his ears, surf spraying against rocks, boulders tumbling into the sea. "I think we'd better get going," he says. "The children need supper. It will be dark soon and neither of you are in fit shape to drive."

Susan leans back against the sideboard, sucks on her cigarette. Her right hand moves down, splays open, rises slowly, makes circles across the plane of her stomach. Aaron sees a single drop of sweat glide down the right side of Lucius's neck. Pearl on ebony. Aaron is dizzy for an instant, steadies himself against the table, then moves forward, to take Susan by the arm. He wants to be gentle but is not certain that, if she taunts him, he will be able to control himself.

"I said it's time to go."

"Her master's voice," Susan says, and she turns on the stereo. Aaron switches it off. Susan pouts. "See? He is just such a goddamned stick-in-the-mud sometimes, Lucius, didn't I tell you? Can't you see? Couldn't you just fucking *die* from it?"

"Hey," Lucius says. "C'mon now. Aaron's a good old boy. You see that jump shot today? You see the power under the boards? You see the moves? This man, he fall back in time, he be the best man out there. The coach, his face dragging the floor when he find out how old Aaron is, and never played for no college."

"I'll pick you up and carry you if I have to," Aaron says.

"*Really?*" Susan's eyes are suddenly bright, azure. "*Would* you?"

"I mean, Aaron be okay for a white man. How much life a guy have left anyway, a man has to wonder, all the years he been married and stuff? Why *you* getting married anyway, Lucius? Don't you never learn? Freedom now, boy. Freedom now!"

Susan sips wine, tries to sit, nearly misses the chair. Aaron puts an arm round her waist and the instant he touches her, his palm falling on the curve of her hip, he is astonished to find that he begins to harden. Chin uptilted, Susan lets her head rest against his shoulder, swings her arm outward and back, so that her forearm drops across her closed eyes.

"In a swoon," she intones. "But listen. If Jen gets knocked up I'll be a grandmother. Can you imagine? Here I am, in the prime of my life—the books say a woman's peak is between thirty-five and forty—and if I'm a grandmother, then what will that make you?"

"Come on," Aaron says, and feels his erection ease even as his anger grows. "Enough. I'm losing patience."

"Carry me then."

"I said I'm losing patience. Don't force me to—"

"Force *me* then, all right?" Her voice is husky. "Come on, big boy. Force me. Come on. We're among friends—"

"Same book say a man's peak at nineteen, Aaron. Bad news. We way past our prime, I guess."

"Problems," Susan says. "Problems and then more problems." She slips out of Aaron's grasp, slumps down in a chair, smiles up at him. "Hi!" she says. "Glad you could make it to our party. Haven't we met somewhere before? Mmmmm." She reaches up with her left hand. "Remember the first time we met? Oh God, when I saw your eyes I just melted. All those crinkles around them, and you so young I couldn't tell you were so old. Take my hand, please?"

He takes her hand, feels the cold metal of her gold wedding band.

"Hey, you two lovers, tell Lucius about it, we have us some story time. No shit, Aaron—remember all the stuff we be telling each other, coming up from Mississippi? He tell me about how you two meet, him cleaning out the stables at the fairgrounds, you wiping them horses' flanks, wondering how a guy so smart be caught shoveling out hot turds. Only what he don't tell me is how come a smart good-looking guy with all his talent, he be moving from town to town, working the county fairs, taking this job and that. Being a poor orphan boy don't explain *that* now, does it?"

Susan's head is on her arms, on the table. "God, he was so lovely then. You were just so lovely, Aaron. After all I'd been through, with Paul running out on me, all his crazy games. The second I saw your eyes, I knew I was safe. Home free."

"Come on," Lucius says. "Come on now, Aaron. I tell you true all about Carrie, so now you gotta tell me about what you doing there, and about them fingers. You don't, then I got nothing left but to believe in Paul's tales and I don't think you be wanting that. Oh yeah. Never could figure that either, when we were working for him, fixing that old house up all fancy, how it don't bug you none that he, you know, had *her* all them years."

Susan lifts her head. "Susan," she says. "Susan. In my presence kindly use my name."

"Come on," Lucius says. "Come on and 'fess up, hey, Aaron. Didn't it bother you just a little, knowing he plowed your fields before you got there?"

"Gentlemen," Susan says. "Proceed as if I were absent. Please. Frankly, I love it."

Lucius reaches up, touches a ceiling beam. "Remember how I teased you 'cause of your fingers, how you could put in all the cripple studs,

and me, the strength and size I got, I'd put in jack studs. Jack studs and
cripple studs, we got 'em all, Aaron, you and me."

"Aaron Levin is not the possessive type," Susan declares. She makes
a V with her hands, rests her chin in the V, stares at Lucius. "Jealousy
is the illusion of possession, so saith Aaron Levin. Didn't he ever teach
you that?"

"And you believe it—that he never be jealous of sharing your body
once upon a time with that other man?"

"Never never never never never. And I quote. *Lear*. Again: to see
feelingly—that is the aim of life. The end."

"Oh man, you too good, Aaron. Like always. You just too good to be
true. I mean, I see guys around used to know Louise, I still feel something twitch inside, and you got to remember all I was able to endure
down there with Carrie. And you know what? Louise, she be happy I
feel that way. A woman *need* that, Aaron. A woman like to be pursued,
see—like you to *crave* her—"

"Shh," Susan says. "Everybody quiet now. Listen. I'm having an idea.
Shh. Maybe after you get married, Lucius, you could wait a while and
then get divorced. Then Aaron and I could get divorced. Then we could
all switch around, like in *Couples*. Then maybe—"

"Hey, hey," Lucius says. "Don't you be tempting me with shit like
that. Louise, she take a rolling pin to you, she hear you talk that kind of
stuff." He turns to Aaron and his manner is suddenly sober, good-na-
tured. "Come on, hey—don't you want to celebrate just a little? All the
hard times gone by for us, friend. Joseph and his brothers, they be
embracing all over the place, happy for us too, see? Moses, they even
gonna let him into that promised land now, no matter he kill some son
of a bitch. That's the way my heart's feeling today. The Lord been good
to me, give me life, so I want to be good to the people I love, see?
Anything's possible, Aaron, if you just open your heart. *C'mon*—"

"Heresy," Susan says. "Lucius heresy. Rewriting texts. Emendations.
Taking God's name in vain, and the man claims to *believe*—"

"Oh I do, I do, and He be forgiving me when I get fancy 'cause He
loves me, don't you see? The way He loves us all. And when one of us
love somebody else, there be a little bit of the Lord in us—when you
love somebody truly it makes everything else all right."

"Disappear," Susan says. "Lucius believes that love makes the world
disappear, that evil is the absence of love, that when a man loves a
woman and a woman loves a man it is our imitation of God, and that
nothing else on earth matters except that love." She grins. "Doesn't he
make religion sound wonderfully romantic, sweetheart?"

"What God loves, see," Lucius says, "is that we got so much to celebrate we be celebrating *Him* too: we got me getting married and Louise and Jen graduating and Susan in her big play. So come on, brother. Ain't you got something too?"

"Yes, but for now I think we should all go. We'll celebrate when we'll be fit to remember what we did."

"That's true too," Lucius says. He cups his hand around Aaron's ear. "Love you like a brother, Aaron. That be love too, see. She left that out —a man's love for his brother. Only problem is, for most of us, it don't start the sap flowing the way the *other* love does—don't move in us like His spirit moves—"

Susan stands, leans on Aaron. "What?" she asks. "I heard you. What is it? Don't tease. Come on—what do *you* have to celebrate?"

"I've decided to register for two art courses at the university. It's the real reason I was there today—"

Susan moves away. Neither she nor Lucius says anything and in the silence Aaron feels suddenly small and awkward, as if he is a little boy asking permission to do something. Have they heard what he said? Do they care?

"I was picking up registration forms before I went to the gym," he offers. "If things go well I'm thinking of enrolling full-time in the fall."

"Hey, hey—!" Lucius says. "Hey! After all them years, that takes courage, man. That be the biggest news of all, cause it's *new*. We didn't know that before, did we?"

"You're right," Susan says, and she wobbles her head from side to side, to clear it. "But now. But *now*. Why now? I mean, why now? Why now, fair Aaron?"

She blows Aaron a kiss from the palm of her hand, then turns her eyes to Lucius.

"Oh come *on*, lady," Lucius says. "That all you can say, you get news like that from him? That all you can say, he gonna do what you and me been wanting him to, what he been dreaming about since who knows when, what I been *praying* for—?"

"I saw snow on the ground this morning," Aaron states. "Out there. The meadow was covered with it. It was very beautiful."

"Yeah," Lucius says. "Saw your tire tracks. Figured. Saw the new wood piled up. Jack studs and cripple studs, I think. Trusses and tie beams. Toe-nails and tie rails. Footings and furrings. Lucius and Aaron. Looks like we gonna be in business again, by and by, only I can't figure out what we be doing this time."

"A surprise."

"For me?" Susan asks.

"For us."

"I work here too, you know." Susan touches a stack of books, on the sideboard. "Susan's tutoring center. Upward bound. I didn't need to go down to Mississippi to help the poor colored folk. I can do that right here in the house my husband built for me. Never leave my family that way. This is the house that Aaron built. See, then, how good he is to me? See what a gift he brought home—a big, tall, handsome disadvantaged colored boy of our very own! That's Aaron for you—my faithful, thoughtful Jewish husband."

"Easy now," Lucius says to Susan. "Maybe that husband be right. Maybe we best be getting on home. Both of us. Maybe we best let him drive."

"God, but those smothering Jewish mothers train them well, don't they? Nice Jewish boys, ever eager to please, to win the smiles and love of women who—who know how to hold out on them, yes? Would one of them ever come home empty-handed?"

"Sorry," Lucius says to Aaron, his eyes sad and bloodshot. "I guess I started something I can't finish. We just thinking on having a little good time, me and Susan, is all."

"But Aaron didn't have a Jewish mother like that, did he?" Susan says. "He had a whole fucking orphanage full of Jewish mothers, you see, except that the mothers were all little boys. Little boys he could please by being the best little boy of all. Little boys he—"

"Don't mock me," Aaron says, grabbing her arm. "I won't permit it."

"Hey, lay off, mister," she says, pulling away. "You don't own me."

"You can come too," he says to Lucius. "If you want."

"Only you got to relax more, man," Lucius says. "She has a point. That's what I been hoping. To see you relax some the way you do when you at work, when you get *that* rhythm going. I be telling you to relax, though, ever since we meet, us and Nicky, you being so god-awful *serious* all the time. Oh you be a good man, Aaron Levin, only you want to *play* more, like the good woman says."

"He relaxes by working," Susan says. "Another Jewish Calvinist. He relaxes by locking his studio door. By dwelling in dark rooms. By hiding. By following his wife around."

"You came out here to work, didn't you?" Lucius says. "All that new wood—you were planning to work today, right?"

"Yes."

"You don't let us get in your way then. We put the shit away while you work, get some air. Sober up."

"It's too late," Aaron says. "Light's almost gone. I was going to work outdoors. I'll come back tomorrow."

"Oh Aaron," Lucius says, and when he does his voice is natural, full of affection. "We just came out here to unwind some, is all. All them pressures, hey—hard day practicing. Stuff. Classes. Louise. I get behind in my courses, Louise she have my ass on the carpet. Only I got me some good stuff, Acapulco gold, from this guy hangs around the team, best stuff I get in a long time, and I just up to my ears in Louise—"

"Up to your fillings," Susan says.

"That too. And Susan, she beat from all her stuff, and we say, what the hell, we entitled sometimes. Don't mean to offend, brother. You go work a while, give us ten-fifteen minutes, the stuff wear off. Then we all be friends again, okay?" Lucius shivers. Aaron says nothing. "You still my friend, Aaron?"

"Of course I'm your friend."

"Love you like a brother, no matter what. You know that?"

Aaron nods, watches tears slide down Lucius's cheeks.

"Don't," Susan says, her hand on Lucius's hand. "I'm too dizzy. Please? I can't take all the damned *feelings!* Turn them off. For me, all right? Everything is just spinning too much. Goddamned wine."

"What did Paul know?" Aaron asks.

"Too much. That man was no good, Aaron—evil through and through. I thought so first time I saw him, knew his game the minute I looked in his eyes."

"Double agent," Susan says.

"Lay off," Lucius says.

"Double trouble," Susan says. "Susan and Paul. Paul and Debbie. Debbie and Lucius. Lucius and Susan. Susan and Aaron. Aaron and Lucius."

"Cool it," Lucius says. He turns to Aaron. "Sorry, man. She'll be okay as soon as the stuff wears off. You go out there and work, like you wanted. You too pissed at us, all the time just standing there, glaring. We a sorry sight, for sure. You don't get out of here, give us some space, somebody gonna get hurt by and by."

"He certainly works hard," Susan says. "But he has no ambition, you see. That is what you must pay close attention to. That is why he might be a double agent too, see?"

"Cool it, lady," Lucius says.

Aaron glances at Lucius, recalls the photo he saw while on campus, in the student newspaper, of a black man lying in bed, sheets rolled across his hips, blood splattered everywhere. "BLACK PANTHER SHOT IN HIDEOUT." Who ratted on him? Are the black students who say their brothers are being killed in their sleep and not, as the police claim, in shootouts, correct? Is it true that the Movement is full of blacks being paid by the government to bore holes, to bring everything down? Are the guns sold to the dead men sold to them by the same men who then go and tip off the F.B.I.?

"Why is it," Susan is saying, "that Aaron Levin works and works, yet wants to stay close to home, safe forever within the little world he's built? Why does a man with such talents, such natural leadership abilities, spurn leadership itself? People would follow him. People *do* follow him. Lucius followed him. I followed him. Carl and Larry follow him. Nicky followed him."

"I followed him—"

Jennifer's voice comes to him at the exact instant her hands are across his eyes.

"Guess who—?"

Before her question is out, he has whirled and whacked her on the shoulder, knocked her against the stove.

"Get out. I want all three of you out of here. Do you hear me or do you hear me? Now you move, and move fast!"

Jennifer clutches her shoulder, forces back tears.

"You *hurt* me!"

"Damned right. And I can do worse."

"Uh-oh," Susan says to Lucius. "Now children, do you recall that temper I told you about—the temper that can kill?"

"What the hell are you doing here?"

"Having a good time," Jennifer says, her eyes defiant. "Or at least I was until *you* got here."

"Answer my question without being fresh. What are you doing here?"

"She rode chaperone," Susan says.

Aaron looks at Jennifer's eyes, realizes that she is stoned too.

"I said to move. Do you hear me? Get your butts out of here. Fast."

"The king hath spoken," Susan says, and she curtsies. Aaron raises his hand, as if to strike her. She lifts her face toward him, smiles. "Please do. We won't mind. I mean, we're into all kinds of shit, aren't we, Lucius? To hell with the superego, right?"

"You shut your mouth and do what the man says. He may not own you, but he's as close as you can get. Let's move on out, hey—"

Jennifer leans down, tries to kiss Lucius's cheek. Aaron grabs her arm. Lucius grins and Aaron is astonished suddenly by how much of the man's face seems to be taken up by teeth. He is confused, frightened, furious. He looks at Susan, imagines her talking with him later when they are alone, telling him that his problem is ever the same—he continues to idealize women too much, to believe that in *their* love lies *his* salvation—and he finds himself asking why it is that he has often, in his mind, made himself jealous by imagining Susan's past—her years with Paul, with other men—but never her future. If he had already imagined the scene he is now living in, would he be less furious, less frightened, less confused?

"Same old Aaron," Lucius says. "Don't you like young folks to have fun no more, hey? Fucked up world we living in, friend. Have to take what pleasures we can, like Paul says. Never know when a body's gonna live or die, or if somebody be around after to care. You and me, brother, we know that better than most. You and me and Nicky, sitting on Rose Morgan's porch. How many years gone by was that, hey—?"

"The Movement's dead," Aaron says.

"Maybe yes, maybe no," Lucius says. "Still, we got some scores to settle, got some asses we want to kick before we go. Paul wasn't *all* wrong. The man made sense now and then."

"We're leaving," Aaron says.

"I don't want to." Jennifer rests her hand on Lucius's shoulder, lets her fingers drift lazily along the side of his neck. "I want to stay with Lucius and Mom. Lucius is my special friend now. He teaches me things. That's part of the revolution, of turning things upside down, see, like Dad said. Instead of me teaching a black, a black is teaching me."

"You're coming with me and you're coming now."

Aaron grabs for Jennifer. She slips behind Lucius and Aaron finds that he is holding Lucius's arm. Lucius twists away angrily.

"Hey—lay off. You want trouble, you can get all you want right here. No shortages, man. We can finish *everything*, here and now, that what you want."

"He's not my father anyway," Jennifer says. "I can do whatever I want."

"Freedom now, baby," Lucius says, bloodshot eyes glaring at Aaron.

"Freedom," Susan says. "Freedom is a constant struggle." She blinks. "Who said that?"

"Made you feel real good to set me free, didn't it?" Lucius says. "Oh yeah. Took you three years before you could do for yourself what came so easy when you did it for me—putting me in school and the rest. You don't think I figured that out way back—that you let me live your life for you so you didn't have to face up to why you couldn't set your own self free? Only trouble is, hey, once you set me free, I free to be free *my* way, and that gonna please you less than you ever think on." Lucius rubs his eyes. "Freedom now, friend. Freedom now. Oh yeah. Freedom got you paralyzed all to hell, don't it, Aaron? You don't know which way to move, whether to try to take me or not, you sober and straight and poor Lucius strung out on all the good things of this world. You coming? You gonna try to take me now?"

Lucius laughs at Aaron, and when he does Aaron imagines the side of his hand smashing upwards against the bridge of Lucius's nose, so that bone pushes in, penetrates brain. What enrages him most, he realizes, is being taken by surprise. But why? Doesn't he agree with what Susan often says—that, like any good story, life is most interesting when most surprising, when what-happens-next is *not* predictable? Why, then, when he is surprised this way is he also terrified? What he wants, he knows, is to be able to stop thinking so much, to be able to get away, to be able to let his mind wander freely so that it will be able to work out of instinct, habit. Then, he thinks, he will be safe. . . .

Jennifer sits, lets her head drop back, swivel. Her hair, like her mother's, is fine and wild and uncombed. The light from the ceiling catches a patch of its gold, makes it look like spun glass.

"Didn't have the heart to tell you," Lucius says. "They moving back in, seems. They all back in town for a visit." Lucius shrugs. "Hard times, man. We need to forget life the best we can sometimes, don't you see? That's what I was trying to tell you all this time."

Lucius takes Jennifer by the arm, leads her from the house. Aaron and Susan file out behind them, into the darkness, into the cool, spring air. Aaron tries to remember the snow, its feathered softness. He feels his heart pumping hard, imagines rolling balls of blood that surge forward, glide and stop, swell, roll through him as if his arteries have hand grenades inside them.

"It's okay, hey," Lucius says. "Still love you, Aaron. Love you like a long-lost brother."

"I just wish to hell you'd fall flat on your face for once in your life," Susan says to Aaron when they are home. "Jesus! Do you know how god-awful it feels to be married to a man who never falls apart, who's always so damned brave and noble and good? Talk about grace under pressure. Listen. What the hell were you trying to start with Lucius—?"

"There was no danger," Aaron says. "Everything was under control."

"See what I mean?"

She lies on their bed, a cold washcloth across her eyes.

"No."

"No," she repeats. And then: "There was no danger. Things are under control. The Movement is dead. Sure. Aaron knows everything. Aaron always does the right thing, the brave thing. Aaron trusts his instincts. Aaron protects us all. Malcolm X is dead. Medgar Evers is dead. Martin Luther King is dead. The king is dead, so long live the king, and right here in my own home, right? Right on. Now *there's* personalized service for you—"

"I'll say it one more time," Aaron says. "If I ever catch you acting that way again with Lucius, or with any other man, I'll—"

She takes the cloth from her eyes, sits up, leans on her elbows.

"You'll *what*, sweetheart?"

Silence. She is, he sees, merely amused by him.

"Come on. Enough bluffing, all right? Just what will you do?"

"I don't know."

"I figured. Good. It's good you don't know something for a change. It's a relief."

He turns away, goes to the door.

"Let's just forget the whole thing, all right? You rest up while I make some supper for the kids."

"But you're not possessive or jealous, are you? Jealousy is the illusion of possession. Sure. Tell me another one."

He turns, feels the rage surge again. "You will *not* humiliate me, is that clear? Not ever again. You will not degrade me or mock me. Not ever again. Do you—?"

"Do I hear you or do I hear you," she intones, anticipating his words. "I know all about it. Oh Aaron, don't you see that it's all *right* for you to blow your cool once in a while, that it's all right for you to be jealous and human and angry? Sweet Aaron. My dear, sweet Aaron. For a brief moment there in the country I thought I finally had a flesh-and-blood husband. Even a few seconds ago it seemed that he might actually be angry with me, that—"

"Don't you talk about me as if I'm not here."

"You're right. But can you understand that it does comfort me to have you yell at me at last, that it consoles me to see you enraged? That it actually makes me *love* you to know that you get frightened?"

"No."

"I didn't think so," she says. "Listen then. There's nothing to be afraid of. I *love* you, sweetheart—I chose you and that doesn't mean that all the other men in the world are eunuchs. As a species, men still interest me greatly. Would you have it otherwise? How often have you told me what an attractive man Lucius is, how you yourself were drawn to him at first in an almost physical way—so why shouldn't *I* be attracted to him?"

"That's not the point."

"But it is, damn it. It is! And you're such a child you can't even admit it." She turns onto her side, rests her cheek on her palm. "Is that why I love you so, because you're so much of a man and so much of a child all at once? My sweet, serious Aaron. My little orphan boy. Lucius has a point, you know, about how serious you are—"

"I don't need lessons from Lucius."

"My God—you really *are* jealous, aren't you?"

Silence.

"Well—aren't you?"

"I suppose."

"I suppose." She smiles, sits up, hugs her knees. He wants to say something about how young she looks—how much like Jennifer—about how he loves her for a parallel reason, because of how much of a woman and a child she can seem to him sometimes. But he says nothing. "Listen, Aaron: sure I was flirting with Lucius and he was flirting with me and we both loved it. But what in heaven's name is wrong with a little harmless flirting? I got high and he got high and there he was and there I was and he's a man and I'm a woman—life's *like* that, sweetheart—I mean, do you think that *ever* stops? Just because you and I were married once upon a time? Do you think the glands and hormones have gone into a state of permanent rest, of—"

"That's not what this discussion is about. You won't fool me by getting into that man-woman talk. Into all your psychological crap. You just listen to me for once and lay off Lucius, do you hear? You don't know what his life was like—what it means for a beautiful white woman like you to show kindness toward him, to tempt him. You weren't there. He's about to get married to a fine—"

She sits up, waves his words away. "Oh come off it." Her voice is hard. He imagines her putting on the black wig, stepping out on stage: a daughter becoming a mother, a mother becoming a widow. "Lucius can take care of himself. Damned well too, believe me. He's no innocent. *You're* the innocent one, if you ask me. You're the one we need to take a long, hard look at."

"Forget the whole thing." He starts for the door. "You're after me for something, and I don't like it or understand it or have to take it. What do you want from me? Come on! What is it you *want?*"

"Everything," she whispers. She laughs, runs her hands along either side of her neck, lifting hair. *"Everything."*

"See what I mean?" he says. "This is all so crazy, you and Lucius out there, and Jennifer in the woods, and then Jennifer with her ridiculous talk all the way home about Malcolm still being alive and how she saw him—how the F.B.I. sank him and gave him a new life, how Malcolm was too smart to die young—I mean, did I dream it all? Did *you*—?"

"Did Jennifer really say that?"

"Yes."

"I must have been asleep."

"She said she saw him in downtown Northampton—that he had put on weight and had a beard, but that she recognized the red hair in the beard and—"

"Aaron?"

"Yes?"

"Lucius agrees with me about you, that the rage is there and that it's something you need to do something about. You were ready to *kill* the two of us out there, don't you think we saw that? And for what? Out of what childish fantasy about men and women and sex? Lucius is a good friend to you and he loves you more than he loves anyone in the world and I don't blame him most of the time, but where in heaven's name, in an otherwise mature and trusting man, does such rage and fantasy *come* from? You were right about doting Jewish mothers, about not having had one. I forget sometimes, you're so good at *pleasing*. Who doesn't like and admire Aaron Levin? And yet, never having had one of them to teach you to worship and idealize women, you do idealize me, and I'm just so tired of it I could die sometimes. I am just so tired of it."

She crosses her arms, smiles sadly. He says nothing.

"I'm just a woman, Aaron," she says. "Beautiful, talented, loving, perceptive. Sure. But just a woman. Human and imperfect. Don't make me out to be more than I am. Please? Promise me that, for all the rest of our years together. The favorite son of a doting mother goes through life with the feeling that he is a conqueror. Who said that—Freud, right? Well, Old Sigmund was wrong once again. That son goes through life with the feeling that he must *become* a conqueror—I read that recently and I buy it. That son goes through life with the feeling that he must conquer the whole damned world and lay it at the feet of that mother or she won't love him, don't you see? He must be a good little orphan boy and lay the world at the feet of an insatiable woman, thereby hoping to win her love, a love nobody can ever win, in truth. A love nobody should ever *want* to win."

She smiles at him.

"I do love you," he says. "It's only—"

"Do you see what my smile does? God! Do you see its power over you?" She taps on a front tooth with a fingernail. "It's only a set of thirty-two small oblongs of calcium and enamel and nerve tissues, well aligned by thirty-four months of excellent orthodontia, the set ringed by a few square inches of skin, yet this smile changed your life, didn't it? What won't men do for the smile of a beautiful woman!"

She shakes her head sideways, as if pitying him. He feels as if he is a child being scolded by a teacher. He has never imagined her talking to him in quite this way. Control is everything, Abe said. To imagine one's future is to try to control it, Aaron thinks. What happens, then, if you suddenly find yourself living inside a future you haven't imagined?

"I wish you could have seen your eyes out there," Susan says. "Rage like that doesn't come from a moment's anger, and it doesn't go away in a moment either. What in heaven's name did you think was going *on* in the woods? So Jennifer took a few tokes—so what? She's eighteen years old now and at least she did whatever she did with her mother nearby and her father's best friend there too. Lucius innocent? Listen. I have a question for you that I probably should have asked years ago. But better late than never. Here goes: in all the years of our marriage haven't *you* ever been tempted to make love with another woman?"

"No."

"No." She laughs. "No? That's *all*? I didn't ask if you ever made a genuine pass or did have an affair with a woman—just if you ever felt *tempted*? And you say you never did. Not even once?"

"No. I *notice* women, but—"

"Oh dear sweet Lord," she says, her head against the headboard. "All those lonesome ladies you've been building houses for. All those pretty young faculty wives sending out their forlorn signals. All those years! *Never*? All those days and months with young long-haired college students bound to save the souls of black men. Come on, sweetheart—like Lucius says, 'fess up, huh? Let's have a real truth session. You tell me your worst secret—which is really your best secret, right?—and I'll tell you mine. No one will ever know except us. Come on. Don't you think we know each other well enough for that?"

"Stop," he says. "I think you're hurting me. I think you're trying to. I think you're being very mean, only I—"

"No. Just talk to me, all right. Talk to *me*. Come on, sweetheart. Look into that noble heart of yours and tell me what it really wants, what it did once-upon-a-time that it never told pretty Susan. We're friends, after all. We're best friends, aren't we?"

"Yes."

"Nicky. Nicky then. Weren't you tempted with her? Anyone with eyes could tell how much in love with you she was. In Mississippi, didn't you—?"

"I'm telling the truth. Why should I ever have wanted another woman when I had you? Why should I have risked *hurting* you—?"

"Oh God, Aaron, but you're a prince."

"I suppose."

"I suppose. Listen: sex exists, honey, and Lord knows but you are a very sexy man. I mean right now, even while my mouth patters along verbalizing all the stuff that drives you nuts, I look at you and I want you. I *desire* you, sweetheart."

She leaves the bed, comes to him. She kisses him, unbuttons his shirt, whispers to him. He feels numb. But why? He smells her. Lilacs and fish, he thinks, and he realizes that he inhaled the same familiar fragrance in the car when they were coming home, while Jennifer was going on about Malcolm X having gone underground. Susan kisses his breastbone, slides her hands downward, continues to unbutton his shirt, to stroke him. She begins to talk again, in a low, even voice. She tells him that she is going to say things, tell him things. She hopes he won't be frightened. She hopes he won't leave or become too angry to enjoy himself. She wants him to know *everything*—to clear the air, to set them both free of the past, to tell him whatever comes to mind. He wants to be close to her? She'll let him be as close as any human being can. He wants them to have some kind of inviolable independence? Once he knows everything, what choice will he have but to love her, not for some dream he has of her, but for who she truly is?

She tells him that Paul used to make her do all kinds of things—wild things that other people might think were perversions. She was so young when she married him, and she had never had much sexual experience before him. Will Aaron be angry with her if she talks about the things she and Paul did together? About the things they tried with some of Paul's friends? Would he like an illustrated catalogue? The truth is that she was afraid *not* to do them, afraid Paul wouldn't love her if she didn't do what he said. She was against group sex and held out for a while, but it was either join in or leave Paul. And there she would be, pregnant, her husband taking his pleasures elsewhere. Full womb and empty arms, right? She was only twenty years old. How could she be a beautiful young actress gliding across a stage if she had to drag a full womb with her? So she overcame her hang-up. She joined in. Jennifer arrived in the world, and afterwards Paul showed her more games. Anything one could imagine—all possible combinations—they tried. Possibilities. Paul believed in possibilities, in a world of endless possibilities. With a vengeance, Paul quoted Aristotle: character may determine men's qualities, he said, but it is by their actions that they are happy or the reverse, and Paul was determined to be happy by his actions. Who would be hurt? Weren't we born with free will? Then she bore Benjamin into the world, and between nursing and diapering and sleeping and walking and cooking and cleaning and Paul's inventions, how was she to have time for herself, for decisions? Free *will?* Don't make me laugh, she would say, one infant at the breast, the other with diarrhea running down its leg. The two of them bawling, colicky. Still, Paul *was* exciting when she was alert enough to notice. She never did know what to expect from him. He did know how to be tender to her, how to take the children at precisely the moment when she believed she could not go on with life a moment longer. Well. He had a way with the children too. Could quiet them, soothe them. No perversion there. She and Paul did laugh and have fun. She did try out enough in the way of sex and drugs so that by the time she left him she knew what it was she did and didn't want in life.

But she left Paul before she met Aaron, and she met Aaron before she had the chance—or desire, or energy—to know other men. Did he know that? Does he believe it? Between the time she walked out on Paul and met Aaron, she had no other men. Does that please Aaron? If she'd had lots of men and adventures between marriages, would Aaron be less jealous *now?* Jealousy? Sure. To see one you love give affection of the same kind to another is surely cause for pain and anger and hurt. But is it actually possible to be jealous of another human being's *past?*

From Paul to Aaron to heaven, she says. That will be the story of her life. And the children. They'll be in that story too. Children, one after the other, arriving just before exhaustion could depart. Was she happy? Was she sad? Who could tell? She used to hope each time she began to swell that the child within would heal her unhappiness—that enormous emptiness in which, within her, she began to dwell—but the child never did. Not Jennifer or Benjamin. Not Larry or Carl. Aaron *began* to heal her. Love began to heal. . . .

She strokes his thighs gently, cups his balls in the palm of her hand. He realizes that he has not moved, has not touched her with his hands. He is astonished at how enormous he is below, and if she continues to touch him and stroke him he is afraid that, within a minute, he will explode. She is telling him that she *is* sorry if she hurt his feelings. Can he forgive her? Can he *ever* forget? She chose him, after all. She knows that men look at her all the time, that she is a beautiful woman, as beautiful as most of those who fill the screens and fantasies of millions of Americans. She can't help having been born with the features she was born with. Slav cheekbones, flaxen hair, full Russian mouth. Blood shows. Passion shows through, drives the life. She does love Aaron more than any other man on the face of the earth. She knows that now. She knows that she can be happy with him. She doesn't need to have children anymore. That ache has not been there for years. He is the father of her children. He is her lover. He is her man.

It *excites* her when he becomes jealous. She is not at all sorry that he followed her and found her at the house, with Lucius. She likes the idea of him pursuing her still, as he did when they first met. She wants him to look long and hard at his rage and jealousy, but not quite yet. Not until she is finished with him. It has been a long time since she has gone completely wild and she wants to. She wants to go wild with him the way she went wild with him in her mind before they ever made love the first time. Is there any desire like the desire for sex? Any hunger that is as fierce? She wonders: if she is vulgar and truthful with him, will he reject her? Or, his suspicions covering his jealousy, has he already decided to do that? Preemptive rejection. Same old Aaron. Same old Susan. She has often feared—can he believe her?—that she will never be able to satisfy him, that she is going to fail him. Why? He has never really judged her or controlled her, and yet . . . Well. She is going to try to satisfy him now in a way that he will never forget. If she expresses her doubts and desires, she believes they will lose the power to make her afraid. Who knows? Maybe Paul is right. Why not a life of possibility? Why not endless surprises? She rubs her cheek against his chest. She takes her hair and brushes his chest with it, as if painting him. She pushes her forehead against his chin. She licks his nipples, sucks on them. She wonders if it turned him on as much as she thought it did, to see her giving her smile to Lucius? Does it excite him now—she rings his penis with thumb and forefinger, applies pressure—to hear her tell him about her life with Paul? What does he want more—to hurt her or to be gentle with her? Does he want to be kind, or violent? To control, or be controlled? She tells him to feel free to tell her what he really wants to do, what wonderful small attentions she can pay to him.

She slips his shirt backwards, turns him around. She removes the shirt, unbuckles his belt. She is on her knees, untying each of his shoes, taking off each sock, pulling his pants down. She folds the pants, sets them across the back of a chair, over his shirt. *We can do anything we want*. She locks the bedroom door, takes his hand, leads him to the bed, puts a finger to her lips. She reaches backwards, unzips, lets her summer dress fall around her feet. She climbs onto the bed, turns her back to him, lies on her stomach, arches her rear-end and begins to roll from one side to the other. She urges him to come on, to come on and give her whatever he wants.

He shivers, but is afraid that if he says anything to her she will begin to talk the way she was talking to him before. To his surprise, his fear makes her seem, despite her words, more beautiful than ever. Is she right, then, about how much he idealizes her? That the more distant and pure she becomes the more he desires her; that the more he desires her and fears he can't have her, the more he comes to fear her rejection; that the more he fears her rejection, the more he needs to suspect that she has already betrayed and rejected him . . . ? What scares him most of all is to find himself thinking this way at the very moment in which she is ready to tell him everything, to give him anything he may want. Is *this* what he has feared all along? For if, in his mind, he can find reason to reject Susan, then he can be free *in* his mind to hold onto the wish that he and Gail might someday be reunited, that there is still some way to retrieve his other life.

He thinks of leaving. He is as frightened of hurting her as he is of being hurt. How, if he tells her about David Voloshin—about Gail and Emilie—can life with her ever be the same again? And yet he does not want to be fooled, or to play the fool. He needs time, he tells himself. Time and distance. He needs to see his life more clearly, to figure out how much of his confusion—his lack of trust—comes from within, and how much from the world. Susan reaches across, blindly, finds his hand, takes his fingers into her mouth, sucks on them one at a time, chews on knuckles. She moans, rolls from one side to the other, reaches below, sticks a finger into herself, then offers it to him, under his nose, wipes it on his lips. She moves onto her side, presses against him, the backs of her legs tight against his bent knees. He starts to enter her but she pushes him back, laughs, blocks the passage with her hand, whispers to him that she wants him in her other hole this time. She bites down on one of his good fingers until it hurts. She tells him that Paul liked it better in there—that he would usually have to get high on something, or be angry, or have just had another woman, but that when he was most sexed up, when his desire for power and control were at their height—that was where he most wanted to be, and that she wants Aaron there now too, where things are dark and dirty and secret. Danger from within and danger from without, right? She laughs. From *going* without? He shouldn't worry. She can control her muscles. Bearing four children has given her that power. Power and control is what it's all about, she says. The idea of power made into flesh. Come on, she urges. Come *on*.

She intones his name into the pillow. She arches her neck, forcing her ear back to his mouth, begins chanting his name—then Paul's name, then Lucius's name—and he finds that he has grabbed her hair in his hand, has rolled a gold hank of it around his fist and that he is pulling on it. She groans. Her smell is stronger than before, the lilac scent mixing now with something rank and familiar. She grinds her hips in slow circles, talks to him, keeps telling him to do anything he wants, anything at all. He is such a good, sweet man. She knows he wouldn't want to hurt his pretty Susan. There is nothing to fear. She tells him not to be jealous of Paul or Lucius any more than is absolutely neces- sary. She chose him, after all. He shouldn't worry about Jennifer or the boys. Hasn't he ever read Norman Mailer? Don't all nice Jewish boys want to be mean to the mothers whose smiles they want to win? He should be as mean to her as he can.

She tells him that he is bigger and harder than any man she has ever known. She tells him to go on and fuck her brains out, and when she does, and when he hears her laugh the way she did when he saw her whisper in Lucius's ear, in the car—laughing *at* him—he finds that his desire to hold back is gone. He yanks down on her hair, snapping her head back even as he lets go and he rams into her as far as he can, feels her convulse. She clamps her teeth down on her forearm, her fists opening and closing on the pillow, in spasms, and he cannot believe how tight she is around him, how raw she feels. He bangs away at her until the sweat is slick between them, until she is crying for him to give her more—more! more!—until he is licking and biting and clawing at her, wherever he can grab, while she whips her head from side to side and makes strange husky sounds from deep inside her chest. Rasping.

Growling. She is gone, off by herself in a wild mix of pain and pleasure from which, not being face to face, he feels strangely distant, as if, he thinks, he is a mere accessory.

When he releases and pulls out of her, wet and limp and bruised, and when she rolls onto her back and smiles up at him, there is a look of happy exhaustion on her face that is unlike any expression he has ever seen there before and, gazing at it, he feels the strangest sensation: that she is a woman he has been intimate with for the first time. He looks away even as she clings to him, tells him how wonderful he is, even as he knows that something is over between them.

But why now? And why so soon? Will they ever do it again like this? Will they ever be able to talk about it? He feels spent, dizzy. He watches her face, her breathing. She moves closer to him. Her eyelids drop, she nuzzles against his chest, says his name once, and then is fast asleep. He holds her, her breasts against his, and he stares across the bedside lamp at the painting on the wall. Vermeer's kitchen maid with downcast eyes. Still pouring her milk, still bathed in pale yellow light.

The sweat begins to dry on him. He imagines them doing what they have done in August, in broiling weather, and he wonders how long it would take until they would pass out. The sun glows orange in the haze. It hangs above the bell tower of Holy Cross Church, will soon drop from view. It is the kind of weather his father called steaming. A *steaming day in Brooklyn*. He thinks of his father telling him to let cold water run across his wrists, to drink warm tea with lemon. He reaches down, pulls the sheet up over them. Has the world, in fact, gone mad on him? Can he float away into some other life? He feels as if he is traveling into a foreign country through veils of mist and steam. Can one ever *forget?* Is the life he was believing, a few short hours ago, to be the life he had desired, found, and loved, an illusion, and if so, is the illusion inside the life itself, or in *him* somehow, in the fact that he believed in it?

In a few minutes, he knows, he will leave the room and go downstairs. Ordinary life will resume. Paul and Debbie will lay their plans, enact their schemes. Lucius and Louise will be married. Jennifer will go off to the Cape for the summer, to college in the fall. The boys will go to their camps. Lucius will get his teeth straightened and filled.

He sees the dentist's drill, in Louise's father's office, coming down on pulleys and wires, hissing and whirring. Then he is closer, staring, and the drill is boring into the back of a man's head, where there is no bone. That happened, he knows. He stood next to Abe and watched. Turkish Sammy and Big Jap Willer held the man down. The man began to talk, to sing. He sees the meat cleaver, coming down on his own splayed fingers. That happened too. The cleaver was in his own hand. He hardly felt the pain. The severed digits looked like fat, pink worms. If Susan thought him a fool today, what would she think were he ever to tell her *that* story? Or would she sympathize with him and love him, not for his loss, but because, so helplessly and stupidly afraid, he had panicked.

Paul, he thinks, is like those men. He is capable, without second thoughts, of throwing acid in Susan's face. Aaron is certain of it, even while he is less certain about the man who made him maim himself, who had been shadowing him from one county fair to another. Did the man work for Fasalino? For the police? For the feds? For the state racing commission? The man saw Aaron sitting there, in front of the horse's stall. He watched for a while, admiringly. He asked Aaron where he had learned to draw so well. He told him he had real good hands, healthy hands. The man wore a black silk vest over a gray polo shirt. He looked like a deadbeat, yet his eyes gave him away, were too alert; his shoes, though scuffed and unpolished, had good soles and heels on them. The man took Aaron's hands in his own, told him he should protect a pair of hands that could draw as well as that. He asked questions, passed the time of day, talked horses and odds and handles. Aaron knew the man's game, knew it well. Or thought he did.

Aaron drank heavily with the other stable boys. He passed out, tried to wash the vomit from his clothes, passed out again. He let them carry him to the stable, where they set him down outside the stall, on blankets. One of the boys kissed him on the forehead. They were all laughing. In the morning he did it. But can he even recall why at the time he *thought* he did it, what in the world it was that he thought he could gain or prove by setting his hand on the chopping block and whacking? What he recalls most of all is how hard it was to get his damned head to stop spinning so that he could concentrate. He didn't want to miss. Aim. Lift. Whack. No hesitation. Was he punishing his fingers for having drawn so well, for having given him away? Why let the world—others— take away what you love? Far better, if you sense they will, to do the job yourself first.

Or was he merely trying to add to his disguise? Was he merely confused and foolish? He had the ice ready nearby. He left the stubs, plunged the bloody stumps into the ice, quickly knotted the tourniquet above his biceps, heard the roaring in his head that must have come from his mouth also. He did not resist when the others came running, when they raced him to the local hospital in an old jalopy. He had identification papers, enough cash to pay for the stitches.

Then he was in a new town, working in the slaughterhouse where they brought the old race horses. He felt sorry for them, but he didn't mind cutting them up once they were dead. They drugged the horses like mad at the end, so that they could stumble around the track, and if nobody claimed them and they couldn't pay their way any longer, they sold them for dog food.

Midways and ferris wheels and kewpie dolls and cotton candy and teenagers holding hands and guys winning teddy bears for their girlfriends. Hot dogs and ox-drawing contests and stock car races and 4-H exhibits and horse races and pills and syringes. Hay and shit and wine. Time blurred. Pain gone. America! It was the same in all the small towns. Upstate New York. Massachusetts. Vermont. New Hampshire. Maine. Some of the owners cared about their horses, but most of the horses were old, half-crippled, their legs splintered even if their hearts still pumped. If they didn't shoot them up with drugs the pain would have been worse for them. Aaron let himself grow a beard, let his hair get bushy, let the foul odors sink into him. He worked the slaughterhouses for a while, then restaurants and diners. He stayed away from the fairs. When the fingers were calloused and brown, he went back.

Two years. Jackie left baseball during those two years. Curious that he hadn't remembered that for a long time. While he was wandering, Jackie retired. Thirty-seven years old. Less than a decade in the major leagues. Lifetime batting average of .311. Not bad for a pigeon-toed black man who played his first game in the majors at twenty-eight years old. Outsmarted O'Malley, who tried to trade him to the Giants for thirty thousand and a pitcher. Lived out in Stamford, Connecticut, where he and Rachel built their own home and where there were no black kids for his children to play with.

Two years. Aaron drank less. He liked hard physical labor, getting in shape. Picked apples in Upstate New York, tobacco in Hatfield. Moved furniture in Worcester. Wherever he was he would cut out in the early afternoon when he could, find a playground or schoolyard, shoot baskets. He shaved his beard, kept the mustache, wore sunglasses, learned to walk differently, at a slower gait. He met Susan. Yet he wondered: if the guy who had been following him discovered what he had done to himself, would he have given up the chase for that very reason? Would he have figured there was nothing Aaron would *not* do in order not to be taken back? If they wanted him at all, Aaron figured, they wanted him back alive. If not, why hadn't the man made his move?

In the fall of 1957 he returned to Northampton—worked at the Three County Fair again. Jackie was now a Vice President for Chock Full O'Nuts, working for a white man named Walter Black. Aaron liked that, figured he and Jackie could laugh over it. Jackie with white hair and black face, Walter Black with black hair and white face.

Aaron never saw the man again. And if the man had been merely curious? If he were merely a state dick on the prowl, seeing what information he could pick up playing hunches? If the man knew nothing, had just been sniffing around, had just been trying to scare Aaron a bit, to see what he could frighten loose . . .

What difference now, Aaron thinks.

He recalls a wide gold band on the fourth finger of the man's left hand, a tiny diamond chip set into it. Family happiness. Aaron smiles. Sure. Maybe in exchange for information about drugs or fixes on one of the other drifters, the man would have helped Aaron. Or maybe he had no idea in the world who Aaron was and didn't care. Maybe he just liked to follow the fairs and watch people draw. Maybe he was on the make. Who knows? What difference now? What difference.

Susan's chest rises and falls. She breathes easily. Her cheeks glow. In a few weeks, summer coming, her hair will begin to lighten, her skin to darken, so that she will appear to be even younger, more beautiful. He has had that for a dozen years now: the smile of a truly beautiful woman. Just for him. Personal happiness. Susan has always believed that, given how awful the world is—the world beyond their door and windows—they are entitled to what she refers to as personal happiness. They are entitled, as in Leverett, to cultivate their own garden and to take joy from it. Guiltlessly. They do what they can, when they can: with their children, with their friends, with Lucius. *Personal* happiness—in *this* life? Aaron laughs. Perhaps the mists are in his head. How foolish can a man be, he wonders. How foolish, and how innocent. The problem, he sees, is not that he began imagining his life before he lived it—it was, after all, a life he had never imagined could be his—but that, when things occurred in his new life that he had not imagined, that surprised and astonished him, he was not ready for them.

He slips from the bed, covers Susan, goes to the bathroom and washes himself. What he feels, he realizes when he returns, is that he has been used.

He dresses and leaves, goes downstairs. He hears Carl and Larry outside, arguing about whether or not Larry was hacked as he shot or if he cried foul *after* he saw that the ball was not going to go into the basket. Aaron looks out the window. Moths flutter, hit the screen, try to get inside. Benjamin lies on a plank of wood that rolls forwards and backwards under the front of a friend's jacked-up car. Benjamin will turn out fine, Aaron thinks. Just fine. Amazing how, short of death, we can and do survive. No magic really.

The children's schoolbooks are on the hallway buffet, in four separate piles. At Susan's suggestion, Jennifer has been reading *The Diary of Anne Frank*. When she was a senior at Northampton High School, Susan played Anne Frank in the stage version of the book.

Jennifer emerges from the kitchen. She has changed into a pair of

dungarees and an old green sweatshirt. Her hair is now braided, pinned
to either side of her ears in what he thinks she calls Dutch braids. He is
surprised at how young she looks, how unformed. The line of her jaw is
soft. She is eating a sandwich, carrying a plate. Aaron smells tuna fish.

"Hi," she says. It is as if what happened at Susan's house never happened. There is neither shame nor guilt nor anger in her manner or
voice or eyes.

"Hi," he says.

"Want some?" she asks, offering him half her sandwich. "I was starv-
ing."

"No thanks," he says, and then: "Your mother is taking a nap. I'll go
fix some supper for everybody. Ask Ben if his friend wants to stay and
eat with us, all right?"

He looks out the window and realizes that it is night, and that the
boys are playing and working by artificial light, using the floodlights
Aaron installed on top of the garage. He wonders if any of them heard
the noises from the bedroom, if they smiled at one another knowingly,
realizing just why it was their mother and father were locked in there,
were not downstairs on time for supper.

"Sure thing," Jennifer says, and then adds, "We all snacked around."

Aaron picks up *The Diary of Anne Frank*, sees that the bookmark
sticks up at about the two-thirds point.

"How do you like it so far?" he asks.

"It sucks," Jennifer says. "I mean, who really gives a shit if—"

He punches. She flies away from him, clutching at her mouth, letting
the sandwich spray across the floor. She sits against the wall, under the
window, eyes wide. The front door swings open and Aaron realizes that
she must have screamed when he hit her. She spits out a tooth, catches
blood in cupped hands. Aaron feels cold. How awful, he thinks, that in
this life happiness should turn so swiftly to misery, that love should turn
to meanness, that trust should turn to betrayal, that beauty should turn
to ugliness. Wasn't there some other way? He nods to the boys, but says
nothing. They stare at him, open-mouthed. He thinks of Susan, asleep
under the white sheet, her mouth half-open, the room suffused in
amber light. What can he say? If what he senses is true—is *actually* true
—what will he ever be able to say to them.

"Jesus!" Larry exclaims.

"You probably shouldn't have said that," Aaron says to Jennifer, and
he walks past his children, out of the house.

15

OCTOBER 24, 1972. Tuesday morning. Aaron is driving along
Route 9 in Hadley on his way to the university when he hears the news
on the car radio: Jackie Robinson is dead. The newscaster says that
Jackie suffered a heart attack in his Stamford, Connecticut, home and
was taken to Stamford Hospital, where, at 7:10 A.M., he passed away. At
7:10 A.M., Aaron thinks, he himself was in the kitchen, frying eggs for
Carl and Larry.

Jackie *dead?* Aaron listens to the newscaster recite words from the
wire services: about how the son of a Georgia sharecropper and grandson of a slave made baseball history by becoming the first black player
in the major leagues; about how he was elected to the Hall of Fame in
1962; about how he worked in recent years for an insurance firm, a bank,
a food-franchising outfit, an interracial construction company; about
how his son, Jack Junior, was killed sixteen months ago in a car crash;
about how he was active in national campaigns against drug addiction
and had been, on this very day, planning to speak at a drug symposium
in Washington, D.C.

When Aaron realizes that his tears are blinding him, he pulls to the
side of the road and waits. He imagines Jackie looking into the casket at
Jack Junior. He imagines Rachel's arm around Jackie's waist, her cheek
against his shoulder. Jack Junior's neck is broken. What did Jackie *feel*
when he looked down at his son? Jack Junior was returning home to
Stamford along the Merritt Parkway in his brother David's M.G. when,
according to the newspapers, his car skidded, spun wildly, slammed into
a concrete abutment, severed steel guardrails, turned over, and pinned
him under the wreckage. He was twenty-four years old. He had been

working late in New York City, arranging a jazz festival which was to benefit the Daytop Program. During his four years at Daytop House in Seymour, Connecticut, he had cured himself of the drug habit acquired in Vietnam and since his cure he had been employed by the Daytop House as a counselor for other addicts. In his dead son's wallet, Jackie found, to his surprise, an old newspaper photograph of himself in a Dodger uniform. In the photograph that Aaron imagines—it was not reproduced in the newspaper—Jackie is diving for a line drive. His body is suspended in flight, hurtling through space at a seemingly impossible angle, nearly parallel to the ground yet at a slight rising diagonal, his arms outstretched, his gloved hand curved backwards at the wrist as it strains to reach the small spheroid of white.

Why is it, Aaron wonders, even as he lets the tears flow, that he is so moved by the death of a man he has never known, yet has been unable to weep for the two men he has been closest to in his life: his father and Abe. Why has he seemed to feel—to show—so little for the loss of the others who were dear to him: Gail, Emilie, Lucius, Susan.

He wipes his eyes with the backs of his wrists. To his right a construction crew is building a new shopping mall. He watches a giant crane slowly lower a long orange girder. Workers in yellow hard hats move deliberately, almost eagerly in the cool morning air. A year before, the land that is now laid over with tons of flat black asphalt was covered with acres of high straw-yellow cornstalks. The Holyoke Range, rising behind the skeleton of the new mall, seems chiseled into the pale early morning sky. The spectacular blaze of autumn color has come somewhat early this year, and now, most trees bare, the landscape stretches away on all sides in browns and lavenders and russets and pale greens. Should he try to paint the picture, not of the half-built mall, but of the mountains and fields behind it—of the Holyoke notch—Aaron would, he decides, do so in watercolors, in washes that might suggest the enormous mass of snow-white air that seems to lie behind the cold blue sky, cushioning it.

This is, as ever, Aaron's favorite time of the year. The crops are, for the most part, already harvested or plowed under, and snow has not yet covered the earth. The landscape opens gradually to wide horizons, endless vistas. Mornings, heading north towards Montague, where he is building a house for a young couple—the wife a social worker, the husband a dentist—he loves seeing the Connecticut River, hidden by trees all through the spring and summer and early autumn, become slowly visible: he likes seeing the full expanse of the river; he likes looking across the river to the rich, flat farmland of Deerfield. It is as if, at this time of year, between the end of autumn and the beginning of winter, his heart opens—as if his mind sheds its dry leaves, sucks in cold air, expands, begins to reveal itself, to fill with bright white light.

He considers going on, as he has planned—to his drawing class, and after his class to the house in Montague. His two coworkers, George and Norm, will be finishing up the framing. Next week, ahead of schedule and in plenty of time for first snow, they can begin to put the roof on. It will be good, he thinks, to lose himself in the steady rhythm of hammering twelve- and sixteen-pound nails into posts and beams and studs and trimmers. But he wonders what the right thing to do is: to stop and to try to recall as much of Jackie's life as he can and thereby to feel the loss—to grieve, to mourn—or, by going on with the ordinary tasks of his own life, to give honor to Jackie's.

Jackie was only fifty-three years old, yet Aaron finds that he is not surprised by the fact of the man's death. Jackie was suffering from hypertension, arthritis, diabetes. He had previously recovered from a near-fatal septicemia and from two earlier heart attacks. He was blind in one eye and, as a result of retinal bleeding caused by diabetes, rapidly going blind in the other. All efforts to stop the deterioration by cauterizing the ruptured vessels with laser beams failed. He had lost his firstborn son.

In an adult education course that Aaron is taking at the synagogue in Northampton—he joined two and a half years before, in the month immediately following his divorce from Susan—the rabbi has explained that the Mourner's Kaddish is not, in fact, a prayer for the dead, but a prayer for the living in which we declare our faith in the fact that life goes on, that the generations renew one another. Jews do not believe in an afterlife. The only immortality we have, the rabbi says—the only way in which we can live on beyond our time on earth—is in our children, or in our works, or in the memories others have of us.

But who, Aaron wonders, is still alive who can remember what he was like before he reached the age of twenty? Who is still alive who ever thinks about the boy named Davey Voloshin, about the young man who married Gail, who loved Emilie, who disappeared . . . ?

The rabbi has explained that there are three levels of mourning. The first level is that of tears. The second and higher level is that of silence. And the third and highest level is that of song. Aaron recalls walking with Lucius and Nicky through downtown Meridien, holding hands while they approached the church in which James Chaney's body waited, but he cannot hear the sound of their voices. He cannot summon up the sound of the hymns they sang in the church. He cannot hear Nicky's voice as she sang by the lakeside, though he can recall the dark oval of her open mouth, the blood along her cheek and jaw. We shall overcome? Not a chance, he thinks. Not in this life. He starts the car, pulls out into traffic.

Just past the Zayre's Shopping Center, at the Hadley-Amherst town line, he makes a U-turn, drives east, back towards home. He knows what it is he wants to do, knew it really in the first instant in which he heard the news on the radio: he wants to be there. He lets his rage subside and admits to himself that he wants to go to New York—to the funeral and to the cemetery—so that he can be with others who mourn and honor a man Aaron once loved with all his heart. He wishes Carl and Larry had not already left for school. He wishes he could sit with them now in his living room, or on the hard ground outside his studio window, and tell them the story of Jackie Robinson's life.

That story is now complete, isn't it?

He recalls sitting in Beau Jack's apartment when he was a boy no older than his own sons, listening to a Dodger game on the radio, Red Barber calling the play-by-play as if he were there in the ballpark, as if he were not in a radio studio looking at words curling across his desk on a narrow strip of ticker tape. Aaron reminds himself to tell the boys about that, about how the announcers would have to invent the action, about how boys like himself would have to imagine the games on the screens inside their heads.

Aaron is thirty-seven years old, the same age Jackie was when Jackie retired from baseball. Aaron is thirty-seven years old and he is living his second life and for the first time in a long while it occurs to him, with force, that he can never cross back over to that first life. The pain is sudden, as if fists have entered an enormous wound in his side and are now opening and closing inside his stomach. Stone seems to grind against stone. His body is rigid, as if poised for a blow that may never come. Yet the pain is bearable. Why? Has the other life and self died then? And if so—if they are gone at last, if he can never go back—why does the pain still come so sharply from time to time, and why can there never be an end to memory, to the sense he has that, as now, he will never be done with mourning?

Because you loved that boy as much as you loved Jackie.

He feels his body relax. Whose voice is he hearing? Is it true—does he love the boy he himself was in the same way that he once loved Jackie, in same way that he loves each of his own sons? He wonders: is the love more intense *because* he has lost that boy forever?

Aaron crosses over the Coolidge Bridge. The fall has been dry and the sandbars in the river below are wide. No boys sit on the railroad bridge that spans the river thirty yards or so to the north. The river's surface is calm and flat, unmoving, as if it is a lake. Aaron hears no music inside his head. Still, he can summon up the sound of Jackie's falsetto voice. Had Jackie come to recognize the sound of that voice as his own? Aaron recalls how surprised he was in Ohio when he listened to himself on tape. Why is it, he wonders, that we always sound so different to ourselves than we do to others?

Aaron can see Jackie, stone-cold in a pine coffin, his snow-white hair like lamb's wool, his skin like hard black leather, and the picture gives neither peace nor comfort. Aaron thinks of how conservative Jackie had become—of how he had, in his newspaper columns, attacked Martin Luther King and Malcolm X and James Baldwin; of how he had become a Republican and supported Nixon and Rockefeller; of how he had shilled for Chock Full O'Nuts—and what he wishes he could have done to this white-haired pigeon-toed half-blind old man, he realizes, was to have kidnapped him and blindfolded him and carried him south again. He wishes he could have stripped him from his business suit and handed him a bat and a ball and a glove and put him on a scrabbly field with a bunch of black kids in the hope that his being there might remind Jackie of the boy he had once been, and of what it was he did so well.

When Aaron arrives home, he telephones Nicky, asks if she can come to his house.

"I'll be right there. But listen—did you hear about Jackie?"

"Yes. It's why I'm calling."

"I'm sorry, Aaron."

"Me too."

"Remember the night you told Rose Morgan's kids all about him, about seeing him with the Dodgers that first year?"

"Yes."

"I love you, Aaron."

Aaron walks through the rooms of his house, down to his studio, sits at his drawing table, gazes out the window at the lawn, the stone wall, the trees. Past the wall, some maples still hold a few scarlet leaves, and the beech trees, at the east end of his property, are filled with brittle silver leaves, as they will be through most of the winter. Aaron tries to hear his own voice talking to Rose Morgan's children and the other civil rights workers about what it was like to watch Jackie take the field, and scuff the dirt with his spikes, and pound his glove. When Jackie took the field, Aaron said to them, there was something about his bearing that reminded us *all* that it was our birthright to be free. Here I am, Jackie seemed to say by the way he stood and moved and gazed at others. Here I am. I'm a man—are you?

Yes sir, that's right, Rose Morgan said.

Aaron looks at the woman in the upper right-hand corner of his table. Her downward glance has not changed. Her kitchen is still filled with pale yellow light, with soft blue and green cloths, with loaves of warm

bread, with the glazed bowl that receives fresh milk. Her forearms and
wrists and cheeks and forehead are still bright with the same gentle light
that will, from the window to her left, shine upon her forever. And the
life outside that window?

Aaron is glad that Nicky is coming to visit—pleased that he called her,
that he didn't resist the impulse. Aaron likes Nicky's husband Mark, a
small bear of a man, blinded in one eye during a civil rights march in
Selma, Alabama. Mark, on sabbatical leave from Dickinson College, is
working at the University of Massachusetts library, where W. E. B.
DuBois's papers are stored, on a book about DuBois's African years.
Nicky is using the year to work on a master's degree in special education.
Afternoons, she works in Northampton at a home for delinquent teen-
age boys, mostly Puerto Ricans. In less than eight months, when she
and Mark return to Pennsylvania, Aaron will graduate from the university.

Aaron tries to imagine what it is he will feel when Nicky is gone. His
mind drifts. He tries to remember August weather in Mississippi. Does
time, he wonders, move more slowly through heat and darkness? He
sees his father on the roof of their apartment house, sitting on the edge,
feet dangling above the street. His father wears a green bathing suit and
a sleeveless undershirt that is too large for him. His father calls down to
neighbors who sit in front of the house. His mother shouts at his father
to get off the edge, to stop showing off. She turns to a neighbor, Mrs.
Ellenbogen. How the hell can he smoke his crappy Chesterfields in this
weather is what she wants to know. Aaron wants to go to his father, to
take his father's hand before his father leans over too far and loses his
balance. Aaron sees steam, like morning mist, rising from the sidewalk,
giving off the heat that the concrete has absorbed all day. He wonders
what he sounded like to others then, when he was a boy. If there is a
difference—a distance—between the self we struggle to make and the
self that others claim to know, is it possible to enter that space—to lie
down in it, to dwell there?

"I like the barns."

"The barns?"

Nicky kisses him on the cheek. He turns to face her and she does not
move back. Her lips, cool and soft, are light against his skin.

"There!"

She points to the drawing on the table, in pencil, of three Hadley
tobacco barns, so much longer than they are high, set low on the horizon, their vertical slats, which run the full length of the barns, open to
the autumn air.

"Oh. The barns," Aaron says. "Yes."

Nicky laughs. "Were you asleep? I kept knocking, but you didn't come to the door."

"No. I was daydreaming, I guess."

"You don't mind my coming down here."

"Why should I mind?"

"Larry says it's your sanctuary, that you get angry sometimes if—"

"Maybe." He takes her hand, kisses it. "But no. I don't mind. Not today. No secrets here—not from you, Nicky. I do like to come here, though—to be by myself, to let my mind drift, to remember things, to imagine—"

"Jackie?"

"Sure."

"Jackie and what else?"

"Jackie and me as a boy, idolizing him, rooting for him, wanting him to show the bastards just how good he was, how much of a man—"

"Did the other guys at the orphanage feel the same?"

"I suppose."

"I suppose. With the same intensity—with *your* intensity?"

"I doubt it."

"Me too."

Aaron laughs. "Listen, Larry came up with this during the summer when I took the kids camping in New Hampshire. 'Do you know what I figured out, Dad,' he said to me one day. 'What?' I asked, and he began to smile the way he does. 'That camping is a very in-tents experience.' Get it?"

Nicky groans.

"But how did Jackie do it, Nicky? How did he let that talent loose day after day when he knew thousands—millions—of people were waiting for him to fail? Every time he came to bat, every time a ball was hit toward him. What kept him going?"

"His belief in himself."

"Maybe." Aaron shakes his head. "He was a cold man, really. I've been remembering that. When he played, and after."

"Like you, right? All talent, no heart."

Nicky kisses him on the forehead. Aaron lets his left hand rest on her stomach.

"The baby's kicking. Can you tell?"

Aaron presses lightly, searches for the baby's shape, for the feet.

"I think so. How many months now?"

"Thirteen weeks to go, but the doctor says it might come early this time. Second children often do."

"Where's Samuel?"

"Upstairs. I parked him in front of the TV. I thought you might want to be alone with me first and I didn't want him to be tempted to put his sweet little hands on your drawings. Those barns are wonderful! How do you get the details? The tobacco leaves peeking out of the openings with their curled edges—they—" Nicky stops. "You're very upset, aren't you?"

"Yes. I'm very upset."

"How would you feel about us just holding each other for a while?"

Aaron stands, puts his arms around Nicky, holds her. He thinks of Gail, of the kitchen on Ocean Avenue, of a moment—perhaps ten days before Emilie was born—when he held to Gail this way. Well, he thinks. Did he love her or did he love her?

He leaves the studio, walks upstairs, Nicky's small fist tight around two of his good fingers. He should know more than most that life is never predictable. Why, then, is he always surprised—frightened— when the unexpected occurs? Is it ever possible to feel ready—to *be* ready—for *whatever* may happen, for *any* of life's possibilities? He says hello to Samuel, lifts the boy in the air and tosses him toward the ceiling the way he remembers Abe doing with him, before the war.

"More!" Samuel says. "More! More!"

"You look very pale," Nicky says. "I'll fix you something. Did you have breakfast?"

"Yes."

"Have a second then. On me."

Aaron sets Samuel down, nuzzles the skin between Samuel's chin and shoulder. Samuel has Mark's build, Nicky's intense gray eyes. He tries to imagine Samuel at seventeen or eighteen, grinning, showing a chipped front tooth. What will news of Mississippi in the summer of 1964 mean to him by then, in 1986 or 1987? How will he ever understand that a moment in history—Malcolm and Martin alive, moving closer to one another in belief and spirit—had been missed, and that an entire nation was, forever after, doomed? Despite his knowledge—the history his father and mother and others can give to him—how will he ever feel that things might, for so many, have been otherwise.

In the kitchen, Nicky moves efficiently, gracefully—taking eggs from the refrigerator, putting bread in the toaster oven, pouring orange juice, fixing Samuel a snack, setting the table. She asks Aaron about his courses, about his work in Holyoke. Aaron travels there three times a week—two afternoons and Saturday mornings—helping out in Operation Renewal, teaching carpentry to blacks and Puerto Ricans. The project seems sensible: if poor people restore condemned and abandoned buildings according to conditions set down by the city's housing commission, the buildings will become theirs. Nicky wonders how

Aaron finds the time to do all he does—to take care of the boys and the
house; to oversee the construction work; to be part of Operation Renewal. . . .

"Do you miss having Susan around?"

"No."

"You manage very well." Nicky turns. "For a father you make a pretty
damned good mother. How are Jennifer and Benjamin? Do you hear
from them? Do they hear from you? Is Paul still alive and kicking?"

"Susan writes to them occasionally. The last time was from San Fran-
cisco. She was living with a man ten years younger than herself—an
actor she met in a repertory company she's part of."

"And—?"

"And what?"

"And what do you *feel* about her, you big dope—what do you feel
about all that being gone, about Jennifer and Benjamin being away,
about the boys growing up without a mother?"

"Do you mean, do I wish I had *you* here instead of Susan?"

Nicky hesitates, a cracked brown eggshell cupped in the fingers of her
right hand. Her look darkens—changes from one of delight to one of
concern, and it is as if, in the instant between the time Aaron has asked
the question and she has thought of answering it, she changes from the
young girl he once knew to the woman she actually is. He calculates:
they met more than eight years ago. She has been married to Mark for
six years. Samuel is almost four.

"No," she says, and she turns back to the stove, drops the eggshell
into the sink. "Not at all."

"You're happy with Mark?"

"Very."

She cracks more eggs, swirls them with a whisk, leans to the left and
lifts toast from the toaster oven.

"Would you butter these, please? Timing. Everything's timing—getting everything there and warm at the same moment."

Aaron goes to the counter, butters the toast. He opens the refrigerator, takes out a jar of blackberry jam.

"I made this with the boys, in August."

"Paul?"

"He sends them a postcard every six months or so. He's living in the
south of France, supported, as near as I can make out, by his father's
money and—if we can believe the stories he told Ben—by the C.I.A.
Who knows? Jennifer says that he claims to be living with a woman
who's some kind of princess, utterly gorgeous and about two years older
than Jen is."

"Still courting Susan then."

"Susan?"

"Women the same age Susan was when he met her. Like Debbie."
Nicky passes him, moving to the kitchen table, a frypan in one hand, a
spatula in the other, and as she passes she jabs him with an elbow.
"Sensitive women of that age are often irresistibly drawn to attractive
older men, or haven't you noticed?"

"I noticed," he says, and he smiles, realizing that sometimes Nicky's
voice reminds him, not of Susan's, as he used to think, but of another.
How strange, he thinks. How obvious.

Fun by the ocean with Davey Voloshin . . .

"I saw Louise the other day," Nicky offers. "Shopping in Louie's. She
had the child—hers and Lucius's—in an umbrella stroller. She's pregnant again. Did you know that? Did you know that she remarried—?"

"Yes."

"Do you ever hear from Lucius? Do you know where he is?"

"No."

"Should I shut up?"

"I don't know."

"But you were thinking about him before, when I mentioned Susan's
name, weren't you? I could tell from your eyes, from—"

"Enough. Okay?"

"Sorry. After all this time, I didn't think what happened could still get
to you."

"It doesn't, usually. It's just that with the news about Jackie and—"

"Shh," Nicky says. She bends over, kisses Aaron on the forehead, and
when he feels her warm lips on his skin, he finds that he is forcing
himself to see the scene again, in Susan's house—so that he will be able
to make it go away? so that he will feel even more depressed than he
already is?—when, three months after the first time he found her there
with Lucius, he discovered them again, but not in the kitchen. Why
didn't he kill them? Why, when he saw them—Susan's hair across Lucius's cheek like a soft gold curtain—did he feel as if he had already
witnessed the scene before? Did they *want* him to discover them? Were
they so weary of their secret and their guilt? Did they merely, in some
strangely kind and deliberate way, want to give him enough time to
make sense of the knowledge that he had taken in, if dimly, the first
time he found them together?

"I don't mind living alone," Aaron says. "I was scared at first—the first
month or two. Did I ever tell you?"

"You wrote. But tell me again."

"I was scared that without Susan I'd be incomplete somehow, that
without her on the other side of the kids—for balance, as it were—there

wouldn't *be* any family. But there is. Me and the boys—that's family enough. And Ben and Jen, when they come home."

"Does Ben like it at M.I.T.?"

"He loves it."

"No regrets?"

"Regrets?"

"About turning down all those athletic scholarships and becoming the great college athlete his father could have been and never was?"

"No."

"Following in his father's footsteps, is that it? Renunciation as a way of life."

"I hope not." Aaron laughs, stares hard at her eyes. "Though there are some pleasures in renunciation."

"You bet. But listen. I remember you once told me that being an only child, and then an orphan, used to make you feel that you were incomplete somehow, as if your parents hadn't finished *making* you."

"Did I say that?"

"Don't play naïve. You said it and you know it. Did you feel that more when you were younger, or after you were put in the orphanage?" Nicky scoops eggs out of the frypan, sets the buttered toast, cut on the diagonal, onto the edges of their plates. She sits. "And speaking of renunciation, are you seeing anyone these days?"

"Now and then." He shrugs. "It doesn't seem important."

"What does?"

"The children. My work. My friends. You."

"Think you'll ever marry again, given this new and enthusiastic attitude toward women?"

"I don't know. Once the first year passed and I saw we'd be fine—me and Larry and Carl—I haven't thought about it much. If it happens, it happens."

"I heard you before. You know that, don't you?"

"Sure."

"Sure."

She reaches across, takes his hand in her own, rubs the stubs of his missing fingers.

"I love you very much, Aaron, but not in that way. I'm not the girl I once was. You're not the man you once were. Can I say it all now? Oh sure. I suppose I could let myself fall in love with you that way again—what grown-ups can't, if they decide to let themselves?—but what *for* now? Think of the mess it would make. And think of this too—what I feel most of all—of how we can get so much more out of *friendship*."

Aaron smiles, but not easily. "Sure," he says. "I suppose."

"I suppose." Nicky stretches, one hand moving past her hip, towards the small of her back. "Oh Aaron, you are such a wonderful man. Jesus!" Her hand moves forward, hesitates, drops. She takes up her fork, begins eating her eggs, motions to him to do the same. "I mean, I can see the whole thing, right? I leave Mark and he goes to California and meets Susan and then we spend the rest of our lives shuttling the kids from one coast to the other—Paul and Susan's, Mark's and mine, yours and Susan's, Mark's and Susan's, yours and mine, Paul and Debbie's, Paul and his princess's—how many families worth by now?—and if we can't figure out whose turn it is, we send them off to France. So do you know what I really think? I think it would be a goddamned shame if even a small part of you stayed so wounded that you didn't let some good and lucky woman into your life again. There are a few of us around, you know. Scared?"

"Maybe."

"Scared," Nicky asserts. "But listen. Would you want more children? Would you be willing to have a second family?"

"A *second?* I don't understand. I already—"

"Besides the one you have now, I mean."

"Yes." Nicky does not seem to notice his confusion. "Sure."

"I mean, think of the waste, Aaron. A man like you and all those good women out there wondering why you're not in their lives. You *could* imagine having a new family?"

"Yes."

"It'll happen then. Okay. Tell me this—are you happy these days, all things considered?"

"Yes."

"Still a man of many words. What was it you said they called you at the Home—the silent one? Like Lou Gehrig, right?" She goes to the gas range, brings more coffee. "The difference always amazes me, though. Still. How silent you can be—not withdrawn, really, but just silent in a warm way, especially when you're around the people you love—and then the way you can suddenly talk like no one else I know, the way—" She stops, licks a scrap of egg from between her upper teeth. "So tell me —why am I here and why did you call this meeting?"

"Because I decided that I want to go down to the city to Jackie's funeral, and I wondered if you'd be able to stay here with the boys for a day or two."

"Why don't you take them with you?"

"To a *funeral?*"

"Sure. You can tell them more about Jackie."

"I think I'll be too upset, and—"

"Why *shouldn't* you be upset? Let them see your heart, dear one. Let them know you care."

"Or I thought that maybe you could have them stay with you and Mark. I'd really like to go, Nicky, and—"

"Did you hear what I said before? Goddamn. Should I shout it? *Why-don't-you-take-your-sons-with-you?* It would be good for them to see where you grew up. That's what I think. It would be good for them to know that part of you, to see where your passion and strength of character come from. From *whence* you came, right? It would be good for them to gather in some clues they could use in beginning to figure their father out, in *beginning* to understand why he cares about things the way he does. You're not eating your breakfast."

"I'm not hungry."

She touches his hand again.

"It's only a suggestion, so don't be offended and defensive. We can still say anything at all to one another, can't we? *Can't* we, Aaron? Have we ever held back, in all the years since we met?"

"No."

"Okay then. It's only a suggestion, but take my word for it, it's a goddamned good one."

About fifteen miles south of Hartford, Larry, resting in the back seat, wakes up. He leans forward, puts his hand on Aaron's neck, lightly.

"How long did I sleep?"

"An hour."

Carl is next to Aaron, his head against a pillow, the pillow wedged between the car's seat and the door. Carl's feet—he is fifteen, almost six feet tall, with long legs—almost reach Aaron's thigh. The sun is beginning to rise in the east, lavender streaks spreading gently above low, rolling hills.

"I bet there'll be lots of famous athletes there today."

"The funeral's tomorrow."

"Then why did we leave so early today?"

"To see Jackie. His body will be in Harlem for viewing at a funeral chapel there, and that way we can walk by the coffin. In the church tomorrow, we wouldn't get a chance."

"To see him?"

"To say goodbye."

"How dangerous will Harlem be? I mean, for white people."

"Not very."

"Do you mind if I ask you questions?"

"No. Not really."

"Did you see Jackie play a lot when you were a boy?"

"Sure." Aaron smiles. "My friends and I used to have a way of sneaking into Ebbets Field once it got past the second inning."

"Was it because you were all orphans—I mean, that they felt sorry for you and let you in?"

"No. After school we'd ride the Flatbush Avenue trolley down to Empire Boulevard. My friend Tony had a cousin who worked one of the turnstiles. There'd be eight or ten of us and we'd chip in, give him two or three bucks and he'd let us all in."

"Sounds great. Sometimes I wish I'd grown up in a big city, the way you did—"

"The big stars will be there. You can look in the newspaper—I left it on the seat next to you—where it tells the names of the pallbearers."

"Bill Russell will be one, won't he?"

"Yes. Russell will be there. Do you know what he said? He said that even though he never saw Jackie play, he'd go halfway around the world to honor him because he was a *man*—because of what he did for all black athletes."

"Will Muhammad Ali be there, do you think?"

"Probably. Jackie's old teammates, though—those are the ones I'm hoping to see. Don Newcombe and Jim Gilliam and Ralph Branca and Pee Wee Reese and Joe Black and Carl Erskine. They were my heroes when I was your age, the way Carlton Fisk and Carl Yastrzemski are yours now."

Larry leans closer. "Was Pee Wee Reese the one you told me about, in the story about how they made the crowd get quiet after they were calling Jackie a nigger?"

"Yes. Pee Wee was from Kentucky, and when he—"

"I remember the story, how I thought Pee Wee got his name from being small, and how you told me about him getting it from shooting marbles—from being a marbles champion in Louisville when he was a kid. But, Dad?"

"Yes?"

"When I was younger—I was afraid to ask—but why did the kids in school used to say that Jews had horns?"

"*Horns?*"

"Some of the Polish kids used to say we had horns and that they must of cut them off when we were born, when we were circumcised."

Aaron talks for a while about anti-Semitism, and about what he himself has only recently learned—about how Michelangelo confused the Hebrew word for beams of light with the word for horns. In the rear view mirror he sees that Larry has stopped listening, is looking out the window.

"Then too," Aaron says, "there are some people who just hate Jews because they like to hate people. The way people hate blacks."

"Well, fuck them," Larry says.

Aaron smiles.

"But what made Jackie so special? Really. There are lots of great black ball players. Why was he the best, the way you always say he was?"

"I don't know. One of the sportswriters pointed out that even though he never hit more than nineteen home runs in a single season on a team that had great home run hitters like Gil Hodges and Duke Snider and Roy Campanella, they always let Jackie bat clean-up. Does that answer your question?"

"I suppose. Will Campanella be there?"

"Yes."

"Carl once did a book report about him. I forget the title."

"*It's Good to Be Alive*," Aaron says. "He'll be an honorary pallbearer. Fat and chubby and always stood with his foot in-the-bucket. He and Jackie never really got along—Jackie thought he was too much of an Uncle Tom—but he was the greatest catcher I ever saw. After the car accident, when he was paralyzed and forced to live in a wheelchair, his wife divorced him."

"Will seeing Jackie dead upset you a lot?"

"It might."

"Yeah. Nicky told us. She said it would be good for you to get it out of your system. Only—?"

"Yes?"

"Does it bother you, that you never really had the chance to be a college or pro ballplayer?"

"Not really."

"Not in baseball maybe, but in basketball, let's say." Larry hesitates for a split-second, then continues: "Lucius used to say you were as good as any of the pros, that if you'd gone to college and played pro you could've been like some of the great white players, like Jerry West or Bill Bradley or Bob Cousy or Dave DeBusschere."

"Not true," Aaron says, and he hears the note of irritation in his voice.

Carl stirs but does not wake.

What Aaron wants to do, he knows, is simply—yet again—to tell the story of Jackie's life to his son. He smiles. Would his father, or his father's brothers, be pleased with him? At Passover, when the children ask the reasons for certain rituals—eating unleavened bread and bitter herbs, dipping greens in salt water, reclining at the table—the father answers by telling the story of the going forth from Egypt. *Because we were slaves to the Pharaoh in Egypt and the Lord our God brought us forth with a strong arm and an outstretched hand. . . .*

"Listen," Aaron says. "When Carl wakes up we'll talk some more, okay? You rest now. It's going to be a long day. We might have to wait in line a while before we can go in to see him."

"He was a lot like you, wasn't he?"

"Who?"

"Jackie Robinson. I mean, like when you're determined to do something—like going back to school at your age and becoming an artist—nothing ever stands in your way, does it?"

"I suppose."

"I suppose." Larry laughs. "You always say that, don't you?"

"I suppose."

They both laugh.

"And anyway, what I figured out a long time ago—it disappointed me—was that you were too old to be a famous athlete anymore. Players as old as you are usually retired already. So maybe you'll be a famous artist instead, right? A lot of famous artists are pretty old—"

"Not as old as me."

Larry laughs again, ruffles his father's hair, then sits back, closes his eyes. Aaron drives on, past Middletown, past New Haven, his boys sleeping in the car. The funeral parlor is at Seventh Avenue and 135th Street, and Aaron doubts that any of the famous players and dignitaries and movie stars will be there, in Harlem. Today will be more of a family day, he hopes. He begins to think of which highways to take, of how he will route himself into the city, of what else he might do with the boys while they are there together.

He has promised to take them to his old neighborhood, to show them where the orphanage and Ebbets Field were. They want to see Radio City Music Hall, the Empire State Building, the Museum of Natural History. Aaron imagines seeing Jackie's wife Rachel and her children, David and Sharon, at the church. He imagines seeing Jackie's two brothers, Mack and Edgar. He knows that everyone will be there: Governor Rockefeller and Joe Louis, Mayor Lindsay and Willie Mays. Movie stars and politicians and civil rights leaders. Bayard Rustin and A. Philip Randolph and James Farmer and Roy Wilkins and Ralph Abernathy. Aaron tries to see Jackie out on the desert—the one he had imagined for Malcolm X and Martin Luther King so long ago—but he does not let his mind dwell on the picture for long.

He imagines, instead, the day of the funeral. After services at Riverside Church, they will drive from Manhattan to Brooklyn, past the street where Ebbets Field used to be, past the New Lots and East New York sections, toward Queens, to the Cypress Hills Cemetery. Aaron's father grew up in East New York, is buried in the Machpelah cemetery nearby, on the other side of the Ridgewood reservoir.

Aaron reaches over and touches Carl's hair. Carl sleeps soundly. Carl has his books of magic tricks with him in his backpack. Carl intends to be a professional magician someday and he reads all the books he can, has begun to give shows for his friends, at school, at parties. The night before, while they were packing, Carl said that he was glad Aaron had never become famous, because if he were, the way Susan and Nicky and Lucius said he could have been, as an athlete or a civil rights leader, then he would have to have been away from home a lot while they were growing up.

By the time they reach southern Connecticut and cross over, along the Merritt Parkway, just past Stamford, onto the Hutchinson River Parkway and into New York State, Aaron knows what he will do after they go to the funeral home. This is doubtless what he had planned to do—sensed he would do, from the first—though he did need Nicky to edge him toward the decision. He will drive from Manhattan into Brooklyn. He imagines Gail's parents still living in the same house. He will get out of his car with Carl and Larry and go up to the front door. He will knock. Ellen will open the door. He will say, "Hello, Ellen—it's David Voloshin." She will start to move toward him, but before her fingertips can read his face, he will tell her that his boys are with him. He will give her their names. Then, as if she is in her garden reaching for flowers, she will put out her hands and, in order to know them, touch the faces of his two sons.

And if she is not there? He smiles. If she is there or if she is not there, he will go back. And if he goes back things will begin to happen that he has yet to imagine. If she is there or if she is not there, he will get in the car with his boys and they will drive along Bedford Avenue and turn right onto Martense Street. He will take his boys to his old neighborhood and show them his street and his house and the courtyards and the alleyways. He can see the four small rooms of his apartment, can see himself walking through them with his boys, room by room. The rooms are clean and white and empty, freshly painted and full of pale morning light—the way they might have been, he thinks, before his life began.

About the Author

Jay Neugeboren is the author of five highly praised novels: *Big Man*, *Listen Ruben Fontanez*, *Sam's Legacy*, *An Orphan's Tale*, and *The Stolen Jew*, which won the American Jewish Committee's Present Tense Award for Best Novel of 1981. In addition, he has written a collection of prize-winning stories, *Corky's Brother*, and a memoir, *Parentheses: An Autobiographical Journey*, and has also served as editor of Martha Foley's memoir, *The Story of STORY Magazine*. His short stories and articles have appeared in *The Atlantic*, *Esquire*, *Sport*, *TriQuarterly*, *Ploughshares*, *Commentary*, *The American Scholar*, as well as many other periodicals, and have been reprinted in several dozen anthologies. Mr. Neugeboren lives in North Hadley, Massachusetts, and is Writer-in-Residence at the University of Massachusetts in Amherst.